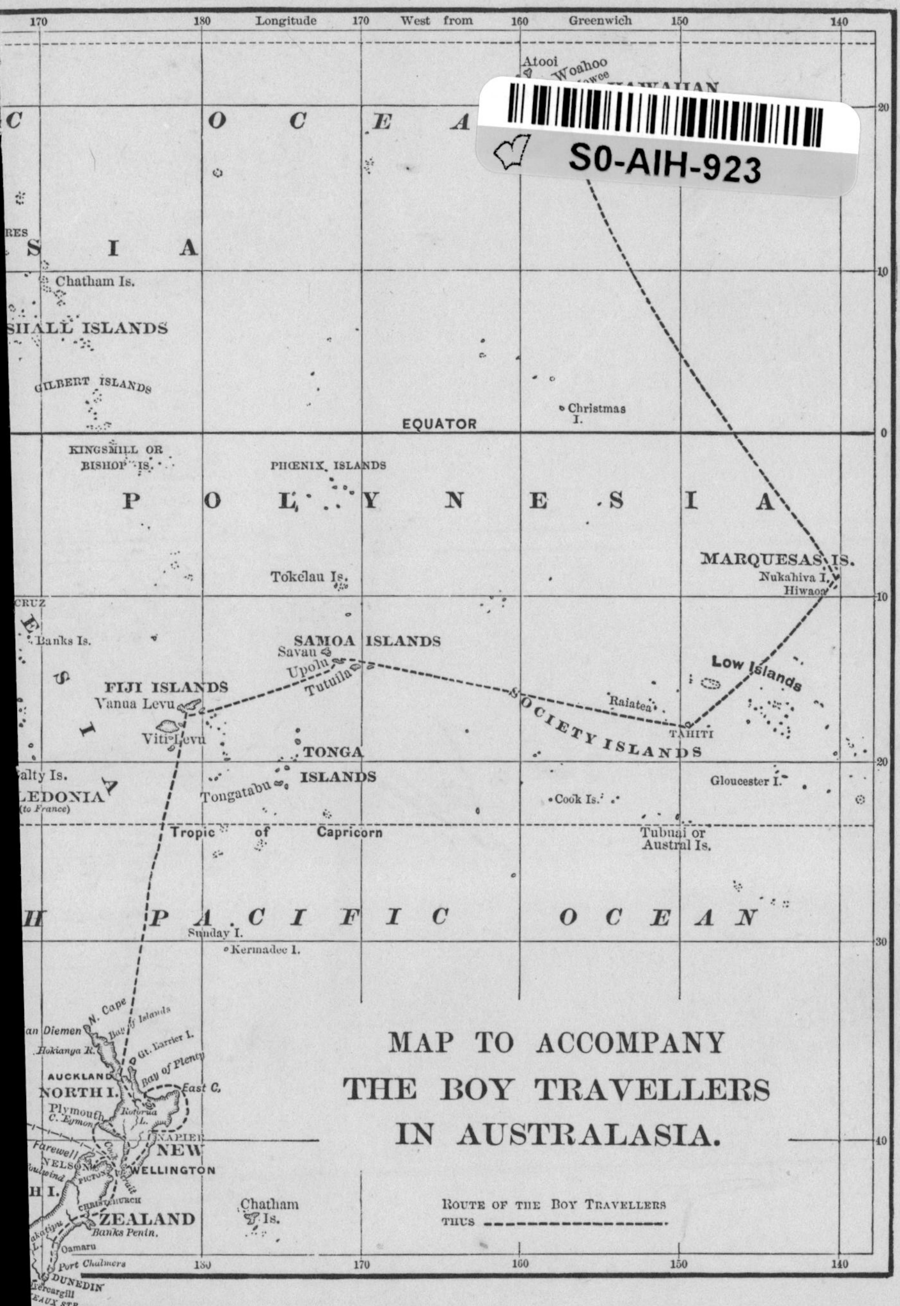
Longitude West from Greenwich
OCEANIA
POLYNESIA
PACIFIC OCEAN
EQUATOR
Tropic of Capricorn
Chatham Is.
GILBERT ISLANDS
KINGSMILL OR BISHOP IS.
PHŒNIX ISLANDS
Christmas I.
MARQUESAS IS.
Nukahiva I.
Hiwaoa
Tokelau Is.
SAMOA ISLANDS
Savau
Upolu
Tutuila
FIJI ISLANDS
Vanua Levu
Viti Levu
TONGA ISLANDS
Tongatabu
SOCIETY ISLANDS
Raiatea
TAHITI
Low Islands
Gloucester I.
Cook Is.
Tubuai or Austral Is.
Sunday I.
Kermadec I.
Banks Is.
Atooi
Woahoo
N. Cape
Bay of Islands
Hokianga R.
Gt. Barrier I.
AUCKLAND
Bay of Plenty
East C.
NORTH I.
Plymouth
C. Egmont
NAPIER
Farewell
NELSON
PICTON
NEW
WELLINGTON
CHRISTCHURCH
ZEALAND
Banks Penin.
Oamaru
Port Chalmers
DUNEDIN
Chatham Is.
LEDONIA (to France)
MAP TO ACCOMPANY THE BOY TRAVELLERS IN AUSTRALASIA.
ROUTE OF THE BOY TRAVELLERS THUS

THE BOY TRAVELLERS IN AUSTRALASIA

Drahému Jeníčkovi
babička, v máji 1959.

C. Graham

THE BOY TRAVELLERS IN

AUSTRALASIA

ADVENTURES OF TWO YOUTHS IN A JOURNEY TO

THE SANDWICH, MARQUESAS, SOCIETY, SAMOAN, AND FEEJEE ISLANDS, AND THROUGH THE COLONIES OF NEW ZEALAND, NEW SOUTH WALES QUEENSLAND, VICTORIA, TASMANIA, AND SOUTH AUSTRALIA

BY

THOMAS W. KNOX

AUTHOR OF "THE BOY TRAVELLERS IN THE FAR EAST" "IN SOUTH AMERICA" "IN RUSSIA" AND "ON THE CONGO" "THE YOUNG NIMRODS" "THE VOYAGE OF THE 'VIVIAN' " ETC.

WITH A NEW APPRECIATION BY CHARLES V. S. BORST

CHARLES E. TUTTLE CO.: PUBLISHERS

Rutland, Vermont & Tokyo, Japan

Representatives
Continental Europe: BOXERBOOKS, INC., *Zurich*
British Isles: PRENTICE-HALL INTERNATIONAL, INC., *London*
Australasia: PAUL FLESCH & CO., PTY. LTD., *Melbourne*
Canada: M. G. HURTIG LTD., *Edmonton*

Published by the Charles E. Tuttle Company, Inc.
of Rutland, Vermont & Tokyo, Japan
with editorial offices at
Suido 1-chome, 2-6, Bunkyo-ku, Tokyo, Japan

Library of Congress Catalog Card No. 71-94041

International Standard Book No. 0-8048-0072-3

First Tuttle edition published 1971

PRINTED IN JAPAN

TABLE OF CONTENTS

CHAPTER I.

CHAPTER II.

CHAPTER III.

CHAPTER IV.

CHAPTER V.

CHAPTER VI.

CHAPTER VII.

CHAPTER VIII.

CHAPTER IX.

CHAPTER X.

CHAPTER XI.

CHAPTER XII.

CHAPTER XIII.

CHAPTER XIV.

CHAPTER XV.

CHAPTER XVI.

CHAPTER XVII.

CHAPTER XVIII.

CHAPTER XIX.

CHAPTER XX.

CHAPTER XXI.

CHAPTER XXII.

CHAPTER XXIII.

THOMAS WALLACE KNOX

An Appreciation

It is curious that modern popular historians and historical novelists, in their often frantic search for colorful but forgotten figures from our American heritage, should have overlooked one name that would exactly fit their specifications for a dashing hero. This man is Thomas Wallace Knox (1835–96) who, at the height of his career in the 1880's, was one of the most popular literary figures of the New York scene but who today is only remembered by those aficionados of 19th-century boys' books. Journalist, best-selling author, inventor, world traveller extraordinary, Thomas Wallace Knox had a career almost as romantic and varied as those of his Victorian contemporaries, Sir Richard Burton and Richard Harding Davis.

The author's introduction to *The Boy Travellers in Australasia* at once suggests an intimate knowledge of the area based on both travel and careful research. One would hardly guess that the cosmopolitan and literate writer was the son of an obscure New Hampshire shoemaker who had never wandered more than a few miles from the small town of Pembroke, New Hampshire. If Mr. Knox, *père*, thought that Thomas (born June 26, 1835) would follow his calling as a cobbler, he was early disappointed when Thomas, tiring of the apprenticeship to his father, left his bench and went on the first of his many trips.

His first trip was only to Boston to attend public school, where his inquisitive mind was undoubtedly first stimulated by a desire to explore both his country and the rest of the world. However, he soon returned to the provincial world of Pembroke, where he continued his education by reading all he could while working on a farm. Largely, therefore, a self-taught man, Thomas became a teacher at the age of fourteen and then four years later established an academy at Kingston, New Hampshire, where he was the principal.

However, he could not long resist Horace Greeley's compulsive cry

"Go West, young man." Thomas went in 1860 when he was lured to Denver by the gold rush in Colorado. He reported the tragicomic happenings from the field so well for the *Denver Daily News* that he was soon chosen city editor. Far more portentous events, of course, were taking place, and immediately on the outbreak of the Civil War in 1861, Knox foresook the glamour of the gold fields for military service. Enlisting as a volunteer aide, he served through two southwestern campaigns in Arkansas and Missouri, where he was wounded during a skirmish. The governor of California recognized Knox's gallantry by appointing him to his staff.

During this time, Knox also served as a correspondent for James Gordon Bennett's *New York Herald*. He went as far as Shiloh with the federal forces in the invasion of Tennessee, but because of his frank dispatches he became *persona non grata* to Halleck, who banished him from the area. Knox then was associated with army movements up and down the Mississippi incident to the subsequent capture of Vicksburg. The brash young reporter also incurred the wrath of General Sherman and, in the subsequent court martial, Knox was convicted of disobeying military orders and excluded from the military department under Grant's command.

Since he was now a reporter without a beat, Knox attempted to manage a plantation near Waterproof, Louisiana. His experiences here, together with his collection of dispatches from the field, formed the material for his first book, *Camp Fire and Cotton Field: Southern Adventure in Time of War, Life with Union Armies and Residence on a Louisiana Plantation* (New York, 1865), a work described by one recent authority as possessing outstanding value for both its accuracy and its objectivity—all qualities which later distinguished his more famous books of travel.

A year later, the *Herald* rewarded its ace reporter with a choice assignment—a trip around the world, which sparked his interest in exotic places as well as invention. In Siberia to accompany an expedition sent by an American company to build a telegraph line for the Russian government, he travelled 3,600 miles in sledges and 1,400 miles in wagons. His fascination with the telegraph led to a system he later patented for the fast transmission of battlefield plans. Knox continued his interest in the telegraph for several years. In Ireland for the international rifle match at Dollymount (1875), he telegraphed the score by means of a device of his invention, indicating by the use of Morse signals the spot in which each ball struck the target. This he developed into a system of topographical telegraphy, which was sold to the United States government for the transmission of weather maps.

Two years later, in 1877, Knox embarked on his most productive world tour, after first serving as a member of the international jury at the Paris Universal Exposition of 1878. He leisurely explored many remote parts of the Orient, but perhaps the country he enjoyed most was Siam. Here the traveller found a receptive audience in the royal court, which had been fascinated with Western civilization ever since the famous visit of Anna Leonowens in the 1860's.

He recalled his earlier experiences as a teacher to the king, who was inspired to adopt a system of public instruction modelled on the ideals and methods of American education brought out in his conversation with Knox. This friendship with the king also resulted in the award of the decoration of the Order of the White Elephant for Knox's book *The Boy Travellers in the Far East: Part 2: Adventures of Two Youths in a Trip to Siam*, which the king declared to be the best description of the country ever written. After several other trips, in 1879 Knox settled in New York, where, until his death in 1896, his prolific outflow of best sellers averaged two a year. He produced some biographies, but his reputation was built on his travel books, especially the many volumes of the "Boy Travellers" series.

All these works are inspired by Knox's philosophy of travel which is expressed in his little guide *How to Travel* (New York, 1881): "To an observant and thoughtful individual, the invariable effect of travel is to teach respect for the opinions, the faith, or the ways of others, and to convince him that other civilizations than his own are worthy of consideration." This lack of condescension—rare for the often patronizing Victorian traveller—of course contributed to the accuracy of Knox's reporting in such a book as *The Boy Travellers in Australasia*. Combined with this accuracy is his insatiable curiosity about all aspects of life in the countries he visited—his work indeed foreshadowing the writing of modern anthropologists.

The net result is a work which, in the case of the book in hand, gives an intimate picture of late 19th-century Australian life during a particularly interesting time—a period when a civilization with a distinctive flavor all its own was emerging from the primitive frontier conditions which formed such a dramatic contrast to the great cities then being built. Knox's trenchant study provides ample material for any American student of westward development who would like to apply Frederick

Jackson Turner's famous frontier thesis to Australian history. His work, especially written in commemoration of the centennial celebration of settlement, gains added significance when one realizes, as Knox notes in his preface, that here is the first illustrated book descriptive of Australia and the neighboring colonies, New Zealand and Tasmania, to be written by an American and done by an American publisher.

Although the book is chiefly concerned with the Australian region, it is worth noting that over one-third of the text actually is devoted to Hawaii and the Polynesian area of the Pacific. An especially charming picture of Honolulu and Oahu is given in those idyllic last years of the Hawaiian monarchy. Here also is a detailed description of the French colony of Tahiti which is all the more interesting since this was the very time when Paul Gauguin was here painting his masterpieces of native life.

Many of the older American juveniles are now being reprinted for no other reason, I suspect, than that they are engaging and nostalgic period pieces. This, however, is a truly significant book, a work which undoubtedly first awakened the interest of many young Americans in a region, which as Knox forecast, would someday greatly affect their country's destiny. It is high time that we now share vicariously the adventures of Knox's youthful "veterans of travel," Frank Bassett and Fred Bronson, who will tell us what they learned on their long trip with their informative guide, Dr. Bronson, who is, of course, none other than Thomas Wallace Knox himself. This book was originally published in 1889 by Harper & Brothers, New York.

Charles V. S. Borst

PREFACE

THE first settlement in Australia was made in 1788; consequently the inhabitants of the great southern continent are this year celebrating their centennial. Three millions of people settled in five great colonies, possessing all the characteristics of an advanced civilization, with the unity developed by a common language and a common allegiance, and the rivalry that springs from the independence of each colony by itself, are uniting in the centennial celebration, and contrasting the Australia of to-day with that of one hundred years ago.

Previous to the discovery of gold in Australia, in 1851, Americans had but little knowledge of that far-away land. The opening of the auriferous fields attracted the attention of the whole civilized world to the antipodes, and many Americans joined the multitude that went thither in search of wealth. Since that time our relations with Australia have, year by year, grown more intimate. Railways across our continent and steamship lines over the broad Pacific have brought Sydney and Melbourne in juxtaposition to New York and San Francisco, and in this centennial Australian year we may almost regard the British colonies under the Southern Cross as our next-door neighbors.

The writer of this volume is not aware that any illustrated book descriptive of Australia and its neighboring colonies, New Zealand and Tasmania, by an American author, or from an American press, has ever yet appeared. Believing such a book desirable, he sent those youthful veterans of travel, Frank Bassett and Fred Bronson, over the route indicated on the title-page, with instructions to make careful note of what they saw and learned. Under the guidance of their mentor and our old friend Doctor Bronson they carried out their instructions to the letter, and the results of their observations will be found in the following pages. Trusting that the book will meet the favor that has been accorded to previous volumes of the "Boy Traveller" series, they offer their present work as their contribution to the Australian centennial, and hope that the boys and girls of their native land will find pleasure and profit in its perusal.

The method followed in the preparation of previous volumes of the series has been observed in the present book as far as it was possible to do so. The author's personal knowledge of the countries and people of Australasia has been supplemented by information drawn from many sources — from books, newspapers, maps, and other publications, and from numerous Australian gentlemen whom he has known or with whom he has been in correspondence. During the progress of the work he has kept a watchful eye on the current news from the antipodes, and sought to bring the account of the condition of the railways, telegraphs, and other constantly changing enterprises down to the latest dates.

Many of the books consulted in the preparation of "The Boy Travellers in Australasia" are named in the text, but circumstances made it inconvenient to refer to all. Among the volumes used are the following: Wallace's "Australasia," Forrest's "Explorations in Australia," Warburton's "Journey Across the Western Interior of Australia," Alexander's "Bush-fighting in the Maori War," Smyth's "Aborigines of Victoria," Bodham-Whetham's "Pearls of the Pacific," Murray's "Forty Years of Mission Work in Polynesia," Cumming's "At Home in Fiji," Markham's "Cruise of the *Rosario*," Palmer's "Kidnapping in the South Seas," Buller's "Forty Years in New Zealand," "Australian Pictures," Harcus's "South Australia," Eden's "Australia's Heroes," Trollope's "Australia and New Zealand," and Nordhoff's "Northern California, Oregon, and the Sandwich Islands."

The publishers have kindly allowed the use of illustrations that have appeared in HARPER'S MAGAZINE and other of their publications, and these illustrations have admirably supplemented those that were specially prepared for the book. The maps on the front and rear covers were specially drawn from the best authorities, and are intended to embody the most recent explorations and the latest developments of the railway systems of the Australian colonies.

T. W. K.

NEW YORK, *July*, 1888.

LIST OF ILLUSTRATIONS

THE BOY TRAVELLERS

IN

AUSTRALASIA.

CHAPTER I.

FROM SAN FRANCISCO TO HONOLULU.—SIGHTS ON THE PACIFIC OCEAN.—A PORTUGUESE MAN-OF-WAR.—NEARING THE SANDWICH ISLANDS.—THE MOLOKAI CHANNEL.—SURF-BEATEN SHORES OF OAHU.—ARRIVAL AT HONOLULU.—A PICTURESQUE PORT.—DISCOVERY AND HISTORY OF THE SANDWICH ISLANDS.—CAPTAIN COOK.—HIS TRAGIC DEATH.—HOW THE PEOPLE HAVE BEEN CIVILIZED.—WORK OF THE MISSIONARIES.—SCHOOLS AND CHURCHES.—PRESENT CONDITION OF THE POPULATION.—OLD CUSTOMS.—SIGHTS AND SCENES IN HONOLULU.—TARO AND POI.—A NATIVE DINNER.—THE COSTUMES OF THE ISLANDERS.—PECULIARITIES OF THE CLIMATE.—THE HULA-HULA AND OTHER DANCES.

"LAND, HO!" from the mast-head.

"Where away?" from the bridge.

"Dead ahead, sir!" was the reply; but it was almost drowned by the buzz of excitement which the announcement produced. The passengers, who had been strolling about the decks or listlessly lounging in their chairs, rushed hastily forward, in their eagerness to catch a glimpse of the land which had been reported "dead ahead."

ROYAL SCHOOL, HONOLULU.

This happened on board the steamship *Alameda*, early one pleasant afternoon as she was nearing the Sandwich Islands on a voy-

THE PHYSALIA.

age from San Francisco. There were three passengers who did not join in the scramble towards the bow of the ship, but remained quietly seated in their chairs. They had been through the experience of sighting land from a steamer at sea too many times to regard it as a novelty.

They were our old friends, Doctor Bronson and his nephews, Frank Bassett and Fred Bronson, whose experiences and adventures in various parts of the world are familiar to many American youths. Not content with what they had seen in Asia, Africa, and Europe, they were now bound on a voyage to the antipodes with the intention of adding another volume to the series in which their wanderings are recorded.*

It was on the eighth day of a voyage over the lovely azure waters of the broad Pacific that the *Alameda* neared the land, and many of her passengers half regretted that they were about to separate. The weather had been delightful, the breezes were light, the sky was nearly always clear, and the temperature high enough to make thick clothing uncomfortably warm, and an awning over the deck desirable. Since

* "The Boy Travellers in the Far East" (five volumes), and "The Boy Travellers in South America," "The Boy Travellers in the Russian Empire," and "The Boy Travellers on the Congo" (three volumes). See complete list at the end of this book.

the second day out from San Francisco not a sail had been seen, as the sailing-ships take another track in order to obtain stronger and more favoring winds. Four or five whales had shown themselves, and a few schools of porpoises played around the vessel from time to time as though they wished to make the acquaintance of the strange monster.

Flying-fish were numerous, and so were those curious denizens of the deep popularly known as "Portuguese men-of-war." One of the latter was caught by means of a bucket; a verdant passenger who admired its beautiful colors took it in his hand for a careful examination, but on feeling a stinging sensation he dropped it immediately. Doctor Bronson consoled him with the information that the scientific name of the Portuguese man-of-war is *Physalis pelagica*, and its power of stinging enables it to benumb its prey. It consists principally of an air-sac which floats it upon the water, and has long tentacles hanging down at various lengths. These tentacles are armed with stings; they paralyze any small fish that comes within their reach, and then act as fingers to sweep up the prize. It is a favorite trick of sailors to induce a novice to pick up a captured physalia, so that they may enjoy his haste in dropping it.

As the *Alameda* continued her course the outline of the land grew more and more distinct, revealing the rugged volcanic cliffs of Oahu, and reminding the passengers of the burning mountains for which the Sandwich Islands are famous. The course of the vessel lay through the Molokai Channel, leaving Molokai Island on the left, and hugging closely against the surf-beaten shores of Oahu, on which the capital, Honolulu, is situated. Near the water there were occasional groves of cocoanut-trees; but on the whole the shore was less tropical in appearance than our young friends had expected to find it.

THE ISLAND OF OAHU.

Every eye was straining to catch a view of Honolulu; but when its position was pointed out most of the passengers were unable to discover any marked indications of the presence of a town. After a time the steamer made a sharp turn to the starboard, and passed through the narrow channel which leads into the pretty harbor of Honolulu. Then the town appeared rather suddenly in view; its houses surrounded by groves of palms and tamarind-trees, interspersed with other tropical

GENERAL VIEW OF HONOLULU.

growths in rich profusion. The harbor is a deep basin in a coral reef, and so perfectly landlocked that it is ordinarily as smooth as a mill-pond, and is safe in all winds that blow. There is good anchorage for ships, and when the *Alameda* entered there was a fleet of sufficient size in the port to give it a very prosperous appearance. Numerous small boats were darting about, and almost before the engines were stopped the little craft swarmed in great force about the steamer.

Back of Honolulu rises a series of volcanic mountains three or four thousand feet high, and from the town itself to the foot of these mountains the ground rises in a gentle slope, so that the view from the harbor is an excellent one. Doctor Bronson called the attention of the youths to a valley opening through the mountains, and to the contrast between the cliffs and slopes, and the bright waters immediately around them. All agreed that the place was very prettily situated, and the view was a great relief after the monotonous voyage from San Francisco.

As soon as possible the party left the steamer and proceeded to the hotel, and, without waiting to see the rooms assigned to them, started out for a sight-seeing stroll. They desired to make the most of their time, as they expected to continue their journey in a week or ten days at farthest. The *Alameda* was to return to San Francisco as soon as she could land her cargo and receive another; the regular mail steamer for Australia would touch at Honolulu at the time indicated, and it was by this steamer they were to proceed southward.

IN THE HARBOR OF HONOLULU.

As they walked along the streets, accompanied by a guide whom they had engaged at the hotel, Doctor Bronson gave the youths a brief history of the Sandwich Islands, which Fred afterwards committed to paper lest it might escape his memory. Substantially it was as follows:

"The famous navigator Captain Cook has the credit of discovering these islands in 1778, but they were known to the Spaniards more than a century before that time. The death of Captain Cook served to bring the islands into prominence; he named them after Lord Sandwich, who was then First Lord of the Admiralty, but they are known here as the Hawaiian Islands, Hawaii being the largest of the group."

"That is the island where Captain Cook was killed, is it not?" inquired one of the youths.

"Yes," was the reply. "It was at Kealakeakua Bay, in sight of the great volcano of Mauna Loa. The famous navigator did not get along well with the natives, who, like nearly all savages, were addicted to thieving. One of his boats having been stolen, he determined to seize

QUEEN'S HOSPITAL, HONOLULU.

the King and hold him a prisoner until the boat was returned. For this purpose he landed with a lieutenant and nine men; the natives suspected his intentions, and a fight ensued, which resulted in his death."

"And they devoured him, it is said," Frank remarked.

"As to that," replied the Doctor, "there has been much dispute. Captain King, the successor of Cook, and historian of the expedition after the latter's death, positively declares that the body of Cook was eaten, along with the bodies of the sailors and marines who were killed at the same time. On the other hand, the islanders declare with equal positiveness that cannibalism did not exist here at that time; and though great indignities might have been perpetrated, the horrible accusation is untrue. At this distance of time it is impossible to say what happened, and we will dismiss the subject. But it is generally conceded that the great navigator owed his death to his severity in dealing with the natives, and his imprudence in venturing on shore with the small force which accompanied him.

"But we'll leave the famous captain at rest," continued the Doctor, "while we give our attention to more modern things. Great changes have taken place in the hundred years or so that have elapsed since

Captain Cook's death. Then the people were savages and idolaters; now they are civilized and Christianized, and may be considered a harmless and kindly disposed race. Education is universal among them, hardly a native of Hawaii being unable to read and write. Every child is obliged to attend the public schools, and there is a special school-tax of two dollars on every voter, in addition to a general tax for educational purposes. Schools are in every part of the islands where there is any population, and the teachers are paid out of the taxes I have mentioned."

KEALAKEAKUA BAY, WHERE CAPTAIN COOK WAS KILLED.

"I suppose the missionaries are to be credited with the spread of education here, are they not?" one of the youths asked.

"Yes," was the reply; "and there have been no more earnest and energetic missionaries anywhere in the world than those that came to the Hawaiian Islands. The first missionaries arrived here in 1820, and for thirty-three years the mission enterprise was supported by contributions in the United States and elsewhere. In that time the donations of Christian people in the United States for the conversion of the inhabitants of the Hawaiian Islands amounted to more than nine hundred thousand dollars."

"What was done at the end of that time?" Fred asked.

"In 1853 the missionaries reported that the people of the Hawaiian Islands had been converted to Christianity, and that idolatry no longer

MRS. THURSTON, ONE OF THE MISSIONARIES OF 1820.

existed among them. Then it was voted by the American Board of Missions that 'the Sandwich Islands, having been Christianized, shall no longer receive aid from this Board.' From that time the churches have been practically self-supporting, though they have received some aid from America. At present the Hawaiian Islands have a missionary society of their own which is sending missionaries and teachers into other islands of the Pacific; and they have a printing-office, where Bibles are printed in several Polynesian languages—just as Bibles were formerly printed in New York for the use of the Sandwich Islanders."

Here the guide interrupted them to point out Kawaiaho church, which he said was the first native church in Honolulu, a substantial and well-built edifice that reminded the strangers of many churches they had seen in the New England States. In reply to Frank's remark to this effect Doctor Bronson said that the most of the early missionaries came from Boston and its vicinity, and it was therefore to be expected that the churches would be of the New England pattern.

KAWAIAHO CHURCH—FIRST NATIVE CHURCH IN HONOLULU.

Fred asked if the church they were passing was the first ever built in the islands. The guide explained that it was the first *native* church, but not the first American one. That honor belongs to the Seamen's (or Bethel) church, which was sent from Boston in a whale-ship around Cape Horn; it was brought in pieces, and set up soon after the ship arrived here. Honolulu has been for a long time a great resort for whalemen, and about 1846 special attention was paid to their needs by the establishment of a Bethel church and society.

The most famous man in connection with this branch of the missionary enterprise was Rev. Mr. Damon, who obtained the reputation of an earnest friend of the seamen, and was generally called "Father Damon,"

BETHEL CHURCH.

in consequence of his paternal care and his kindness towards all who came within his influence. He established a Seamen's Home in connection with the church, and it has been of great use in keeping the sailors away from the evil influences that are found in most ocean ports.

"Go where you will on these islands," said the Doctor, "you will

NATIVE SCHOOL-HOUSE IN HONOLULU.

find churches everywhere, and not far from each church there is a native school-house where the children are taught to read and write. On Sunday the churches are filled with worshippers, and there is no more devout people anywhere than on these islands. There are now more churches than are needed by the population, for the reason, not that there is any decline in religious zeal, but because of the decrease in the number of inhabitants. At the time of Captain Cook's discovery the islands were estimated to have a population of not far from two hundred thousand. Small-pox, measles, and other diseases have made terrible havoc, and at present the native population is little if any above fifty thousand. It has been declining with more or less rapidity ever since the beginning of the century, and the last census showed a considerable falling off since the one that preceded it.

THE COURT-HOUSE IN HONOLULU.

"Not only are the islanders diminishing in numbers," he continued, "but the people of to-day are said to be smaller in stature than those of a century ago. The missionaries and other old residents say that when they first came here they used to meet great numbers of natives of high stature and majestic figures, belonging generally to the old families of chiefs and nobles. Occasionally at this time you may see them, but not often."

"I suppose the chiefs and nobles were of a different race," Frank remarked, "otherwise they would all be of the same general height."

"That was formerly supposed to be the case," was the reply, "and even now the theory is sustained by many people. But I believe the general opinion is that all were of the same race, and the superior development of the chiefs and nobles was due to their easier life and better food, which could hardly fail to have an effect through many generations."

NATIVE GENTLEMAN OF HONOLULU.

One of the youths asked if the people received the missionaries kindly, and showed a desire to be instructed and civilized.

"In a general way they did," was the reply, "though that was by no means always the case. Some of the chiefs looked suspiciously upon the coming of the strangers, fearing, and not without reason, that their power would be diminished as their subjects became enlightened. The King was favorable to the work of the missionaries, and consequently the hostility of the chiefs could not be exercised with severity. Before the advent of the missionaries the Hawaiians had no written language. The missionaries reduced the language to writing, prepared school-books, a dictionary, a hymn-book, and a translation of a part of the Scriptures, all in the native tongue, and they trained the native teachers who were needed for the management of the schools then and afterwards established.

"In this way the missionaries gave the Hawaiian people the benefits of civilization, and year by year saw the old superstitions and customs disappearing. Some of them still remain, but not many; just as in New England you may to this day find people who believe in witchcraft, and all over the United States persons who have implicit faith in supernatural things. The Hawaiians are by no means perfect in their morals and beliefs, and you can find iniquity in Honolulu, just as you may find it in Boston or Philadelphia. Murder and theft were very common a hundred years ago; now the former crime is quite as rare as in the United States, and as for the latter, it is even more so. Nearly all the stealing in the islands is done by Chinese or other foreigners, and not by the natives."

Our friends passed near the court-house, which bore a marked resemblance to an American town-hall in a prosperous town, and stood at the edge of a well-kept garden. The Doctor remarked that court-houses and jails were some of the adjuncts of all civilized lands, and therefore they were needed in Hawaii as well as elsewhere. "But I am told," he continued, "that the majority of the inmates of the jail at Honolulu are of other races than the Hawaiian, and that Americans and English form a good proportion."

A little way beyond the court-house our friends met a man carrying two covered baskets slung at the ends of a short pole which rested on his shoulder. Frank turned to the guide and asked what the man was carrying.

HAWAIIAN POI-DEALER.

"He's a poi peddler," was the reply, "and I wonder you have not met one before, as there are many of them. He peddles poi, and the people buy it to eat."

He then explained that poi is the national dish of the islands, and is made from the taro-root, which is the Sandwich Island form of the potato. He pointed out a taro-garden, and said that there were many such gardens in and around Honolulu, as the natives did not consider a home complete without one.

The taro-root is baked in an underground oven, and then mashed very fine, so that it would be like flour if the moisture were expelled. After it has been thoroughly mashed it is mixed with water, and in this condition is ready for eating. It has an agreeable taste when fresh, and most foreigners like it upon the first trial. For native use it is allowed to ferment; when fermented it suggests sour paste to the

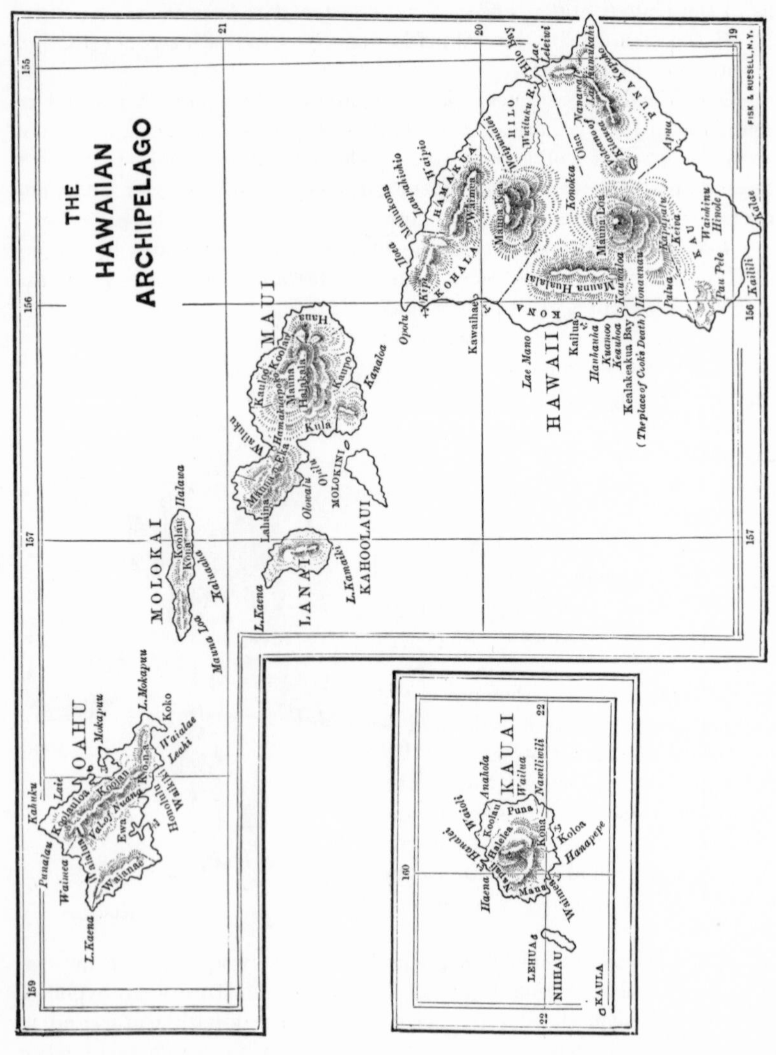
THE
HAWAIIAN
ARCHIPELAGO
HAWAII
MAUI
MOLOKAI
OAHU
LANAI
KAHOOLAUI
MOLOKINI
KAUAI
NIIHAU
LEHUA
KAULA
Mauna Kea
Mauna Loa
Mauna Hualalai
HILO
Hilo Bay
KONA
KOHALA
HAMAKUA
PUNA
KAU
Kawaihae
Kailua
Kealakeakua Bay
(The place of Cook's Death)
Haleakala
Lahaina
Wailuku
Kanaloa
Halawa
Honolulu
Waikiki
Ewa
Waianae
Koko
L. Kaena
L. Mokapuu
Waimea
Koloa
Hanapepe
Hanalei
Nawiliwili
155
156
157
159
160
19
20
21
22
FISK & RUSSELL, N.Y.

uneducated palate, and is nauseating to the novice. Natives greatly prefer it in this form, and a good many foreigners cultivate their taste until they too would rather have their poi sour than fresh.

Soon after the islands were settled by foreigners an ingenious Yankee saw a chance for making money by importing machinery for making poi, in place of the old form of hand-crushing. Now there are factories in various parts of the island where poi is made in large quantities, chiefly for the use of planters and other large consumers. It forms quite an article of export to other islands where Polynesian labor is employed, and especially to the guano islands, where nothing can be cultivated. A former king of Hawaii established a poi factory at Honolulu, and by so doing became very unpopular with his subjects, just as has been the case with other kings who have introduced labor-saving machinery into their dominions.

HAWAIIANS AT A FEAST.

At dinner that evening Frank and Fred asked for poi and were promptly supplied. It was explained to them that the native way of eating it was to insert the forefinger in the dish, twirl it around until it was well coated with the sticky substance, and then draw the finger through the mouth. Both the youths concluded that they would allow the natives to monopolize that form of eating, which was hardly to be reconciled with civilized customs. They contented themselves with spoons, which answered their purpose completely.

NATIVE HAY PEDDLER.

Poi, fish, and pork are the principal articles of food among the Hawaiians; but at a feast several articles are added that do not come into the daily bill of fare. The guide took Frank and Fred to a native *luau*, or festival, and pointed out the following dishes: poi, fish and pork, as already mentioned; baked ti-root, which bore a striking resemblance to molasses-cake, of which New Englanders are fond, and the resemblance included both appearance and taste; raw shrimps and limu, which is a sea-moss smelling and tasting very disagreeably to the novice; kuulaau, which is an agreeable compound of cocoa-nut and taro-root; paalolo, a combination of cocoa-nut and sweet-potato, of a sweetish taste; and two or three additional mixtures of the same sort. Then there were cuttle-fish raw and cooked, roasted dog, and a small quantity of pickled salmon, liberally dosed with red pepper. Fred suggested that as the salmon was imported, and therefore expensive, the red pepper was freely added in order that the article would be sparingly eaten.

The guide, who was a native, explained that the feast was for the purpose of enabling the giver to build a new house, and each guest was expected to pay fifty cents for his entertainment. He pointed out a calabash bowl lying on the ground as the receptacle of the money, as it was a matter of etiquette for the master not to receive the cash directly from the hands of his guests. The affair had been arranged some time beforehand, and the price of the feast was mentioned in the invitation. Everybody was in new clothes, it being one of the Hawaiian customs that every garment worn at a feast must be quite new, and a native would rather be absent from the entertainment than violate this point of etiquette. Five or six men who served as stewards were dressed exactly alike, each of them wearing a green shirt and red trousers, made for the occasion. In addition to this, they had green wreaths on their heads, and most of the persons present had their heads decked with flowers or leaves.

The diners sat on the ground, and as they took their places their portions of roast pig, neatly wrapped in ti-leaves, were distributed to them. They were expected to be satisfied with their allowance, and etiquette forbade their asking for more of this article, though they could help themselves freely to anything else. When the feast was over each one carried away whatever of his roast pork was unconsumed. The guide said it would be very impolite to leave any portion of it, and even the bones were carried away. The feeding was not done in a hurry; a native feast lasts for several hours, the guests pausing two or three times to get up a fresh touch of appetite, and occasionally walking about, singing, dancing, talking, or laughing, in order to increase the capacity of their stomachs.

Our young friends tasted some of the dishes, and each dropped a half-dollar in the calabash bowl that was designated as the receptacle of the contributions of the guests. They carried away their portions of roast pig, and gave the packages to some urchins whom they encountered a short distance from the scene of the feast. The latter immediately sat down to enjoy the toothsome delicacy, and no doubt imagined themselves to be for the time the most favored beings in the land. Their appearance indicated that roast pig did not often enter into their bill of fare, and the rapidity with which they attacked the contents of the packages showed that they had not dined.

Frank thought it must have been a great change for the people of the islands when they abandoned their old custom of going without clothing and adopted the dress of civilization. When it is remembered that a hundred years ago the islanders were naked savages, the remark of the youth is not to be wondered at. The missionaries say that in the early days the attempts of the natives to adopt European dress were decidedly ludicrous; they could not understand the necessity of three or more garments, but thought a single one sufficient to begin with. A hat, a shirt, and a pair of trousers were considered enough for three, and some of them used to argue that these garments

DRESS OF HAWAIIAN WOMEN.

were altogether too numerous for one individual, when there were so many others without anything.

Fred made a sketch of a group of women, and afterwards procured several photographs showing how the feminine natives of the islands are ordinarily clad. On the back of the sketch he wrote as follows:

"The dress of the women can hardly be called picturesque, but after being seen a few times its oddity is not as apparent as at first. Most of the women go bareheaded, or with wreaths of leaves and flowers in their hair. Their dress hangs from the shoulders without being gathered in at the waist, and quite closely resembles the morning wrapper of civilized lands, though it is not so ornamental. Black, dark, and pink are the usual colors of the dress, but on festive occasions something gayer can be frequently seen. You would be surprised to see the grace and dignity with which the older women carry themselves, and I think much of it is due to the loosely flowing dress."

The climate is so mild that heavy clothing is not needed. The heat is of course greater in the lowlands than among the mountains, whose highest peaks are covered with snow for a considerable part of the year. Honolulu is said to be the hottest place in the kingdom, and thin clothing, but not the thinnest, is worn there the entire year. White is worn a great deal, but it is so easily soiled that a good many prefer to wear garments of blue serge, or blue or gray flannel. Flannel is desirable for the winter months, but the islands are so near the equator that the difference between winter and summer is not very great.

In December and January the temperature sometimes falls to 62° Fahrenheit in the early morning, but by noon, or 2 P.M., it generally reaches 75° or 76°, and remains between that point and 70° until midnight. In July the highest point reached is 86°, and on a few occasions 87°. The extreme range of the thermometer is not more than 26° or 28°, which makes it a very comfortable climate to live in. It is said to be an excellent one for persons suffering from pulmonary complaints, though it is somewhat debilitating for healthy men and women accustomed to the rigorous climate of the northern States of America.

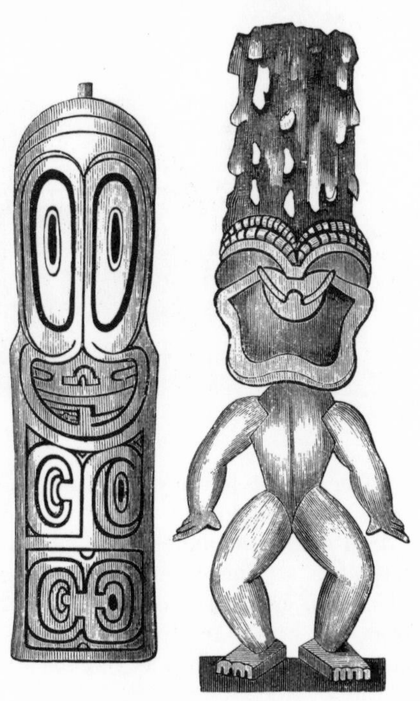

ANCIENT IDOLS OF HAWAII.

Residents of the islands say there are regions among the mountains where the nights are invariably cool enough for a fire all the year round, while the days are never hot. Even in Honolulu the air is not as sultry as that of New York or Philadelphia in July and August, and the greatest heat experienced is almost always tempered by a breeze. There is more rain in winter than in summer, but there is no really dry season. It is a circumstance that strikes the stranger curiously that there is much more rain on the windward side of the islands than on the leeward; sometimes the former will have a great deal of rain, while the latter gets little or hardly any. The trade-wind controls the rainfall, and by ascertaining where it strikes a new-comer may have much or little rain accordingly as he selects his place of residence.

GRASS HOUSE, HAWAIIAN ISLANDS.

The guide told the youths that they could sit on the veranda of the hotel at Honolulu and see the rain fall every day, but without getting a drop within the limits of the city. "You may be here all day in the sunshine," said he; "but if you are going to the windward side of the island you must take your rubber overcoats. The showers that you see from the hotels are from the clouds that have been blown over the mountains, and as soon as you cross the range you will be in the midst of them."

Doctor Bronson said that the decrease in the population of the islands had been, by some people, attributed to the adoption of clothing by the natives. "It is argued," said he, "that the people are very careless, and have not learned the sanitary laws which govern the use of clothing. A native thinks nothing of lying down with his wet clothes upon him when he has been soaked by a rain or dipped in the surf; it is hard to make him understand that such a practice is dangerous, and many of the inhabitants have died of the severe colds contracted in this way."

In the outskirts of the city our friends came to a house which the guide said was a good specimen of the native dwelling, and they obtained permission to enter and examine it. It had a door, but no windows; was a single story in height, and its sides were made of upright sticks interwoven with palm-leaves, while the roof was thatched with grass. The floor was of solid earth covered with mats, and at one end there was a sort of platform raised a foot higher than the rest. This platform was the sleeping-place of the inmates, and was elevated in order to insure its freedom from dampness in case of a heavy rain. In front of the house was a bench, where one might sit in the shade during the afternoon, and where no doubt the owner idled away a considerable part of his time. The islanders are not fond of hard work, and in fact they have no occasion to labor as industriously as do the inhabitants of more rigorous regions.

Around Honolulu the expense of living is greater than it is away from the port, owing to the increased price of the products of the fields.

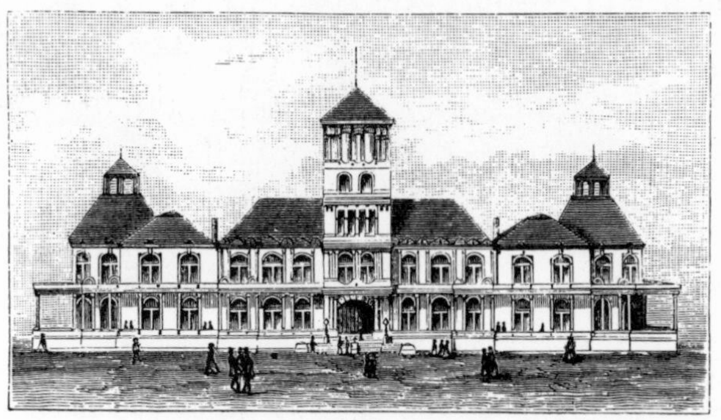

GOVERNMENT BUILDINGS, HONOLULU.

In the country it may be said that a man who works two days in the week can support his family comfortably, especially if he is near the sea-coast, whence he can obtain a supply of fish at any time he chooses to go for them. Fishing, taro-planting, and making poi are his chief occupations, and to these he generally adds mat-weaving, which is neither difficult nor laborious. His wants are few and easily supplied, and it is no wonder that the islander displays an unwillingness to wear himself out in constant toil. The conditions of life do not require him to do so, and he lacks the ambition to accumulate a fortune solely for the sake of accumulating it.

After dinner the guide proposed that the strangers should witness a *hula-hula*, or native dance. It was quite unlike the dancing of European countries, consisting principally of more or less active movements of the limbs while the body of the dancer swayed from side to side.

HAWAIIAN DANCING-GIRLS.

The dancers were girls dressed in short frocks like those worn by American school-girls; they had wreaths in their hair and around their ankles, and their dresses were loosely gathered in at the waist, where they were held by cords. The music was supplied by two men who struck their hands upon large calabashes and sang or chanted a low monotonous air. A very little of the dance satisfied the curiosity of the visitors, and they returned to the hotel at an early hour.

The Hawaiians have another dance, which can be seen at their festivals; it is performed by men and women, usually elderly people, and is accompanied by singing, in which all may join. Then there are dances for the younger people, but they are not generally practised, owing to the opposition of the missionaries, and possibly to the unwillingness of the people to indulge in active exercise unless they are paid for it. All the dances have descended from the days before the advent of the foreigners, and therefore have an interest for any one who desires to learn whatever he can about the history of the islanders.

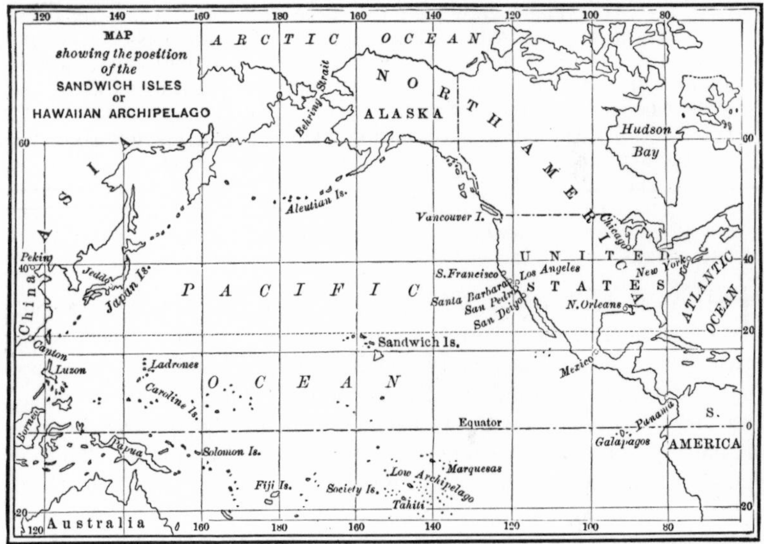

CHAPTER II.

IN AND AROUND HONOLULU.—PUBLIC BUILDINGS.—THE THEATRE.—ROAD TO THE PALI.—A MAGNIFICENT VIEW.—VILLAS NEAR THE CITY.—GIRLS ON HORSEBACK.—TARO-FIELDS.—THE WATER SUPPLY.—MOUNTAIN-PASS.—HAWAIIAN COW-BOYS.—HILO AND THE VOYAGE THITHER.—APOCHRYPHAL STORIES ABOUT THE RAIN.—SURF-SWIMMING.—THE GREAT VOLCANO OF KILAUEA.—OVER THE LAVA-FIELDS.—DIFFICULT ROADS.—THE VOLCANO HOUSE.—A DISTURBED NIGHT.—BURNING LAKES.—SIGHT-SEEING UNDER DIFFICULTIES.—TERRIFYING SCENES.—KILAUEA AND MAUNA LOA.—THE GREATEST VOLCANO IN THE WORLD.—HISTORIC ERUPTIONS.—CRATER OF HALEAKALA.—SUGAR CULTURE IN HAWAII, ITS EXTENT AND INCREASE.—OTHER INDUSTRIES.—RETURNING BY SCHOONER TO HONOLULU.—LEPER ISLAND OF MOLOKAI.—A DAY AMONG THE LEPERS.

THE next day was devoted to excursions in the immediate vicinity of Honolulu, a carriage-drive through the principal streets of the town, a visit to the palace and other Government buildings, and two or three calls to present letters of introduction. The visit to the palace included an introduction to the King, Kalakaua, who received his visitors politely and devoted a short time to their entertainment. The conversation referred mainly to the United States, and barely touched upon matters connected with the islands.

In their drive about the city Frank and Fred found that Honolulu is a well-built town with narrow streets. The houses are mostly of wood, dropped down rather carelessly in many places, with little attempt at uniformity, and not much decoration. The amount of tropical verdure, which almost concealed many of the villas and detached residences in the side streets and outskirts of the place, recalled Ceylon and other regions near the equator which they had visited in their former travels. Frank thought he could readily imagine himself in the suburbs of Colombo, while Fred was inclined to close his eyes for a moment and think he had been transported on the enchanted carpet of the Arabian Nights to Batavia or Buitenzorg, in Java. In many of the court-yards fountains were playing, the drops of water sparkling in the bright sunshine, and adding materially to the beauty of the scene.

There are some fine residences in Honolulu, but none that would be considered of much consequence in a wealthy capital of Europe. The best buildings are the public ones, and in the list we must include the Hawaiian hotel, as it was built by the Government at an expense that was considered a heavy one for the country to bear. Near the hotel is the theatre, which is also a Government affair, and brings very little revenue to its owners. It is in use occasionally whenever a strolling company on a voyage between Australia and America happens along and gives a few performances. Honolulu is hardly able to support a theatre through the entire year, as the portion of the population able and willing to patronize it is very small.

LAHAINA, ISLAND OF MAUI.

Frank and Fred were amused at the equestrian performances of the natives, and particularly at the dash and energy with which the laughing girls pushed their horses at full speed. They rode "man-fashion," bestriding the horse instead of sitting on a side-saddle, and few of them seemed contented with any but the most rapid pace. The horses of the Hawaiian Islands are small but strong, and capable of great endurance;

in fact, if they were otherwise it is evident they would not live long, when the habits of the natives are remembered. In travelling in the Hawaiian Islands it is necessary to carry your saddle, as carriage-roads are not numerous, and a good many places that one wishes to visit cannot be reached by wheeled vehicles. Of course it is possible to hire saddles when hiring horses, but this is by no means universally the case.

WOMEN ON HORSEBACK, HONOLULU.

The afternoon drive was extended to the Pali, a mountain-pass six miles out of the town, and one of the chief attractions to visitors who can only make a brief stay at Honolulu. Outside of the business portion of the place our friends entered upon a straight and very dusty road, which for the first two miles and more led among the villas belonging to the merchants and other well-to-do people who make Honolulu their home. Each villa stands in a garden by itself, and the houses are often rendered invisible by the masses of foliage that surround them, and the creeping and climbing plants that rise to their very tops. The road steadily rises, and consequently the occupants of the houses have fine views of the bay and town; while the mountains rise behind them to form a background. Fred was so charmed with the beauty of the scene that he wished to sketch some of the villas, but the recollection of their limited time prevented his carrying the desire into execution.

Beyond this region of villas the carriage entered the foot-hills, where the road wound with a steep grade among taro-fields, in which men were at work up to their knees in water tending the plants which yield to the Hawaiian the staff of life. The water which irrigates the taro-fields is brought by innumerable streams from the sides of the mountains, to which it is supplied by the clouds borne by the trade-winds. Honolulu receives its water from the mountains, and there is certainly an abundance of it.

Beyond the taro-fields there is good grazing for cattle and sheep, of which there are numerous herds and flocks. Frank called attention to a water-fall some distance away, which made a pretty contrast with the dark sides of the mountain, and was evidently nearly, if not quite,

A MOUNTAIN VALLEY.

two hundred feet in height. At one of the turns of the road the carriage came in contact with a cart which was descending the slope too swiftly for safety; the damage was trifling, but for a few moments things wore a serious aspect, as there was a good chance of being tossed over the side of the almost precipitous slope.

There were not many travellers along the road, the most picturesque being groups of girls on horseback and the herders who were driving cattle to market or for a change of pasture. The girls were generally in bright-colored robes, which were gathered in at the waist with brighter sashes that streamed behind them as they dashed along

HAWAIIAN TEMPLE.

(*From a Russian Engraving about* 1790.)

the road. Most of them wore straw hats on their heads, and generally the hats were adorned with flowers in wreaths and festoons, which were most liberally bestowed. Now and then Frank's attention was drawn to a pretty face which surmounted a neck adorned with a string of blossoms of gaudy colors; the necklace formed an admirable setting for the complexion, but sometimes the blossoms were not chosen with due regard to the contrast of colors.

The Hawaiian cow-boys, or cattle-drivers, were not unlike their American prototypes, as they wore broad-brimmed hats and bright-colored scarfs; they were mounted on tough little horses, and sat in saddles of the American cow-boy pattern, the pommel rising high, and the stirrups made of wood. Then there were strings of pack-mules and horses coming down from the points in the mountains inaccessible to wheeled vehicles, and now and then our friends met a Chinese gardener taking the produce of his little patch to market on the back of a pack animal, and in some instances on a wheelbarrow. A few groups of men and women on foot were encountered, but the number was so small that Frank and Fred concluded that the Hawaiians were a home-loving people, and did not wander about much.

Near the Pali the road passed through thickets of how-trees, which resembled the growths of manzanita on the slopes of the California foot-hills. These thickets are so dense that it is impossible for man or horse to pass through them; in fact they are impenetrable to any but the smallest animals. Frank thought he would like to cut a cane as a souvenir, but refrained from doing so when reminded by Fred that he could probably buy all the canes he wanted in Honolulu.

MOUNTAIN SCENE IN THE SANDWICH ISLANDS.

Suddenly from the other side of the narrow pass a wonderful panorama was presented. Around on each side were the rugged cliffs of the mountain range, while in front they looked from a height of eight or nine hundred feet above the sea-level upon a picture which included every variety of scenery. In the distance was the blue Pacific washing the sandy shores and curving reefs of coral, and between the ocean and the point where our friends were standing were grassed and wooded foot-hills, and long stretches of lowlands dotted with coffee and sugar plantations, taro-fields, and other evidences of careful cultivation, together with villages and clusters of huts that marked the dwelling-places of the men engaged in this tropical agriculture.

"We could almost say that we had the colors of the rainbow in this bit of landscape," said Fred, afterwards, while describing the scene. "The blue sky and sea were tinged with purple, the distant mountains varied in shades of blue and gray, the foot-hills and plains gave us every verdant tinge that you can name, from the bright green of the mountain grass to the dark foliage of the vegetation that surrounded the villages; and as for yellow, you had it in every variety, from the reddish tint of the sinuous roads to the bright and almost white belt of sand that separated land from sea. We recalled several similar views in different parts of the world, but could give none of them preference over this. It was the view from the Baidar Gate in the Crimea, combined with Wockwalla near Point de Galle, and a bit of the scene from the Righi Culm in Switzerland."

Whoever goes to the Hawaiian Islands will consider his visit incomplete unless he includes the island of Hawaii and the great volcano of Kilauea in his tour. Doctor Bronson desired that the party should proceed thither at the earliest moment, and found on inquiry that a steamer was to leave for Hilo on the second morning after their arrival at Honolulu.

"Prepare for wet weather," said his informant, "as it rains all the time at Hilo. They say they have seventeen feet of rain there annually, and sometimes there are days and days together when it rains without letting up a minute. Gum-coats and water-proofs are in order, and the more you have of them the better."

Continuing, the narrator said that a Hilo man once made an experiment by knocking out the heads of an oil-cask, and it rained in at the bung-hole faster than the water could run out at the ends! Frank asked for the documents in the case—the affidavits before the justice of the peace, and the certificate of the resident clergyman—but they were not forthcoming. Another story was that the fishes frequently swam up into the air a distance of three or four hundred yards before discovering they were not in the bay, the showers being so dense that it was impossible for them to distinguish the one from the other. Fred declared himself skeptical on this subject, as the showers consisted of fresh water, while the bay was salt, and a salt-water fish does not usually show a willingness to swim up a fresh-water stream except in the spawning season.

The run to Hilo was made in about forty hours, the steamer making several stops on the way. It rained "cats and dogs" when the party landed, but as all the baggage had been wrapped in water-proof coverings, nothing was damaged. Arrangements were speedily made for departure on the following morning without regard to the weather; horses and guides were engaged, the best animals being selected for the saddles and others for packing purposes, and a substantial lunch was made

HILO.

ready for the mid-day meal. Doctor Bronson insisted that the horses should all be freshly shod before starting, and an extra supply of shoes and nails carried along. The road goes over the lava-beds for nearly the whole distance, and if a horse loses a shoe he will go lame in a very few minutes, so rough and cutting is the lava.

Fortunately the morning was fine, and the bay of Hilo presented a pretty appearance. Groves of palm and other tropical trees lined the shore, the surf broke in regular pulsations upon the curving stretch of beach, and was made animate by dozens of men and boys at play in the waves. For the first time our friends saw some of the sport in the water for which the islanders are famous, though less so at present than in the days that are gone. Fred thus described it:

"Each man had a surf-board, which was a thick plank twelve or fifteen feet long and perhaps thirty inches wide, and said to be made

SURF-BATHING AT HILO.

from the trunk of a bread-fruit tree. There were five or six of the natives to whom we had promised half a dollar each for the performance. They pushed out with their planks to the first line of breakers and managed to dip under it and swim along by the help of the undertow. They passed the second line in the same way, and finally got beyond the entire stretch of surf into comparatively smooth water.

"Then they tossed up and down for a while, waiting for their chance. What they wanted was an unusually high swell, and they tried to find a place in front of it so that it would sweep them towards the shore just where it broke into a comber. They tried several times but failed, and we began to get out of patience.

"At last they got what they had waited for, while some were kneeling on their planks and others lying extended with their faces downward, and just ahead of the great comber they swept on at a speed of little, if any, less than forty miles an hour. There they were just ahead of the breaker, and apparently sliding downhill; one of them was swamped by it, but he dived and came up behind the wave and made ready for the next. The others kept on, and were flung high and dry by the surf, and as soon as they could rise from their planks they ran towards us to receive their pay. One of the fellows stood erect on his plank while in the surf, just as the Nubians at the first cataract of the Nile stand up while descending through the foaming water."

Meanwhile the guides were busy getting the cavalcade in readiness, and a little before eight o'clock the party was under way for the great volcano. From Hilo to the Volcano House is a distance of thirty miles. The horses go for the most of the time at a walk, and though the ride has been accomplished in six hours, it is better to allow not less than ten for it, and "take things easily." This will give time for a rest of an hour for lunch at the Half-way House—the lunch being the one which we have already prepared.

THE VOLCANO HOUSE.

Frank wanted to try the effect of a gallop, but to guard against accidents Doctor Bronson suggested that gallops would be out of order for the day. The path over the lava is full of holes, and very rough and broken in many places. The natives trot and gallop along the road, but the novice should refrain from so doing. At a walking pace there is little discomfort and practically no danger, and parties of ladies and children can make the journey without excessive fatigue. "Chi va piano va sano," as the Italians say.

The youths found the ride from Hilo to the volcano full of interest. They amused themselves by comparing the lava-fields with those of the volcanoes they had visited in other parts of the world, and they studied the ferns, of which there were many varieties, the largest of them having stalks three or four feet in diameter and a height of fifteen or twenty feet. Other ferns were very small, and between the small and large there were all shades of colors and all possible sizes. One of the guides showed that the ferns were not altogether ornamental plants, as he plucked from one of them a woolly substance he called *pulu*, and said it was used for stuffing beds and pillows. Many tons of pulu are exported every year to America and other countries.

At the Half-way House everybody was hungry, and the lunch was speedily disposed of. A little after six o'clock in the evening the Volcano House was reached, and here the party spent the night. A good supper was prepared and eaten, and the incidents of the day and plans of the morrow were discussed; then the youths joined Doctor Bronson, at the suggestion of the latter, in a sulphur vapor-bath of Nature's own preparation, and after it all retired to sleep. The accommodations were limited, but everybody was weary enough to be willing to put up with the most primitive style of lodging, provided nothing better could be obtained.

Here is what Frank wrote concerning the visit of our friends to the crater of the volcano:

"We took a hearty breakfast and left the house about half-past eight o'clock in the morning, to make acquaintance with the crater. We put on our strongest shoes but did not encumber ourselves with heavy clothing, as the guide said we should not need it. The house is quite near the crater, almost on its edge, and so we didn't have far to go to begin sight-seeing; in fact, we had begun it on the previous evening, and all through the night, as the light of the volcano was almost constantly in our eyes. Two or three times during the night we saw the lava spurting up like a fountain above the edge of one of the small craters, and altogether the scene was an exciting one.

"It is fully three miles from one side of the crater of Kilauea to the other; but you do not walk in a straight course across it, for the simple reason that you can't. The crater is a great pit varying from eight hundred to fifteen hundred feet in depth; its floor consists of lava, ashes, and broken rocks, the lava predominating. It is rough and uneven, and in several places there are small craters sending up jets of flame, smoke, and steam, and there are numerous cracks from which smoke and steam issue constantly. In many places the lava lies in great rolls and ridges that are not easy to walk over, and some of them are quite impassable. Consequently the path winds about a good deal, and you may be said to walk two miles to get ahead one.

"The floor of the crater is hardly the same from week to week, and if I should make a map of it, and describe the place very carefully, you might not know it if you come here a year from now. In many places it is so hot that you cannot walk on it. Lava cools very slowly, and the thicker the bed of it the longer the time it requires for cooling.

VIEW OF ONE OF THE BURNING LAKES.

"The Hawaiians say that the volcano is under the control of the Goddess Pele; she is a capricious deity, and you never know for any great length of time beforehand what she will do. Whenever the mood strikes her she orders an eruption, and straightway the fires are lighted, the mountain trembles, and the earth all around is violently shaken. Flames burst forth from the crater and shoot high in air, and sometimes the floor of the whole area is lifted and tossed like the waves of the sea. Kilauea may be said to be constantly active, as the fires never cease; but there are periods of great activity followed by seasons of comparative quiet.

"Over the floor of the great crater we picked our way for nearly three miles to the Burning Lakes; and what do you suppose these lakes are?

"Their name describes them, as they are literally burning lakes—lakes of fire so hot that if you should be foolish enough to try to bathe in them, or so unfortunate as to fall into their waves, you would be burned up in less than a minute. We had to climb up a steep bank of lava to get in sight of them, and then what a spectacle was presented!

"There were two little lakes or ponds, five or six hundred feet in diameter, and separated by a narrow embankment which the guide said was occasionally overflowed, and either covered entirely or broken down for a while. These lakes are on the top of a hill formed by the cooling of the lava, and at the time we saw them their surface was perhaps one hundred feet below the point where we stood on the outer edge or rim. The wind blew from us over the lakes, and carried away the greater part of the smoke and the fumes of sulphur; but in spite of the favoring breeze we were almost choked by the noxious gases that rose from the burning lava, and the numerous crevices in the solid banks where we stood.

"I said the bank was formed by the cooling of the lava; I should rather say by its hardening, as it was far from cool. It was so hot that it burned our feet through the soles of our thick shoes, and we stood first on one foot and then on the other, as turkeys are said to stand on a hot plate. Fred sat down to rest, but he stood up again in less than half a minute, as it was like sitting on a hot stove. We had brought a canteen of water which the guide placed on the ground near us; when I went to pick it up for a drink, the air and exertion having made me very thirsty, it was so hot that I burned my fingers in trying to hold it. The water in the canteen was like a cup of tea as good housewives like to pour it steaming from the kettle.

"Our faces were blistering with the heat that rose from the surface of the lakes, and then we scorched our hands in trying to protect our faces. We were blinded and suffocated; we coughed and spluttered, and found it difficult to speak, and in a little while concluded we had had quite enough of the lakes. We used our eyes rapidly, as there was a great deal to look at, and the whole scene was such as does not often come into one's opportunities.

"The molten lava seethed, bubbled, boiled, and rolled below us, its surface covered with a grayish and thin crust, out of which rose irregular circles and patches of fire that seemed to sweep and follow one another from the circumference to the centre of the lake. Every minute or so the lava in the centre of the lake bulged up and broke into an enormous bubble or wave which sometimes rose twenty or thirty feet into the air, and then broke and scattered just as you see a bubble breaking in a kettle of boiling paste or oatmeal porridge. I know the comparison is a homely one, but I can't think of anything that will better describe what we saw.

"The bank of the lake down near where the lava came against it was red-hot, and so you may imagine if you can a mass of liquid fire rolling and surging against a solid one. One of the lakes was much more agitated than the other, and the liquid lava seemed to break upon its sides very much like a sea upon a rocky shore. Owing to the half-plastic condition of the lava, it could not break into surf and spray like the waves of the ocean, but it made a dull roar, something like that of the Pacific on the beach near San Francisco just after the subsidence of a storm.

VIEW ON A LAVA FIELD.

"The surface of the lava changes its height from time to time. The guide said it occasionally rose until it overflowed the sides of the basin enclosing the lakes, and formed streams that spread out over the level area of the great crater. Sometimes it sank so that it was fully four hundred feet from the edge of the rim down to the lava; but whether it was high or low, there was never a time when it was wholly inactive.

"The guide called our attention to cones which had formed on the rim of the lake; they were caused by the cooling of the lava around vent-holes, and as successive jets of lava were thrown up and cooled they had formed cones fifteen or twenty feet high, and some of them as much as thirty feet. When the height became so great that the lava sought an outlet elsewhere, it generally left a hole in the top of the cone. We looked down some of these holes and saw the seething mass

HAWAIIAN WARRIORS OF A CENTURY AGO.

of lava threatening each moment to rise and destroy the very frail foundation where we were standing. The guide said there was little real danger, as the lava had receded since the cones were formed. I observed that the crust where we stood was not more than a foot or so in thickness; and as the lava is very brittle, the spot was certainly not a safe one. Besides, the fumes that rose from the vent-holes were absolutely stifling; and though the sight was a fascinating one, it was impossible to remain there long, owing to the difficulty of breathing.

"We have visited volcanoes in other parts of the world, but none that equalled this, and never have we seen anything to compare with the Burning Lakes of Kilauea. What a magnificent sight it must be to see an eruption of Kilauea or Mauna Loa—especially the latter, as it is much the larger of the two. Just now it is quiet, but when it does break out it is, I believe, the greatest volcano in the world. Let me give you a few figures:

"Mauna Loa has had eight great eruptions in forty years, an average of one eruption every five years. It is 13,700 feet high, and in several of its eruptions it has sent streams of lava fifty miles in length to the sea. The flow of these streams is slow, usually requiring eight or ten days, and sometimes longer, to cover the distance from the mountain to the sea. In one eruption it was estimated that 38,000,000,000 cubic feet of lava were poured out, and in another 17,000,000,000. Kilauea is properly a spur of Mauna Loa, and less than 4000 feet high, but nevertheless it is the largest constantly active volcano in the world.

CHAIN OF EXTINCT VOLCANOES, ISLAND OF KAUAI.

"When the lava from Mauna Loa reaches the sea there is an immense cloud of steam rising from the point where the molten mass enters the water; the ocean is heated for miles around, and fishes by millions perish from the heat. The ground all over the island is devastated, earthquakes are frequent, and altogether Hawaii must be an unpleasant place of residence at that time.

"We got back to the hotel about five o'clock in the afternoon, thoroughly tired out with the day's excursion, which had given us so many curious and terrible sights. It has been an experience which we shall long remember."

Our friends wanted to visit the great crater of Haleakala, on the island of Maui, in order to be able to compare an extinct volcano with a live one, but time did not permit. They talked with a gentleman who had been there, and that, said Fred, was the next best thing to seeing with their own eyes. Here is the substance of what they learned concerning Haleakala:

"You have a ride of about twelve miles to reach the summit, and you ought to go up so as to sleep at the top and get the view at sunrise. There is no house there, but of this there is no need, as there are several caves in the lava—they are really broken lava-bubbles, which are each large enough to shelter half a dozen persons comfortably. Of course you must have a guide and must carry plenty of blankets, or you will suffer from the cold. Water and wood can be found near the top of the mountain.

"The crater of Haleakala is thirty miles in circumference, or ten miles across, and it is two thousand feet from the edge of the rim that surrounds it to the floor of the crater; over this floor are spread ten or twelve smaller craters and cones, some of them large enough to be good-sized mountains by themselves, as they are nearly, if not quite, a thousand feet high.

"You can descend into the great crater if you wish, and there is a path by which you can traverse it; but it is very necessary that you should not turn from the path, as the lava is so sharp that it would endanger your horse's feet to go even a few yards over it. Stick to the route, and implicitly obey your guide."

Fred obtained a map of Haleakala, which we give on the following page. It shows the shape of the crater and the openings at either end, where the lava is supposed to have made an outlet for itself; these openings are called Koolau Gap and Kaupo Gap, the former being something more than two miles across, and the latter a trifle less.

Before leaving Hilo, Doctor Bronson arranged for a schooner to meet the party at a point on the Puna coast, which was easily reached in a day's ride from the crater of Kilauea. Before sunset they had paid the guide for the hire of the horses and his own wages, and the evening saw them dashing through the waters on the way to Honolulu. The trade-wind bore them swiftly along; Hawaii is to windward of Oahu, and while it takes a schooner or other sailing-vessel four or five days to beat from Honolulu to Hilo, the return journey can be made in from twenty-four to thirty hours. The second morning from Puna saw the schooner anchored in the harbor of the capital, and our friends had the satisfaction of breakfasting at the spacious and comfortable Hawaiian hotel.

Through the courtesy of a gentleman engaged in the sugar culture, our friends made a visit to a sugar plantation, the culture of the saccharine product being the principal industry of the Hawaiian Islands. We have not space for an account of all they saw and heard, but will give a summary from Fred's note-book.

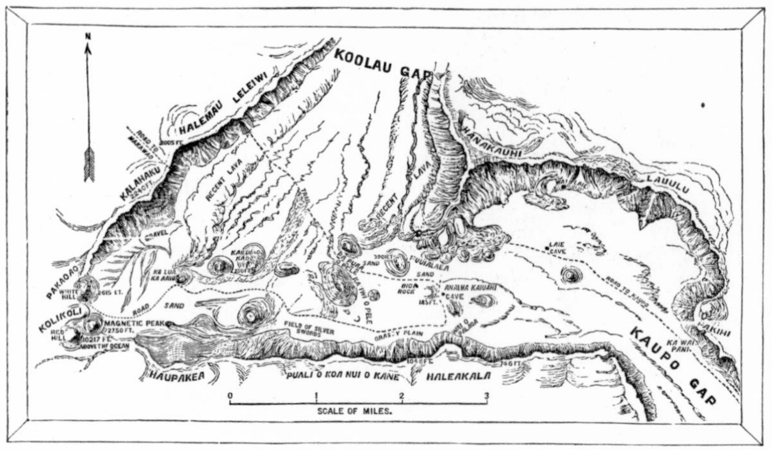

MAP OF THE HALEAKALA CRATER.

"Sugar is grown on all the four large islands of the group, but the principal seat of the industry is on Maui, which seems peculiarly favorable to it. We were told that the yield was sometimes between five and six tons to the acre, four tons was not an unusual amount, and it would be considered a poor plantation that did not give two or two and a half tons. The volcanic soil seems to be just what the sugar-cane loves; the seasons are such that planting can be done in many places at any time of the year, and there is not the least danger of frost, as in the sugar area of the United States.

"The common custom is to raise two crops, and then let the ground lie idle for two seasons; so that taking a series of years together, allowance must be made for the idle time in estimating the yield of sugar. In some localities, especially those where the ground is artificially irrigated, this plan is not always followed, as it does not appear to be necessary. To show the growth of the industry, let me say that the export of sugar in 1860 was 1,414,271 pounds, while in 1871, eleven years later, it was 21,760,773 pounds. Last year it was in the neighborhood of fifty million pounds.

KAMEHAMEHA I., FIRST KING OF THE SANDWICH ISLANDS.

"In the early years of the sugar culture the work was performed by the natives, but in course of time it grew to such an extent that the local supply of labor was not sufficient. A great number of Chinese and Portuguese were introduced, and laborers have been brought from other islands of the Pacific Ocean, so that the population of the country is now a mixed one. By the census of 1878 the population was 57,985; 44,088 of these were natives, 5916 Chinese, 4561 whites, and 3420 half-castes. In 1882 the population was estimated at 66,895, including 12,804 Chinese. In the two years ending March 31, 1884, there was an immigration of 6166 Portuguese from the Azores Islands. Among the whites the Americans are most numerous, but the Germans are steadily increasing in numbers, a large part of the sugar interest and the commerce dependent upon it being in their hands. The commercial king of the islands is Claus Spreckels, who is of German origin, and practically controls the sugar culture. He owns a steamship line between Honolulu and San Francisco, and the local steamers plying to the various islands are mostly in his hands.

"Rice and coffee are also products of the islands, but they occupy a low position when compared to that of sugar. Hides, tallow, wool, and salt are also exported, but the quantity is not great. The value of the exports of the islands is from eight to ten million dollars annually, and the imports amount to about two millions less than the exports. The principal imports are textile fabrics, clothing, implements, machinery, and provisions."

So much for the commercial condition of the kingdom of Hawaii. Let us now turn to other matters.

Our friends took a day, or rather two nights and a day, for a visit to the famous Leper Hospital on Molokai Island. Leaving Honolulu late one evening, they were landed the next morning on Molokai for their strange excursion. We will let Frank tell the story of the visit.

WATER FALL ON ISLAND OF KAUAI.

"The leper settlement is on a plain, which is surrounded by mountains on three sides and the sea on the fourth. The mountains are so rugged as to be impassable except at a few points, which are always carefully guarded. The sea-front is also watched, so that escape from the settlement is practically impossible.

"Any person in the Hawaiian kingdom suspected of leprosy is arrested by the authorities, and if a medical examination shows that he is afflicted with the disease he is sent to Molokai. The sentence is

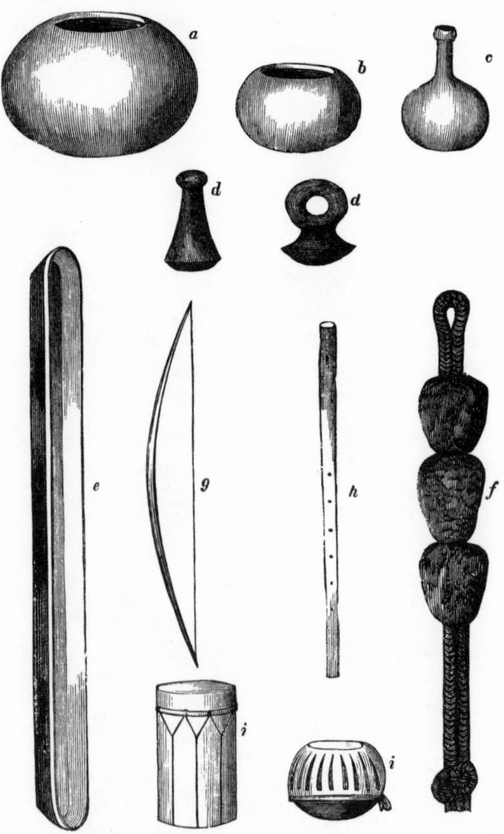

IMPLEMENTS OF DOMESTIC LIFE.

a, Calabash for poi.—*b*, Calabash for fish.—*c*, Water-bottle.—*d*, *d*, Poi mallets.—*e*, Poi trough.—*f*, Native bracelet.—*g*, Fiddle.—*h*, Flute.—*i*, *i*, Drums.

perpetual, leprosy being considered incurable except in its earliest stages. A man sent to Molokai is considered dead. His wife may obtain a decree of divorce and marry again if she likes, and his estate is handed over to the courts and administered upon as though he had ceased to exist. Great care is exercised to prevent the banishment of any one about whose case there is any doubt. There is a hospital near Honolulu where all doubtful cases are sent, and the physician in charge keeps them there until the certainty of the presence or absence of the disease is settled beyond question.

"The doctor who accompanied us through the settlement assured us that leprosy is neither epidemic nor contagious in the ordinary sense of the latter word. It can only be communicated by an abraded surface coming in contact with a leprous sore; and he said that the practice among the natives of many persons smoking the same pipe had done much to spread the disease. He shook hands freely with the victims of leprosy during our visit, and did not take the trouble to wear gloves, even when the hands of the others were covered with sores.

"He told us that the disease first showed itself by a slight swelling under the eyes and in the lobes of the ears; then the fingers contracted like birds' claws, the face swelled into ridges that were smooth and shiny, and later these ridges broke into festering sores. Sometimes these symptoms on the face do not appear, the attacks being principally on the hands and feet. The fingers and toes wither and decay; they seem to dry up and shrink, as we saw several persons whose fingernails were on their knuckles, the fingers having shrunk away and disappeared.

"It is a curious circumstance that the victims of leprosy rarely suffer pain. The decay of the extremities is gradual, and the shiny ridges on the face may be pinched with the fingers or punctured with a pin without giving any sensation. Among the nine hundred and odd persons in the leper settlement we saw very few sad faces. The people were enjoying themselves very much as they would in Honolulu—talking and laughing, walking or lounging about, or riding horses, and in one place they were playing a game that evoked a good deal of shouting and hilarity. Many were at work in the fields and gardens, or making salt along the shore. There is a leper governor for the settlement, and the usual number of subordinates that such a place requires. There is a store where goods are sold at cost, and many of the lepers re-

HAWAIIAN PIPE.

ceive money from their friends and spend it at the store. The Government provides the lepers with clothes and lodging, and gives them sufficient food for their subsistence. Those who can work are encouraged to do so, and all that they produce is bought by the Board of Health and paid for out of the store.

"Then they have two churches—one Catholic and the other Protestant. The latter has a native pastor, and the former a white priest, who has volunteered to seclude himself among these unfortunate people for their religious good. There are three white men and eight Chinese who have been sent here as lepers. It has been charged that the Chinese brought leprosy to the islands, but the doctor says this is not so, the disease having existed here before the Chinese came; and besides, it is quite unlike the malady of that name in China. There it principally attacks the skin, while the Hawaiian form belongs to the blood.

"The location of the settlement is an excellent one, as it is on the windward side of the island, and constantly swept by the pure breezes from the ocean. For those who are unable to move about there are large and well-kept hospitals, where the patients are waited upon by other lepers that have not reached the disabled stage. Access and escape are alike difficult, and everything seems to have been done to make life as comfortable as possible to the unfortunate victims who are sent here."

CHAPTER III.

SUDDEN CHANGE OF PLANS.—THE YACHT *PERA*.—DEPARTURE FROM HONOLULU.—VOYAGE TO THE MARQUESAS ISLANDS.—NOOKAHEEVA BAY.—HISTORICAL ACCOUNT OF THE MARQUESAS.—WHAT OUR FRIENDS SAW THERE.—TATTOOING AND HOW IT IS PERFORMED.—THE DAUGHTER OF A CHIEF.—NATIVES AND THEIR PECULIARITIES.—COTTON AND OTHER PLANTATIONS.—PHYSICAL FEATURES OF THE ISLANDS.—VISITING A PLANTATION AND A NATIVE VILLAGE.—MISSIONARIES AND THEIR WORK.—THE TABU.—CURIOUS CUSTOMS.—PITCAIRN ISLAND AND THE MUTINEERS OF THE *BOUNTY*.—WONDERS OF EASTER ISLAND.—GIGANTIC MONUMENTS OF AN UNKNOWN RACE.

THOSE who have followed the Boy Travellers in their journeys in other parts of the world will remember that their plans were often changed by circumstances which could not be foreseen. At Honolulu one of these changes took place, and this is how it happened:

When the *Alameda* entered the harbor on her arrival from San Francisco our friends observed at anchor a trim-looking yacht displaying the English flag. They were too busy with the novelties of the place to give her any attention, and her presence was soon forgotten.

On the morning of their return from Molokai Doctor Bronson encountered in the breakfast-room of the hotel an old friend, Doctor Macalister, of Cambridge, England. Their greetings were cordial, and all the more so as neither had the least idea that the other was in the Hawaiian Islands or anywhere else in the Pacific Ocean. In almost the same breath each exclaimed,

"What are you doing here?"

Doctor Bronson explained briefly how he came to Honolulu, and where he was going, to which Doctor Macalister responded,

"I came here on the yacht *Pera;* she belongs to Colonel Bush, formerly of her Britannic Majesty's army, but for several years in the service of the Turkish Government. I am the colonel's guest, and we came here by way of India, China, and Japan. We leave to-morrow for the South Pacific, where we are to cruise about for several months, visiting the most interesting of the island groups. We go first to the Marquesas Islands, and then—"

LOOKING SEAWARD.

Just at this moment Colonel Bush entered the breakfast-room, and was introduced to Doctor Bronson. A moment later Frank and Fred arrived, presentations followed, and before the morning meal was over the American contingent was fairly well acquainted with the English one.

Conversation developed the fact that two gentlemen who had arrived on the *Pera* had left by the mail-steamer for San Francisco, having received letters at Honolulu which compelled their immediate return to England. Consequently the *Pera's* party was reduced to Colonel Bush and Doctor Macalister.

The party arranged to meet at dinner. Colonel Bush and Doctor Macalister went to the *Pera*, while Doctor Bronson and the youths proceeded to make farewell calls, as the steamer on which they were to continue their journey was due on the morrow, and they wished to be ready for her.

Exactly how it came about we are unable to say, but it is evident that Colonel Bush desired further acquaintance with Doctor Bronson and his nephews, and that Doctor Macalister had heartily approved the colonel's desire. At all events, when the three gentlemen were together after dinner, Frank and Fred having left the table, the colonel invited Doctor Bronson, with his nephews, to accompany him in his voyage to the South Seas.

THE OWNER OF THE YACHT.

"There is plenty of room on the yacht," said he, "and provisions are abundant. The *Pera* is almost identical with the *Sunbeam*, the famous yacht of Sir Thomas Brassey, of which you have read. She relies upon her sails when there is any wind, and has auxiliary steam-power to propel her when needed. The north-east trade-winds will carry us down to the equatorial belt of calms, and then we'll steam through it to the south-east trades, which will carry us straight to the Marquesas. From the Marquesas we'll go to the Society Islands, then to Samoa, and then to Feejee. There you can if you like take the mail-steamer to New Zealand and Australia, or continue with the *Pera* wherever she goes. Beyond Feejee I have not formed my plans very definitely, as they will depend somewhat upon the letters I receive there, and upon the state of things in the New Hebrides, the Solomon Islands, and other of the groups to the west of Feejee."

"GOOD-BY!"

The heartiness of the invitation, the opportunity the voyage would give for seeing groups of islands not on the regular track of travel, and the fact that he was not pressed for time, settled the question with Doctor Bronson, and he accepted at once. He excused himself shortly afterwards to inform the youths of the change in their plans.

Of course they were delighted at the opportunity of making an acquaintance with the islands that were included in the *Pera's* proposed voyage, and earnestly congratulated themselves on their good-fortune.

AT HOME ON THE "PERA."

The baggage of the party was sent on board in the forenoon of the next day; the travellers followed it, and a little before two o'clock in the afternoon the *Pera* steamed out of Honolulu and headed southward. When she had made a good offing her engines were stopped, the fires were put out, and the yacht proceeded at a splendid pace with the strong trade-wind on her port beam. Her course was directed to the south-east, so as to enable her to cross the equator about longitude 140° west, and take advantage of the south-east trades in making the Marquesas.

Frank undertook a journal of the voyage; but like most works of the kind, it abounded in repetitions, and our space will not permit extensive quotations. One day was so much like another that the young gentleman admitted that his narrative would make very tiresome reading, and he doubted if any one would care to peruse it. Suffice it to say the time passed agreeably, as there was a good library on board, and each member of the party tried to do his share towards entertaining the rest. Stories of sea and land, "of moving accidents by flood and field," and discussions upon scientific, social, and all other imaginable topics, served to beguile the hours and shorten the distance between the Hawaiian and the Marquesas groups.

The north-east trades carried the *Pera* almost to the equator, then came a period of calm in a torrid temperature that drove everybody to the shelter of the double awning over the deck, and made them sigh for cooler latitudes. Heavy clothing was at a discount, and the lightest garments were found more than sufficient. Social rules were suspended, and pajamas were worn altogether, except at dinner-time, when light suits of linen took their place. Dinner was served on deck beneath the awning, and the ice-machine was kept in constant action to supply ice for the use of the sweltering travellers. Happily this state of affairs

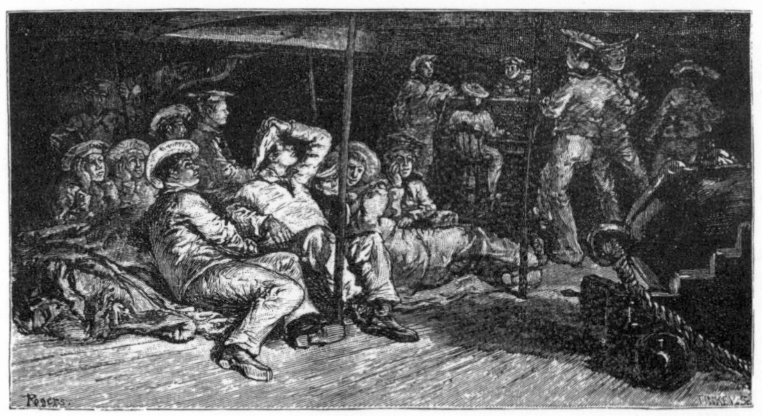

BELOW DECK IN THE TROPICS.

did not last long; as soon as the *Pera* entered the calm belt the funnel was hoisted, fires were started, the equator was crossed triumphantly, and the yacht in due time caught the south-east trades, and was once more turned into a sailing-craft.

As they left the equator behind them the north star disappeared below the horizon, and the Southern Cross, that magnificent constellation of the antarctic heavens, came into view. Frank regretted that they could not look at it with a powerful telescope, when he learned from the captain of the *Pera* that there is a brilliant cluster of stars in the centre of the Cross, invisible to the unassisted eye, and only revealed by a strong glass. Farther south their attention was absorbed by the Magellan clouds, two nebulæ of stars so densely packed together and so far away that they resemble light fleecy clouds more than anything else.

In a direct line it is about two thousand miles from Honolulu to the outermost of the Marquesas group. The log of the *Pera* showed a run of 2180 miles, and on the morning of the sixteenth day of the voyage the lookout gave the welcome announcement that land was in sight. Colonel Bush had given directions for the yacht to proceed direct to Nookaheeva Bay, the best harbor in the Marquesas group, and consequently the travellers contented themselves with distant views of the outer islands that lay in their course. The islands are evidently of volcanic origin, as they present high peaks rising two or three thousand feet, and in some places their sides are almost precipitous. With a glass, or even with the unaided eye, it was easy to perceive that the sides of the mountains and the valleys enclosed between them were thickly clothed with tropical trees and undergrowth, that extended down close to the water's edge.

Frank made the following historical note concerning the islands:

"They were discovered in 1595 by a Spanish navigator, Mendaña de Neyra, who named them Las Marquesas de Mendoza, in honor of the Marquis de Mendoza, Viceroy of Peru. They are sometimes known as the Mendaña Archipelago, in honor of their discoverer; and they are also called the Washington Islands, having been so named by Captain Ingraham of the American ship *Hope*, who visited them in 1791. They are generally divided into two groups, the Northern and Southern, and the Island of Nookaheeva, where we are going, is in the Northern group. Altogether there are thirteen of the islands, with an area of less than five hundred square miles and a population of about ten thousand.

"Properly the name Marquesas belongs to the Southern group only, as they alone were visited by Mendaña; the Northern group was not known until the American captain discovered it, and therefore we shall insist that they are the Washington Islands."

For the description of what they saw at Nookaheeva we will rely upon Fred's account.

"As we neared the island," said the youth in his journal, "we got up steam and went proudly into the harbor, which has a very good anchorage. The French flag was flying from a tall staff at the end of the bay, and you must know that the islands are under a French protectorate, and have been so since 1841. Hardly was our anchor down before the yacht was surrounded by a dozen boats, or canoes; one of them contained a Frenchman in a greatly faded uniform, who said he was the captain of the port. I very much doubt if he ever held the rank of captain anywhere else.

ON THE COAST OF THE MARQUESAS.

"However, he represented the authority of the French Government and treated us politely. Evidently the port was not often visited by pleasure craft like our own, as he seemed somewhat surprised when told that we had nothing to sell, and did not wish to buy anything except fresh provisions. We bought some yams, bread-fruit, bananas, and other fruits and vegetables, together with two or three pigs that the natives brought alongside in their boats. The captain of the port promised to send us a man who would supply us with fresh beef, and then went on shore, whither we followed as soon as we had lunched.

"Both in the boats and on the land we had a good opportunity to study the natives, who are said to be the finest type of Polynesians. They belong to the Malay race, and are distinguished for their graceful and symmetrical figures; the men are tall and well proportioned, with skins of a dark copper color, while the women are considerably lighter in complexion, partly in consequence of their being less exposed to the sun, and partly because of certain pigments which they apply to their faces and arms.

"Tattooing is in fashion here; it prevails among both sexes, though more among the men than the women. It takes a long time to perform it thoroughly. A resident Frenchman with whom we talked on the subject said that the operation began at the age of nineteen or twenty, and was rarely finished until the subject was approaching his fortieth year. It is performed with an instrument shaped like a comb, or rather like a small chisel with its end fashioned into teeth. The figure is drawn upon the skin, and then the artist dips the comb into an ink made of burnt cocoanut-shell and water, until the blunt ends of the teeth have taken up some of the coloring matter. Then the comb is placed on the proper spot, and with a mallet is driven through the skin, eliciting a howl from the subject, unless he is of stoical mood.

"Only a few square inches can be operated on at a time. The flesh swells and becomes very sore, and the performance cannot be repeated until the swelling subsides and the patient has gathered strength and recovered from the fever into which he is generally thrown. We are told that the custom is far less prevalent than when the islands were first discovered, and it will probably die out in another generation or two.

"The marks made by tattooing are permanent, and no application has ever been found that will remove them. We have seen several men whose entire bodies were tattooed, others whose arms and faces had alone been wrought upon, and others again who had kept their faces free from marks but had their bodies covered. One old fellow consented to stand for his photograph in consideration of being rewarded with a hatchet and some fish-hooks, which we willingly gave him. We added a pocket-knife, which he received with a grunt of satisfaction, but

A VIEW IN NOOKAHEEVA.

without deigning to say 'Thank you,' or anything like its equivalent. He said his name was Gattanewa, and that he was grandson of a former chief of that name.

"The faces of the women are not tattooed, except that now and then they have a black line on the upper lip, which is quite suggestive of a budding mustache. One pretty woman was pointed out to us who was said to be the daughter of a chief; her hands and arms were tattooed, the tattooing on the arms extending nearly to the elbow. At a little distance she seemed to have on a pair of embroidered gloves, and this fact suggested an idea. Why could not the ladies of civilized lands have their hands tattooed in imitation of gloves, and thus save themselves the trouble and expense of donning a new pair so often? An ingenious artist could do it nicely, and he might even tattoo the buttons in their places, so that the gloves could have no possible chance of slipping off or getting out of shape.

GATTANEWA'S PORTRAIT.

"There was a chief of one of the interior tribes who presented an excellent specimen of the work of the Polynesian artist on a living canvas. Circles, squares, and all sorts of curious figures had been delineated on his skin, and then punctured in with the tattoo instrument; and the artist certainly possessed a correct eye, as all the drawing was mathematically exact. The chief allowed Frank to make a sketch of him, as the photograph did not bring out all the lines with distinctness; of course he was rewarded for his condescension, and as he received twice as much as he had expected, we had any number of candidates offering themselves when it was known how liberally we paid for services.

TATTOO MARKS ON A CHIEF OF THE MARQUESAS.

"Doctor Bronson says the custom prevails in many of the islands of Polynesia, though not in all, but is fast dying out through the influence of Christianity and civilization. Tattooing has been practised in almost all parts of the world and in all ages. According to the Bible, it must have existed in the time of Moses, for we find it to be one of the practices prohibited to the Jews. Read what is said in Leviticus, xix. 28: 'Ye shall not make any cuttings in your flesh for the dead, nor print any marks upon you.' It prevailed among the ancient Thracians, and the ancient Britons practised it. It still exists among sailors, and has probably descended through them from the time when it was common in Great Britain, though they may have adopted it from the barbarous countries to which their occupation carries them.

"Frank says these people are like a French salad, as they are dressed with oil; they use cocoanut-oil for polishing their skins and anointing their hair, and it is applied with great liberality. One of the presents we gave to the chief who stood for his picture was a flat bottle like a pocket-flask; he said through the interpreter that it was just the thing for carrying oil, and he will no doubt use it for that purpose until it goes the way of all bottles and is broken. The effect on the skin is less disagreeable than you might suppose, as it makes it shine like a piece of mahogany, and brings out the tattoo marks just as varnishing a picture brings out its strong points more clearly than before.

"Turmeric and other coloring substances are used with the oil. Turmeric gives a reddish tinge to the natural brown, and when it is applied to the skin of a pretty woman the effect is like that of the tint of an American belle who has spent a summer at the sea-side or on a yachting cruise, and has not been careful of her complexion. Here is a hint for the ladies who pretend to go to the sea-side or the mountains in summer, but are really obliged to remain at home: Make a cosmetic of cocoanut-butter and turmeric, and apply it in place of cold-cream night and morning. In this way you can get up a 'sea-side tan' at a trifling expense.

"Before civilization came here the natives wore very little clothing, and even at the present time they do not spend much money on their wardrobes. The native cloth, tappa, is made by pounding the inner bark of a species of mulberry-tree with a mallet after soaking it in water. Tappa enough for an entire dress can be made in a day, and when it is done it will last five or six weeks. For a head-dress it is made of a more open texture than for garments to cover the body. The women wrap three or four yards of it around the waist to form a skirt or petticoat, and then cover their shoulders with a mantle of the same material. European cotton goods have partially replaced tappa, and the old industry is dying out. It is a pity, too, as tappa is prettier than cotton cloth, and the natives look better in it than in more civilized material.

"In another way civilization has destroyed the picturesqueness of the Marquesas Islands. The natives formerly wore necklaces made of hogs' and whales' teeth, and the men bored their ears, in which they inserted ornaments of bone or teeth. These snow-white necklaces on the skins of the Marquesas women had a very pretty effect, much prettier than that of the cheap jewellery they wear nowadays, and which comes from French or English manufactories. The chief's daughter whom I mentioned had one of these necklaces, but she wore it more as the mark of her rank than because she admired it. Above the necklace she had a double string of common beads. She had a funny sort of ear-ornament that we tried in vain to buy, as it was one of the insignia to indicate her rank in life.

THE CHIEF'S DAUGHTER.

"When the French took possession of the islands they started to make an extensive colony. They sent a fleet of four ships of war with five hundred troops, and hoisted the French flag with a great deal of ceremony. Fortifications were built, and there were some conflicts with the natives; but of course the islanders, with their rude and primitive weapons, were speedily conquered. The French built docks and jetties in addition to their fortifications, but they have been of little practical use. We found that the most of the jetties had rotted away, and in place of the former garrison of five hundred men there are now about sixty soldiers and a few policemen.

"The Governor treated us very kindly, and at our first call upon him he invited us to dine with him, where we met his amiable wife and the officers of his staff. Colonel Bush invited them to dine on the yacht. As the cabin is limited, we had the Governor and his wife on one day and the officers on another, and I am sure they all enjoyed our visit. Strangers come here so rarely that our advent made an agreeable break in the monotony of their lives.

"There are some fifty foreigners living here, and they include several nationalities—English, American, Irish, Scotch, French, German, Portuguese, Spanish, and Peruvian. Some of them are engaged in business, but there is not a great deal of it, as the colony has not been successful. Cotton is the principal article of cultivation, and there is a small trade in beche-de-mer, the famous sea-cucumber of which the Chinese are fond. It brings a high price in the markets of Canton and Shanghai, sometimes selling as high as five hundred dollars a ton. One of the Englishmen, who has a store in the little settlement, said that several of the cotton plantations had been abandoned, owing to the difficulty of getting laborers for them. The natives are disinclined to work, and laborers from other islands cannot be had in sufficient numbers. Several hundred Chinese have been imported, and also some laborers from the Gilbert and Loyalty Islands. The Chinese make very good colonists, and many of them have plantations of their own, which they manage very successfully.

"The same gentleman showed us a fungus that comes from the valleys between the mountains; it looks very much like a scrap of dried leather, and would not be considered worth much to one who did not know about it. It brings a good price in China, where it is used for making soup. We tried some of it at dinner one day, and found it not at all disagreeable to the taste; in fact it was so good that our steward bought nearly a barrel of it for future use.

"There is a road around the head of the bay which was built by the French soon after their arrival, but has been neglected and is not in good repair. Our host took us on a ride along this road, from which the view is delightful. In front is the deep blue water of the bay, while behind us the mountains rose very precipitously, and seemed to shut us out altogether from the rest of the island. The bay is nearly in the shape of a horseshoe, ending in two high headlands, and to follow its shores requires a walk or ride of about nine miles. The entrance is less than half a mile wide, and is guarded by two small islands, each about five hundred feet high.

"Cowper says:

> "'Mountains interpos'd
> Make enemies of nations who had else,
> Like kindred drops, been mingled into one.'

"There is nowhere in the world a better illustration of the truth of this assertion than in the Marquesas. In each island the mountains rise in ridges like the sections of a starfish; some of these ridges are quite impassable, and all of them very difficult to traverse. The result has been that there was formerly very little intercourse between the tribes occupying the different valleys, and until the French came here there was hardly a time when two or more tribes were not at war.

A EUROPEAN'S RESIDENCE IN THE MARQUESAS.

Even at present they are not entirely at peace, and though the most of them have abandoned cannibalism, it is occasionally practised.

"Our host told us that in many of the valleys there are old men who have never been outside the limits of the mountain walls that enclose their homes, and others whose journeys have been wholly confined to short excursions on the water a few miles from shore. The ordinary mode of communication is by water, and in many cases it is the only one possible.

"The gentleman invited us to go to one of the valleys where he has a plantation; we made the excursion in a large sail-boat manned by six or eight natives, but built after an English model and commanded by an English sailor. Starting early one morning, we made the run in about four hours, spent an afternoon and night in the valley, and returned the next day. All these valleys in the Marquesas have a wealth of tropical trees and smaller plants which is not surpassed anywhere else in the world. The cocoa and several other varieties of the palm-tree abound here, and they have the bread-fruit, the banana and taro plants, the sugar-cane, and, as before mentioned, the cotton-plant.

"Close by the landing-place we came to a village of a dozen or twenty huts built of the yellow bamboo and thatched with palmetto-leaves, which the sun had bleached to a whiteness that reminded us of a newly shingled roof in temperate zones. Our guide called our attention to the platform of stones on which each house stood, and said it was a protection against dampness. The rain falls frequently and very heavily, and it is the abundant moisture that makes the vegetation so luxuriant. On the mountain ridges, in whatever direction you look, there are streams tumbling down, and the steep cliffs are whitened by numerous cascades. The moisture nourishes a great variety of creeping plants, and in many places they completely cover the precipitous cliffs and give them the appearance of green water-falls.

"The natives in one respect resemble the Irish peasantry, their chief wealth being in pigs. These animals were introduced by the Spaniards, who were for a long time venerated as gods in consequence of this inestimable gift to these simple-minded people. Before the visit of the Spaniards the islands had absolutely no four-footed animals; hence it is easy to see how Mendaña and his companions were regarded as more than human.

"Now they have some horses and horned cattle, but not many; they have dogs and cats, and unfortunately they have rats, which were brought here in foreign ships, and have multiplied so fast that they have become a great pest. There are only a few varieties of birds on the islands; most of them have beautiful plumage, but none can be properly called song-birds.

A MARQUESAN VILLAGE.

"Near the village is a well-built church of stone; it is in charge of a Catholic priest, and we were told that there is an average of one church to every two hundred inhabitants all over the islands. The first missionaries to the Marquesas came in the London Mission ship *Duff* near the end of the last century, but after a short residence they became disheartened and abandoned the effort to convert and civilize the people. Several attempts were made in the first quarter of the present century, but with a similar result. In 1833 some American missionaries tried the experiment, and in 1834 the London Mission Society sent a fresh party of missionaries, but all to little purpose.

CATHOLIC MISSIONARY.

"In 1853 an English missionary named Bicknell and four Hawaiian teachers, accompanied by their wives, went to the Marquesas at the request of a Marquesan chief, who had gone to the Sandwich Islands in a whale-ship to present the invitation. The French priests opposed the coming of these missionaries, but the chiefs refused to give them up, and so the teachers remained, but they made little progress in converting the natives to Christianity.

"The Catholic mission supports quite a number of priests and a bishop at the Marquesas. The mission has had very poor success in securing adherents to its faith, but it has done much good in the way of showing the natives the result of industry. Around each mission station there is a well-cultivated garden, and some of the finest cotton-fields on the islands may be found there. I have never seen anywhere a prettier cotton-field than at the mission we visited.

"There is a convent at Nookaheeva, where the French Sisters are educating about sixty Marquesan girls, whose ages vary from four to sixteen years. There is a similar school for boys, which is under the charge of the mission; and the bishop hopes that these boys and girls will be of service in educating and converting their people to the religion and civilization of the foreigner. But from all we can learn it will be a long time before his hopes are realized. The Queen is a devout Catholic, while the King is a nominal one, and each missionary has a small flock of followers; but the great majority are as much heathen as ever, and cling firmly to their old superstitions.

"One of the curious customs of the South Sea Islands is the *tabu*, and it prevails much more strongly at the Marquesas at the present time than anywhere else. The word is Polynesian, and singularly resembles in sound and meaning the *to ebah* of the ancient Hebrews. It has a good and a bad meaning, or rather it may apply to a sacred thing or to a wicked one. A cemetery, being consecrated ground, would be tabu, or sacred, and to fight there would be tabu, or wicked. Our English word 'tabooed' (forbidden) comes from the Polynesian one.

"It would take too long to describe all the operations of tabu as it formerly prevailed through Polynesia and still exists in some of the islands, and especially in the Marquesas. There were two kinds of tabu, one of them permanent, the other temporary. The permanent tabu was a sort of traditional or social rule, and applied to everybody. All grounds and buildings dedicated to any idol or god were tabu, and

IN A GALE NEAR THE MARQUESAS.

therefore became places of refuge to men fleeing from an enemy, exactly like the Cities of Refuge mentioned in the Bible. It was tabu to touch the person of a chief or any article belonging to him, or eat anything he had touched. In the Tonga Islands it was tabu to speak the name of father or mother or of father-in-law or mother-in-law, to touch them, or to eat in their presence except with the back turned, when they were constructively supposed to be absent.

COMMODORE PORTER'S FLEET IN NOOKAHEEVA BAY.

"In the Feejee Islands it was tabu for brother and sister and first-cousins to speak together or eat from the same dish. Husband and wife could not eat from the same dish, and a father could not speak to his son if the latter was more than fifteen years old!

"The tabu was a very convenient police system, as any exposed property could be made safe by being tabooed. The chiefs and priests could tabu anything they chose; when a feast was about to come off the chief would previously tabu certain articles of food, and thus insure an abundance on the day of the festival. Violation of certain kinds of tabu was punished with death; other and smaller violations had various penalties affixed, and they generally included sacrifices or presents to the gods, or the payment of fines to the chiefs.

"Well, here in the Marquesas, among other prohibitions, it was tabu for a woman to enter a canoe or boat. Men had a monopoly of all paddling and sailing, and the only sea-voyage a woman could make was by swimming. I have read about women in the South Seas swimming out to ships anchored a long distance from shore, and never understood till now how it was. It is no wonder that sailors used to mistake these Marquesan nymphs for mermaids as they dashed through the waves with their long black hair trailing behind them in the water."

EASTER ISLAND HOUSE AND CHILDREN.

Fred's account of what they saw in the Marquesas pauses abruptly at this point. Perhaps he was interrupted by just such a scene as he describes in the last sentence, but he could hardly fall into the old error of the sailors. The women of the Marquesas are fine swimmers, but no better, perhaps, than those of the Feejee, Samoan, and other tropical or semi-tropical groups.

The *Pera* remained several days at the Marquesas, and then proceeded to Tahiti, in the Society group. Before they left Nookaheeva one of the officers of the Governor's staff pointed out the hill where Commodore Porter hoisted the American flag when he anchored with his prizes in the bay during the war of 1812. "That was a long time ago," said the officer; "but the incident is vividly preserved in the traditions of the people. And it was that incident that greatly aided the French in getting their foothold here."

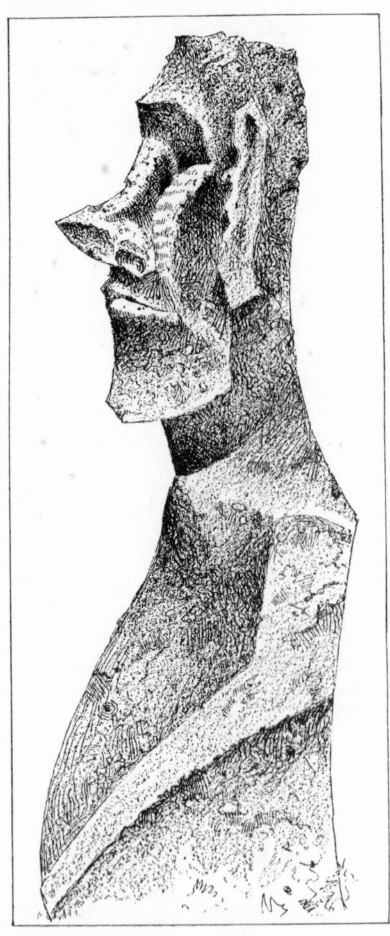

LAVA ROCK IMAGE, EASTER ISLAND.

"How was that?" Frank inquired.

"At the time of Commodore Porter's visit," replied the officer, "the Nookaheevans were at war with a neighboring tribe. The hostile tribe made an incursion one night and destroyed about two hundred bread-fruit trees close to Porter's camp; the next day they sent a messenger to tell him he was a coward, and they would come soon and attack his camp.

"Porter thereupon concluded to teach them a lesson, and so he sent a small detachment under Lieutenant Downs to aid the Nookaheevans to punish their enemies.

"This was accomplished, and the hostile tribe was completely subdued. As soon as he had completed the repairs to his ships Porter sailed away, but he was long revered in Nookaheeva. When the French came here, thirty years afterwards, the natives thought the performance of Porter would be repeated, and the Frenchmen would aid the Nookaheevans to defeat their enemies. They were received with open arms, and the natives were not undeceived until the French had completed their forts and were fully able to defend themselves."

Continuing his reference to the natives, Frank's informant said that great numbers of them were at one time kidnapped and carried away by labor-vessels, of which more will be said in a later chapter. In 1863 small-pox was introduced by foreign ships, and killed nearly one-half of the population. Altogether the people of the Marquesas have no special occasion to be grateful to the white man.

EASTER ISLAND MAN.

During the *Pera's* voyage to Tahiti our young friends devoted their time to a study of that part of the Pacific Ocean and the islands it contained. Fred called their attention to Pitcairn Island, which has been long famous as the home of the mutineers of the *Bounty;* both the youths regretted that they were not to pass in its vicinity, but consoled themselves by reading an account of a visit to it, and a description of the inhabitants.*

One day while they were busy with their studies of the Pacific, Doctor Bronson called their attention to Easter Island, which he pronounced one of the most remarkable islands in the great ocean.

Frank eagerly asked why it was so, and the Doctor kindly explained as follows:

"It is remarkable," said he, "on account of the mysterious origin and history of its former inhabitants, and the sculptured rocks and

* "The Young Nimrods Around the World," chapter xv. Published by Harper & Brothers.

stone images which they have left scattered in great numbers over the island. It has been known since 1722, when the navigator Roggewein discovered it on Easter Sunday of that year, and named it Easter Island in commemoration of the discovery. Some authorities say it was discovered in 1686 by Davis, an English buccaneer, and it was known as Davis Land until Roggewein's visit. Captain Cook visited it about 1772, and it is said he found twenty thousand inhabitants there. The island is about thirty miles in circumference, and is situated in latitude 27° 10′ south, and 109° 26′ west longitude. It has a remarkable isolation, being two thousand miles from the coast of Chili, and one thousand five hundred from any other inhabited island except Pitcairn, and that, as you know, is a small island, about two miles long and not more than a mile broad in its widest part.

EASTER ISLAND WOMAN.

"Easter Island is called Rapa Nui by the natives of Tahiti, and is of unmistakably volcanic origin. There is a large extinct crater on each end of the island, and numerous small ones between, the ground being thickly covered with black volcanic rock and obsidian in the western portion. The largest of these volcanoes is named Rauo Kao; it is over one thousand three hundred feet high, enclosing a fresh-water lake nearly three miles in circumference, the surface of which is partially covered with vegetable matter, over which a man may walk in places. The second one in size is extremely interesting on account of its being the place where the stone images were made from lava rock, a great number of which still remain, some unfinished and attached to the precipitous cliffs. An enormous number of these images is scattered all over the island, while there are ninety-three inside and one hundred and fifty-five immediately outside of the crater. They are in solid pieces, varying from five to seventy feet in height; some of the figures lying prostrate are twenty-seven feet long, and measure eight feet across the breast."

"Very much like the great statues at Thebes and Karnak in Egypt," said Fred.

"Yes," replied the Doctor, "and one of these statues measures twenty feet from the shoulder to the crown of the head. The sculpture is extremely rude, and as works of art the Easter Island statues bear no comparison to the Egyptian ones. The human body is represented terminating at the hips, the head is flat, the top of the forehead cut level so as to support a crown which was cut from red tufa found in one of the smaller craters. They were transported to villages near the sea, and placed upon stone platforms constructed in various heights and different lengths, facing the water. One of these platforms supported thirteen immense images, and all of those examined contained human bones, showing it to be a place of burial. Of these platforms one hun-

STONE TABLET OF CHARACTER WRITING.

dred and thirteen have been counted. On a precipice overlooking the sea is a village of ancient stone huts, where, it is said, the natives lived only during a portion of the year. Near by are also sculptured rocks, covered with curious and extremely interesting carvings.

"The platforms are from two to three hundred feet long, and about thirty feet high, built of hewn stones five or six feet long, and accurately joined without cement. The platforms are at intervals all around the coast, and some of the headlands were levelled off to form similar resting-places for the images.

STONE PLATFORM FOR IMAGES.

"All of the principal images have the top of the head cut flat and crowned with a circular mass of red lava hewn perfectly round; some of these crowns are sixty-six inches in diameter, and fifty-two inches thick, and were brought eight miles from the spot where they were quarried. About thirty crowns are lying in the quarries, and some of them are fully ten feet in diameter, and of proportionate height."

Frank asked if the present inhabitants had any tradition concerning these statues.

"None whatever," was the reply. "At present there are less than two hundred people living there; they seem to be the degenerate remains of a race something like the Maoris of New Zealand, and they speak a language similar to those people. Although undoubtedly a cannibal race—in fact, one old man speaks with enthusiasm when asked regarding the custom—they are at present quiet and enlightened, but retain many superstitious ideas which they have received by transmission. They venerate a small sea-bird, the egg of which is sacred to them, and their season of feast begins in August, when the first eggs of these birds are taken from two barren rocks near the cliffs. Men and youths swim to these rocks, and the one who first secures an egg is held in high esteem; he lords it over the others for twelve months, his food being furnished for him, and he is not permitted to bathe for three months. A recent visitor says the people are so dirty that you could suppose every man, woman, and child had performed the successful feat the last feast-time. The last king was Kai Makor, who died about 1864, when Peruvian ships visited Rapa Nui, and a number of the natives were seized and taken to work the guano on the Chincha Islands, where the greater number died. A few were finally sent back, and they brought with them small-pox, which caused great havoc and nearly depopulated the island. Water is scarce, but the climate is equable, and one of the most delightful in the world, the thermometer seldom registering higher than 75° to 80° during the warmest season.

"An image and some other curiosities were brought away in 1886 by the United States steamer *Mohican*, which visited the island in that year. They are now in the Naval Museum at Washington, and it is hoped that some one will be able to decipher the hieroglyphics, which thus far have remained without an interpreter."

CHAPTER IV.

FROM THE MARQUESAS TO THE SOCIETY ISLANDS.—THE GREAT BARRIER REEF.—THE CORAL INSECT AND HIS WORK.—ATOLLS AND THEIR PECULIARITIES.—ORIGIN OF THE POLYNESIAN PEOPLE.—ARRIVAL AT PAPEITI.—ON SHORE IN TAHITI.—A BRIEF HISTORY OF THE ISLANDS.—WORK OF THE MISSIONARIES.—THE FRENCH OCCUPATION.—VICTIMS FOR SACRIFICE.—OLD-TIME CUSTOMS.—PRODUCTS OF THE SOCIETY ISLANDS.—BECHE-DE-MER FISHING.—VISIT TO THE REEF.—CURIOUS THINGS SEEN THERE.—ADVENTURES WITH SHARKS, STINGAREES, AND OTHER MONSTERS.—GIGANTIC CLAMS.—VISITING THE MARKET.—EATING LIVE FISHES.—A NATIVE FEAST.—EXCURSION TO POINT VENUS.

WHEN well clear of the Marquesas the *Pera* turned her prow to the south-west, in the direction of Tahiti, which lay about nine hundred miles away. The strong trade-wind bore her swiftly on her course, and on the fourth day of the voyage the lofty peaks of Otaheite's isle rose into view. The summits of the mountains seemed to pierce the sky, so sharp and steep were they, and almost to their very tops they were covered with verdure. Luxuriant forests were everywhere visible, and the shore was fringed with a dense growth of palms that seemed to rise from the water itself.

COAST SCENERY, TAHITI.

The central peak of Tahiti has an elevation of something more than seven thousand feet, and from this peak there is a series of ridges radiating towards the sea like the spokes of a wheel. Many of these ridges are so steep on their sides that they cannot be ascended, and so narrow that there is not room for an ordinary path. A man standing on one of these ridges could with his right hand throw a stone into one valley, and with his left a stone into another, whose inhabitants could communicate only by descending to the coast, or to the lowland which borders it. The valleys are luxuriant, and even the ridges are covered with vines and bushes.

As the youths, with their glasses, eagerly scanned the coast they were approaching, one of them called out that he could see a strip of calm water close to the shore.

"We are coming to the great barrier-reef of coral," said Doctor Bronson, "and the calm water that you see is between the reef and the shore.

"Tahiti is one of the best examples of an island surrounded by a coral reef," the Doctor continued. "It extends quite around the island, sometimes only a few yards from it, and sometimes four or five miles distant. There are occasional openings through the reef, some wide and deep enough to permit the passage of large ships, and others practicable only for small boats. Inside the reef the water is calm, and a vessel once within it has a secure harbor."

The boys could see the surf breaking on the reef with great violence, and throwing spray high into the air. Outside was the ever-restless sea; inside lay the placid lagoon, which reflected the sunlight as in a mirror.

"Just think of it," said Frank; "that great reef, which resists the waves of the ocean, and could destroy the largest ship that floats, is built up by a tiny worm which we could crush between our fingers with the greatest ease. The patience of the honey-bee is nothing compared to that of the coral insect."

Fred asked what was the depth of water near the reef, both inside and outside.

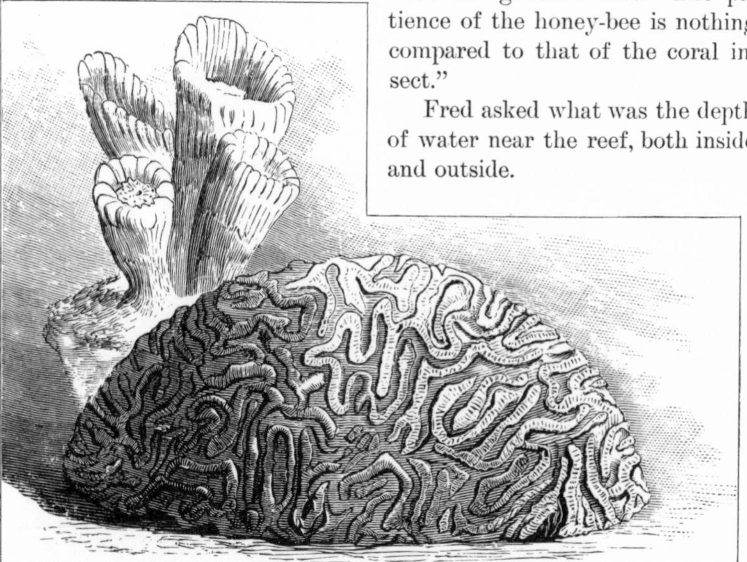

SPECIMEN OF CORAL.

Doctor Bronson answered that it varied greatly, the inner lagoon being sometimes only a few feet, or perhaps inches, in depth, and sometimes two, three, or five hundred feet. Outside there is generally a great depth of water, sometimes so much that the sounding-lead fails to find bottom at a distance of only a few yards. "This constitutes," he added, "one of the dangers of navigation, as a ship may be close upon a reef without being aware of it until too late.

THE CORAL WORM.

"The coral insect," he continued, "does not work at a greater depth than two hundred feet, and he ceases operations when he reaches the surface. When these reefs are more than two hundred feet deep it is supposed that the bottom has slowly receded and carried the reef with it; as the recession went on, the coral insect continued his work of building. It reminds me of what happens sometimes to a railway in a swampy region; the embankment for the track sinks from time to time, and a new one is built above it. After a while sufficient earth has been thrown in to make a solid foundation, and then the sinking ceases.

"The atoll is another curious form of the work of the coral insect," said the Doctor, continuing. "It is circular or oval in shape, the island forming a rim that encloses a lake or lagoon. There is always an opening from the sea to the lagoon, and it is generally on the leeward side. Sometimes there are two, or even three or more openings, but this is unusual; the island rises only a few feet above the water, and is the work of the coral insect upon what was once the crater of a volcano; at least that is the general belief.

"The atoll is not a desirable place for residence, as the ocean during severe storms is liable to break across the narrow strip of land and sweep away whatever may be standing there. Many atolls are uninhabited, and none of them has a large population; cocoa-palms, bread-fruit, and other tropical trees are generally found on the inhabited atolls, and partially or wholly supply the natives with food. In some instances the people support themselves by fishing either in the lagoon or in the ocean outside. The lagoon forms a fairly good harbor for ships and canoes, but sometimes the water in it is too deep for anchoring."

As the minutes rolled on, the outlines of the mountains and ridges, the valleys and forests, grew more and more distinct. Frank and Fred strained their eyes to discover an opening in the reef, but for some time their earnest gaze was unrewarded. At length, however, Frank saw a spot where the long line of spray appeared to be broken; gradually it enlarged, and revealed a passage into the great encircling moat of Tahiti. It was the entrance to the harbor of Papéiti, the capital of the French possessions in this part of the Pacific.

The yacht glided safely through the channel and anchored in front of Papéiti, or Papaete, as some writers have it. Two French war-ships were lying there, and several schooners and other sailing-craft engaged in trade among the islands. Then there were some half-dozen ships and barks from various parts of the world, bringing cargoes of miscellaneous goods for the Tahitian market and carrying away the produce of the islands. Frank looked in vain for an ocean-going merchant steamer, and found, on inquiry, that the Society Islands are not visited by any of the steamships engaged in the navigation of the Pacific.

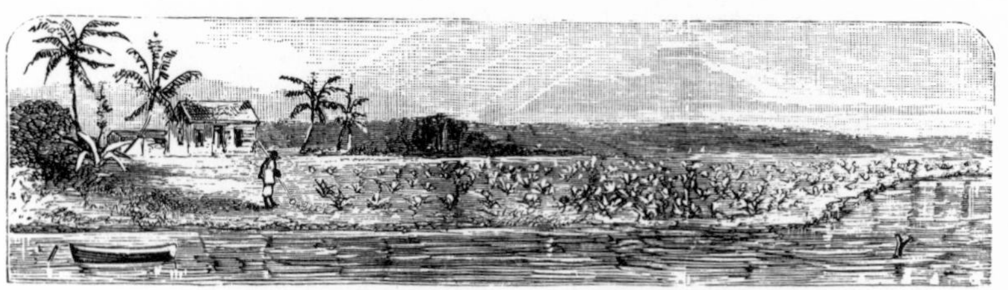

ON THE SHORE OF THE LAGOON.

The Society Islands are a group, consisting of two clusters about seventy miles apart. Some geographers apply the name to the northwestern cluster only, while the other is known as the Tahiti or Georgian group. The latter is the larger and more populous, and is a French colony, while the former is independent. The Spaniards claim to have discovered Tahiti in 1606, and it was visited in 1767 by Captain Wallis, who named it King George's Island. Two years later Captain Cook discovered the north-western cluster, called the whole group the Society Islands in honor of the Royal Geographical Society, and restored to Tahiti its native name.

"Why is Tahiti sometimes called Otaheite, and why is Hawaii, in the Sandwich Islands, sometimes called Owyhee?" Fred inquired.

"Thereby hangs a tale," replied the Doctor, "or rather a great deal of conjecture. Some ethnographers think the islands of Polynesia were peopled from the Malay Peninsula and Archipelago, while others think they were peopled from Japan. Advocates of either theory have a great number of arguments in its support. We haven't time to go over the list; and even if we did we should not be able to settle the question.

A CABIN IN THE SUBURBS.

The theory that the inhabitants of the Sandwich and Society islands came originally from Japan is supported by the use in their languages of the prefix O (signifying "honorable") exactly as it is used in Japan. As the Japanese say O-yama (honorable mountain), so the Hawaiians say O-wyhee, and the Tahitians O-taheite.

"Many Japanese sports, such as archery, wrestling, boxing, spear-throwing, and slinging stones, were in vogue in some of the islands at the time of their discovery; they are rapidly passing away as the people become civilized, and in another generation or two will hardly be heard of. In their language they are nearer like the Malay than the Japanese; that they are of Malay origin is very clearly proven, but exactly how they came here it is not likely we shall ever know."

While this conversation was going on the yacht was visited by a custom-house official, who took the declaration of the captain as to her nationality and name, and her object in visiting Tahiti, and then returned to shore. Our friends followed him, and in a very short time were pressing their feet against the solid earth of Papéiti. For an account of what they saw we will again refer to Fred's journal.

"You cannot see much of Papéiti from anywhere," said Fred, "because of the great numbers of trees that grow in and around the place. Here they are: bread-fruit, hibiscus, cocoa-palms, and half a dozen other varieties, so that nearly every house is hid from view until you are close upon it. The row of shops and cafés near the water is an exception to the rule; they are like the same kind of establishments everywhere in a French colony, and reveal the nationality of the place at a glance.

THE COAST IN A STORM.

"There are mountains in every direction excepting towards the sea, and through a gorge at the back of the town a particularly fine mountain is visible. Most of the houses are only one story in height, especially in the outskirts, where the well-to-do residents have their villas. In the town there are a few two or three storied buildings, belonging to the foreign merchants or used for Government purposes; but these are exceptions to the general aversion to stair-ways. Land is so cheap here that everybody ought to have plenty of room.

"The names of the streets make us think of Paris. The principal one is the Rue de Rivoli, and there we find the hotels, shops, and cafés, or rather the most of them. On the Rue de Commerce are the warehouses, where goods and provisions are stored; and the Rue de Pologne, which is the widest and best shaded of all, is mainly given up to the Chinese for shops and tea-houses. The Chinaman has taken root here, and flourishes; every year the Chinese hold upon business increases, and some of the French residents advocate the expulsion of the Mongolians, through fear that they will soon have a monopoly of the commerce of the islands.

"In the resident part of the town nearly every house stands in its own garden, and the most of these gardens are prettily laid out. There are good roads in and around the place, and we have had some charming drives, sometimes in carriages, which we hired at one of the hotels, and sometimes by invitation of the residents. We have had a most hospitable reception, and everybody from the Governor down has tried to make us enjoy our visit.

"The English consul invited us to dine at his country residence, and afterwards treated us to a moonlight excursion on the water. It was very pretty, as the lagoon was as calm as a mirror, and there were many boats out at the same time. The natives seem to be a careless, fun-loving people. Wherever there is a group of them there is always more or less laughter going on, and they seem to be constantly playing harmless little jokes on one another. The evenings here are delightful, and it is the custom to go out after dinner. The favorite resort is the lawn near the Government-house; a band from one of the ships-of-war plays there every evening, and always has a large audience. The natives are very fond of music, and when it is lively they fall to dancing on the green turf.

"The population of the two clusters that form the Society group is said to be a little less than twenty thousand, three-fourths of them belonging to the Tahitian cluster and one-fourth to the north-western. The native population of this island is about eight thousand. There are about one thousand Chinese on the islands, eight hundred French, two hundred and fifty British subjects, and one hundred and fifty Americans, and perhaps one hundred of other nationalities.

"They tell us that we can drive in a carriage all the way around Tahiti, a distance of one hundred and sixty miles, and that we can hardly go a mile of this distance without coming to a stream of clear water rolling or rippling down from the mountains. Most of these streams are simply rivulets or brooks, but some of them are rivers too large and deep to be forded. Some of these rivers have been bridged, but where this has not been done they must be crossed by ferry-boats. Villages are scattered at intervals of a few miles, and any one who undertakes the journey can be comfortably lodged every night, especially if he sends a courier in advance to arrange matters for him. Colonel Bush had an idea of making the journey, but concluded it would be tiresome long before the circuit was completed, and so the scheme was abandoned.

"One of the early missionaries brought some orange-trees here, and they were found admirably adapted to the soil and climate of Tahiti. You see orange-groves or orange-trees everywhere, and we have never found finer oranges in any part of the world. It is a curious fact that the best trees are those which have grown from seed scattered carelessly about without any thought of planting; in nearly every case they are finer and more productive than those which have been carefully cultivated and transplanted.

"The French have a *jardin d'essai*, or Experimental Garden, where trees and plants from all parts of the world are cultivated with a view to finding those best adapted to Tahiti. As a result of this garden and other importations, the Tahitians now have mangoes, limes, shaddocks, citrons, guavas, custard-apples, tamarinds, peaches, figs, grapes, pineapples, watermelons, cucumbers, cabbages, and other fruits and vegetables of whose existence the people were entirely ignorant a hundred years ago.

A FRENCH BISHOP.

"The French Government has a garrison of about four hundred soldiers in Tahiti, with a large staff of officials of various kinds — naval, military, and civil. The Governor is a personage of great local importance, as he has very liberal powers and can do pretty much as he likes. We found him a very pleasant gentleman. He invited all our party to a reception at the Government-house, and the officers of his staff showed us many attentions.

"The French took possession of Tahiti in 1842; they had been waiting for an opportunity, and it came in that year. Three Catholic missionaries had been expelled by Queen Pomare at the instigation, so the French say, of the English missionaries. A French fleet came to Papéiti and threatened to bombard the town unless her Majesty should pay immediately a large indemnity, and consent to the return of the expelled missionaries. The Queen was quite unable to raise the money, and the French took possession and established their protectorate.

"The protectorate continued till 1880, when the King, Pomare V., was persuaded to cede the nominal sovereignty in consideration of a life pension of twelve thousand dollars annually. The annexation of Tahiti as a French colony was formally proclaimed in Papéiti March 24th, 1881.

VIEW IN AN ORANGE GROVE.

"The first missionaries that came here were sent by the London Mission Society in 1797; but they made little progress in the conversion of the natives, and after a time were driven away in consequence of inter-tribal wars among the people. In 1812 the King invited them to return; they did so, and in the following year a church was established.

"The King was converted to Christianity, together with several of his priests and subordinate chiefs, and from that time on the work of the missionaries progressed rapidly. Long before the French took possession the entire population were nominally Christians, and had burned their idols and destroyed their heathen temples. There is no evidence that they ever practised cannibalism, but they were cruel in war. Prisoners were slaughtered in cold blood, or offered as sacrifices to the gods; human sacrifices were common, and there were certain tribes and families from whom, in times of peace, the victims for sacrifice were taken.

"In olden times these tribes and families were selected, and it is said there was a third of the population whose lives might be taken at any moment. When a victim was called for, resistance was useless, as the whole population, even including a man's nearest neighbors, united to carry him to the *marae*, or altar of sacrifice.

NATIVE BAMBOO HOUSE, TAHITI.

"In the early days of Christianity the victims for sacrifice were taken from among the converts, and sometimes the heathen tribes combined to hunt down the Christians in order to offer them to the gods. It was the story over again of the persecution of the early Christians in Rome and elsewhere in Europe.

"When the French took possession of the islands they oppressed the English missionaries in various ways, and had it not been for the persistence of the natives in adhering to the men who converted them, the representatives of the London Mission would have been driven out altogether. The trouble was finally compromised by allowing the English missionaries to remain under certain restrictions, and establishing a French Protestant mission to work in harmony with the French Catholic one.

NATIVES OF THE SOCIETY ISLANDS FISHING.

"The great bulk of the people are Protestants, as they adhere to the faith to which they were originally converted. The Society Islands as a whole now contain three English missionaries, sixteen native ordained ministers, and more than two hundred other preachers and teachers. There are four thousand three hundred church members, fifty schools, and more than two thousand scholars attending them. The French do not make much interference except on the island of Tahiti, where only one English missionary is allowed to reside. He is not, however, recognized as a missionary to the natives, but as pastor of the Bethel Church at Papéiti."

"That will do for statistics on that subject," said Frank. "While you have been looking up these points in the history of the islands I've been finding out what they produce."

"I was getting around to that," replied Fred; "but if you've found it out I'm glad. What is it?"

"From all I can learn," said Frank, "the colony isn't a very prosperous one for the French. The exports amount to about a million dollars annually, and the imports to seven hundred thousand dollars; there are no import duties except on fire-arms and spirits, but I am told it is proposed to place a duty on nearly everything consumed here, so as to make the colony self-supporting.

"The people have quite abandoned the manufacture of *tappa*, or native cloth, and dress entirely in goods of European make. They have learned how to distil intoxicating liquor from the orange, and this delicious fruit threatens to be a curse to them instead of a blessing. They have given up tattooing, which was never practised to so great an extent as in the Marquesas; there would be no use for tattooing now, as they have all taken to wearing clothes just as in the Sandwich Islands.

"As to the products of the islands," continued Frank, "they consist principally of cocoanut-oil and coppra (the dried substance of the cocoanut, from which oil is extracted after its arrival in Europe), arrow-root, cotton, sugar, and mother-of-pearl shells. The cotton cultivation has not been profitable; and as to the trade in sugar, it has not been anywhere nearly so successful as in the Sandwich Islands."

A SEA-URCHIN.

"You have omitted one thing from your list of products," said Doctor Bronson, as Frank paused. "You have made no mention of beche-de-mer."

"That's so," was the reply; "but the fact is, I wanted to learn more about it than I know now."

"I thought so," said the Doctor, smiling, "and so I've arranged that we will go to the reef to-morrow morning to see how beche-de-mer is taken. We must make an early start, so as to be there at daylight."

Further talk about the Society Islands was indefinitely postponed, and the party adjourned to bed. All were up in ample season on the morrow for the excursion to the reef.

The best time for visiting the reef is at low tide. The tides in the Society Islands differ from those in most parts of the world, by never varying from one day to another throughout the year. At noon and at midnight is the height of the flood, and at six o'clock morning and evening is the lowest of the ebb. Ordinarily the rise is about two feet; periodically twice a year there comes a tidal-wave that breaks over the reef with great violence, and sweeps across the lagoon to the shore.

Frank and Fred sought an explanation of this tidal peculiarity, but were unable to obtain a satisfactory one. A resident of Papéiti said the tides were so certain in their movements that many people were able to tell the time of day very nearly by a glance at the reef.

THE BOTTOM OF THE LAGOON.

To the student of marine life a coral reef is full of interest, and that of Tahiti is one of the finest in the world. Here are some of the curious things that were described by our friends:

"We saw," said Frank, "some enormous starfish with fifteen arms covered with sharp spines of a gray and orange color. These spines were on the top of the arms; the bottom had an array of yellow feelers like fingers, with suckers at the ends. The boatmen cautioned us not to touch these creatures, but their caution was not needed, as we all kept our hands at a respectful distance.

"There were thousands and thousands of sea-urchins, some of them with spikes as large as your fingers and stiff as a nail, down to little fellows the size of a pigeon's egg, and armed with long needles like the quills of a porcupine. It is no joke to step on one of these things when you are bathing in the sea and have your feet unprotected. Somebody has likened them to thistles, and says they more or less resemble hedgehogs and porcupines. Urchin, according to the dictionary, means hedgehog, and therefore the name is not inappropriate.

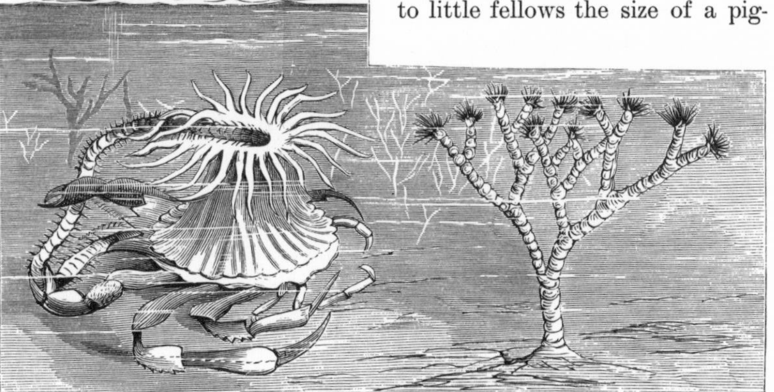

SEA-ANEMONE AND HERMIT-CRAB.

"There are sea-anemones as large as a cheese, and of all the colors you can imagine. An amusing thing about them was that a lot of little fishes, not more than two inches long, were playing hide-and-seek, swimming around among the spines of these huge polyps. The water is very clear, and as you look over the side of the boat into the garden of coral with its great variety of colors, and its numerous inhabitants, finny, shelly, and otherwise, it is like a glimpse of fairy-land.

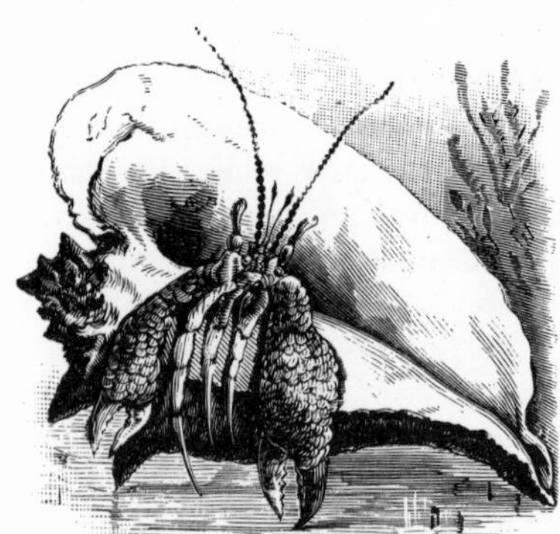

HERMIT-CRAB AND SEA-SHELL.

"It made our flesh creep just a little to see the water-snakes coiling around the branches of coral, and gliding about all unconscious of being gazed at. Then there are gold-fish, blue-fish (not the blue-fish of America, but a little fellow of the brightest sky-blue you ever saw), fish of a pale green, and so on through all the scale of colors. As they swam among the corals they reminded us of butterflies in a garden."

Fred saw a shell travelling along in a most unexpected way, which he could not understand until he ascertained that it was occupied by a hermit-crab. Then there were large crabs in their own shells, and also lobsters, which kept a sharp eye out for danger, and retired to places of security when the boat approached.

The youths had hoped to be able to walk on the reef, but the surf was so high that it was unsafe to venture there. Besides, the walking, even when the reef is comparatively dry, is not of the best, as the surface is rough, and there are many holes in the coral in which the novice may get a dangerous fall.

Many fishing-boats were about, as the time of low tide is the best for fishing, and the water furnishes an important part of the food of the people. Several fishermen, nearly naked, and armed with spears, were in the foaming waters at the outer edge of the reef, waiting, with their weapons poised, ready to strike anything that came within their reach. A dozen or more large fish were taken in this way while our friends were looking on; not once did the spearmen miss hitting their mark, and Frank and Fred both wanted to applaud them for their accuracy of aim.

Inside the lagoon other fishermen were pursuing their prey in boats, the spearmen standing ready in the bow to embrace every opportunity of striking. Men and women were fishing after the ordinary manner of civilization, and with civilized hooks and lines. Formerly they used hooks of pearl-shell and bone, and also hooks of the roots of the ironwood-tree. But in these modern days the ordinary hooks of commerce are almost the only ones ever seen in Tahiti.

Then there were net-fishers in great number, and with many varieties of net. Seines, purse-nets, casting-nets, dip-nets, all were there, and all handled with the dexterity which is only attained by long practice.

The guide explained that some of the fishes which were excellent eating at one time of the year were poisonous at another. The poisonous condition is caused by their crunching the coral at the time it is said to be in blossom, and by eating sea-centipedes,

VIEW AMONG THE CORAL BRANCHES.

which resemble a yard or two of black string with the smallest imaginable legs. All the land-crabs of Tahiti are edible, but several sea-crabs are not; and there is one variety so poisonous that it is only eaten when the eater wishes to commit suicide.

A FISH INSIDE A SEA-SLUG.

Beautiful shells are brought up from the depths of the waters, but they must be touched with great care, as the spines of many of them are poisonous. One of them, scientifically known as *Conus textilis*, a beautiful shell of cone-like shape, has been known to cause death in a few hours, the symptoms being much like those produced by the bite of a rattlesnake. Some of the jelly-fishes of England and America have the same poisonous character, but in a much smaller degree.

The guide hailed a boat which was filled with sea-slugs, sea-cucumbers, tripang, or beche-de-mer, as this article of commerce is variously known, and the youths had an opportunity of examining the curious marine product. They were cautioned not to touch them, as these apparently helpless creatures, which resembled sausages or bags of India-rubber filled with sea-water, were not as harmless as they appeared. The guide said they ejected this water when touched; and if it fell on a wound or scratch, or into the eye, it caused intense pain, and sometimes resulted in temporary or even permanent blindness.

The sea-slugs were of all colors—black, red, gray, and two or three varieties of green. The most dangerous is an olive-green one marked with orange spots, and hence called the leopard. When it is disturbed it throws up long filaments like threads or strings, which adhere very tenaciously; and wherever they touch the skin they raise a burning blister.

Most of the sea-slugs are caught in still water by divers, who use forks with long prongs, with which they secure their prey. There is one variety, the red one, which is taken in the surf, but all the others prefer quiet nooks. When a canoe has been filled with these repulsive-looking objects it proceeds to the drying establishment on shore. There the creatures are thrown into a kettle of boiling water sufficiently long to kill them; then they are cleaned, and stewed for half an hour, and then placed on racks of sticks for smoking and drying.

The smoking must be kept up for three days, and longer if the weather is damp, and then the leathery substance is ready for packing in palm-leaf baskets for transportation to China. Great care must be taken to have it thoroughly dried, as the least remaining moisture will spoil it during its long voyage in the hold of a ship.

Sometimes fishes are found inside the sea-slug, and it seems to be well established that they live altogether in this contracted sea-water tank. When taken out and placed in clear salt-water they soon die, in spite of every precaution.

While looking over the side of the boat Fred saw a large clam, and immediately coveted it. The guide engaged a diver who was near by, and for a small reward the man went below for the prize.

CORALLINE.

The clam was lying with his mouth open, and evidently enjoying his morning bath of sea-water. The diver inserted a sharply pointed stick into the flesh of the mollusk, and the shell closed upon it instantly. Then he severed the filaments which attached the clam to the rock, and with one hand below the shell and another holding the stick, made his way to the surface.

"Most of the diving for clams is done by the women," said the guide, while Fred was gazing at the huge shell, nearly two feet long, which lay before him. "Many a woman, and many a man too," continued the guide, "has been nipped by the shell and drowned there, totally unable to escape. In all parts of the South Pacific you will hear horrible stories of death in this way. These clams grow to a great size, as you see; half a shell often serves as a bath-tub for a child, and in the Catholic churches of Polynesia it is used for holy water.

OCTOPUS, OR DEVIL-FISH.

"Some years ago a native in the Paumotan Islands was diving for pearl-oysters, and while feeling around for them accidentally thrust his hand inside a gaping clam-shell, which closed on him instantly. The shell was in a hole in the coral, so that he could not reach the back to detach it; the only thing he could do was to sever his fingers with the knife in his free hand. He thus saved himself from being drowned, but was maimed for life."

The guide called the attention of the youths to some large eels which were coiled up in the coral. He said they were very voracious, and many natives had been deprived of fingers by these uncanny creatures. They sometimes reach a length of eight or ten feet, and one poor fellow had the whole calf of a leg bitten off by one of them.

Then there are a great many cuttle-fish, and sometimes the girls and women are caught and overpowered by them. The danger from these creatures is so well known that the natives rarely go out alone to dive for them or for clams. Some of the cuttle-fish measure six feet across; they lie in holes in the coral, and throw out their long arms to grasp anything that comes in their reach. They cling around the body of a diver or wrap themselves about his head, and unless speedily relieved by his companions his death is inevitable.

STINGAREE, OR SEA-DEVIL.

"Are there any more dangers among the reefs?" said Frank, when all these had been recounted.

"Yes," was the reply; "there are great numbers of sharks, some of them harmless and others dangerous. The worst is a white shark, thirty feet long, and he is so bold that he has been known to attack canoes, either by overturning them and throwing their occupants into the water, or by seizing an arm or leg which happened to be outstretched, and dragging its owner overboard.

GARDEN OF A SUBURBAN RESIDENCE.

"There is a smaller shark, six or eight feet long, which lives in caves in the coral, and comes out in search of food. Its flesh is good to eat, and one of these sharks is quite a prize. In some of the groups of islands the fishermen dive into the shark caverns while the monster is asleep, and pass a noose around his tail; then the man rises instantly to the surface, and his companions haul up the ugly creature tail first, stunning him with a club or hammer as he comes over the side of the boat."

"But suppose," said one of the youths, "that after the diver has entered the cave the shark should change his position and get across the door-way."

"In that case," replied the guide, "his only mode of escape will be to tickle the shark so as to induce him to move aside. He can only do this when its tail is towards him; if he has turned the other way the man's fate is practically sealed."

Fred concluded that he would never indulge in diving for sharks as a means of livelihood, and Frank fully agreed with him.

Then the guide told them of the stingaree, or sting-ray, which is not unknown in American waters, but grows to a much greater size here than on the coast of the United States. Its tail has a sharp, barbed point, which generally breaks off when struck into the flesh; the point is serrated on both sides, the teeth pointing backward, and so it works its way inward like the quill of a porcupine. Other dangers of the water were described; but it is time to return from the reef, and so we will leave them there.

On their return to Papéiti our friends visited the market, going first to the section where fish were offered for sale. Here is Frank's note upon what they saw there:

"There were fishes of all sizes and kinds: bonito, rockfish, eels, clams, oysters, mussels, turtle, salmon from the rivers, prawns, crabs, and a great many varieties of finny and scally things that have no name in English. The natives are fond of raw fish, and we saw them swallowing little fishes whole and slices of big ones just as we would dispose of a basket of strawberries. One of the first persons we saw in the market was a pretty girl of eighteen or twenty who was crunching live shrimps, or letting them wriggle down her throat as readily as she would swallow so many sugar-plums.

"Some European residents have acquired the taste for raw fish, and they say it is delicious. We have not ventured upon it, though we take clams and oysters raw according to the practice of our own country. The tropical bivalves are not so good as those of temperate regions, and I believe this is the general testimony of travellers.

"The market is well supplied with chickens, turkeys, pigeons, and ducks, which are nearly always sold alive, as the heat of the climate prevents their being kept more than a few hours after slaughtering. Pigs are sold alive, and they are carried about suspended by their hind-legs from a pole. It is painful to hear them squeal, and there ought to be a Tahitian branch of the Society for the Prevention of Cruelty to Animals to put a stop to this barbarity.

GATHERING ORANGES FOR THE FEAST.

"Most of the market-people were natives, but I observed a good many Chinese there, especially in the section devoted to vegetables and fruits. These people take very naturally to vegetable gardens, and their patient industry is well rewarded by the fertile soil of Tahiti."

On reaching the hotel, our friends found an invitation to a feast which one of the merchants was to give the next day at his country residence, in native style. They immediately sent acceptances, and were ready at the time appointed for the carriage which was provided by their thoughtful host.

"When we reached the house," said Fred, "each of us was provided with a new bathing-dress and towels, and proceeded to the river close by, where numbers of guests were already enjoying a bath in the clear water. The party straggled back in twos and threes; and as fast as we returned every one of us was crowned with a wreath of flowers after the Tahitian custom. There was a great deal of fun and laughter about this part of the entertainment, but everybody enjoyed it, and entered heartily into the sport of the occasion. The guests included all our party from the yacht, the officers from the ships of war, every stranger of consequence in Papéiti, and pretty nearly every respectable resident.

"By the time everybody had returned from the bath and received his crown the feast was announced, and we went in procession to the dining-hall. This proved to be a temporary building, made of a slight framework of bamboos and banana-trees, covered with a thatch of palm-leaves and decorated with festoons of leaves and vines.

"The building was erected over a fine piece of lawn, and the table was spread on the grass. Instead of a table as we understand it, fresh banana-leaves were spread on the grass, and on these the good things of the feast were laid. On the grass at the edge of this novel tablecloth mats made of cocoa fibre were spread, and on these mats we sat down native fashion. It was rather awkward getting down to the floor, but of course the awkwardness added to the fun of the occasion.

"The substantial part of the feast consisted of turkeys, chickens, and young pigs, roasted and served cold, and then there were all kinds of fin and shell fish, both raw and cooked. All the fruits of the island were there, and all the vegetables, including yams, sweet-potatoes, cucumbers, and the like. European wines took the place of the native drink, *kava*, which is rapidly going out of use.

"Instead of plates, each of us had a pile of bread-fruit leaves which served as plates, and in front of each guest there were four half cocoanut-shells. One was full of drinking-water, the second full of milk, the third contained chopped cocoanut, and the fourth sea-water. The sea-water was emptied into the chopped cocoanut to form a sauce like the Chinese *soy*, into which the various articles of food were dipped before being conveyed to the mouth, and then the shell was filled with fresh water, and used as a finger-glass.

"We enjoyed the feast very much, though all of us confessed afterwards to a back-ache, from the novelty of our positions. After the feast there was dancing in the spacious parlor of our host, and the festivities were kept up until late in the evening."

TAMARIND-TREE AT POINT VENUS.

An excursion was made the next day to Point Venus, which has a historic interest, as it is the promontory where Captain Cook made the astronomical observations by which he determined the correct position of the Society Islands. The name of the place commemorates his observation of the transit of Venus which he and his scientific party made here in 1769.

It was a delightful ride along the Broom-road, as it is called, shaded by palm and bread-fruit trees, and through groves of oranges, citrons, guavas, bananas, and other tropical productions. Our friends inspected the light-house which is maintained here to direct the mariner approaching Papéiti, and Frank made a sketch of the tamarind-tree planted by Captain Cook near the spot where he made the famous observations.

A GROVE OF COCOANUT-TREES.

CHAPTER V.

FROM THE SOCIETY TO THE SAMOAN ISLANDS. — BEFORE THE TRADE-WINDS.— NOTES ABOUT THE MISSIONARIES. — OPPOSITION OF TRADERS TO MISSIONARIES. — HOW POLYNESIA WAS CHRISTIANIZED. — THE WORK OF THE MISSIONS. — REV. JOHN WILLIAMS. — ROMANTIC STORY OF THE HERVEY GROUP. — THE LONDON MISSIONARY SOCIETY. — THE WESLEYAN AND OTHER MISSIONS.— DEATH OF MR. WILLIAMS.—SANDAL-WOOD TRADERS.—POLYNESIAN SLAVERY.— LABOR-VESSELS AND THE LABOR-TRADE.—HOW NATIVES WERE KIDNAPPED.— "THE MISSIONARY TRICK."—THE MUTINY ON THE *CARL*.—CAPTURE OF THE *DAPHNE*.—HOW LABOR IS OBTAINED AT PRESENT.

THE Society Islands are between latitude 16° and 18° south, and longitude 148° and 155° west; the Samoan Islands, the next destination of the *Pera*, lie in latitude 13° to 15° south, and longitude 169°

RUNNING BEFORE THE TRADE-WINDS.

to 173° west. Consequently the course of the yacht was a little north of west, and gave the party a pleasant run before the north-east tradewind, the crew having hardly anything to do from the time the last peak of the Society Islands disappeared until the mountains of Samoa came into view. All the world over, there is no more delightful sailing than in the trade-winds. A ship bowls along for ten, twenty, or perhaps thirty days, without squaring a yard or changing a brace, and all the time she carries every stitch of her canvas, and the water beneath her bows is a bank of foam.

DR. COAN, MISSIONARY TO HAWAII.

During the voyage our young friends busied themselves as usual in learning something about the regions whither they were bound, as well as perfecting their information about what they were leaving behind. The conversation turned one day upon the work of the missionaries in the South Pacific in redeeming the inhabitants of the islands from their former condition of barbarism.

"The missionaries have not received half the credit they deserve," said Doctor Bronson, in reply to a question which Fred propounded. "It is the fashion among certain men who have had commercial relations with these islands to deride the missionaries and throw ridicule on their work, and sometimes travellers fall into the same way of talking. There are idlers and useless men and women among the missionaries, just as there are in every occupation in life, but this circumstance does not justify the denunciation that has been heaped upon the entire body."

Frank asked why it was that so many men engaged in commerce were opposed to the missionaries.

"Principally for the reason," was the reply, "that the missionaries defend the natives against the dishonesty of certain classes of traders, and thus reduce their profits. There are honest men and dishonest ones engaged in commerce in Polynesia, just as there are elsewhere. When you hear a Polynesian merchant denouncing the missionaries in vehement terms, you may fairly conclude that the missionaries have stood in his way when he was endeavoring to defraud the natives. He is a man not to be trusted, at least that is a fair inference, though in this as in everything else he may be an exception.

"Let me give you an illustration of this," continued the Doctor. "Some years ago I heard a retired sea-captain in New York denouncing the missionaries, and declaring that they had ruined the trade of the South Pacific. It was at a dinner-party, and before the end of the evening the old captain became quite communicative about the ways of commerce with Polynesia and the Malay Archipelago. Among other things he told how they traded with the natives in his younger days. 'We used,' said he, 'to take our old-fashioned balance scales on shore with our fifty-six pound and smaller weights with handles to them. We set up the scales, and then the natives brought forward some bags whose exact weight they knew. These bags were used for testing our weights, to see that they were correct. Of course they were all right; the testing and setting up the scales took the best part of the afternoon, and then we knocked off for the day.

"'We left the scales on shore where they had been set up, but took

NO RESPECT FOR MISSIONARIES.

the weights back to the ship "for safety." They were hollow, and the handles were screwed in; during the night we unscrewed the handles, filled the hollow space with lead, and then screwed the handles back again so neatly that nobody would ever discover anything. In this way we managed to get the cargo to average 160 to 170 pounds a picul

(133 pounds); and in those days a supercargo or captain who couldn't make a cargo come up to at least 150 pounds a picul wasn't wanted another voyage by the owners. Trade went on that way until the missionaries found out all about this and other tricks, and told the natives. They never would have suspected anything if it hadn't been for the missionaries.'

"This man," continued the Doctor, "was no worse than many others in the same line of business; and if all stories are true, he was no worse than many of our forefathers, who made money by their dealings with the savages in the early days of American colonization. The belief that it is no sin to cheat the infidel and heathen is not by any means confined to the followers of Mohammed. It is easy to understand why he was opposed to the missionary labors in the South Seas, as they certainly tended, in his estimation, to the ruin of commerce."

One of the youths asked if this opposition to the Christianizing of the heathen was prevalent among the large mercantile houses, as well as among the small and independent traders.

"It is impossible to answer this question with plain yes or no," was the reply; "but it is safe to say that a very large section of the commercial community of every nation is unfavorable or, at all events, indifferent to missionary enterprises. Even national power is sometimes invoked in the interest of commerce, without regard to the effect upon the heathen. British artillery forced the Chinese to open their markets to the opium of India, and the power of British, French, German, and other arms on the coast of Africa, for purposes of trade, is well known. Even America is not without sin in this respect; American diplomacy, backed by American ships of war, opened the ports of Japan, and the history of our dealings with our own Indians reveals many instances of bloodshed or oppression in the interests of post-traders and other speculators.

"Until its failure a few years ago, the German house of Godefroy & Sons was by far the largest firm or association doing business in the Pacific. It had large fleets of ships, it had branch houses in many parts of the world; in numerous islands of the Pacific its agents were established, and it owned lands and buildings of immense value. In the harbor of Apia, Samoa, they had a ship-yard, where they not only repaired old ships but built new ones, and they owned several excellent harbors in other parts of Polynesia. There was not a single group of islands of any consequence where they were not established, and they had a great influence with the German Government.

"Now, do you suppose this great house was friendly to the missionaries—the men who came here and opened the way for commerce? Not a bit of it. Here is an extract from their general orders to their agents everywhere:

"'Never assist missionaries by word or deed, but, wheresoever you may find them, use your best influence to obstruct and exclude them.'*

"The effect of these instructions is illustrated in the experience of the American missionary ship *Morning Star*, several years ago, in a

TRADING STATION IN THE PACIFIC.

visit to the Kingsmill group of islands, near the equator. A pilot came out to meet the ship, and made her anchor three miles from shore to wait the permission of the King before any one could land. When the King learned that it was a missionary ship, he sent word that he would supply any needed provisions, but on no account could any one come on shore. The traders had told him that if any missionaries were allowed

* New Zealand Blue-book, 1874, evidence of Mr. Sterndale, late employé of Godefroy & Sons.

to land they would bewitch him and his people, and he had determined to protect himself from harm.

"Numerous instances of the demoralizing effects of commerce, when controlled by bad men, can be given. The missionaries were the first to occupy Polynesia, when traders could not venture there; some of these good men lost their lives, but the work of taming the savages went on until commerce could follow in their footsteps. You might naturally expect that commerce would be grateful, but such is far from being the case."

JOHN WESLEY, THE FOUNDER OF METHODISM.

Then the conversation turned upon the history of missionary efforts in the South Pacific from the opening enterprise of the London Mission near the end of the last century. Frank and Fred made copious notes on the subject from the books within their reach, and the information supplied by the Doctor, and from these notes they subsequently condensed the following interesting story:

The London Missionary Society was formed in 1795 by zealous men of different denominations; the call for the first meeting was signed by eighteen Independent clergymen, seven Presbyterian, three Wesleyan (Methodist), and three Episcopal, and the assemblage was held September 22d of that year. The islands of the Pacific were then attracting attention in consequence of the mutiny of the *Bounty* and the death of Captain Cook, and they were selected as the first field of operations.

Many young men offered themselves as missionaries, and of all the number of applicants twenty-nine were selected. The first delegation landed on Tahiti March 4, 1797, and formed the first mission of the Society. From that beginning the South Seas have been gradually covered with missions, and the Society has pushed its work into other fields which we need not consider here. It still adheres to its original plan of avoiding denominational differences of doctrine and Church government, and zealously pursues its work. Nearly all the denominations of Protestants have since organized separate missions of their own, both in Great Britain and America, for spreading the Gospel in the South Seas. In our account of the Sandwich and Society islands the work of the missionaries has been described; we have seen how whole populations have renounced heathenism and its practices, have been provided with written languages, and with schools and churches, and have been changed from savages to civilized men and women. And all this is due to the work of the missionary, who labored for the good of his fellow-man.

MISSION CHURCH AND STATION.

MISSION PARK MONUMENT.

More than three hundred islands of the Pacific have abandoned their heathenism, and nearly half a million of Polynesian savages have been virtually Christianized. Their communicants who have been gathered into the churches number fully sixty thousand, not including the inhabitants of the Sandwich Islands, who are now supporting missions of their own.

One reason of the success of the mission work is the common-sense that prevailed at the outset in dividing the field among the different denominations, so that the minds of the natives should not be confused as to the character of the teachings they were receiving.

This was done through a friendly agreement between the London Missionary Society and the Wesleyan Mission, the former having exclusive charge of the work in the Samoan Islands, and the Wesleyans taking possession of the Feejee and Tonga groups. Other groups were disposed of in the same way as time went on, and the arrangement was found entirely satisfactory. Catholic missions have been established in some of the islands where the Protestant missions were already settled; they have made poor progress, as the natives showed an unwillingness to abandon the faith they had adopted for another.

The American Board of Foreign Missions was organized in Mission Park, Williamstown, Massachusetts, in the early part of this century, and the organization is commemorated by an appropriate monument. It has evangelized the Hawaiian Islands, and carried on work in the Marquesas, Gilbert, Marshall, and Caroline islands. Since 1873 most of the active labor has been performed by the Hawaiian Evangelical Association, which owns a mission vessel, the *Morning Star*.

MISSION SHIP ON HER VOYAGE.

The London Missionary Society has missions in the Society, Tuamotu, Hervey or Cook, Austral, Samoa, Tokelau, Ellice, Gilbert, and Loyalty groups, on Niue and several other isolated islands, and in New Guinea. It owns two vessels, the *John Williams* and the *Ellengowan*.

The Australian Wesleyan Conference supports missions in Tonga, Feejee, Samoa, Rotumah, and New Britain; the Presbyterian churches of Australia have a mission in the New Hebrides, and possess a mission vessel, called the *Dayspring*.

The Melanesian Episcopal Mission is maintained in the Banks', Santa Cruz, and Solomon islands, and has a mission vessel, called the *Southern Cross*. The Catholics have missions on all the islands controlled by the French, and on most of the others, but they did not make their appearance until long after the work had been well under way in the hands of the Protestant organizations.

A considerable proportion of the early missionaries were murdered by the natives, whose good they sought, and others died of disease, privation, and the effects of the climate. But the ranks were steadily filled up, and the work went on; the native converts and teachers were fully as zealous as the white men who had taught them the new religion, and much of the work of instruction was performed by them. Whenever native teachers were murdered by the savages among whom they had taken their residences, others volunteered to fill their places. The following incident is recorded in the history of mission work in Polynesia:

In 1822 the mission ship of the Rev. John Williams anchored off an island which proved to be Mangaia of the Hervey group. Three Tahitian teachers, two of them accompanied by their wives, volunteered to land and establish a mission. No sooner were they on shore than they were attacked and plundered of everything they possessed, and they only escaped with their lives by swimming back through the surf to the ship.

A few months later the mission ship went there again, and two unmarried teachers, Davida and Tiere, sprang into the sea and swam to the shore, carrying nothing but the clothing they wore and a portion of the New Testament in Tahitian, which was wrapped in cloth and tied on their heads. A great crowd assembled at the landing, and as they stepped on shore several warriors levelled spears at them. The King took the swimmers under his protection, treated them kindly, took them to the temple, and pronounced them tabu, or sacred, so that the natives should not harm them.

Within two years Tiere died, but the work of conversion went on so well that one day the King and his chiefs determined to give up idolatry. They carried the thirteen idols which they had hitherto worshipped to the house of Davida, and announced that for the future they would worship the God of the white man. These thirteen idols are now preserved in the museum of the London Missionary Society.

In 1821 Mr. Williams decided to send a mission from Raiatea to the Hervey Isles, of which very little was known beyond the bare existence of such a group, and that it was inhabited by fierce cannibals. Several native converts from Raiatea were landed on the island of Aitutaki; they were well received by the chief and his people, but Mr. Williams had great fears for their safety, owing to the bad character of the cannibal inhabitants.

LANDING ON AN ATOLL OF THE HERVEY GROUP.

In the following year, when the mission ship went there again, great was the joy of Mr. Williams to learn that all the inhabitants had abandoned idolatry, burned their temples, and decided to be Christians; they had built a large church, kept the Sabbath religiously, and on the day following the arrival of the mission ship two thousand of them assembled on the beach in solemn prayer, which was led by the delighted missionary. After the service they brought their idols and carried them on board the mission ship, so that the people of the other islands might see for themselves that they had discarded altogether the worship of the worthless images.

The story of the conversion of the inhabitants of the island of Raratonga, of the Hervey group, sounds like romance. So little was known of this island that Mr. Williams had great trouble in finding it, as its latitude and longitude had not been established. Among the converts on another island were six natives of Raratonga; one of these men told Mr. Williams that if he would sail to a given point on the island of Aitutaki, he could take bearings that would carry him where he wished to go. So, taking the six Raratongans on board, he steered for the point indicated, and by following the directions of the man the island they sought was reached.

The young King came on board, and agreed to take the six natives ashore, and also a Tahitian teacher, who had volunteered to remain. The King, Matea, a handsome fellow six feet high, and with every inch of his skin elaborately tattooed, was one of the first converts. Within a year the whole population had become Christian, and there was not a house on the island where the family did not assemble morning and evening for divine worship. Mr. Williams and another missionary went there with their families in 1827, and were met at the shore by several thousands of natives, who shook hands with them so vigorously that their arms ached for hours afterwards. A few days after their arrival the people came in procession, bringing fourteen enormous idols, for which they had no further use, the smallest of them being fifteen feet high.

A new church was erected capable of containing three thousand people; some of the idols were used as pillars of this building, and the rest were burned. The railing of the pulpit stairs of this church was made of spears which the chiefs contributed, and all the heathen temples, and even their foundations, were completely broken up.

The Hervey Islands are now a centre of missionary work in the South Pacific. The islanders have a theological college, which has sent out nearly two hundred trained teachers and preachers of their own, and about half this number are scattered among the isles of the Pacific where the inhabitants have not yet renounced heathenism or their cannibal practices. In 1881 four of these missionaries, with their wives and children, twelve persons in all, were murdered by the natives of New Guinea, and several others narrowly escaped with their lives.

Shortly after settling in the Hervey Islands Mr. Williams determined to carry the Gospel to the Navigator's, or Samoan group. Having no ship, he built a boat, sixty feet long and eighteen feet wide, with the aid of the Raratonga natives. He wanted a blacksmith's bellows to shape the iron-work, and in order to make it he killed three of his four goats to obtain their skins. In a single night his bellows was devoured by the rats, the only quadrupeds indigenous to the islands, and he then invented a pump by which air could be forced.

His boat took fifteen weeks for its construction. Its sails were of native matting, the cordage was of the bark of the hibiscus, the oakum for calking the seams was made from banana stumps and cocoanut husks, and the sheaves were of iron-wood. To obtain planks, trees were split with wedges, and then cut up with hatchets. One anchor was of stone, and another of iron-wood, and the provisions consisted of pigs, cocoanuts, bananas, and other tropical products. In this vessel he sailed during the next four years to many islands of the Pacific, distributing teachers among them, and doing everything in his power for the good of the people. In 1834 he visited England, and returned in the missionary ship *Camden*, which had been purchased by the London Missionary Society.

Mr. Williams continued his work until 1839, when he, with a companion missionary, James Harris, was murdered by the natives of the

COCOA PALMS IN THE HERVEY ISLANDS.

New Hebrides Islands, whither he had gone to plant a mission. The stories of the conversion of the people of the Tonga, Samoan, and Feejee groups is only scarcely less romantic than what has just been narrated of the Hervey Isles. In all these islands, as well as in the Sandwich and Society groups, it is probable that the proportion of the inhabitants who observe the Sabbath, attend divine service, and gather in their families for morning and evening worship, is greater than among the people of Great Britain or the United States.

In their intertribal wars, which sometimes occur in these days, though far less frequently than before the advent of the missionaries, all parties abstain from fighting on Sunday, and men may safely circulate from one hostile camp to another.

And all this has been accomplished through the self-abnegation of the men who obeyed the divine injunction, "Go ye into all the world and preach the Gospel to every creature." Volumes could be written, as volumes have been written, but even then the whole story of the work and sufferings of the missionaries in the South Seas would remain untold.

Referring to the opposition of the traders to the missionaries, Doctor Bronson said that the death of Mr. Williams was due to the conduct of the seamen, though it was not directly instigated by them.

"One of the products of the Pacific Islands," said the Doctor, "is sandal-wood, which brings a high price in the Chinese market, and so much has it been sought in the last fifty or sixty years that on many of the islands it has entirely disappeared. The sandal-wood traders committed many outrages on the islands that they visited, and these outrages naturally led to reprisals.

"When Mr. Williams and his friend landed on Erromanga, in the New Hebrides, a party of warriors rushed upon them from a thicket where they had been lying concealed. In an instant the missionaries were clubbed, and their bodies were afterwards roasted and eaten by the savages whom the devoted men sought to reclaim. Investigation showed that a sandal-wood ship had visited the island a few weeks before, and her crew had killed several of the natives who opposed the plunder of their plantations and the destruction of their trees. Of course the natives were ready to revenge themselves on the first foreign ship that came there, and this happened to be the one carrying the missionaries.

"In 1871," continued the Doctor, "the death of Bishop Patteson occurred on the island of Nukapu in much the same way. The bishop was widely known and esteemed for his devotion to missionary work in Polynesia, and was greatly beloved by the natives on all the islands he had visited. Shortly before his visit to Nukapu a labor-vessel had been there, and carried off many of the natives against their will. While the natives were thirsting for revenge the bishop arrived, and, not knowing him, they put him to death, as the natives of Erromanga had killed Mr. Williams more than thirty years before."

"Please tell us something about the labor-vessels and the labor-trade," said Frank. "I have read about them, and we heard them mentioned in Tahiti and Honolulu, and would like to know more about them."

"It is quite a long story," was the reply, "but I'll try to give it to you briefly. You remember that in the Hawaiian and Society islands it was necessary to import foreign labor for the plantations, the natives being too indolent, or not sufficiently numerous, for the wants of the planters. Well, the same state of affairs prevailed, and still prevails, in the Samoa, Feejee, Tonga, and other groups, where cotton and sugar plantations have been established, and also in Queensland, in Australia.

NATIVE HOUSES AND CANOE.

"Well, the demand naturally led to an effort to supply the want. Labor-vessels went among the islands and groups farther to the west, especially among the Solomon and New Hebrides islands, to hire men to work on the plantations where they were needed.

"Nearly all of these vessels were English, either from the ports of Australia or hailing from Feejee, Samoa, or Tahiti. Occasionally an American captain went into the labor traffic, and there was now and then a French or German vessel engaged in it.

"The theory of the business was that men were hired on regular contracts to work for a period of years (from three to five years) on designated plantations, for certain stipulated wages, and at the end of the contract they were to be returned to their homes free of expense to themselves. Every man was to understand perfectly what was required of him, and nobody was to be taken except of his own free-will.

"This was the theory and the practice at the outset, but very soon the practice became far otherwise. Some men were hired on the above plan, more were hired from their chiefs without being consulted as to their own willingness in the matter, and a still greater number were kidnapped and sold into slavery."

"Sold into slavery?"

"Yes, exactly that. They were decoyed on board the labor-ships, and when a sufficient number were there they were bound hand and foot, flung into the hold, and the ship sailed away with them. They were delivered over to the planters at so much a head, and very few of them ever found their way back again to their homes."

"Why, that's just like what we used to read about the African slave-trade," said Fred, who had been listening with open-eyed astonishment.

"Quite so," the Doctor answered. "It was the revival of the African slave-trade, and was carried on under the British flag. And many of the men were taken into slavery on British soil as they were turned over to the planters of Queensland, a British colony.

"The matter became so notorious that the attention of the British Government was called to it, and measures were taken to put an end to the outrages. Ships of war were sent to the South Pacific to suppress the illegal trade, and stringent laws were passed to prevent further outrages. At present every labor-vessel must be licensed for her business, and carry an official who superintends the making of contracts, and makes sure that every laborer signs the agreement with his own free-will, and with a full understanding of the terms of the document. Care is taken with regard to the food and treatment of the men while on shipboard, and also when at work on the plantations."

Frank asked what were the means resorted to to obtain men before the Government took these precautions.

"As to that," was the reply, "the tricks and devices were various. The usual plan was for a ship to anchor near an island, and of course she was soon surrounded by the natives in their canoes, ready to barter cocoanuts and other produce for what the white men had to sell. The

MISSIONARY STATION ON ANEITYUM ISLAND.

men were enticed on board, and when a sufficient number was on the deck a signal was given by the captain, and the sailors would knock the victims down as rapidly as possible. Some escaped by jumping overboard, but the rest were secured, and the ship then proceeded to another island to repeat the process until her cargo was complete. Then, with her hold packed like that of an African slave-ship fifty years ago, she steered for Feejee or for Queensland, and the captain and crew made a handsome profit for their work.

TANNA ISLANDER ON A QUEENSLAND PLANTATION.

"After a time the natives became too wary to be enticed on board in the ordinary way, and then other plans were tried. The *Southern Cross*, the mission ship used by Bishop Patteson, was painted white, and the natives were familiar with its appearance. Accordingly the slavers adopted the following plan to obtain their living cargoes:

"About the time the bishop was making his rounds a white vessel appeared and anchored near an island. A boat put off for the shore, and in its stern sat a black-coated individual with a white necktie, green glasses, a book under his arm which would readily pass for a Bible, and an umbrella over his head. The cry went around that the bishop had come, and the natives flocked to the beach to welcome him.

"Instead of the bishop it was a strange missionary, who spoke enough of the language to make himself understood. He told them that the bishop had had a fall the day before and broke his leg, and therefore could not come on shore. He must hurry away to Sydney to see a doctor, and could only stay a little while at the island, but he wanted to see his friends on board, and would like some yams and fruit.

"In the course of an hour or so fifty or more canoes are flying over the water laden with presents for the good bishop. The fruit is passed on board, the men follow and are admitted two or three at a time, to descend into the bishop's cabin.

"At the foot of the cabin-stairs they are met by half a dozen sailors, who put pistols to their heads, threaten to kill them if they make the least outcry, tie their hands, and pass them along into the hold through

GROUP OF ISLANDERS ON A FEEJEEAN PLANTATION.

a hole which has been cut from the cabin for that purpose. When a batch has been thus disposed of another is allowed to descend, and in a little while the hold is full; fifty or more natives have been made prisoners, and meantime the strange missionary has returned from shore, the canoes are cut adrift or sunk by dropping pieces of iron into them, and the pretended missionary ship sails away with a cargo of slaves for the Queensland or Feejee market."

FIRING DOWN THE HATCHWAY.

"And was this really done by Englishmen?" one of the youths asked.

"Yes, not only once, but several times," the Doctor answered; "and of the men thus stolen from their homes very few ever found their way back again. If you wish more information on this point, read 'Kidnapping in the South Seas,' by Captain Palmer, and 'The Cruise of the *Rosario*,' by Captain Markham, both of the Royal Navy. These gentlemen were sent to cruise in Polynesian waters to suppress the slave-trade; and though they made several captures, they did not find themselves supported by the colonial courts. 'In two glaring instances,' says Captain Markham, 'when slavers were seized and sent to Sydney for adjudication they were acquitted, and their captors were themselves condemned in heavy damages for detention and injury done to those vessels.'

"A notorious case," continued the Doctor, "was that of the slaver *Carl*, which has figured prominently in the newspapers and official documents. This vessel left Melbourne in June, 1871, for a cruise among the South Sea Islands, with the object of procuring laborers. Dr. James Patrick Murray was on board as a passenger and part owner of the vessel, which was commanded by Joseph Armstrong. They tried to obtain laborers at the New Hebrides Islands by legitimate methods but failed, and then they resorted unsuccessfully to the 'missionary trick.'

"After this the party captured the natives by upsetting or destroying their canoes. According to Dr. Murray's account, given on the trial of Armstrong and one of the crew, the captain and crew used to smash the canoes by dropping pig-iron or stones into them, and the passengers in their own boat picked the natives out of the water, sometimes stunning them with clubs or slung-shot if they were troublesome.

THE "ROSARIO" CHASING A MAN-STEALING SCHOONER.

"In this way they collected about eighty natives, keeping them in the hold at night, and allowing them to come on deck during the day. One night there was a disturbance in the hold, and the natives tore down the bunks, or sleeping-places, and with the materials thus obtained they attacked the main hatchway.

"An attempt was made to pacify them but it failed, and then the crew began firing down the hatchway. The firing lasted about eight hours, being kept up during the night, one of the men occasionally throwing lights into the hold in order to enable the others to direct their aim. At daylight all appeared to be quiet, and so the hatches were opened and those who were alive were invited to come up. About five came up without help; there were eight or nine seriously wounded, sixteen badly wounded, and about fifty dead. The dead and the sixteen badly wounded were immediately thrown overboard; the ship was out of sight of land at the time, and therefore it was impossible that any of the wounded could have reached the shore.

A WITNESS FOR THE DEFENCE.

"The blood was removed from the hold, all traces of the affair were effaced, and when the *Carl* was overhauled by the *Rosario* shortly afterwards there was nothing suspicious in her appearance, and she was allowed to proceed on her voyage.

"The captain and one of the crew were condemned to death, but the sentence was afterwards commuted to imprisonment. Murray was allowed to be one of the witnesses for the prosecution, and so escaped punishment. Others of the party on board said Murray was the ringleader in the whole business, and that he sang 'Marching through Georgia' while firing at the poor natives in the hold. They further said that he selected those who were the least wounded when the remainder were thrown overboard, and he used to read prayers to the crew and then give the order to go and smash the canoes of the natives."*

"And all this happened in 1871," said Frank, "and was done by Englishmen and under the English flag!"

"Yes," replied the Doctor; "and until the outrages became so notorious that the attention of the civilized world was drawn towards them, many official Englishmen in the British colonies were very lukewarm on the subject, and evidently did not wish to impede the progress of the cotton and sugar industries by interfering with the business of procuring laborers. Let me give an instance of this:

"Captain Palmer, the predecessor of Captain Markham in command of the *Rosario*, seized the schooner *Daphne*, of forty-eight tons burden, fitted up exactly like an African slaver, and with one hundred natives

* This account is abridged from "The Cruise of the *Rosario*," by Captain A. H. Markham, R. N.

on board. They were entirely naked, had not even mats to sleep on, and the hold of the schooner resembled a pigpen more than anything else.

"The *Daphne* had a license to carry fifty native 'passengers,' but it made no mention of Feejee, where she was seized, and whither she had taken her cargo for sale. The natives were landed at Levuka, Feejee, and placed under the care of the British consul, and the *Daphne* was sent to Sydney for adjudication. The Chief-justice of New South Wales, Sir Alfred Stephen, decided in the *Daphne's* favor in the following words, which I will read from Captain Palmer's Book, 'Kidnapping in the South Seas:'

"'... It will not be enough to show that artifice has been used, or even falsehood told, to induce the natives to enter into the agreements or contracts mentioned, if they really did enter into the contracts.

"'The morality of the proceeding cannot be taken into consideration in determining the question raised here. The captor will have substantially to prove that the natives were going to be passed into a state of real slavery by those who had taken them on board the *Daphne*, or were to be put into a state really amounting to slavery, and in violation of the agreement and against their will.'

INDIAN GIRL HOUSE-SERVANT IN FEEJEE.

"The *Daphne* was released, and Captain Palmer was compelled to pay the expenses of the trial, amounting to nearly $900. This money was afterwards refunded to him by Her Majesty's Government, which approved his action in seizing the schooner and placed his name on the list for promotion."

"How do the colonies obtain their laborers at present?" Fred asked.

"They get them from the islands in legitimate ways, as I before told you, and they also import Chinese and Indian coolies. The supply of Polynesian labor is not equal to the demand, and in the last few years, especially in Feejee, there has been a large importation of coolies from India. We will learn something about them when we visit the Feejee Islands."

CHAPTER VI.

THE SAMOAN ISLANDS.—APIA.—ITS POSITION AND PECULIARITIES.—BEACH-COMBERS.—HISTORY AND ADVENTURES OF SOME OF THEM.—CHARLEY SAVAGE.—SAMOAN POLITICS.—ATTEMPT TO POISON MISSIONARIES.—FRENCH CONVENT AND SCHOOLS.—COMMERCE WITH SAMOA.—VISITING A NATIVE VILLAGE.—GAMES OF THE YOUNG PEOPLE.—YOUTHS THROWING SPEARS.—MISSION COLLEGE AT MALUA.—HOW THE STUDENTS LIVE.—PANGO-PANGO.—ADMIRAL WILKES'S DESCRIPTION.—ATTENDING A SAMOAN PICNIC.—DIFFERENCES OF TASTE.—MASSACRE BAY.—LA PÉROUSE.—HOW HIS FATE WAS DISCOVERED.—THE SWORD-HILT AT TUCOPIA.—LOSS OF THE *BOUSSOLE* AND *ASTROLABE*.—VANIKORO ISLAND.

THE *Pera* reached the Samoan Islands without mishap, and anchored in the harbor of Apia. The Samoan group is also known on charts and maps as the Navigator's Islands; the former name is the native one, while the latter was bestowed by Bougainville in 1768, who called the group *Archipel des Navigateurs*, in consequence of the skill displayed by the natives in managing their canoes. There are nine inhabited islands in the group, with an area of about 1125 square miles and a population of something less than forty thousand.

SAMOAN DOUBLE CANOE.

In general effect our friends found the scenery of Samoa not unlike that of Tahiti, though the detail was materially different. The harbor of Apia is an excellent one, affording secure anchorage and safety from all winds; the captain of the yacht told Frank that there was a finer harbor at Pango-Pango, in another island, but Apia was the most important commercially. The trading company that succeeded the German house of Godefroy & Sons, after the latter's failure, has a large establishment at Apia, and controls a great part of the business of the islands. The ship-yard of the company was pointed out, and it needed only a glance to show that it was extensive and well equipped.

CORAL ARCHITECTS IN SAMOAN WATERS.

Apia consists of a long and rather straggling village, stretched along the shore of a crescent-shaped bay; like most of these South Sea island ports, it is concealed by the cocoa palms and other trees peculiar to the tropics, and many of the houses are so well covered by the verdure that the visitor cannot make out their position until he is close upon them.

A BEACH-COMBER.

Back of the town, which contains two or three hundred stores and residences, the horizon is filled with richly green hills, which rise one upon the other to a height of nearly five thousand feet. Streams come trickling down from these hills, and there is one water-fall visible from the harbor large enough to make a well-defined stipple of white against the rich green of the mountains that surround it. Frank and Fred immediately suggested a walk to the water-fall, but their enthusiasm was checked by Doctor Bronson, who thought there would be enough in Apia to amuse them at least for that day.

Hardly was the anchor fixed in the mud before a boat was lowered and the *Pera's* party went on shore. Doctor Bronson and the youths proceeded to the American consulate, while Colonel Bush and Doctor Macalister went to call upon the representative of their country. After the official formalities were over they strolled about the town, and in a short time Frank and Fred had familiarized themselves with a considerable amount of the history of Samoa, as we have ascertained by a perusal of their journals.

"Apia isn't much of a place," said Frank, "but what it lacks in numbers it makes up in variety. Among the residents there are Americans, Englishmen, Germans, French, and several other nationalities, the Germans being most numerous and controlling the best of the trade. Then there is a fair sprinkling of men whose nationality is open to question, and whom any respectable country would not be anxious to claim. Samoa is at present the favorite resort of the beach-comber; perhaps you don't know what a beach-comber is.

"All through the islands of the Pacific there are men whose history is shrouded in obscurity, and who are unwilling to tell the truth about themselves, for the simple reason that the truth would be inconvenient. They are deserters from ships, runaways from home—perhaps in consequence of crimes for which the law would like to lay hands on them—outcasts from decent society or society of any kind, and not at all particular as to how they make a living. They were more numerous fifty years ago than at present, but there is still a sufficient number of them for all practical wants of the country. In the days when England sent its criminal classes to Australia, the South Sea Islands were filled with escaped convicts and ticket-of-leave men; but that source of supply no longer abounds, and thereby hangs a tale which may as well be told here as anywhere else.

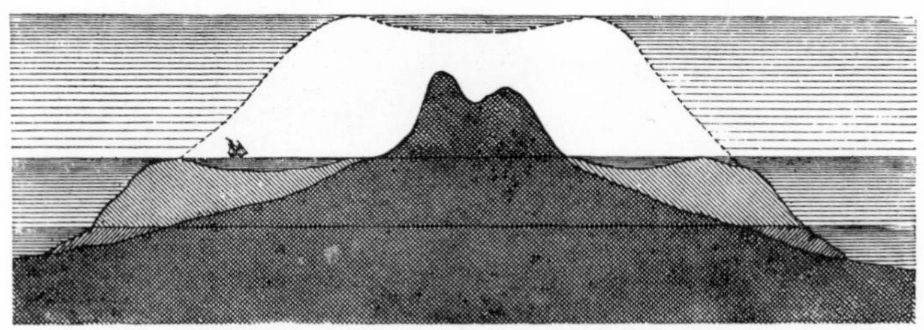

GROWTH OF CORAL ON A MOUNTAIN SLOWLY SUBSIDING.

"The first white settlers of the Feejee Islands was a band of twenty-seven convicts, who escaped from imprisonment in New South Wales, in 1804, on a small schooner which they had captured. They landed in Feejee with a few muskets, and in their encounters with the natives their weapons made them all-powerful. The natives regarded the muskets as something supernatural, and if the white men had conducted themselves with intelligence they could have obtained mastery over the whole population with very little trouble. The natives were ready to acknowledge them as rulers, and did in fact exalt several of them to the position of chiefs. But the fellows quarrelled with the natives and among themselves, and when Commodore Wilkes touched at the Feejees, in 1840, only two of them were alive.

"These wandering or stationary vagabonds are the men who are called beach-combers in the parlance of the South Pacific. They are not fond of law and order, and whenever an island group goes under the control of any European power the beach-combers are very likely to leave and take up their abode on islands where the natives are still independent. When the French occupied Tahiti many beach-combers there fled to Feejee, and when Feejee became an English colony they departed for Samoa. Samoa is still under the rule of its own kings, or rather under their misrule, but the probabilities are that it will soon be in the hands of the Germans. When this happens you may expect an emigration of beach-combers to the islands, if any remain, where there will be no legal restraints.

ASS'S EARS, FLORIDA ISLAND.

"The stories of many of these fellows is full of the most startling incidents, even after making a very liberal deduction for what their imaginations have added to the facts as they occurred. One of them tells how, when he landed in Feejee, he was condemned to be baked and served up at a feast; the oven was being heated for his reception when the chief concluded to keep his prize a while longer until he could be fattened. The man was released, but he ate sparingly of the food that was given him, and at the same time ingratiated himself with the natives, particularly with the chief, by showing him how to make war successfully upon his enemies. The result was he was saved from baking, became a man of importance, had fifty wives, and a goodly number of slaves.

"Another beach-comber named Charley Savage became a man of great importance, and received the honors that were given to the most exalted chiefs. He assisted his tribe in making war, and was nearly always successful. One day, however, his fortune deserted him, as he was killed in a fight, and his body fell into the hands of his enemies. They cooked and devoured him, and made his bones into sail needles, which were distributed among the people in token of the event, and as a remembrance of the victory in which he was slain.

"It must not be supposed from this reference to cannibalism that the Samoans practised it. They seem never to have been addicted to devouring their enemies or anybody else, and in other respects were superior to their neighbors.

"Like nearly all these island groups, Samoa has been, from time immemorial, the scene of almost constant warfare between the tribes inhabiting the different islands. There are generally two or three claimants to the throne of Samoa, and the foreign consuls are kept pretty busy adjusting difficulties growing out of the local wars, and involving the destruction of foreign property. On two occasions the

A HOUSE IN THE TONGA ISLANDS.

protectorate of the islands has been offered to the United States, but it has been declined with thanks. It has also been offered to England, but thus far has not been accepted, and the indications, at the time of this writing, are that Samoa will be a German colony before many months.*

* Since the above was written Samoa has virtually passed into the hands of the Germans. The former King was deposed, taken on board a German war-ship, and carried into exile in New Guinea. A new king was placed on the throne, and is maintained there by a German garrison stationed at Apia.

"The Samoans have been divided into two great factions, and it has never been possible for them to come to an agreement that could be kept for any length of time. Their quarrels have been aided by the scoundrelly white men just mentioned, and our consul says that if all these bad fellows could be driven out there might be a chance for peace.

"It was these beach-combers that in the early days of the labors of the missionaries greatly hindered their work, and in several instances directly caused their deaths. As an illustration I may mention the death of the first three English missionaries who went to the Tonga Islands. There was an escaped English convict living there who persuaded the King that these men were wizards, and that an epidemic which was then raging had been caused by them. The King accordingly murdered the good men at the bidding of the scoundrel.

"When the first missionaries settled in Pango-Pango, in Samoa, some twelve or fifteen of these beach-combers were living there. These rascals were so bitterly opposed to the missionaries that they tried to drive them away, and failing in this laid a plot to poison them. The story is thus told by Rev. Mr. Murray in his book, 'Forty Years of Mission Work in Polynesia:'

"'The plot was wellnigh carried into execution. The opportunity was to be embraced when the teakettle was on the fire. Cooking and boiling of water are carried on in open sheds on the islands. The time fixed upon for carrying the plan into effect was *service* afternoon. The lad who attended to the boiling of the water was accustomed to fill the kettle and put it upon the fire before going to the service. Hence there was afforded the opportunity which our enemies sought. We had all gone to the service, and there was no human eye to watch their movements. The appointed afternoon happened to be windy, and while the man who had undertaken to carry the plot into effect was in the act of doing the deed, another, who had been smitten with remorse, struck his arm and scattered the poison; they had no means of obtaining more, and so the attempt failed. The man who was instrumental in saving our lives remained on the island several years acting as pilot to vessels entering Pango-Pango harbor, and in 1841 he left in our missionary brig *Camden*. It was not from himself that we learned our obligations but from another white man who lived on the island at the time of the plot, and knew of it though he had no hand in it. The occurrence led to the breaking up and scattering of the party of would-be murderers, as they feared the arrival of a man-of-war, and they could no longer trust one another.'

"The Samoans are a handsome people," continued Frank in his journal, "of a deep bronze or copper color, and graceful figures. Some of them have adopted foreign garments; but a good proportion adhere to the native dress, which consists of fine mats or thick handsome tappa, made from the fibre of the mulberry or bread-fruit tree. Their tappa is thicker than that of the Marquesas, but unfortunately the manufacture of it is diminishing year by year, and in a little while no more will be made. Foreign calicoes are taking its place, just as in Tahiti and the Marquesas. Of course the foreigners wish a market for the goods they have to sell, and therefore they encourage the wearing of garments or materials of European make.

"The most lightly clad Samoans were those that came out in boats when we lay at anchor and wanted to dive for money. They are excellent swimmers and divers, and when a piece of silver is thrown into the water they are after it instantly, and catch it before it reaches the bottom. The best of the divers was a girl who appeared to be about fifteen years old; when she caught a coin she held it between her teeth till she rose to the surface, and after taking breath for half a minute or so was ready for another dive. The performance was exactly like what we saw at Singapore, Malta, and other ports, where there are always plenty of natives ready to dive for the coins that passengers throw over for them. The water is perfectly clear, and though it is fully a hundred feet deep, every object on the bottom can be seen.

NATIVE TEACHER, UPOLU, SAMOAN ISLANDS.

"In our stroll about Apia we passed the convent where four French Sisters and as many Samoan ones have charge of the education of some sixty or more native girls, many of them the daughters of chiefs or belonging to the high caste families. As we passed the convent the girls were singing very sweetly, and we paused to listen; it was easy to imagine that we were passing a school in Rouen or Dijon, so much was the singing like what one hears in France. The French Sisters are said to be very much devoted to their work, and as the Samoans are fond of music they readily receive instruction in singing. The girls are taught in all the branches customary in schools of this sort in other parts of the world; sewing and other home duties are not neglected, and when the pupils leave the school they are in a position to do a great deal of good among their less accomplished sisters.

"There is a similar school for boys, under the charge of French priests, and there are Protestant schools in every village. The Catholics have made greater progress here than in any other of the island groups; they have between three and four thousand adherents, and among their converts are some of the most influential men of the islands. The representatives of the London Missionary Society claim about twenty-five thousand followers, and the Methodists something more than five thousand, the latter having come into the field much later than did the London society. Nearly all the adult population can read and write, and there is scarcely a child ten years old that cannot read its own language.

"There are groves of cocoanut-trees everywhere, and we were not surprised to learn that the principal product of the islands is from the cocoa-tree. Ten thousand tons of copra are shipped every year to the markets of Europe, where the oil is extracted, and there is besides a large production of cocoanut-oil in Samoa, which some have estimated as high as two thousand tons. The Germans have extensive cotton plantations, and there are smaller plantations belonging to English and American companies and individuals; coffee and sugar are cultivated, but the culture of these articles has not thus far been very extensive.

"As at Tahiti and in the other islands, it has been necessary to import laborers from elsewhere to work the plantations, as the Samoans are not fond of exerting themselves any more than are those of the Society group. Thus far most of the laborers have been imported by the Germans, and they come from all the islands where the German vessels trade. The Polynesian Land Company and the American Land Company have also made some importations of the same sort, but up to the present time they have not equalled the Germans.

"While walking in the outskirts of the town we were thirsty, and asked the native boy who accompanied us where we could find some water to drink. He immediately suggested cocoanut-milk, and on our acquiescing he hailed a boy who was lounging under a cocoanut-tree close by, and said something to him in Samoan.

"Immediately the second boy took a small piece of rope which had

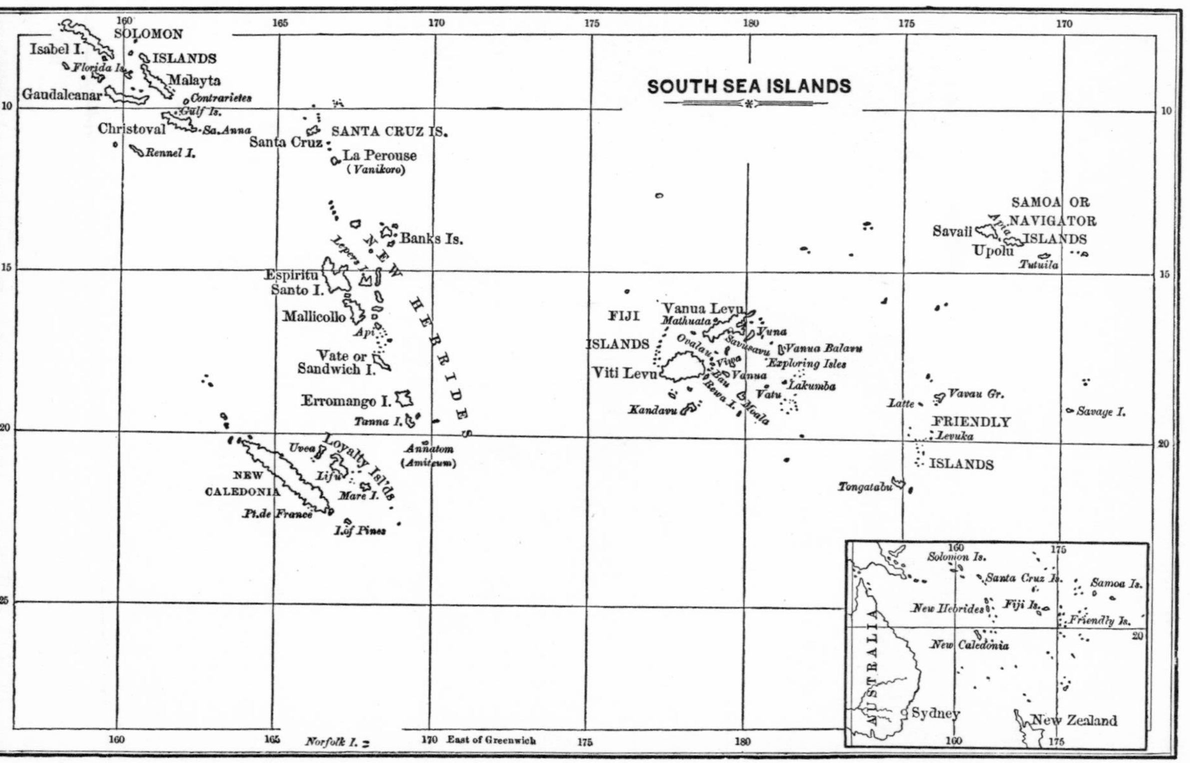
SOUTH SEA ISLANDS
SOLOMON ISLANDS
Isabel I.
Florida Is.
Malayta
Gaudalcanar
Contrarietes
Gulf Is.
Christoval
Sa. Anna
Rennel I.
SANTA CRUZ IS.
Santa Cruz
La Perouse (Vanikoro)
Banks Is.
NEW HEBRIDES
Lepers I.
Espiritu Santo I.
Mallicollo
Api
Vate or Sandwich I.
Erromango I.
Tanna I.
Annatom (Amiteum)
Loyalty Isl'ds
Uvea
Lifu
Mare I.
NEW CALEDONIA
Pt. de France
I. of Pines
FIJI ISLANDS
Vanua Levu
Mathuata
Yuna
Savusavu
Vanua Balavu
Exploring Isles
Ovalau
Viga
Vanua
Bau
Lakumba
Vatu
Rewa I.
Moala
Viti Levu
Kandavu
SAMOA OR NAVIGATOR ISLANDS
Savaii
Apia
Upolu
Tutuila
Vavau Gr.
Savage I.
Latte
FRIENDLY ISLANDS
Levuka
Tongatabu
Norfolk I.
East of Greenwich
Solomon Is.
Santa Cruz Is.
Samoa Is.
New Hebrides
Fiji Is.
Friendly Is.
New Caledonia
AUSTRALIA
Sydney
New Zealand

been twisted out of cocoa fibre, and prepared to ascend one of the trees. By means of this rope and his hands and feet he went up about as quickly as we could have ascended a staircase of the same height, and threw down several nuts, with which we quenched our thirst. Any one who has been in the tropics knows how refreshing is the milk of the green cocoanut when he is weary and thirsty.

CRABS EATING COCOANUTS.

"We saw some crabs feeding on cocoanuts, which are about the last thing in the world you would suppose a crab could eat. Perhaps you'll laugh and be incredulous, but they really do eat cocoanuts, and get the meat out without any assistance. Cocoanuts are their principal food, but they do not refuse other fruits, such as figs, candle-nuts, and nutmegs. This is the way they do it:

"The crab climbs a tree and pushes down a ripe cocoanut, which is easily detached, and he shows a great deal of sagacity in selecting only the ripe nuts. Then he comes down to the ground and tears the husk from the nut, and he always begins at the end where the eye-holes are.

If the tree is a sloping one, and there are rocks underneath, he climbs up again, carrying the nut with him, and drops it on a rock, where it will be broken. If the situation is not favorable for this performance, he digs into the eye-holes until he makes an entrance sufficiently large to admit his pincers, with which he withdraws the meat.

"These land-crabs are excellent eating, though they are rather too oily for a delicate stomach. They live in large holes, which they dig themselves and line with the fibre torn from the cocoanut-shell. They grow to a great size, and sometimes a single crab will yield a quart of oil. They are distinctively land-crabs, and the natives say they only

A PLANTATION IN THE SOUTH SEA ISLANDS.

use the sea to bathe in. We asked our guide if all crabs in Samoa are good to eat, and he answered that all land-crabs were, but the sea ones were doubtful, some of them being poisonous at certain seasons of the year.

"We went into some of the native houses, and found them neat and clean. The roofs of the houses are very high, and supported on low posts; Fred said there was a great deal of roof and very little wall, and this exactly describes a Samoan house. The roof is thatched with palm-leaves, and when well and properly laid will exclude the heaviest rains. The houses have no doors, mats being suspended at the entrance; the result is, the dogs and chickens may walk in when they choose, though in many houses the chickens are not allowed to enter.

A FAIR WIND.

"It is the custom to place screens of plaited palm-leaves around the houses at night, but they are always removed at daylight. In the interior of the houses screens of cloth are suspended from the roof to divide the space into rooms where the inmates sleep. The couches are piles of fine mats of cocoa fibre, and the pillows are simply sticks of bamboo or other wood, on which the neck, not the head, is rested. It is about as uncomfortable as the Japanese pillow, which it closely resembles, and is no doubt the cause of the early-rising habits of the natives.

"All the cooking is done out-of-doors, and there is very little inside the houses that can be called furniture. In one house we found a group of young people playing a game which was something like our game of forfeits. They sat in a circle and spun a cocoanut around on its sharp end; when it fell the person towards whom the three black eyes pointed was adjudged the loser. When they are to decide which of them is to do anything, leaving the others free, the lottery of the cocoanut is used to determine the matter.

"Warfare being more prevalent here in later years than in the Society group, we found the games of the young men much more vigorous than at Tahiti. We saw a party of boys playing at *totoga*, or reed-throwing; they had reeds five or six feet long, with points of hard wood, and the skill of the game consisted in making the reeds skim as far as possible along the grass.

"In another spot some young men were throwing spears at the stumps of trees, and in this game the skill consisted in a youth's ability to force out the spear of some one else while fixing his own in the stump. They have several games in which spears and clubs are used, and sometimes they are accompanied by a good deal of risk. Spears are thrown so as to hit the ground and then glide upward to the mark, and sometimes a man stands up armed with only a club and allows half a dozen others to throw their spears at him in rapid succession. By a dexterous handling of his club he turns the spears aside, but it is evident that the slightest mistake may have serious consequences.

BREAD-FRUIT.

"When we came back to the landing-place we thought we would take a ride in a native boat instead of calling away the boat of the yacht. So we hired an outrigger canoe, and were quickly paddled to the side of the *Pera*. These boats are not by any means new to us, as we have seen them in Ceylon, the Malay Archipelago, and other parts of the world. The Samoans handle them with a great deal of skill, and I do not wonder that Bougainville recognized their ability by calling this group the 'Navigator's Islands.'

"I forgot to say," added Frank, "that we saw several cases of elephantiasis, which the natives call *fé-fé*, and is said to be quite common in all the islands of the group. The arms and legs of the victims are swollen to a great size, but, happily for them, the disease is not attended with pain. The cause of *fé-fé* is as unknown as is that of goitre in Switzerland."

Apia is on the north side of Upolu Island, which is the most important and the most populous of the group. It has an area of about three hundred and thirty-five square miles, and a population of not far from fifteen thousand, or more than one-third the entire number of inhabitants of Samoa. In the middle of the island is a chain of broken hills sloping towards the sea, and these hills up to their very tops are green with verdure. The harbor of Apia is sheltered by a natural breakwater; but, though the principal seat of commerce, it is not considered as fine as that of Pango-Pango, on Tutuila Island, whither our friends proceeded when their inspection of Upolu was completed.

The day after their arrival at Apia they made an excursion to Malua, about twelve miles distant, to see the college of the London Mission, which is located at that point. Of this journey Fred wrote as follows:

"We hired a boat with six strong natives to row it, but they didn't have much to do, as the wind favored us both ways, and the greater part of the distance we were under sail. The journey seemed a very short one, as we were busy studying the scenery, which is very pretty and changed every few minutes as the valleys opened to our gaze and revealed their wonderful richness of tropical productions. We kept a sharp watch for the college buildings, but didn't see them until we were quite close to the village.

"The fact is the college is not a huge edifice such as you find in Europe or America, but a collection of fifty or sixty one-story cottages, which are built around a large square, with a hall or class-room at one side. In another respect it is unlike a college in civilized countries, as each student is generally accompanied by his wife and family; we were told that married men were preferred to single ones, as the wife and children could be educated at the same time that the student pursued his studies, and they are useful afterwards in instructing the women and children in the places to which they are assigned.

"Every cottage has a garden attached to it, which the student is required to cultivate sufficiently to support his family. Any surplus stock he raises is sold and placed to his credit, and nearly all the students feed and clothe their families out of the proceeds of the garden. The college was founded in 1844 by Doctor G. A. Turner; it has educated more than two thousand teachers and preachers, and in consequence of the system I have just mentioned is almost self supporting. There are several thousand cocoanut, bread-fruit, and other life-supporting trees on the grounds, while the gardens are devoted to taro, yams, bananas, and similar plants. Here, as elsewhere in the South Pacific, the banana-plant is very productive, and requires comparatively little labor to take care of it.

"The rules of the institution are very strict, and any student who repeatedly disobeys them is requested to make way for some one who will not. The bell rings at daylight for morning prayers, after which the students go to work in their gardens or at their trades, or fish in the lagoon in front of the settlement. At eight o'clock the bell rings again for bath and breakfast, and at nine it summons the classes for recitation and instruction, which continue until four in the afternoon. Then more work till sunset, when the bell calls to family prayer. After this the students study by themselves till nine o'clock, when the bell tells them to extinguish their lights and go to bed.

WAR CANOE OF THE OLDEN TIME.

"The majority of the students are Samoans; the rest are from all the islands of the South Pacific, whence they have been sent by the local missionaries. They study arithmetic, geography, and of course learn to read and write, and besides these ordinary branches of education they devote considerable time to the Scriptures and to theology.

"Every Saturday evening there is a prayer-meeting, at which the students make short exhortations. On Sunday there are three services

—morning, afternoon, and evening; and there are Sunday-schools for the children and Bible classes for the older folks. On the first Sunday of each month there is a communion-service, after the manner of churches in England and other civilized lands. We have not seen anywhere in the Pacific a finer assemblage of native men and women than

CANOES DRAWN ON SHORE.

the class at this college; they had bright, intelligent faces, and we were told that they were all so anxious to progress in their studies that they rarely infringed any of the rules of the institution, the one most frequently violated being that which required them to stop studying at nine o'clock and go to bed.

"It was getting quite dark when we returned to Apia and found our old quarters on the yacht. They wanted us to stay all night at the mission school; but there were so many of us that we thought it best to come back to Apia lest we might incommode our hosts by thrusting such a large number of visitors on them at once. You may be sure we slept soundly in our cabins, as we were all thoroughly tired out with the long but very interesting excursion."

After a few days at Apia the yacht proceeded to Pango-Pango, in Tutuila Island, a distance of about eighty miles. Under her steam-power she made the journey in a single day; had she relied on her sails it would have been far different, as Tutuila lies dead to windward of Upolu, and there are several currents which add their force to make a passage difficult. Sailing-vessels are often five or six days making this trip, which can be covered in a few hours by steam.

Our young friends thought they had never seen anywhere a more beautiful harbor than this; Frank sat down to describe it, and after writing a few lines said he would abandon the attempt, and fall back upon the account of Admiral Wilkes, who visited it in 1839. Accordingly he copied the following from the history of the famous expedition:

"The harbor of Pango-Pango is one of the most singular in all the Polynesian isles. It is the last point at which one would look for a shelter; the coast near it is peculiarly rugged, and has no appearance of indentations, and the entrance being narrow, is not easily observed. Its shape has been compared to a variety of articles; that which it most nearly resembles is a retort. It is surrounded on all sides by inaccessible mural precipices, from eight hundred to one thousand feet in height. The lower part of these rocks is bare, but they are clothed above with luxuriant vegetation. So impassable did the rocky barrier appear in all but two places, that the harbor was likened to the valley of 'Rasselas' changed to a lake. The harbor is of easy access, and its entrance, which is about a third of a mile in width, is marked by the Tower Rock and the Devil's Point."

CAPTAIN JAMES COOK.

"He might have added," said Frank, "that there is a coral reef on each side of the entrance, with the surf breaking heavily over it, or at any rate it was doing so at the time we entered. Pango-Pango is a splendid harbor, and could hold a great many ships. Its principal disadvantage is that the prevailing trade-wind blows directly into it, so that while a sailing-ship can get in without much trouble she has a hard time to get out unless she has a steam tow-boat to help her."

Doctor Bronson told the youths that at one time the King of Samoa proposed to present the harbor of Pango-Pango, and an area of land surrounding it, to the United States Government for a coaling and naval station; but as the acceptance of the proposal would involve political relations that might be troublesome in future, the offer was practically declined. The commerce of Pango-Pango is not as important as that of Apia, for the very simple reason that the island of Tutuila contains only four thousand inhabitants, and their productive energies are not great. Copra and cocoanut-oil are the principal articles of export; there are some small plantations devoted to cotton, sugar, or coffee, but the lack of native laborers and the high cost of imported ones has kept these industries in a backward state.

AN AMERICAN RESIDENT.

The first European vessel to enter this harbor was the *Elizabeth*, an English whaler, commanded by Captain Cuthbert. He gave it the name of Cuthbert Harbor, but the appellation never adhered to it. Pango-Pango is its native name, and will probably be maintained long after Cuthbert is quite forgotten.

The settlement at Pango-Pango was so much like the one at Apia that we will not risk wearying the reader with a description. Suffice it to say the yacht remained two or three days there, and then proceeded on her voyage in the direction of the Feejee Islands.

Before their departure they were invited to attend a Fa-Samoa party, and the invitation was promptly accepted. Frank asked what a Fa-Samoa party was.

"You might put it in French," said the American consul, by whom the invitation was given, "and say *a la Samoa*, or, to come to plain English, you may render it 'Samoan fashion.' 'Fa-Samoa,' 'Fa-Feejee,' or 'Fa-Tonga,' mean after the manner of Samoa, Feejee, or Tonga. It is a convenient feature of the language, and I can assure you the party will be an enjoyable one."

"The consul was right," said Frank, in telling their experience, "as the party was a jolly one. It reminded us of the dinner at Tahiti after the native style, but was more like a picnic than anything else we have at home. In fact it was a good deal of a picnic, as each person who was invited contributed something to the supply of eatables for the table, so that those who did not fancy the native dishes need not go hungry.

"The picnic ground was just outside the town, on a pretty bit of lawn shaded by grand old bread-fruit and cocoanut trees, and in the midst of a grove of bananas, which extended on three sides of the lawn and served as a sort of hedge. Banana-leaves were spread thickly on the grass, and on this lowly table the edible things were spread, and what do you suppose we had to eat?

"We had sucking-pigs roasted very much as they are roasted at home, or folded in taro-leaves and baked in hot ashes; the steam from the green leaves cooks them thoroughly, so that the joints fall apart at the merest touch of the knife, or a slight strain of the fingers. They gave us pigeons cooked the same way, and I remark, by-the-way, that

CAVE NEAR THE PICNIC GROUND.

there are pigeons in the Samoan Islands, and it is one of the native pastimes to catch them. We had several kinds of scale-fish, some cooked and others raw, and we had crawfish and prawns and Samoan oysters; but I'm bound to say I didn't think much of the oysters when I remembered those of my native land. They gave us a salad made of the young and tender shoots of the cocoa-tree, and very nice it was, and everywhere we turned there were bananas, oranges, pineapples, and other tropical fruits.

"The dishes that most attracted our attention were the puddings made of bananas, bread-fruit, taro, and similar things. The consul told us that each of the ingredients was beaten fine and baked separately, and then they were all worked in together and covered with the thick cream from a ripe cocoanut. Cocoanut-cream is wonderfully rich; when taken by itself it is apt to cloy the stomach and disturb digestion, but used as a sauce for the puddings it is delicious; but you must touch it sparingly, as it is full of oil.

"We sat on the ground to partake of the feast, and had a back-ache afterwards, just as we did in Tahiti. For drink we each had a freshly opened cocoanut-shell, and we took the cocoa-milk as we would take tea or any other beverage in civilized lands. There were some cakes made of putrid bread-fruit, but we did not touch them any more than we did the equally vile-smelling Limburger cheese which one of our entertainers had brought along. The bread-fruit is in season for about half the year; the natives store the fruit in pits lined with banana-leaves, and thus stored the stuff ferments, and soon smells so badly that any person with a sensitive nose cannot bear to come within odoriferous distance. When walking where there are any of these bread-fruit pits we always try to keep to windward.

"Taste and habit are everything. The Germans are nauseated by putrid bread-fruit, while the Samoans are equally intolerant of Limburger. They are horrified when told how long game is kept in England and America before being cooked and eaten, and the merest taste of Worcestershire sauce would spoil their appetites for a whole day at least."

The course of the yacht carried her near Massacre Bay, and Fred naturally inquired why the spot was so called.

"It was so named," replied Doctor Bronson, "because of the massacre of several of the crew, together with the captain, of the *Astrolabe*, one of the ships of La Pérouse, the ill-fated navigator whose death was so long a mystery."

"What were the circumstances of the affair?" was the inquiry which followed this explanation.

"The ships of La Pérouse, the *Boussole* (compass) and *Astrolabe* (quadrant), were off the island, and Captain De Lange, who commanded the *Astrolabe*, sent four boats on shore to procure water. They carried sixty soldiers and sailors, and were commanded by De Lange in person.

The boats made their way through the reef, and reached the beach without opposition. While the work of watering was going on the natives appeared friendly enough, until suddenly they gave a loud shout, and attacked the Frenchmen with stones and clubs. Captain De Lange was killed, and with him eleven of his men. The rest escaped to the ships, leaving one of their boats aground. La Pérouse endeavored to get inside the reef to punish the natives, but after several days he gave up the attempt and proceeded to Botany Bay, whence he sent an account of the affair to his government."

"And that was the last heard of him for a long time?"

"Yes; he sailed from Botany Bay with the *Boussole* and *Astrolabe* in March, 1788, and for thirty-eight years nothing was known of him or his ships, or what became of them."

MASSACRE BAY.

"Did the French Government try to find out anything about their fate?"

"Oh, certainly. They sent an expedition to the South Seas, but it returned without the least information. Then they sent a circular to ambassadors, consuls, and other officials, at the courts of all the powers of the world, and to scientific societies and commercial associations, asking them in the name of humanity to search for any trace of the missing expedition, and offering to reward any one who rendered assistance to survivors, or gave any information about the fate of La Pérouse and his companions."

"And it took thirty-eight years to get the desired information?"

"Yes. All inquiries of navigators and others came to nothing, and gradually the fate of La Pérouse was considered a problem impossible of solution. On the 13th of May, 1826, an English trading-ship from Calcutta, the *St. Patrick*, Captain Peter Dillon, touched at the island of

A VILLAGE IN VANIKORO.

Tucopia, in latitude 12° 21′ south, longitude 168° 33′ east. Find its position on the map, and then I'll tell what Captain Dillon discovered there."

Frank and Fred eagerly scanned the map, and by following the lines of latitude and longitude they speedily located Tucopia. It is between the Solomon and New Hebrides groups, and lies nearly due north-west from the Feejees, and a little north of west from Samoa.

"Captain Dillon," continued the Doctor, "found there a Frenchman named Martin Buchert, whom he had known at the Feejees thirteen years before, and also a Lascar sailor who had landed at Tucopia with Buchert. The meeting of Dillon and Buchert was an interesting one; and so much was Dillon absorbed with it, that he did not at first notice a silver sword-hilt which the Lascar wore suspended by a string around his neck. While he was talking with Buchert, the Lascar sold the sword-hilt to the ship's armorer for a few fish-hooks. The natives that swarmed around the ship had many articles of European manufacture, and questions concerning them led to a remark about the sword-hilt, which was speedily obtained again from the armorer.

"Captain Dillon learned that the things were brought from an island called Vanikoro, about two days' sail to leeward of Tucopia, and that the natives there had many articles of European manufacture, which were obtained from two ships that had been wrecked there long before.

HAT ISLAND, WEST OF VANIKORO.

"Captain Dillon thought of La Pérouse, and of the reward which the French Government offered. Then he bought all the European articles which the natives of Tucopia possessed, and as soon as this was done he made sail for Vanikoro.

"When his ship was under way he carefully examined the sword-hilt with a magnifying-glass. There was a monogram so badly worn that the letters were indistinct, but he finally made it out 'J. F. G. P.'—the initials of the name Jean François Galaup de la Pérouse.

"He had found the hilt of the great navigator's sword!"

"And what did he find at Vanikoro?" said one of the youths, eagerly.

"Owing to contrary winds," the Doctor replied, "he was unable to visit the island at that time, and returned to Calcutta without doing so. He reported his discovery, and exhibited the sword-hilt and other relics; the East India Company fitted out a ship and placed it under his command, and he proceeded to Vanikoro, where he obtained a great many relics, including anchors, cannon, chains, and other heavy things, and learned from the natives the story of the wreck of the *Boussole* and *Astrolabe*."

"What was it?"

"The ships went ashore in a severe gale. On one of them every one of the crew was drowned in the surf or killed by the natives. On the other, supposed to be the one commanded by La Pérouse in person,

LOUIS XVI. AND LA PÉROUSE.

friendly terms were established with the people, and the crew were unharmed. They built a small vessel from the wreck of the larger one, and a part of them sailed away. They were never heard of afterwards; those who remained on the island died one after another, and it is supposed that the last survivor perished only a few months before the sword-hilt was found at Tucopia."

"And what became of Captain Dillon?"

"The French Government kept its promise. It created him a chevalier of the Legion of Honor, gave him a life pension of four thousand francs, and appointed him consul to Tahiti, where he remained until the establishment of the protectorate over the Society Islands. Then he returned to England, and lived on his pension until his death in 1846."

CHAPTER VII.

THE FEEJEE ISLANDS: THEIR EXTENT AND POPULATION.—TERRIBLE FATALITY OF THE MEASLES.—ROTUMAH AND ITS PEOPLE.—KANDAVU AND SUVA.—VITI LEVU.—SIGHTS OF THE CAPITAL.—PRODUCTIONS AND COMMERCE OF FEEJEE.—GROWTH OF THE SUGAR TRADE.—THE LABOR QUESTION.—OBSERVATIONS AMONG THE NATIVES.—FEEJEEAN HAIR-DRESSING.—NATIVE PECULIARITIES.—CANNIBALISM, ITS EXTENT AND SUPPRESSION.—HOW THE CHIEFS WERE SUPPLIED.—A WHOLE TRIBE OF PEOPLE EATEN.—LEVUKA.—INTERVIEWS WITH MERCHANTS AND PLANTERS.—THE BOLOLO FESTIVAL.—ANCIENT CUSTOMS.

DURING the voyage to the Feejees Frank and Fred informed themselves concerning that famous group of islands, which formerly had a dark reputation for being the scene of the grossest forms of cannibalism. What they learned was substantially as follows:

"There is really no such group of islands as 'The Feejees;' the word Feejee comes from Viti, or Vee-tee—Viti Levu being the largest island of the group, which consists of something more than two hundred islands and islets. The number is variously placed at from two hundred to two hundred and fifty, and of these about one hundred and forty are inhabited. Viti Levu

A NATIVE OF FEEJEE.

measures about ninety-seven miles from east to west and sixty-four from north to south, and its area is computed at 4112 square miles. Vanua-Levu, with an area of nearly 2500 miles, is the next largest, and then come Taviuni and Kandavu, the former of 217 square miles, and the latter of 124. None of the other islands have areas equalling one hundred square miles, and it would be tedious to name them all.

A ROYAL ATTENDANT.

"Altogether the Feejee group has an area estimated at 7400 square miles, or about 400 square miles less than that of the State of Massachusetts. Its population is estimated at—"

Fred was about to write 200,000, taking the figures from a book before him, when he was interrupted by Doctor Bronson.

"Wait a moment," said the Doctor, "and I'll tell you something on that subject.

"Twenty or twenty-five years ago," he continued, "the population was estimated at fully that figure, and some authorities put it as high as 250,000. Of course there has never been a careful census, and in the interior of the larger islands it is not easy to get even a close approximation of the number of inhabitants. Since the occupation of the islands by the whites the population has followed the general law of all Polynesia, and diminished with more or less steadiness.

"In 1874 it was estimated that it had been reduced to 180,000, and in the following year fully one-third of this number died from the scourge of measles."

"Measles!" exclaimed Frank and Fred, in astonishment. "I didn't know," Frank added, "that this disease was a deadly one."

"It is not usually so considered in civilized lands," the Doctor answered, "nor would it have been so here but for the ignorance of the people, and their persistence in doing exactly what they should not have done.

"In the latter part of 1874 Thakombau, King of Feejee, and his sons went to Sydney in an English man-of-war, to pay their respects to the Governor of New South Wales. At Sydney the two youngest boys took measles, but the disease showed itself in such a mild form that nothing was thought of it. On the return voyage in January the King had a slight attack, but it was considered of no consequence, and on his arrival at Levuka he went ashore at once.

"His relatives and subjects came to pay their respects, and according to custom smelt of his hands or his face, and thus took in the poison of the disease. A few days after his arrival there was a meeting of chiefs and other high dignitaries from all the tribes of the group, and the same ceremonies were gone through. In this way the disease was spread through the group, and when it developed it caused the death of nearly every chief who had attended the ceremonial.

ANCIENT FEEJEE TEMPLE.

"All through the Feejees people died by the thousand; in some instances whole villages were struck down, and there were not enough well people to care for the sick or bury the dead. Medical directions were published and sent abroad as soon as possible, but the superstitious people had been told by some of the beach-combers and other scoundrels infesting the islands that the disease had been imported in order to kill them off and get their lands, and that the medicines of the white men were intended to spread rather than check it. The medical directions were ignored; some tribes who had become Christian renounced the new religion and drove out their teachers. In one instance where a teacher died of measles his Christian disciples concluded that it was best to follow the old custom and bury his wife and children with him, in order to propitiate the demon of the scourge."

"Why was the disease so fatal here when it is not so in our own country?" one of the youths inquired.

"You are aware, I presume," the Doctor answered, "that care should be exercised in measles against taking cold, and thus driving the disease to the lungs. These people are continually bathing, and it was the most natural thing in the world for them to rush to the cooling streams as soon as the fever came on them. In this way thousands doomed themselves to death, and besides, there came an unusual rainfall that converted great areas of country into swamps, and rendered it impossible for the people to keep dry even if they had tried to do so.

"As an illustration of the effect of bathing, I may mention the case of the native police at Levuka. A hundred and fifty men were seized with measles, and the officer in charge, an Englishman, immediately established a hospital and ordered those who were least affected to care for the rest. They were forbidden to bathe or allow any one else to do so; all the patients recovered except ten, and of these every man was found to have disobeyed orders and indulged in a bath in the tempting sea which was close by.

"An English resident says that whole villages were swept away by the scourge, the dead were buried in their own houses, and to this day many of the platforms on which the Feejeean houses are built are simply family tombs. The coast towns suffered more than those of the interior, probably in consequence of their being in more swampy ground, and thus more affected by the dampness. The measles were afterwards carried to other groups, where the effect was severe, but not so fatal in proportion to the population as in the Feejees."

With this explanation Frank put down the number of native inhabitants of the Feejees at 120,000; afterwards he obtained at Suva the figures of the census of 1884, which were as follows: European residents, 3513; native Feejeeans, 115,635; Polynesian laborers, 5634; Asiatics, about 5000; and Rotumah men, about 2600.

"What is a Rotumah man?" said Fred, when the above figures were obtained and read aloud by Frank.

"Rotumah," said the Doctor, "is a small island lying in mid-ocean about four hundred miles north of Feejee, and recently made a British possession. The natives are a kindly race; the women are prettier than most other Polynesians, and the men strong and of good size. They make excellent sailors, and you find them in ships all over the South Pacific, and even in other parts of the world. A gentleman who visited Rotumah told me it was no uncommon thing to find natives who had been in New York, London, Liverpool, or Hamburg, and they could discuss the relative merits of sailing and steam vessels with an intelligence not always found among white sailors.

A POLYNESIAN IDOL.

"Though living in an island where nature is kindly and the wants of man are few, the Rotumah men are not unwilling to work; they are consequently sought as laborers in the Samoan, Tahitian, and other groups, and especially in Feejee. So many men have been taken from the island that the supply has been practically exhausted, and the planters are compelled to look elsewhere. Some of the laborers were kidnapped in the manner described in our discussion of the labor-trade, but the most of those who emigrated were fairly and honestly obtained."

The outlying islets of the Feejee group were first sighted by our friends on the yacht, and in due time the peaks of the larger islands came into view. The Feejeean Archipelago is situated between the fif-

A COAST SCENE IN KANDAVU.

teenth and twenty-second parallels of south latitude, and the meridians of 177° west and 175° east longitude, and scattered over an area of ocean some two hundred miles from north to south, and three hundred from east to west. Its exact extent is not known, as there has been no complete survey of the islands; one is now in progress under the direction of the colonial government, but it will take some time for its completion. Surveying in Feejee is slow and difficult work, owing to the dense tropical vegetation that is found everywhere.

The first island of importance which was sighted by our friends was Kandavu, the fourth largest of the group and containing something like 10,000 inhabitants. As they expected to see it later, they did not stop there, and the youths contented themselves by studying its well-wooded slopes and fertile valleys, and the towering head of Mount Washington 3000 feet high on its western side. The captain told them that Kandavu was the stopping-place of the mail-steamers on their way between San Francisco and Australia, as it was more convenient and less dangerous for them than either Suva or Levuka. He added that it abounded in fine timber, and was a favorite resort for whalers in search of supplies and water.

Steam was made as soon as Kandavu was sighted, and in a few hours the *Pera* was at anchor in the harbor of Suva, the capital of the British colony of Feejee. It was selected in 1880 by a commission appointed to secure a site for a future capital, the former one, Levuka, having been found disadvantageous in some respects. Levuka is more centrally situated in the archipelago than Suva, but its harbor is not so easy of access, and a ship approaching or leaving it has more dangerous navigation. Levuka is on the small island of Ovolau, while Suva is on the south side of Viti Levu, which is, as before stated, the largest and most populous of the group.

A PLANTER'S RESIDENCE.

On shore our friends found a prosperous-looking place, when its age was taken into consideration, and Frank said it reminded him of a town in California or Colorado. There were half a dozen hotels, several churches, which represented the Catholic, Episcopalian, Presbyterian, and Methodist faiths, a great number of shops and stores, and many well-built warehouses, cottages, and other dwellings. They went to the principal hotel before proceeding to call upon their consuls or make any acquaintances, and the proprietor immediately offered to show them the sights of Suva.

A NEW ARRIVAL.

He pointed out the Governor's residence, the jail, hospital, custom-house, and lunatic asylum, together with other public edifices. Doctor Bronson suggested that there was every indication of a fixed community when so young a place could boast of a jail and a lunatic asylum, not to speak of the custom-house and the hospital.

"We needed a jail here before anything else," was the reply to his remark. "All the riffraff of the South Seas seemed to be collected in Feejee before the annexation, and there was nothing but the powerful arm of law, with jails and other paraphernalia, that could preserve order."

"They had been gathering here for a long time, I presume," said the Doctor, "and were most numerous just before the annexation."

"There had been a fair sprinkling of beach-combers and idlers," was the reply, "ever since the islands were first occupied by white men. After them came men who wished to engage in planting cotton, sugar, and other things for which the islands were supposed to be favorable; there were some adventurers among them; but, on the whole, they were a good class of citizens, as they were nearly all of birth and education, and most of them brought some capital with which to go into business.

"But in the latter part of the sixties we were inundated with a different lot of adventurers. A few came with the design of planting cotton, or engaging in some other honest employment, but the great majority were penniless fellows, with no fondness for decent occupations. Many of them had left the Australian colonies to avoid arrest for swindling or other crimes, and there was a fair share of men for whom the prisons yawned for offences of the most serious character. Down to that time San Francisco had been the haven to which these fellows emigrated, but it was easier to go to Feejee than to America, and therefore Feejee got the benefit."

"I think I heard something about it at the time," the Doctor remarked.

"Quite likely," responded his informant. "About 1870–71 Feejee was a word of contempt in Australia. 'Gone to Feejee' had the same meaning in Sydney and Melbourne that 'Gone to Texas' had in the United States forty or fifty years ago; but now, under colonial rule, it is an orderly land, and life and property are as safe as in Australia or California."

In the conversation that followed Frank and Fred learned that the late King Thakombau, who died in 1883, offered the sovereignty of the islands to the Queen of England under certain conditions, but the offer was declined. Another offer was made in March, 1874, which was also declined; but in October of the same year a deed of cession gave the sovereignty of the islands to Great Britain. A charter was shortly after issued, making Feejee a colony of Great Britain, and the first governor, Sir Arthur Gordon, arrived in June, 1875, and assumed authority.

GOING TO FEEJEE.

The colony has been, on the whole, a prosperous one, though there have been periods of depression. Year by year the capabilities of the islands are becoming better known, and it would seem that there is every known kind of productive soil in Feejee. Its swamps will produce rice in abundance, and the other lands are adapted to sugar, cotton, coffee, sweet-potatoes, yams, and all other tropical productions, while in many localities pease, beans, cabbages, apples, and other fruits and vegetables of the temperate zones are successfully grown.

Frank asked about the cocoanut and bread-fruit trees, and was told that the former was indigenous, and the latter had been grown there so long that it was practically so. The cocoanut-tree was an important article of cultivation, and thousands of acres have been planted with it.

SCENE ON A COTTON PLANTATION.

For a long time the chief article of export was copra, but latterly it has been exceeded by sugar. In 1875 the export of copra was 3871 tons; in 1884 it was 6682 tons, or nearly double the amount of nine years before. As the young trees come into bearing the exportation of copra will be greatly increased.

"The growth of the sugar-trade," said his informant, "has been very rapid, as you will see by the figures. In 1875 the export of sugar was 96 tons, and in 1876 it was 265 tons; in 1884 it was nearly 9000 tons; and in 1885, 10,586 tons. Molasses shows about the same increase as its first-cousin, sugar, though the product of later years is not as valuable as some that preceded it, owing to the diminished price of the article.

"Cotton has not been a profitable crop on the whole," he continued, "and the production has fallen off from 386 tons in 1879 to 150 tons in 1884, and only 45 tons in 1885. Many cotton-bushes have been destroyed to make place for the cultivation of sugar; coffee has been little, if any, more profitable than cotton, and many of the coffee plantations are now devoted to bananas, which are an important article of export. In 1875 less than $500 worth of fruit was sent from the islands, while the exports for the last three years have exceeded $100,000 worth annually.

"The other exports are beche-de-mer, tobacco, cocoa-fibre, tortoise-shell, wool, hides, and pearl-shell, but none of them amount to a great deal. The industries of the colony are somewhat hampered by restrictions upon the importation of foreign labor; in consequence of former abuses the Government is very severe, and some of us think needlessly so."

Frank asked in what particular he thought the authorities ought to be more lenient.

"The laborers are engaged for three years," was the reply, "and under the old regulations a laborer could be re-engaged for another period of three years if he was willing to do so. At present the employers are compelled to return him to his home, even though he is desirous of remaining here for another term. This is the rule as to imported labor; if a planter hires Feejeeans to work for him he is obliged to make his engagements from month to month. The proba-

SUGAR-CANE MILL.

bility is that coolie labor from India will in time drive out Polynesian labor."

"Why so?" Fred asked.

"Because of the lower relative price of it. Polynesians must be fed, clothed, and cared for by the employer, and consequently it is not easy to calculate exactly the cost of this kind of labor. The coolies feed and care for themselves, and besides they are better and more steady laborers. A Polynesian laborer costs about eighty dollars a year, a Feejeean one eighty-five dollars, and a coolie from India or China ninety-five to one hundred dollars. But, all things considered, the Asiatic is preferable to the Polynesian."

FEEJEEAN HEAD-DRESS.

There was further conversation relative to the labor-trade, which has already been discussed in this book, and so we will not repeat it. Our friends then took a stroll along the Victoria Parade, a wide and handsome avenue nearly a mile in length. Frank and Fred were interested in everything they saw, and particularly with the passing kaleidoscope of Englishmen, Germans, Americans, and other white nationalities, together with Chinese, Indian coolies, Feejeeans, Rotumah men, and natives of half the islands of the Pacific. Of course the Feejeeans were more numerous than any other race or kind of people that passed before their eyes.

"The Feejeeans," said Frank, in his account of their visit to Suva, "are considerably darker than the Samoans or Tahitians; Doctor Bronson says they belong to the race of Papuans rather than to the Malays, though possessing characteristics of both. They are superior to the Papuans in physique and in their degree of civilization, but they have the frizzly hair and beard and the dark skin which indicates their Papuan origin. Then, too, they use the bow and arrow for weapons, and make pottery, neither of which is characteristic of the true Polynesian.

"What struck us as odd about them was their immense heads of hair, some of them being fully three feet in diameter. Hair-dressing seems to be one of the fine arts in Feejee, and the barber is a most important personage, though less so to-day than formerly. And how do you suppose they managed to get such enormous mops on their heads?

"Well, the naturally frizzly hair is 'improved' by the barber. Each particular hair is seized and pulled with tweezers until it stands out straight, helped of course by the other hairs which have been served the same way. The hair-dressing of a Feejeean dandy takes the greater part of the time, and when he wishes to appear in specially fine style he must be for a whole day at least in the hands of his barber. When the hair has been stretched out to the proper degree, it is wrapped with fine tappa or imported muslin, and in this condition presents a very curious appearance.

"The office of barber to the King was such a sacred one that the royal barbers were tabu, or forbidden to do anything else. They could not even feed, dress, or undress themselves, or do anything whatever with the hands which were to be used solely on the royal coiffure. And yet there were plenty of men who coveted this honorable occupation in spite of its manifest inconveniences.

"They are a polite people—at least we are told so, and certainly have seen nothing to lead us to think otherwise. The hotel-keeper says the Feejeean boys make excellent table servants, and the native policemen along the streets seem fully equal to any we have ever seen outside of a European or American city. Like all Polynesians, the Feejeeans are very ceremonious, and great sticklers for etiquette. The chiefs and nobles are surrounded with ceremony, and one needs to be as careful in approaching them as in approaching the Queen of England or the Emperor of Russia.

AN ACCOMPLISHED LIAR.

"Here in Suva most of the people have adopted European dress, or a modification of the native one, but back in the mountains they adhere to their primitive garments. These are strips of cloth around the waist, and owing to this enormous array of hair I have just told about they sleep on a pillow consisting of a stick like a thick lath, with legs four or five inches long. It is like taking a section of a two-inch plank a foot long and four inches wide, and resting one's neck on the edge. A Feejeean pillow is by no means an inconvenient weapon in a fight, and 'very handy to have in the house.'

"It is said the Feejeeans look upon lying as an accomplishment, and I have been told that one of the worst stumbling-blocks in the way

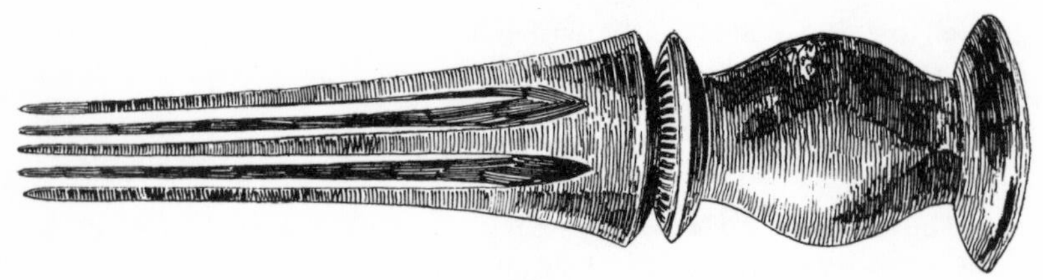

FORK OF A CANNIBAL KING.

to their conversion to Christianity was to have them understand that it was wrong to tell deliberate falsehoods. They have improved a great deal under missionary teachings, and there is still plenty of opportunity for more improvement in the same direction. When angry, they are sullen rather than noisy; when a chief is offended, he puts a stick in the ground as a mark by which he remembers the cause of his anger. After a while he may pull up the stick as a sign that his anger is relenting, and he is ready to be propitiated with gifts.

"We look upon this people with a great deal of curiosity, as we have all our lives associated them with terrible stories of the most horrible forms of cannibalism. Happily this is a thing of the past, but it is by no means so very long ago. Even now the people among the mountains are said to indulge in it occasionally; but if they do, the extent of the practice is very small by comparison with fifty years ago.

"How it was adopted no one knows; the Feejeeans have a tradition that it began in an effort to prevent the incursions of people from other islands, and as a result of battle, which is quite likely to have been the case. In course of time it was not confined to enemies and foreigners, but extended to those who were offered as sacrifices in the temples. Sacrifices increased in number year by year until, as in Tahiti, a considerable part of the population was liable at any time to be offered up at the bidding of the priests or chiefs.

"In every village there were particular ovens and pots devoted to cooking the flesh of men, and the cooks were as skilled in the cannibal art as are the Parisian *chefs* in theirs. It was not uncommon to see twenty or thirty human bodies cooked at a time for a great feast, and the chiefs used to sacrifice their wives or their friends to gratify their tastes for this horrible article of food. When a chief demanded *bakola* (long pig), the customary name for human flesh, his attendants used to rush out and kill the first person they met in order to gratify his wish!

"The bakola was not eaten with the fingers like other kinds of food, but with wooden forks with long prongs, and these forks were tabu for any other purpose. Each fork had a special name, like an individual; the fork of one of the cannibal kings was named *undroundo* ('a dwarf carrying a burden'), and was presented in 1849 to one of the missionaries by Ra Vatu, the son of the King referred to. Ra Vatu talked freely about his father's love for human flesh, and showed to the missionary the line of stones which registered the number of bodies he had eaten. One of the native teachers who accompanied the missionary counted the stones, and found they numbered eight hundred and thirty-two! Thakombau, the last King, was a cannibal until the latter part of his life, and his father, Tanoa, continued a cannibal till the day of his death.

TANOA, FORMER KING OF FEEJEE.

"Here is a story that I find in Doctor Seemann's report of his visit to Feejee:

"'A peculiar kind of taro was pointed out as having been eaten with a whole tribe of people. The story sounds strange, but as a number of natives were present when it was told, several of whom corroborated the various statements or corrected the proper names that occurred, its truth appears unimpeachable.

"'In Viti Levu, about three miles north-north-east from Namosi, there dwelt a tribe known as the Kai-na-loca, who, in days of yore, gave great offence to the ruling chief of the Namosi district, and as a punishment for their misdeeds the whole tribe was condemned to die. Every year the inmates of one house were baked and eaten, fire was set to the empty dwelling, and its foundation planted with taro. In the following year, as soon as this taro was ripe, it became the signal for the destruction of the next house and its inhabitants and the planting of a fresh field of taro. Thus house after house and family after family disappeared, until the father of the present chief pardoned the few that remained. In 1860 only one old woman was the sole survivor of the Na-loca people. Picture the feelings of these unfortunate wretches as they watched the growth of the ominous taro! There was no escape, as they would only hasten their doom by fleeing into territories where they were strangers.'

"When the Wesleyan missionaries came here in 1835 they found cannibalism in full sway, and it now seems a wonder that they were not immediately killed and eaten. They partially owed their exemption to the fact that the flesh of white men is considered insipid, or tainted with tobacco, and therefore they were not regarded as desirable prey. Their progress in converting the natives was at first very slow, but they were patient and determined, and in course of time they were rewarded for their efforts. At present the great majority of the people are professing Christians, cannibalism has ceased since 1878, polygamy is rare, and idol worship is no more. After a time the Roman Catholics established a mission, and since the annexation the Church of England has sent its representatives to Feejee.

A CANNIBAL DANCE.

"In 1885 the Wesleyans reported that they had 906 churches and 347 other preaching-places in the islands, 25,932 church-members, and 104,806 attendants upon public worship. They had 1749 day schools, and 40,313 scholars in these schools, and they had nearly 42,000 children attending Sabbath-school. The Roman Catholics have about 8000 church-members, and the Church of England has a much smaller number, its adherents being principally Englishmen and other foreigners.

"So much for what the missionaries have accomplished in this group of Pacific islands in the short space of fifty years. At present the Wesleyans say the expenses of maintaining their missions in Feejee is about $25,000 a year; and of this amount $15,000 is contributed here, the balance coming from abroad. Reading, writing, and arith-

SKULL FOUND AT THE BANQUET GROUND.

metic are taught in the common schools; there are higher schools in each missionary circuit, where persons are trained for the ministry, and others can be educated. There is a central college at Navuloa, where a superior education, both native and English, is given to those who are preparing for ordination, and also to others who may desire it. The Government has established industrial schools, where the sons of chiefs are taught reading and writing as in the common schools, and also instructed in house-carpentering, boat-building, and other trades.

"I think I hear you asking how the English manage to govern the islands when they are so few and the natives so numerous. Well, Feejee is a crown colony, and its affairs are administered by a governor and executive council; the laws are prepared by a legislative council of

VIEW IN A VALLEY OF THE INTERIOR OF THE ISLAND.

thirteen members, seven of whom are official and six are nominated by the Governor. In legal matters the imperial laws are followed, except where there has been local legislation. All jury cases are decided by the judge, with two assessors; the system of trial by jury was abolished by the first governor, Sir Arthur Gordon, at the suggestion of Sir John Gorrie, who was then chief-justice. The natives have a system of local self-government which is recognized by the colonial authorities; there are twelve salaried superior native chiefs exercising executive functions under the Government, and also twenty-six native magistrates."

Our friends found enough in and around Suva to interest them for several days. They visited some of the cotton, sugar, and coffee plantations in the vicinity, examined some of the sites of the ancient temples of the Feejeeans which were the scenes, of horrible slaughters in the days of cannibalism and idolatry, went through some of the native villages, where they were kindly received by the chiefs, and did other things which were very natural for visitors to do. There was nothing especially new about the plantations, with the possible exception of the groups of laborers from the islands of Polynesia and Melanesia, some of whom were of races strange to the eyes of our friends. There were men from Tanna, from the Solomon Islands, from New Guinea, and also representatives of other groups of islands, until the whole made quite a formidable list.

The owner of the largest plantation that they visited told Frank and Fred that the men from the different islands would not fraternize with one another any more than will Germans, Irish, and negroes in America or England. They do not trust one another, and their huts are in different groups, in widely separated parts of the plantation. Many of them are cannibals, particularly the men from the Solomon and New Hebrides islands, and occasionally get into open warfare for the purpose of capturing somebody whom they can eat. This very distrust of one another is to the advantage of the planter, who could not easily manage them if they were united and harmonious.

Fred thought the Solomon Islanders were the most repulsive looking of the lot, and their employer said they were treacherous and revengeful in addition to being murderous. In times past, before the establishment of the Colonial Government, they used to make raids on the villages and kill any unfortunate Feejeean they met, whom they carried away and devoured. Of late years they have been restrained from this practice, but not without some severe lessons.

"The Tanna men are not much unlike them," their informant continued, "but they are less treacherous and sullen, and are better workers. They eat the flesh of men when they can get it, but they are also fond of dogs, cats, lizards, rats, and flies."

As he spoke he pointed to a pen containing several puppies which the Tanna men were fattening, and would make the basis of a grand feast on their next holiday.

From Suva the party went by a local steamer to Levuka, Colonel

Bush being unwilling to risk the *Pera* among the rocks and reefs, which render navigation far from safe in these waters. They found the harbor of Levuka smaller than that of Suva, but in other respects equal to it, as the anchorage was good, and the place well sheltered from gales. The barrier reef which forms the harbor is about a mile from shore, and has two passages by which vessels may enter or leave port.

AVENUE OF PALMS.

Of course the removal of the capital to Suva was a severe blow to Levuka, but the place has a good commerce of its own, and being more centrally situated in regard to all the islands of the group, it is in no danger of decay. It contains three or four hotels and several boarding-houses, and its mercantile establishments are generally of a substantial character. There are Wesleyan, Catholic, and Episcopalian churches in Levuka, several branch buildings of the Government offices, and a well-kept hospital for the use of such European strangers as may need medical attention.

"The founders of Levuka were not altogether happy in one respect," said one of the residents, who was pointing out its features to our friends. "The hills around it are so steep that it was not practicable to extend the town over them; we could build our dwellings there, but it was out of the question to establish stores and shops where people

A PART OF LEVUKA.

must climb to reach them, so we extended along the base of the hills, and in some cases out into the sea, where we made land by filling in.

"You see," he continued, "that Levuka consists practically of a single thoroughfare which we call Beach Street, for the very practical

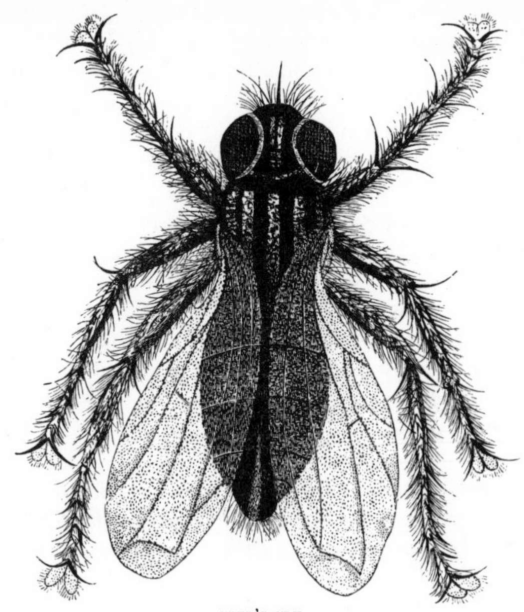
FRED'S FLY.

reason that it follows the course of the beach. Outside the town it is prolonged into a road that nearly surrounds the island of Ovolau, and will completely encircle it in time. Two or three years ago we started to build a street railway; we made surveys and subscribed for the stock, but the Government opposed the project, and it was given up."

Our friends found accommodations at one of the hotels, and were fairly comfortable, or would have been if they could have escaped the flies and mosquitoes. These insects were numerous enough to form a veritable plague, and seemed to take special delight in annoying strangers. A planter who was stopping at the hotel declared that the flies had sentinels stationed to give notice of the arrival of a stranger so that all could pounce on him at once, and that whenever the flies grew weary of their work the mosquitoes came forward to relieve them. Frank made a sketch of a Feejee mosquito, while Fred took the likeness of a native fly. These works of art were laid carefully away where the subjects thereof could not reach them with intents of destruction or mutilation.

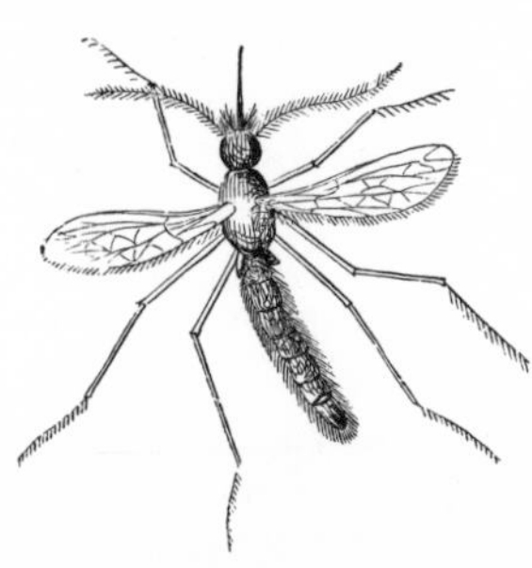
FRANK'S MOSQUITO.

Dinner was taken at the hotel-table, and proved, on the whole, a pleasant affair. The youths made several acquaintances among the planters, merchants, and others who were stopping there; Frank and Fred added materially to their stock of information relative to the agricultural and other advantages of Feejee, and also to the mode of life among the residents. The dinner consisted of pork, salt and fresh beef, chicken, yams, taro, and other vegetables, together with English and American preserves, and potted things that are found wherever Englishmen are settled in the eastern or southern hemisphere. "You may not think much of it when compared with a dinner in New York or London," said one of the planters, "but if you go and live six months or a year on a plantation you'll think a dinner here is the very height of luxury. Salt beef and occasional chickens and pigs are our only meats on the plantations, backed up by yams and taro in one unvarying round. Where we can afford it we have potted and canned things, but they are expensive, and very often cannot be had at any price. It has repeatedly happened that men who had been living on the rough fare of the plantations came to Levuka after an absence of months, and overfed themselves at the hotel-table to such an extent as to bring on a fatal illness."

After dinner they sat on the veranda of the hotel and enjoyed the land-breeze which sets in a little after sunset, and is considerably cooler than the day breeze from the sea. It is also free from flies and mosquitoes, which at this time retire to the sleeping-rooms of the hotel to make ready for the arrival of the lodgers. On the veranda the conversation was continued, and many features of Feejeean life were touched upon.

"It's a pity you are not to be here at *balola* time," said one of the residents to Fred, when the latter had explained that their visit was to be a very brief one.

Fred thought the gentleman said *bakola*, and immediately his thoughts ran on the cannibalism of the Feejeeans in times past. He remarked that he supposed those days were gone forever, but his informant answered, to the great astonishment of the youth, that they had the festival every year, and it was something not to be missed.

Then the gentleman went on to explain, and Fred soon ascertained the difference between *bakola* and *balola*.

"The balola, or balolo," said he, "is a sea-worm whose scientific name is *palolo viridis*. It looks like a string of vermicelli, being little larger than a thread, and varying from an inch or two to a yard in length. It lives somewhere in the sea, no one knows where; on two days of the year it comes to the surface, and all the rest of the three hundred and sixty-five it keeps carefully out of sight. The natives know exactly when it will come; it first appears in October, the date being fixed by the position of certain stars, and its second appearance is at the full moon, between the twentieth and twenty-fifth of November.

"The worms are far more numerous in the November than in the October appearance, and hence the October one is called the 'Little Balola,' while the November coming is the 'Great Balola.' At the great festival the sea is covered in some places to the depth of several inches with these worms, which are red, green, and brown in color, and form a writhing and wriggling mass not altogether pleasant to look at. They come a little past midnight, and when the sun rises they sink down out of sight and remain there until the next year."

"How curious!" exclaimed the youth, in astonishment.

ONE VARIETY OF SEA-WORM.

"No one has been able to explain the phenomenon," was the reply, "nor tell how and where the worm passes the rest of his time. Why he appears on these occasions and no other, or why he appears at all, nobody has yet found out, and you may be sure the worms won't give up the secret.

"The natives go out in their boats in great numbers; every native boat that can float is occupied, and the Europeans go along at the same time to see the fun. As long as the worms remain every native is busy with baskets and ladles trying to fill his boat with them; there is a great deal of excitement and laughter, as the people steal from one another and have as much fun as they can out of the festival. Then there are shoals and shoals of fish of all sizes and kinds that are feeding on the worms, and seem to understand that they must make the most of their opportunity.

GOING FOR BALOLA.

"As soon as daylight comes, and the worms sink out of sight, the people return to the shore, wrap the worms in taro-leaves, and cook them in ovens after their manner of roasting. The supply is so great that there is enough for everybody for several days, and baskets of balola are sent to friends in the interior, just as you send fruit and game in America. The stuff is not agreeable to European taste, but isn't so bad after all when you can conquer your prejudice against eating worms."

"To show the force of the religious convictions of the Feejeeans," said another resident, "let me say that when the festival comes on Sunday not a single canoe of the natives goes out except those of the Roman Catholic Church members. The Methodists obey the religious requirements so closely that not a canoe will go on the water on Sunday except to carry a preacher to church. You cannot hire one of these people to climb a cocoanut-tree on Sunday, or do any other work that is not strictly one of necessity."

"What an immense change," said another, "from the days when cannibalism prevailed throughout the islands, and when all public ceremonials were attended with human sacrifices. On the death of a chief his wives and servants were buried alive with him, in order that he could have their company in the spirit world. When a chief's house was built a slave stood in each post-hole to support the post, and was buried there alive. War-canoes were launched or drawn ashore over the bodies of living prisoners, who served as rollers and were crushed to death by the weight. Life was held of no consequence, and parents who were ill or felt the weakness of age coming used to ask their children to bury them. A missionary was once invited by a young man to attend the funeral of the latter's mother; she walked cheerfully to the grave, and sat down in it to have the earth heaped about her by her children, and was much surprised when the missionary interfered to prevent the proceeding.

ANCIENT FEEJEEAN WAR-DANCE.

"And I have heard," he continued, "of a young man who was ill and feared he would get thin and be laughed at by the girls of his acquaintance. He asked his father to bury him, and the latter consented. When the youth had taken his place in the grave he asked to be strangled. The father scolded him, and told him to sit still and be buried just like other folks, and make no further trouble. Thereupon the youth became quiet, and the burial was completed."

"Can this really be true?" queried the youth.

"The story is found on page 475 of Erskine's 'Journal of a Cruise among the Islands of the Western Pacific,'" said his informant, "and I have no doubt whatever of its truth. The evidence as to the former customs of the Feejeeans is so direct and positive that it cannot be doubted."

Fred lay awake for some time that night, his thoughts busy with the changes which had been wrought in the islands of the great ocean through the labors of the missionaries. Afterwards he watched the effect of the moonlight on the waters, and while watching fell asleep.

MOONLIGHT ON THE WATERS.

CHAPTER VIII.

ATTENDING A NATIVE CHURCH.—A FEEJEEAN PREACHER.—DINNER WITH A FEEJEEAN FAMILY.—THE SEASONS IN FEEJEE.—A TROPICAL SHOWER.—A HURRICANE.—A PLANTER'S ADVENTURES.—SCENES OF DEVASTATION.—THE CLIMATE OF THE FEEJEE ISLANDS.—WRECKED ON A REEF.—ESCAPING FROM THE JAWS OF CANNIBALS.—A WALKING ART GALLERY.—A TATTOOED WHITE MAN.—RETURNING TO SUVA.—THE FRIENDLY, OR TONGA, ISLANDS.—TONGATABOO.—THE KING OF THE TONGAS.—HOW HE LIVES.—A REMARKABLE CAVERN AND A LOVE STORY ABOUT IT.—FROM FEEJEE TO NEW ZEALAND.—HAURAKI GULF.—AUCKLAND.—A FINE SEAPORT AND ITS COMMERCE.—HOW NEW ZEALAND WAS COLONIZED.—THE MAORIS.—CURIOUS FACTS ABOUT A CURIOUS PEOPLE.—MISSIONARIES IN NEW ZEALAND.—HOW THE MAORIS MAKE WAR.

THE second day of the stay of our friends at Levuka was Sunday, and the party attended the Episcopal church in the forenoon, where service was conducted by a clergyman who had recently arrived from London. In the afternoon they strolled to the native village outside the town, where they found some fifty or sixty Feejeeans squatted on the mat-covered floor of the neat and well-swept church listening to a preacher of their own race. They were amused to see a tall man armed with a long stick with which he occasionally touched the heads of those who were inattentive, and sometimes his touch was far from light. Frank thought the idea would not be a bad one for churches nearer home, where worshippers have been known to go to sleep during the sermon.

The preacher was a tall, fine-looking man of at least fifty years, and he spoke with an eloquence that indicated his earnestness and fervor. Of course his language was unknown to our friends, but they all agreed that the Feejeean tongue is capable of much expression. It contains many guttural sounds that do not always strike the American or English ear agreeably, and the orator seemed to speak with more rapidity than is compatible with a clear understanding on the part of his hearers. When the sermon was ended the preacher offered a prayer, and then a hymn was sung by the whole congregation. The air was a familiar Methodist one, but the words were Feejeean. Whether the meaning of the original hymn was preserved with the air no one of the listeners was able to say, and there was no interpreter present to tell them.

As soon as service was over the strangers were surrounded by a group of natives, and there was an attempt at conversation; but as our

MISSION CHURCH IN THE FEEJEE ISLANDS.

friends were totally unlearned in Feejeean, and the vocabulary of the natives was principally confined to the word "shillin'," there was not much interchange of thought. Nearly every Feejeean understands "shillin'" well enough to pronounce it. He has a clear idea that it means money, and it is in this sense that it is used. Ask a native what he will sell his house for, and he will answer "shillin';" ask him the price of a cocoanut, and the reply is the same. In the former case he would of course decline the offer if actually made, and in the latter he would bring you twenty or fifty cocoanuts for the figure named.

In strolling around as the congregation dispersed Frank and Fred became separated from the rest of the party, but without any misgivings as to their safety or loss of way, as they were accompanied by several natives, one of whom invited the youths to his house. This was an invitation not to be ignored; it was accepted at once, and the man led the way along a path to where he lived. It was a hut of dried reeds lashed to a framework of poles, and stood with a dozen similar huts in the shade of a grove of cocoa-trees. The thatched roof was high and arched, while the sides were very low, and had no windows. There were two doors on opposite sides, but the door-way was so low that it was necessary to stoop almost double in order to enter. In front of the hut was a lot of bones and all manner of refuse, and a couple of pigs were lying across the door-way They showed no inclination to move as the master of the house approached; but on catching sight, and possibly smell, of the strangers, they were up and off very quickly.

GOING TO CHURCH.—RIVER SCENE.

Inside the hut the floor was covered with plaited rushes, and there was a low partition of reeds dividing it into two nearly equal spaces; one of these was used as kitchen and sitting-room and the other for sleeping; but there was no furniture in either place beyond three or four of the wooden pillows already described. In one corner of the

FEEJEEAN HEAD.

kitchen was a rough hearth, with some clay pots in which fish and yams were cooked.

Partly by signs and partly by the words "want eat," the host invited the youths to stay to dinner. They accepted, more to see how and upon what the natives live rather than on account of having an appetite. Fire was lighted on the hearth, or rather it was stirred up from some slumbering coals, fish and yams were put on to boil, and in a little while the meal was ready. Frank and Fred made friends with the children, to whom they showed their watches, and made a few presents of silver coin as an indirect compensation for their dinner, and when the meal was ready they proceeded to enjoy it. One of the children had been sent for some banana-leaves, which served as plates; on these leaves the fish and yams were dished up, and a piece of rock-salt was brought out, together with a shell, with which each guest could scrape off as much salt as he liked, and whenever he wanted it. The youths made a practical demonstration of the truth of the adage that fingers were made before forks, though not without some inconvenience. To end the repast they had some ripe bananas, and of course the drink that accompanied the meal was the juice of freshly picked cocoanuts.

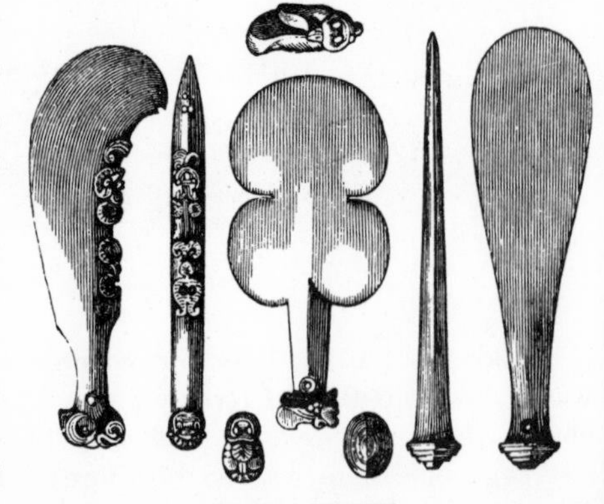

FEEJEEAN WEAPONS.

As soon as Frank and Fred rose from the mats the youngsters of the family attacked what they had left, and in a very few minutes nothing remained save the lump of salt and the empty banana-leaf plates. Then there was handshaking all around, and the visitors took their leave. The host accompanied them to the road leading back to town, and there left them, but not until he had pocketed a shilling which Frank tendered him.

Clouds were forming in the sky, and the youths thought it would be prudent to return to the hotel. They did so, and found the rest of the party on the veranda waiting for the promised shower. In a few minutes the rain came down thick and fast, and the wisdom of returning was no longer in doubt. The shower was soon over, however, and then the sun came out as brightly as ever, though there was no apparent change in the temperature.

"You are in the best season of the year," said one of their new acquaintances; "it's fortunate for you that it's not hurricane time now."

"We have here," he continued, "a dry season and a wet one. The former is cool, and lasts from May to October; the latter is hot, and lasts from October to May. During all the dry season, and for a month at each end of the wet one, the climate is delightful, the temperature varying from 70° to 76° or 78°, and the heat of the sun being tempered by breezes from the sea. The mean temperature is about 80°, the extreme ranges thus far recorded being 60° and 122°. From Christmas to March is called the 'hurricane season;' the air is moist and sticky, the temperature averaging 84°, with a humidity so great that one seems to be constantly in a Russian steam-bath. This is the unhealthy season, and fevers and other diseases due to the heat and moisture are common."

TELLING THE STORY.

Frank asked if hurricanes were frequent during the season.

"Not at all," was the reply, "but when they do come they are in dead earnest. From 1879 to 1886 we didn't have a really severe hurricane; but this is, I believe, the longest interval known to any of the European residents. One old settler told me there were several years when not a season passed without at least one hurricane."

"Are they very destructive?" Fred inquired.

"I can best answer that question," said the gentleman, "by describing the first hurricane I ever passed through in the Feejees.

FORMATION OF CLOUDS BEFORE A FEEJEEAN HURRICANE.

"I was on a plantation in which I had bought an interest, and during the whole of the month of March the weather was very calm and sultry. One day, towards the beginning of April, the wind turned to the north-west, which was quite unusual; squalls and showers followed, and then the breeze freshened into a gale. Heavy clouds covered the sky, thunder sounded loud and long, the barometer fell, and the clouds seemed to sweep just above the tops of the trees. Then the rain came in torrents, flooding all the level ground, and turning the brooks into rivers. Our party took shelter in the largest and strongest house in the neighborhood—one that had stood through several hurricanes, and was thought to be proof against them.

"For two days the wind blew, and every hour it increased. By the second night it was a fully developed hurricane whose velocity we had no means of measuring. The rain fell tremendously; the lightning was vivid, and almost continuous. The thunder followed the course of the storm; and altogether the noise was so great that we had to shout to one another to be understood. Our house shook like a rickety bird-cage, and many times it seemed to be half lifted from the ground; but it stood through the storm, and was the only one that did so.

AFTER THE STORM.

"On the following morning the wind had died down to a moderate gale, and we could venture out. The picture that presented itself cannot possibly be described with anything like vividness. Cocoanut and bread-fruit trees by the thousand had been thrown down or stripped of their leaves; banana-plants were in the same condition; the grass was levelled, and covered with mud and water, and not a house in the neighborhood remained standing. In the cotton-fields not only were the leaves and bolls stripped from the plants, but in many places the plants had been torn up by the roots and lay in heaps. In Levuka many houses were blown down; vessels were driven ashore, or broken to

COAST SCENE IN A CALM.

pieces at their moorings; and the whole windward coast of the islands was strewn with wrecks. Many foreign vessels that were known to be in Feejee waters, or near the islands, were never heard of again, and they doubtless went down on that terrible night. At Macuata, on Vauna Levu, the wind lifted a small vessel bodily from the beach and blew it into a native village two or three hundred yards away!"

LOST IN THE HURRICANE.

The story of the hurricane led to various anecdotes of the South Seas, and in this way the afternoon was passed until dinner-time. One man told how a ship on which he once sailed was driven before a hurricane and thrown upon a reef, where the waves dashed her to pieces. He was carried into the comparatively smooth lagoon inside the reef, and saved himself by swimming, all his companions being drowned. Fortunately for him, the islanders among whom he landed were not cannibals, or he would have been condemned at once to the oven. The cannibals of the South Pacific have always regarded people shipwrecked on their shores as special gifts or windfalls, just as the inhabitants of certain parts of the coast of the United States are said to have regarded the cargoes of wrecked ships less than a century ago. Of course he

MOTA, OR SUGAR-LOAF ISLAND.

taught the natives many useful things, and eventually married the daughter of the chief, and became a chief himself when his father-in-law died.

Another man, who claimed to have visited half the islands of the Pacific, endeavored to prove his assertion by asking our friends to step inside for a few moments, where he removed his clothing and exhibited samples of the tattooing of pretty nearly every group. "That clouded pattern on my left leg," said he, "was done in the Kingsmill group, while those squares and fancy stripes on the right leg were put on in

TWO-TREE ISLAND.

Samoa. My right arm and shoulder were done in the New Hebrides, while the left side was the work of the best artist of the Marquesas Islands. The fancy embroidery on my breast is of New Zealand, and that down my back was done in Tahiti."

Truly this man was a walking art-gallery of the Pacific Islanders, only his hands and face remaining unmarked by the tattoo. When the inspection was completed, and our friends had left the man to resume his dress, Frank suggested that he would be a fine prize for a medical museum, where his skin could be preserved after his death. Doctor Bronson agreed with him, but the suggestion was not offered to the subject of the conversation.

A YOUNG STUDENT.

The party returned to Suva by the steamer that brought them to Levuka, and there a change of plans occurred. Doctor Bronson, with Frank and Fred, proceeded to New Zealand by the regular mail-steamer, while Colonel Bush, with the *Pera*, continued his cruise among the islands of the Pacific. Our friends were sorry to part with their pleasant companions and the splendid hospitality of the yacht, but they did not feel justified in protracting their stay among the islands, since there is a general similarity of the groups to each other, though they may differ greatly in detail.

Frank and Fred regretted that they could not visit the Friendly, or Tonga, Islands, the first destination of the *Pera*, but they consoled themselves by reading what they could find on the subject. They learned that the Tonga group was discovered by Tasman and visited by Cook, who gave the isles the name of Friendly, on account of the apparently amiable disposition of the inhabitants. They have a population of about twenty-five thousand, and are farther advanced in civilization than their neighbors of Feejee or Samoa. The Wesleyan missionaries have converted them to Christianity; many of them can speak English, and have learned reading, writing, arithmetic, and geography, and on the whole stand high in the scale of education. The products of the Tonga Islands are similar to those of the Feejees, and the group is also subject to hurricanes, which are often very destructive.

The principal island is Tongataboo, which is low and level, of coral formation, and about twenty miles long by twelve broad. Here the King resides, and here, too, is the principal mission station, the King being an earnest Christian, and a regularly ordained preacher in the pulpit. He wears European clothes, has European furniture in his house, employs an Englishman as his private secretary, and altogether is quite a civilized gentleman. He has caused good roads to be made around and across the island, and in other ways has made his little kingdom know the advantages of the lands beyond the seas.

STONE MONUMENT, TONGATABOO.

Fred was particularly interested in reading about a curious monument of former days that is to be seen in Tonga, and of which the natives have no tradition. It reminded him of the monuments of Easter Island, and he made the following note on the subject:

"It stands on a grassy lawn in the interior of the island, and is so surrounded by tropical growths that it is concealed from view until the visitor is close upon it. It consists of three huge stones, two of them upright like pillars, and the third resting upon them. This upper stone is eighteen feet long, twelve feet wide, and fifteen feet above the ground; resting upon it is, or was, an immense bowl of hewn stone, which is supposed to have been connected with some of the religious ceremonies of the people who erected this monument. But how they put the three stones in their places is an unfathomable mystery."

A VOLCANO IN THE PACIFIC.

Fred also wanted to see a famous cavern in one of the Tonga Islands which can only be reached by diving into the sea, as the mouth is completely under water at all times. A young Tongan found it while diving after a turtle, and he afterwards utilized it as the place of concealment of the girl with whom he had fallen in love, and who was the daughter of a chief whose displeasure he had incurred. He persuaded her to flee with him and follow him into the water; these women swim like dolphins, and she dived after him and rose into the cave, which is beautifully lighted by the phosphorescent rays from the water, very much as is the famous Blue Grotto near Naples.

Here she remained for months, everybody wondering what had become of her, and also wondering why the young man absented himself so frequently, and always returned with wet hair. He carried her fruit and fish to eat and a supply of mats for carpeting the stone floor at one side of the cavern. One day his companions followed him, and dived where they had seen him disappear. Thus they found the cave; but what became of its inmates is not clearly recorded in the history of Tonga.

It takes an excellent swimmer to make the visit to the cave without danger of death from drowning. The entrance bristles with sharp points of rock, and when a native dives he turns on his back and uses his hands to keep himself clear of these dangerous obstructions. The captain of an English man-of-war tried to enter the cavern, but was so severely injured against the sharp rocks that he died in consequence.

We will leave the *Pera* to pursue her course among the islands of the Pacific, while we accompany Doctor Bronson and the youths on their voyage to New Zealand and Australia. The mail-steamer *Zealandia* carried them swiftly along, and on the morning of the fifth day they were in sight of the shores which were their destination. From Suva to Auckland, the former capital of New Zealand, is a distance of about one thousand miles, and there is regular communication both ways monthly between the two points. There is also steam communication between Sydney and Feejee, about sixteen hundred miles—sometimes direct from one port to the other, and sometimes by way of New Caledonia, which lies a short distance out of the direct track.

AN ISLAND CAVERN.

The *Zealandia* entered Hauraki Gulf, passing between the Great Barrier and Little Barrier islands, and holding her course almost due south; then, through the Rangitoto Channel, she turned, and the harbor of Auckland was before her.

"Shall we have to wait for the tide?" Frank asked, as they passed Great Barrier Island. "It often happens that we have to wait several hours for a tide when we're all impatience to get on shore."

"We don't have to wait for tides at Auckland," replied an officer of the *Zealandia*, to whom the query was addressed. "We can come in at dead low-water and steam to an anchorage, or to the dock if we're ready to go there. The least depth is thirty-six feet at dead low-water of the spring-tide, and at the highest tides we have fifty feet.

"There is hardly a finer seaport anywhere," he added, "than Waitamata, as the harbor of Auckland is frequently called by the New

Zealanders. It has, as I've told you, plenty of water at all times, and its entrances are superb. Rangitoto Channel is the one generally used; the other is Hieh Channel, and would be considered first-rate in many a place I know of. Rangitoto is about two miles wide; the section of the harbor between North Head and Kauri Point is about a mile across, and therefore is easily fortified in case we have to defend it against a hostile fleet."

ISLANDS ON THE COAST.

"I see," said Fred, who had been studying the map, "that the island is very narrow here."

"Yes," was the reply; "it is only six miles across; and if you examine carefully you'll see a good harbor on the other side. That is the harbor of Manakau, and there's a railway connecting it with Waitamata."

"It reminds me of Corinth, in Greece," said Fred, as he continued the contemplation of the map.

"No doubt it does," said the officer, in response. "Auckland is called the Corinth of the South Pacific; Corinth is now having a canal made through its isthmus, and we hope to have one for ours in due time."

The steamer made her way direct to the wharf, and as soon as she had made fast and the gang-plank was out, our friends stepped on shore in New Zealand. Under the guidance of a fellow-passenger, they entered a carriage and were driven up Queen Street, the principal thoroughfare, to the hotel they had selected for a resting-place during their sojourn in Auckland. They were favorably impressed with the activity that prevailed on the streets, and the general evidences of business prosperity. "A Missourian would call it 'a right smart place,'" said Frank, as they were alighting from the carriage at the end of their drive.

"Yes," responded Fred, "and even a New Yorker would treat its beautiful bay with respect after seeing it as we did."

"Where did the city get its name?" one of the youths asked Doctor Bronson.

"It was named after Lord Auckland, First Lord of the Admiralty, and afterwards Governor-general of India, by Captain Hobson, who

AUCKLAND IN 1840.

founded the city. Captain Hobson was sent here, in 1838, to organize a colony. He saw this was a good site for a city, and accordingly he established the capital here. It remained the capital until 1865, when a royal commission moved the seat of government to Wellington, the latter place being more centrally located. Of course the Aucklanders were not at all pleased at the change, but their city is so well established commercially that there is no danger of their being ruined by it."

From various sources Frank and Fred found that Auckland had a population of nearly forty thousand within the municipality, and seventy thousand in the city and suburbs. "It has," said Frank, in his journal, "handsome streets, a great number of well-constructed public buildings, such as post-office, custom-house, exchange, courts, Government offices, and the other paraphernalia of a well-established city, and it has also a fine museum, a public library, and a park and botanical garden. No city would be complete without a cemetery, and Auckland is not behind in this respect, as it has a very pretty one, and, as the French say, it is well peopled.

"We were much interested in the Queen Street wharf, where we landed; it extends nearly two thousand feet into the harbor, and affords facilities for thirty or forty vessels to discharge or receive cargoes at once. There are several other wharves, including a fine one, nearly completed, at the end of Hobson Street. I have heard often of 'Hobson's Choice,' and never knew exactly what it was. This city seems to have been Hobson's choice, since Captain Hobson founded it; all I can say is, that I shall have more respect for the old saw than I ever had before.

"You can get an idea of the commerce of the place when you know that about two hundred and fifty sailing-vessels are owned here of an aggregate burden of twenty thousand tons, and sixty-five steamers of seven thousand tons altogether. It has regular steam communication with Australian ports by the vessels of the Union Steamship Company, has a monthly line to Feejee, and is a port of call for the mail-steamers between Australia and California. The Northern Steamship Company of Auckland has a fleet of thirteen steamers, principally engaged in coast navigation, so that New Zealand is well served by its own boats.

"Of course the port has graving or dry docks for the accommodation of the ships that need them. There was one three hundred feet long, and forty-two feet wide, but it was found inadequate after a few years, and now they are completing another five hundred feet long and ninety feet wide. This ought to be long and wide enough; but if ships go on increasing in size as they have been, it won't be a great while before another and longer dock will be needed at Auckland as well as in other ports."

While Frank was noting the foregoing points in regard to Auckland, Fred was writing a few paragraphs relative to New Zealand. And first he wondered how it came to be New Zealand instead of New England or New Britain.

"That's easily explained," said Doctor Bronson, "by the fact that it was discovered by the Dutch navigator, Tasman; the French and Spaniards both lay claim to a previous discovery, but the evidence they offer is very doubtful. Tasman was sent in 1642 by Van Dieman, Governor-general of the Dutch East Indies, to explore the coast of New Holland. He made the exploration and called the country Van Dieman's Land, in honor of the Governor-general, but the name has recently been changed to Tasmania. On this voyage he discovered this country, which he called New Zealand, in honor of the province of his birth; he also discovered the archipelagos of the Feejee and Friendly isles, and returned to Batavia, having been absent only ten months.

VIEW OF AUCKLAND FROM MOUNT EDEN.

"Look at the map," continued the Doctor, "and you will see that New Zealand is divided nearly in the centre by a channel of the sea known as Cook Strait. The two islands thus formed are known as North Island and South Island, the former containing forty-eight thousand square miles, and the latter fifty-seven thousand. Beyond South Island is Stewart Island, which is triangular, and measures about thirty-six miles on a side; taken together the three islands remind you of Italy, and are shaped not unlike a boot with its toe towards the north.

South Island is sometimes called Middle Island, from its position between North and Stewart islands.

"Cook Strait commemorates the great navigator who was killed on the Sandwich Islands. He landed here in 1769, and took possession

MISSION STATION AT TANGITERORIA, NEW ZEALAND.

of the country in the name of England. He made five visits altogether to New Zealand, and introduced pigs, potatoes, sheep, goats, and other animals and vegetables."

"Hadn't Tasman already taken the country for Holland?" said Frank.

"No," replied the Doctor, "he did not set foot at all in New Zealand. He anchored in a bay in South Island, next to that in which the town of Nelson now stands, and had an encounter with the natives who opposed his going on shore. He lost four men in the fight, named the place Massacre Bay, in memory of the occurrence, and sailed away without landing."

"How soon after Captain Cook's occupation of the country did the British Government establish colonies?"

"Not for some time," replied Doctor Bronson. "In the latter part of the last century and the beginning of this many American and English whalers visited New Zealand, and year by year the knowledge of the country was increased. Visitors usually got along well enough with the natives, and were kindly treated; whenever there were encounters with the New Zealanders they were generally caused by the misconduct of the visitors themselves. Thus, in 1809, the captain of the English ship *Boyd* flogged and otherwise ill-treated a native chief, and the followers of the latter took a terrible revenge by killing no less than seventy of the crew and passengers.

"On some parts of the coast the natives were for a long time hostile, probably in consequence of outrages that had been committed by whalemen and others. Some of their ideas of the white men were curious.

EARLY DAYS IN NEW ZEALAND.

The natives paddle their boats with their faces towards the bow, and when they saw the foreign boats coming to the shore they thought the men had eyes in the backs of their heads because they rowed with their backs in the direction of their course. Some of them thought the ships were great birds, and their boats the birdlets or chicks.

"As in Polynesia, the missionaries were the pioneers of civilization in New Zealand. They came here in 1814, and previous to that time only one European, a shipwrecked sailor, is known to have lived among the natives. The Church Missionary Society established a mission in that year at the Bay of Islands, now called Russell—the mission party consisting of Rev. Samuel Marsden, chaplain to the Government of New South Wales, and three other ministers, Kendall, Hall, and King. They were kindly received by the chiefs, and held their first service on Christmas-day, 1814. Eight years later the Wesleyans established missions in New Zealand, and sixteen years after that (in 1838), the Roman Catholics did likewise."

"Then the missionaries were in advance of all Government colonization?" said Fred.

"The Church Missionary Society and the Wesleyans certainly were," was the reply, "as the Government did not send a resident official here till 1833. He had no power beyond that of writing reports of what he saw and heard, and was felicitously styled by somebody 'a man-of-war without guns.' There had been an attempt to form a colony in 1825, but it was given up, and the sixty emigrants who came out from England returned in the ship that brought them. The mission establishment at Kororareka, in the Bay of Islands, became the nucleus around which a good many lawless adventurers gathered. The bay was the resort of whale-ships, and in 1838 it was visited by fifty-six American, twenty-three English, twenty-one French, one German, and twenty-four New South Wales ships. There was so much lawlessness and crime that a vigilance committee was formed, very much like the institutions of that name which have been famous in California history.

"In 1837," continued the Doctor, glancing occasionally at a book he held in his hand,* "an association was formed for the purpose of colonizing the country, very much as India had been colonized by the East India Company. It was styled the New Zealand Company, and was founded by Lord Durham, and after some delay a surveying ship was sent out, followed by several ships carrying emigrants. This was the beginning of the colonization of New Zealand; the first settlement was made at what is now Wellington, the capital, though it was then named Port Nicholson. Auckland was founded soon after; and with the foundation of that city and the establishment of a government, the colony was well under way. It prospered for a while, and then, owing to quarrels with the natives, there was a long period of gloom.

* "Forty Years in New Zealand," by Rev. James Buller.

"We will talk more on this subject by-and-by," said the Doctor; "just at present we will use our eyes in studying the present rather than the past."

With this hint the youths closed their note-books and returned them carefully to the pockets where they belonged.

The youths were curious to see a Maori (pronounced mow-ry, the first syllable rhyming with "cow"), and they had not left the steps of the hotel before their desire was gratified. Their fellow-passenger from the *Zealandia* pointed out several of the aborigines of New Zealand, and among them he recognized an acquaintance, who greeted him cordially.

IN A STATE OF DECADENCE.

Frank was disappointed at seeing the man dressed in European garb, and looking altogether so much like an Englishman that he was not readily distinguished from the men of British origin. He was fully six feet high, muscular and well-formed, and had a slight tendency to corpulence. His face was darker than that of the average Englishman, and about the complexion of a native of the middle or south of France, and certainly lighter than the southern Italian. Frank thought it could be described as a light brown; but he was informed that these people are of different hues, and the Maoris have twelve names to indicate as many shades of color.

The eyes of this specimen native were black, and his hair was also black and slightly curly. As he talked he displayed a fine set of teeth; and as dentists are unknown among the Maoris, it is to be supposed these teeth were natural. His features were regular and symmetrical, the nose having a slight tendency to an aquiline form, the lips large and well developed, but not thick like those of the negro, and the mouth capacious enough for all practical purposes.

After a short conversation with his friend the Maori passed on, and then Frank learned that he belonged to one of the families of chiefs, and could therefore be considered as belonging to the aristocratic branch of the race.

"There are about forty thousand, or perhaps forty-five thousand, Maoris in New Zealand at present," said the gentleman. "Two or three thousand of them live on South Island, and all the rest upon North Island. The families of the chiefs are readily distinguished by their superior grace and dignity, just as the aristocratic part of a race is distinguished in any other part of the world. When Captain Cook came here the Maoris were savages and cannibals, though they had a patriarchal form of government, and in several ways had made an approach to civilization."

"They practised tattooing, did they not?" one of the youths asked.

"Certainly," was the reply; "and some of them still do so, though the habit is dying out. In another generation it will hardly be heard of any more. The Maoris are becoming assimilated to the European population around them. Many of them own houses and farms, have large herds and flocks, and there are several Maori merchants and ship-owners. Many of them are employed by the English settlers and merchants, and you will find them on the railways and in the coasting steamers, where they make good sailors and are generally liked by their employers."

Frank asked whence they were supposed to have come, and how long it probably was since they settled in New Zealand.

"They are of Malay origin," said the gentleman, "and according to their traditions, which are unusually clear, they came here from either the Sandwich or the Samoan islands, four or five centuries ago, in a fleet of thirteen large canoes, which were followed by others. The names of their canoes, the chiefs that commanded them, and the places where they landed are carefully preserved in their traditions. They say that they came from an island called Hawaiki, in the Pacific Ocean, and this is thought to be either Savaii, in the Samoan group, or Hawaii in the Sandwich Islands. Their language is so nearly like that of the Sandwich Islanders that the two people can understand each other after a little practice.

"They had no written language until one was made for them by the missionaries, and the nearest approach to it was a knotted stick, by which the wise men transmitted the names of successive chiefs. They had a great many songs of love, war, religion, and other things,

A KAINGA MAORI (NATIVE VILLAGE).

but these are fast dying out, and so are their traditions and legends. Sir George Grey collected many of their poems, myths, and fables, and published them in a large octavo volume, and if you wish to know more on this subject you can see the book in our public library."

CARVED NEW ZEALAND CHEST.

Fred asked if they were diminishing in numbers as rapidly as the people of the South Sea Islands had diminished since the advent of the white strangers.

"Yes," was the reply, "but civilization has had less to do with their reduction than the quarrels among themselves. When Captain Cook took possession of the islands, it is thought there were 120,000 Maoris living here; to-day there are less than 50,000. Before the whites came here the Maoris were divided into eighteen nations or great tribes, and the nations were subdivided into tribes, of which each had its chief whom it acknowledged. Each tribal chief regarded the head of his nation as his lord and obeyed his orders.

"The nations were constantly at war with each other, and then, too, the tribes of any one nation might be at war among themselves. The Maoris loved war for its own sake, vastly preferring it to peace, however much it might inconvenience them. Some of their ways were peculiar, and quite at variance with European notions or customs. Shall I tell you some of them?"

The youths expressed their desire to hear more about this interesting people, and their informant continued:

"Their wars were conducted with great ferocity, and the vanquished were either enslaved by the victors or killed and eaten."

"That is not so very strange," said Fred, as the gentleman paused; "savages in many parts of the world do the same thing."

"Of course they do," was the reply; "but they do not divide their ammunition and supplies with their enemies in order that they can fight on equal terms."

"Did the Maoris do that?" Fred asked in astonishment.

"Certainly they did, on several occasions that are known to the white residents. While they were at war with the English they used to send notice whenever they were about to make an attack, and they thought we did not treat them fairly in not doing the same. After the last war one of our officers asked a Maori chief why it was that when he had command of a certain road he did not attack the ammunition and provision trains. 'Why, you fool!' answered the Maori, much astonished, 'if we had stolen your powder and food, how could you have fought?'

"Once when one chief insulted another, the latter remarked that if chief number one had not known his own superiority in arms and ammunition, he would not have dared to behave in such a manner. Thereupon chief number one divided his fighting material into two equal parts, and sent one part to his enemy with an invitation to war.

"Sometimes two villages would get up a little war, and after fighting each other all day, the inhabitants would come out of their forts towards evening and talk over the day's sport in the most friendly way. The next morning they would begin again, and keep it up during the daytime, to meet in the evening for a social conference. An old missionary used to tell how, in one of these local wars, he had known the defenders of a fort to send out to their assailants that they were short of provisions, and the latter would immediately send in a supply of food. The same missionary said he had performed divine service one Sunday between two hostile forts, the inhabitants of which came out to worship, meet in the most perfect amity, and return, to resume fighting on Monday morning.

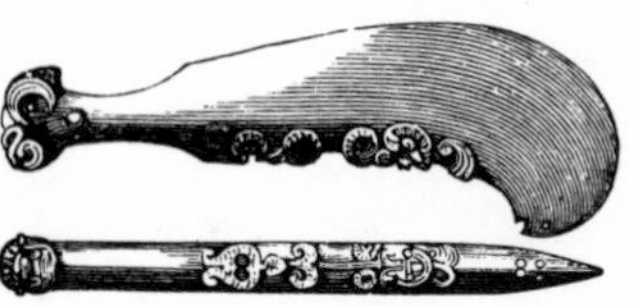

MAORI WAR CLUBS.

"It is estimated," said the gentleman, "that between the years 1820 and 1840 more than thirty thousand Maoris perished in these inter-tribal wars. Many perished in the wars with the English, and many others have died in consequence of their contact with civilization, as in the islands of the Pacific, some from intemperance, and others from small-pox, measles, and kindred diseases, which were brought here by the whites. At present wars among them have ceased, cannibalism is unknown, fully one-half of the adults can read and write, and two-thirds of them belong to the churches."

CHAPTER IX.

THE SUBURBS OF AUCKLAND.—EXTINCT VOLCANOES.—MAORI FORTIFICATIONS.—A KAURI FOREST.—KAURI LUMBER AND GUM.—HOW THE GUM IS FORMED AND FOUND.—TREES OF NEW ZEALAND AND THEIR VALUE.—FERNS AND THEIR VARIETY.—A PAKEHA MAORI.—HIS REMINISCENCES.—CURIOUS NATIVE CUSTOMS.—BUYING HEADS.—SALE OF A LIVING MAN'S HEAD.—THE LAW OF MURU.—NEW ZEALAND BIRDS.—THE GIGANTIC MOA, OR DINORNIS.—NATIVE WEDDINGS.—KAWAU ISLAND.—SHARK FISHING.—OYSTERS.—VISITING THE THAMES GOLD-FIELDS.—SIGHTS AND SCENES.—GOLD MINING IN NEW ZEALAND.—POPULATION OF THE COLONY.—ENCOURAGEMENT TO IMMIGRATION.—JOURNEY TO THE HOT LAKES.—CLIMATE OF NEW ZEALAND.

AFTER a glance at the interior of Auckland, our friends naturally turned their attention to its surroundings. They were reminded of Naples, as Auckland is in a region of extinct volcanoes, one of which, Mount Eden, rises only a mile from the city. Following the advice of the landlord of the hotel, they drove thither, passing numerous villas of the well-to-do residents, with which the sides of the mountain are dotted. From the edge of the crater there is a fine view of the city and its surroundings, and the view takes in several volcanoes.

LAKE IN THE CRATER OF AN EXTINCT VOLCANO.

The Maoris had formerly a fortification on the top of the mountain; it surrounded the crater, so that a whole tribe could be concealed there, if necessary, for purposes of defence. Frank and Fred traced out some of the terraces that formed the original fortification, and Doctor Bronson said the works showed a good deal of military skill.

Within a radius of ten miles of the city no less then sixty-two points of eruption have been found, the greater part of them being only insignificant cones or hills. The largest and best specimen of the extinct volcanoes of Auckland is Rangitoto, which rises from a great mass of black lava, presenting a forbidding appearance. Unfortunately for the beauty of the landscape, the forest that once covered this region has been nearly all cut or burned away, and Auckland will doubtless regret in the near future the desolation which her settlers have made.

The youths were anxious to see the famous Kauri pine (*Damara Australis*), which is confined wholly to Auckland, and is the most renowned of New Zealand trees. Before returning to the city they were driven where they saw a single specimen, and before their departure from the district they had the satisfaction of seeing a Kauri forest. Frank's note on this subject is interesting, and we are permitted to quote it:

SAWING A KAURI PINE.

"The peculiarity of the Kauri pine is that the trunk does not appear to diminish in size from the ground to where the limbs begin to spread. We saw some trees more than two hundred feet high; they were eight or nine feet in diameter at the base, and had no limbs within forty or fifty feet of the ground. They reminded us of the famous big trees of California, but were taller in proportion to their diameter. We don't think we ever saw more graceful trees anywhere. They haven't a great deal of foliage, and it grows in little tufts very much like bushes.

"The wood is full of gum, and is very valuable as timber. They told us it was the finest wood in the world for shingles, as the gum preserved it from the effects of the weather. A great deal of the lumber from the Kauri pine is shipped to other parts of New Zealand, and also to Australia, China, Feejee, and other places where it can find a market.

STOCK-FARM IN THE SUBURBS.

Many of the sticks have been sent to England to serve as masts and spars for her Majesty's ships of war, and altogether the trade in Kauri lumber is very large. The result is, a great deal has been cut away, and the time is not very distant when the Kauri forests will be gone.

"While we were walking among the Kauri trees our guide prodded the earth with a spear that he carried, and he kept doing this so frequently that we asked what it meant. He answered that he was looking for Kauri gum, and after a time he struck a hard substance, which he dug down to and brought to light.

"It was a lump of Kauri gum, and looked more like amber than anything else; in fact, it is said to be used very often in place of amber for the mouth-pieces of pipes and cigar-holders, and for other purposes where amber is ornamental. It is worth eight or ten cents a pound, and the shipment of Kauri gum from Auckland amounts to nearly a million dollars annually.

"'How do you get the gum?' one of us inquired of the man who was showing us through the forest.

"'In just the way you see,' he replied. 'The gum cannot be obtained from the tree by any process of tapping or reducing from the wood. The tree falls and dies, and then, when it decays, the gum collects in lumps in the ground. It takes years and years for it to collect, and this little lump, which I have just taken from the ground, has probably been lying here for centuries. A new forest has risen where the old one stood, and has taken a long, long while to grow.'

"We asked what other timber-trees there were in New Zealand, and our informant mentioned the Kahikatea, or white pine; the Rimu, or red pine; the Totara, which is claimed to be impervious to the attacks of the teredo; and the Tanekaha, which has a handsome, close-grained, and durable wood, and whose bark furnishes a strong dye. Then there is the Matai, which is much like the English yew, and is used for making furniture; the Miro, which has a beautiful red fruit on which pigeons grow fat; and the Kawaka, which has a remarkable leaf and a durable wood.

"There is a great variety of tree-ferns, some of them reaching a height of forty feet, and a diameter of twelve inches or more. The most tropical of all the trees of New Zealand is the Nikau, which is the only representative of the palm family. The ferns are more tropical than the trees, and add very much to the beauty of the forest, though they impede locomotion in many places. As for fruit-trees, there are very few indigenous to the country, but nearly everything that grows in the United States or England flourishes, and they have many things here that are strangers to us at home. Peaches, apples, apricots, figs, oranges, strawberries, pears, and other fruits are abundant in their seasons, and some of them reach a luxuriance and perfection surpassing that of the countries whence they came.

A WATER-OAK.

"Near the Kauri forest we were shown a Maori *pah*, or fort, that is said to have been the scene of severe fighting in the early days of the colony. While we were looking at it a man joined our group, and our guide told us he was a *pakeha* Maori. You will wonder, as we did, what a pakeha Maori is.

A PAKEHA MAORI.

"Well, he's a white man who lives among the Maoris, and in former times, before the colonization, there was a goodly number of them, for the simple reason that unless a man was a missionary he couldn't easily stay in the country without living among the natives. *Pakeha* means stranger, and is applied to any white man, and a pakeha Maori is a white man living among the natives. The tribes were very desirous of having pakehas among them, for the reason that they could learn useful matters from them, but more particularly they could buy muskets, gunpowder, tools, and other trade goods, of which they were in great need. A pakeha who had trade goods was always welcome, but a man who had nothing was of little consequence, and sometimes had a hard struggle to keep his head on his shoulders.

"With a judicious present of a few shillings we got on the right side of this man, and induced him to talk about what he had seen or knew among the Maoris. I have written down some of the things he said. I can't vouch that they are all absolutely correct; but his statements are corroborated by intelligent white men who have long lived in the country."

Here we will close Frank's journal for a few minutes and listen to the pakeha Maori.

"You see I'm an old man; I came here when I was very young, and have seen a great many changes. I was in Sydney, and heard New Zealand was a good place for trade, so I loaded some goods on a schooner that was coming this way, and in due time was landed in the country. At first I made my home with one of the whites, who had come here before me and got on friendly terms with the tribe where he lived; it didn't take long to do it, as the Maoris were very anxious to buy my goods."

A PAKEHA MAORI'S HOME.

Frank asked what goods they wanted most.

"Muskets and ammunition," was the reply, "and for these they paid fabulous prices in wild flax, which was the principal product worth shipping away. They were constantly at war, and the tribe that possessed the white man's weapons could destroy any tribe that was without them. This happened in many cases, and whole tribes who were without guns were destroyed by their more fortunate adversaries. They were literally eaten up, as the natives were cannibals in those times.

"To get muskets they impoverish themselves, neglecting their agriculture in order to gather flax to buy them with, and literally starving themselves. Many died of starvation in consequence, and in another way muskets proved the death of those who owned them. In the times of clubs and spears the Maoris had their pahs and villages on high hills,

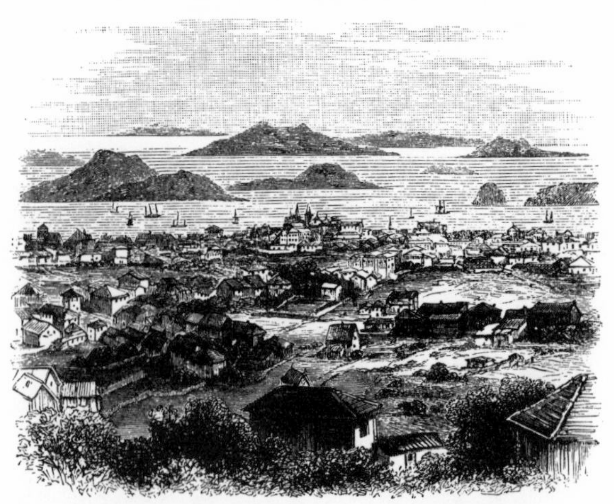

VIEW OF A PART OF AUCKLAND AND ITS HARBOR.

where the air was pure and the ground dry; when they got muskets they moved into the low ground, where they were carried off by the dampness and its consequent fevers. I have known whole villages and tribes killed in this way, so that not one man, woman, or child remained. The musket was as fatal to those who owned it as to those who did not; it was deadly either way.

"Now about some of the customs of the Maoris. They used to be tattooed very finely, and some of the fighting-men were beautiful to look at. The warriors used to bring back the heads of those they killed in battle, and some of the traders got to buying these heads provided they were finely tattooed. They gave a musket for a good head, and as soon as this was known some of the tribes began to make war on others just for the sake of getting tattooed heads to sell.

"You may think it strange, gentlemen," said the pakeha, "but I've known the head of a live man to be sold and paid for beforehand, and afterwards honestly delivered according to the agreement; and one time when the heads of warriors were not equal to the demand for them, some of the chiefs tattooed the faces of several slaves whom they intended to kill whenever the traders arrived who had agreed to buy the heads. But the slaves were not faithful to their masters, as they all ran away into the bushes just as the inflammation in their faces was passing away and they were getting in good condition to be marketable.

"They had the tabu in its most rigid form here," he continued; "but as you probably learned all about it in the South Sea islands I won't take your time to talk about it.

"Another curious custom of the Maoris was the *muru;* the word means 'plunder'—and some folks might call it robbery, which it amounted to, though it was the custom, and practically the law of the country.

"If a man's child fell into the fire and was severely or perhaps fatally burned, he was plundered of nearly everything he possessed, and the same was the case if his canoe upset while he was fishing, or any other accident happened to him. The people of the tribe assembled and gave him notice that they would be there for the muru on a particular day. He prepared a great feast for them, and after the feast they sacked his house and carried away pretty nearly everything he had. Sometimes he did not have enough left to live upon, but he had the opportunity of getting even by joining in a muru against somebody else. These performances were never opposed, and in fact a man would feel insulted if a serious accident of any kind happened to him and no notice was taken of it. The greater the robbery, the greater the honor conferred upon the victim.

MAORI TATTOOING.

"If a man killed another through malice and with deliberate intent, the act was generally considered of no consequence, or it might even be meritorious. If it was his own slave that he killed, it was considered his personal affair entirely; if the victim was of another tribe, it was a matter of tribal revenge or retaliation; and if of his own tribe he would

INLAND SCENERY.

be defended by his family or section, and nothing came of it. But if he killed a man of his own tribe by accident, such as the discharge of a gun, then the law of muru had full force, and the man and all his relatives were plundered of everything they possessed."

Fred asked if the Maoris were given to the ordinary kind of thieving, like most savage nations.

"Much less than you might suppose," was the reply. "Of course there were pilferers; but, on the whole, private property was pretty safe from burglary and sneak-thieving. The muru gave an opportunity for plundering, and so did the warfare between the tribes; but a man could exempt himself from the muru if he wished, by giving up all claims to its advantages on his own account. When I first came to New Zealand I was the subject of a muru, and afterwards joined in one upon a Maori friend; but I found so many disadvantages, losing so much more than I gained, that I stipulated to have nothing to do with these affairs in future.

"In actual honesty the Maoris have been injured by their contact with Europeans. They will steal and do other improper things more than formerly; but against this we must offset the abolition of slavery, cannibalism, tribal wars, polygamy, and many of their superstitious and cruel practices. When anything is stolen from you the chief can recover it, and will do so if you apply to him. Custom requires that you should tell him to keep it as a reward for his trouble, and so you don't gain much by the recovery of the plunder.

"They were not favored by nature," continued their historian, "as they did not have the bread-fruit, banana, and cocoa-tree to supply them with food, and they did not even have the pig until it was given to them by Captain Cook. Dogs and rats were their only quadrupeds, and they ate both. The native dogs are extinct, as the Maoris did not care to preserve them when pigs became plentiful.

CAPTAIN COOK'S GIFT TO THE MAORIS.

"It used to be the custom to make human sacrifices on the death of a chief; prisoners of war were used for this purpose, their blood being sprinkled on the grave, and the flesh roasted and eaten. There was a grand feast at a funeral, and even now this custom is kept up, though they have no longer any human sacrifices. The festivities at a Maori funeral are very much like those of an Irish 'wake,' and something like an Arab burial ceremony. They eat and drink all they can get, and the mourning is performed by the women, who howl and cry for hours, simply because it is the custom to do so."

As the time of our friends was limited, they bade adieu to the pakeha Maori, and left him to meditate upon the changes that had taken place since his advent into New Zealand.

"He might have told you," said their guide, "that the native rat has been killed off by the European one, which was introduced from ships, and the European house-fly has driven away the native blue blow-fly. The foreign clover is killing the ferns, and European grasses generally are supplanting the native ones very rapidly. The English sparrow has become very common in New Zealand, and will doubtless destroy some of the native birds."

Fred asked about the birds of the country, but his informant could not describe them with any degree of accuracy. Later the youth learned that there are one hundred and thirty-six varieties in all, of which seventy-three are land birds. One of these, the Apteryx, or Kiwi, is wingless, and lives in the mountains. He is very scarce, and only rarely captured or even seen. There are six varieties of parrots, and two of falcons—one about the size of a pigeon, and the other a very active and industrious sparrow-hawk. There is one owl, and there is a blackbird, which is called the "parson bird" by the settlers, for the reason that it has two white feathers under its chin like the ends of a clergyman's neck-tie.

Fred asked if New Zealand was not the home of the now extinct Dinornis, the largest bird of which we have any positive knowledge.

"Yes," replied his informant; "the bird was called *Moa* by the natives, and it is pretty clearly established that he was abundant when the Maoris came here, but was wiped out of existence some two hundred years ago. Skeletons of the Moa have been found, and show that the largest of these birds must have attained a height of fourteen to sixteen feet."

"Were they dangerous?" was the very natural query which followed.

"Not by any means; they were wingless, and belonged to the ostrich family, and the naturalists say they were stupid birds, that could easily fall a prey to man. This fact accounts for their extinction in the first two or three centuries of the presence of the Maoris in New Zealand. It is fortunate that their skeletons have been preserved in the earth, so that we can know positively that such great birds existed."

"How do you know the Maoris lived upon these birds?"

"Partly through their traditions, and partly from the discovery of many of the bones of the Moa in the ovens and in the heaps of rubbish around the ruins of ancient villages. The natives devoured any birds they could catch; parrots, pigeons, parson-birds, anything and everything edible was legitimate food. Those that dwelt on the coast lived chiefly on a fish diet, and those in the interior made annual or more frequent migrations to the sea-side for purposes of fishing. The rivers abound in eels, and they grow to an enormous size; I have seen eels weighing fifty pounds each, and have heard of larger ones."

SKELETON OF THE EXTINCT MOA (DINORNIS).

Frank asked what the clothing of the natives was made of before the Europeans came to the country.

"It was made from the fibre of the flax," was the reply. "There are several kinds of flax, and it grows everywhere and near every village. Not only did it supply the material for garments, but for nets,

DRESSING FLAX.

baskets, lines, mats, dishes, cordage, and other things. They used cords made from it for binding the walls and roofs of their houses together, and thus made it serve in place of nails. Great quantities of flax are raised here nowadays, as you will understand when you know there are some forty and odd flax-mills in the colony, and considerable flax is exported every year.

"Most of the Maoris that you will see during your stay in New Zealand wear clothes of European style, as they find them more convenient than the cloaks and mats of former days. On ceremonial occasions the old finery is displayed, and the cloaks of some of the chiefs are really magnificent. Cloaks and mats or blankets were the ordinary dress, one mat being wrapped around the waist, and the other thrown over the shoulder. Men wore their mats on the right shoulder, and women on the left, and they sometimes adorned their heads with the gayest feathers they could find. Children went naked in their early years, except in the coldest weather, when they wrapped themselves in any old garments they could lay hands on."

The youths learned many other things about the Maoris, but we have not room for all the notes they made on the subject. Frank asked particularly about the marriage ceremonies of the natives, probably for the information of his young lady friends at home. He learned that children might be betrothed by their parents when very young, or if not so betrothed they could marry very much as in civilized lands. Sometimes the parents and families, and more frequently the whole tribe, discussed any proposed match, and made all sorts of hinderances to it. Courtship was begun by the girl quite as often as by the young man, and when marriage was decided there were great preparations for a festivity, and the bride and bridegroom were provided with new mats and many other articles of household use. The funny part of the business was that during the marriage-feast everything movable was carried away by the friends, under the law of muru already described. The young couple started in life with nothing except the clothes they wore and the house that had been built for them.

During their stay at Auckland our friends visited some of the islands in the bay, including that of Kawau, where Sir George Grey, a former governor of New Zealand, has a fine residence. The house is quite English in appearance and character, and contains a good museum of Maori and other curiosities. The grounds around the house abound in pheasants of several kinds from Europe and Asia, kangaroos from Australia, tree-kangaroos from New Guinea, and several members of the deer family. Near Kawau they saw a fleet of boats manned by Maoris engaged in the capture of sharks. The creatures they pursued were not the ordinary shark, which is abundant in New Zealand waters, but a smaller variety measuring about six feet in length.

As the sharks were hauled into the boats they were killed by sharp blows upon the nose, and then flung into the hold. When a boat was filled it proceeded to an island, where the prizes were hung up to dry;

and Frank was told that from twelve to twenty thousand of these sharks are taken in the bay of Waitamata every year, and either dried for winter food or eaten fresh. Out of curiosity our friends took a luncheon of shark steak, which had been baked on a hot stone after the

FAMILY OF DEER ON KAWAU ISLAND.

native fashion. They found it palatable, but rather tasteless, and so dry that Fred suggested oiling each mouthful, or smothering it with butter. It was unanimously voted that shark with the Maoris was not half as enjoyable as salmon with the Indians of the Columbia River, or shad with the fishermen of Delaware Bay.

More palatable than shark steak were the oysters which abound in the bay. The island of Kawau has a coast-line of about thirty miles, and all around it there are oyster-beds, some of them of great extent. Not only do the oysters grow on the rocks and in the water, but they cling to the overhanging limbs of the trees, and grow there quite contented with their immersion of a few hours twice a day during the rising of the tide. Frank and Fred found the oysters of good flavor, and soon became quite expert at opening the shells with the oyster-knives which were opportunely brought along in the boat.

"Don't fail to visit the gold-mines and the Hot Lake district," was the injunction repeatedly made to Doctor Bronson and his young companions. As soon as they had exhausted the sights of Auckland and its neighborhood they proceeded to follow the foregoing advice.

First in order were the Thames gold-fields. A steamer carried them in five hours from Auckland to Grahamstown, and as soon as they were on shore they began their inspection of the mines. There are no placer diggings here, the mining being almost entirely confined to the veins of quartz in the mountains, which rise abruptly from the shore

PROSPECTING FOR GOLD.

of the bay on which Grahamstown is built. For this reason Grahamstown, which takes its name from Robert Graham, its founder, has a more permanent and substantial appearance than the ordinary town in a newly opened mining country. It lies along the shore of the bay, and the numerous reduction-works, founderies, and similar establishments were suggestive of a manufacturing centre rather than a mining one only a few years old.

Doctor Bronson had a letter of introduction to a gentleman interested in one of the largest mines, and the trio of travellers were at once made welcome. Clad in appropriate costumes, they were taken into the mine, where they walked a long distance through a tunnel, and were then conducted through a perfect maze of shafts and levels, where the

STAMP-MILL AT GRAHAMSTOWN.

workmen were busily occupied in removing the auriferous rock, which was carried directly to the reduction-works, where it was crushed and the precious metal extracted. The gold contains a large amount—thirty per cent.—of silver, and consequently has an appearance of pallor when turned out from the retorts. As the work of gold-mining has been described elsewhere in the wanderings of the boy travellers, it is hardly necessary to give it here, the processes of mining and reduction being practically the same all over the world.

Frank and Fred obtained the following information relative to gold-mining in New Zealand, and especially in the region now under consideration:

" Gold-mining in New Zealand properly dates from 1861, when gold was discovered by Mr. Gabriel Read at Tuapeka, in the province of Otago. The existence of the precious metal was known nine or ten years before that date, it having been found at Coromandel by a Mr. Ring, who reported his discovery to the authorities at Auckland. Since 1861 it has been found in many places, and is now an important industry of the country. Some of the mines are wholly alluvial, or placer, diggings, others are wholly quartz-mines, which are called reefs in New Zealand and Australia, and others are combinations of alluvial and quartz mining.

"For the enlightenment of some of my younger readers I will here explain that alluvial, or placer, mines are those where the gold is found

"STRUCK A POCKET."

in the earth or soil and is separated from it by washing. Quartz-mines are those where the gold is in the ledges of the mountains and requires to be removed by tunnelling or blasting, or both. The rock containing the rock must be crushed to powder, and the gold separated from the powder by washing and mingling it with quicksilver. Quartz-mining requires a great deal of money to carry it on; so much, indeed, that it is generally conducted by companies, and these companies, it is proper to say, very often take more from the pockets of the stock-holders than they do from the mines. Alluvial diggings are the resort of the poor man, who needs only pick, shovel, and pan to set him up in business.

"During the year ending March 31, 1886, the mines of New Zealand yielded 233,068 ounces of gold, which was valued at more than four millions of dollars; at least this was the amount entered at the custom-house for exportation; some was doubtless absorbed in the colony, but no one can tell how much.

"The yield of the Thames district for the same time was 61,939 ounces, or more than one-fourth the entire amount for the colony. During the month of May, 1886, 3039 ounces of gold were taken from 2574 tons of rock. Some of the mines have paid good dividends to their owners, but others have never made any returns. The ups and downs of mining in New Zealand are about the same as in other parts of the world.

"There are nearly five hundred mining companies registered in New Zealand, with a paid-up capital of about ten million dollars. Down to the end of 1885 more than two hundred million dollars' worth of gold had been exported from New Zealand, so that there can be no question of the importance of the colony as a mining region. According to the official returns there are more than eleven thousand men engaged in mining; two thousand of these are quartz-miners, and the rest, including three thousand Chinese, are in the placer mines.

"The placer miners do not confine themselves to the valleys of the rivers among the mountains, but seek gold along the west shore, where they find it under the bowlders and other stones embedded in the sand of the beaches. The popular idea is that this gold is washed up from the sea during severe gales; the scientific men say it is really washed up by the lifting power of the waves on the sand that has been brought down by the rivers and drifted along the shore. Some of this gold is obtained by washing the sands in sluice-boxes, just as in operations among the mountains; and deposits, or 'pockets,' are occasionally discovered in the sand under the loose stones. Sometimes these deposits are of considerable value, and we have been told of a miner who found a single pocket containing nearly thirty ounces of gold. Similar pockets exist in the mountains, and it is the height of a miner's ambition to find a well-filled one and secure its contents without anybody's help.

"The alluvial mines in North Island are less extensive than those of South Island. It is estimated that these mines cover an area of twenty thousand square miles in South Island alone, and as very little capital is required for working them, they are more popular than the others.

"The principal quartz-mines are in the Coromandel and Thames districts; the reefs have been prospected to six or eight hundred feet below the sea-level, and also to a height of two thousand feet above it.

GOLD-MINING ON THE SEA-SHORE.

In some places the rock has yielded six hundred ounces to the ton; at least it has assayed to that extent, but the amount obtained upon working it in quantities is far less. Of course such rock as this is a rare exception in New Zealand as everywhere else.

"In the province of Otago there are rich reefs, and in some places gold has been found at elevations of six and seven thousand feet above the sea. The highest mine in New Zealand is on the summit of Advance Peak, near Lake Wakatipu, in South Island.

"The mines have been beneficial to the country in two ways: first

A MINER'S CAMP IN THE MOUNTAINS.

by the yield of gold, and secondly by attracting attention and emigration to New Zealand. Like the colonies of Australia, New Zealand offers inducements to emigrants, and is very desirous of promoting emigration from the overcrowded countries of the Old World. An agent-general is maintained in London, and a vast amount of printed matter setting forth the advantages of the colony to actual settlers is issued annually from his office. Emigrants with families are carried to New Zealand at a reduced rate of fare, and at one time they were transported almost free of charge, so anxious was the Colonial Government to increase its population. The colony now has nearly if not quite six hundred thousand inhabitants, which is certainly a good showing when we remember that the settlement had its beginning in 1840, when its first governor came out from England."

Our friends remained at Grahamstown over Sunday, and observed a state of affairs which was an improvement over that of American mining towns in general on the first day of the week. All work was suspended, and the whole population turned out in its best clothes. There are churches of nearly every denomination at Grahamstown, and all were well filled with worshippers; one of the churches has a stained-glass window which cost some fifteen hundred dollars—certainly an unusual sight for a mining town.

Monday was spent among the hills and in the mines of the Thames, and the youths retired to bed that night thoroughly wearied with the exertions of the day. On Tuesday the party returned to Auckland, and immediately arranged for a visit to the Hot Lake district. The trip was planned as follows: Their heavy baggage was sent by steamer to Tauranga, which is on the east coast, and the nearest port to the district they were to visit. Then, with only their hand-bags and some rough garments and necessities for mountain travel, the trio proceeded by rail, coach, and horseback to their destination. By this plan they were enabled to see the country and avoid travelling the same route twice over. The route for the ease-loving tourist is from Tauranga by coach to the Hot Lakes, a distance of about fifty miles, and back again over the same route. It is proper to say that travellers who come as far as New Zealand for the sake of sight-seeing are greatly disinclined to repetition,

VISITING A MINE.

and nearly all visitors go by one route and return over another. The Government has established a sanatorium and laid out a town in the centre of the Hot Lake district. It is building a railway from Oxford to this town, and the promise is confidently made that by the end of 1888 travellers may go by train from Auckland direct to the Hot Lakes without the fatigue of a coach-ride over the present rough road.

"We had a charming ride," said Frank, "over the railway to Oxford, where we took the coach in the direction of the famous region of New Zealand geysers. Much of the country through which the railway passes resembles England both in scenery and products; English fruit-trees grow well here, and English grasses seem adapted to the soil. American pines have been introduced and are doing well; they make a pleasing contrast to the New Zealand wattle-tree and cabbage-palm and the ferns which abound everywhere. The country is thinly settled, but will undoubtedly support a large population in course of time. Villages with European houses alternate with Maori encampments, the latter abounding with lazy aboriginals.

"One of the advantages claimed for New Zealand is its similarity to England in climate and products, with the great point in its favor that while the climate has all the mildness of that of England it lacks its severity. The average temperature of London is said to be seven degrees colder than that of North Island, and four degrees colder than the temperature of South Island.

"They tell us that snow seldom lies on the ground at the sea-level on North Island, and not very often on South Island; but the summit of Ruapehu, the highest mountain in North Island, and also the tops of the peaks of the great mountain chains in South Island, are perpetually covered with snow. The snow line is about seven thousand five hundred feet high.

"The sun was shining brightly and there was a genial warmth to the air when we left Auckland, but within an hour we were in a terrific rain that beat heavily against the windows of the railway-carriage and pattered like hail on the roof. 'This is our one drawback,' said a gentleman who accompanied us, when the rain began to fall. 'The changes of weather and temperature in New Zealand are very sudden. The alternations from heat to cold, from sunshine to storm, from calms to gales, are so frequent and marked as to defy calculation and prevent our saying with truthfulness that there is any uniformly wet or dry season throughout the year.'

"Then he went on to say that compared with Great Britain the climate seemed to be far superior when the death-rate was considered. It was less than eleven in one thousand annually, and lower than in any of the colonies of Australia. He claimed that the salubrity of the cli-

INLAND SCENERY.

mate was due in great measure to the breezes for which New Zealand is noted, there being no less than one hundred and twenty-six gales or high winds in a single year (1885), and good winds for nearly all the rest of the time. The prevailing winds are from the north-west and south-west, with occasional storms from the opposite quarters. The annual rainfall is twenty-eight inches at Auckland, thirty-six inches at Wellington, and twenty-five inches at Dunedin, and there is more rain on the east coast than on the west."

We will learn in the next chapter what our friends saw among the Hot Lakes of New Zealand.

CHAPTER X.

THE HOT LAKE DISTRICT; ITS EXTENT AND PECULIARITIES.—MEDICINAL SPRINGS. —ANALYSIS OF THE WATERS.—FRED'S NARROW ESCAPE.—SCALDED TO DEATH IN A HOT POOL.—LAKE ROTOMAHANA.—THE WHITE TERRACES; HOW THEY ARE FORMED.—THE PINK TERRACES.—BOILING LAKES.—NATURE'S BATH-TUBS. —PETRIFIED BIRDS.—A TABOOED MOUNTAIN.—THE TABU ON DUCKS.—NATIVE DEMORALIZATION. — WAIROA. — DESTRUCTION OF THE TERRACES. — TERRIBLE ERUPTION, WITH LOSS OF LIFE.—A VILLAGE THROWN INTO A LAKE.—TAURANGA AND THE GATE PAH. — MAORI FORTIFICATIONS. — SHORT HISTORY OF THE MAORI WAR; ITS CAUSES AND RESULTS.—FROM TAURANGA TO NAPIER.— A PASTORAL COUNTRY.—ATTRACTIONS OF NAPIER.—OVERLAND TO WELLINGTON.—FARMING AND HERDING SCENES.—A CURIOUS ARTICLE OF COMMERCE.

"THE volcanic region of North Island is a large one," wrote Frank in his journal, "and as I can't find any two persons who agree as to its extent, I won't attempt to give its area in square miles or acres; but it is large enough to meet the wants of everybody, and hot enough to suit the most fastidious.

"Long before you reach the neighborhood of the Hot Lakes you find steaming springs, and there is hardly one of them that is not credited with some wonderful healing properties. On an area of a hundred and fifty square miles there are many thousands of hot springs of all temperatures from tepid to boiling, and of all sorts of composition. Only a few have been analyzed, but enough of them to show that hardly any two are alike. All the mineral springs of the world seem to be represented in this district, and when they have been properly catalogued they will form a sanatorium to which the entire globe can send its invalids for relief and healing.

"To make a list of the chemicals they hold in solution would be to copy the index of an exhaustive work on chemistry, and therefore I refrain.

"These springs have been the resort of the Maoris for centuries, and for white people ever since New Zealand could boast a white population. Wonderful cures are recorded or reported, but it is evident that an invalid should have the advice of a competent physician before trying the springs in earnest. To come here and take the baths indiscriminately, when the number and variety are so great, would be much like turning one's self loose in a drug-store and tasting the contents of all the jars in succession. Thus far the principal diseases treated have been gout and rheumatism, and many a sufferer has found relief and been cured of his malady. One bath has been so successful in curing skin diseases that it is known as the 'pain-killer;' its ingredients are sulphate of potash, sulphate of soda, chlorides of sodium, calcium, magnesia, and iron, silica, hydrochloric acid, sulphuretted hydrogen, and traces of alumina, lithium, and iodine. What disease could stand such a combination as that?

AMONG THE HOT SPRINGS.

"Most of the villages are near hot springs, not so much for the curative properties of the waters as for the convenience of cooking food without the trouble of collecting fuel, or even building a fire. At one village where we stopped for dinner there were twelve or fifteen springs of all temperatures from tepid to boiling; we bathed in one spring while the potatoes for our dinner were being boiled in another not a dozen yards away. Around the springs, and along the path by which

THE BATHS AT ROTOMAHANA.

we walked from them to the house, there were cracks and holes in the ground from which steam issued, and occasionally little jets of boiling water. It gave us an uncanny feeling to walk along this path, and we agreed that it was not a nice place for promenading in the dark.

"The proprietor of the hotel accompanied us, and said it was not safe to stray from the path, as one was liable to break through the thin crust and find his feet plunged into hot water which had accumulated beneath the surface. He showed us a pool which is the special resort of the Maoris, and where half a dozen of them were bathing, the bathers being watched by as many more of their kinsmen, who were squatted on flat stones erected over the steam-jets at the edge of the pool. The temperature of the water is about ninety degrees, but it rises occasionally to a hundred and more. We found a secluded pool, and took a bath there; after the bath we greatly enjoyed a luscious melon which our host brought us.

"It is a curious sensation to stand on a hill and look over a considerable area of country which may easily be imagined to be undergoing a cooking process from one end to the other. Jets of steam rise from the ground in a great many places; some of them continuously, others

HOTEL LIFE AT THE HOT LAKES.

in quick or slow jets, and with intervals of a second or so, or perhaps fractions of a second, and others with dignified intervals of several minutes. Some of the geysers threw up columns of water fifteen or twenty feet in height; but, on the whole, they were less interesting than the geysers of Yellowstone Park in America. At one place the sulphur fumes were so stifling that it was next to impossible to look into the holes in the ground, and only possible by holding the nose firmly and looking while the breath was retained.

"And these sulphur fumes came very near causing a horrible death to Fred. We were among the boiling springs, where the greatest precaution was necessary to avoid falling into the pools, as they were only short distances apart, sometimes less than a foot. Our guide had called attention to one of the geyser holes, where the water at the bottom was boiling furiously. Fred was looking into it, when suddenly there rose a puff of sulphur that half stifled him. He sprang backward as he threw his head in the air, and in doing so stepped within three inches of the edge of a pool of water that was quiescent, though almost at the boiling-point. Had he fallen into it he would have been scalded to death in a few moments.

"Accidents of this sort are by no means uncommon. A child of the hotel-keeper fell into a pool a few months ago, and was scalded so badly that it died within an hour. They told how a native woman dropped her baby from her arms; it fell into a pool of scalding water by the side of the path. The woman went in to rescue it, and both mother and child were drowned in the pool. Men, horses, and dogs have fallen into these pools, or more frequently broken through the thin crust that lies above the accumulated hot water or hot mud beneath the surface.

"One Maori village where we stopped is so completely built on a volcanic foundation that the steam rises in every house; and the little open space in the centre, where the village councils are held, is half paved with broad stones, which are all kept warm by steam from the earth. Close to the village are several mud-baths, where one may sit up to his neck in hot mud for hours, and then wash off the adhesive stuff in a neighboring pool. These *solfataras*, or mud-baths, are very numerous, and in many instances very dangerous. Where they are small the hot mud simply boils and bubbles, and slowly oozes out of the ground; and the chief danger lies in breaking through the crust near them and finding yourself plunged in the scalding mush. The larger solfataras are like the mouth of a well, the mud bubbling up in the centre and forming a ring of dirt that solidifies and offers a good footing, so far as the eye can perceive; but woe betide the unfortunate stranger who ventures to step upon it; the crust gives way, and he will be fortunate if he escapes with his life.

"We reached Rotomahana, the famous little lake of this district, without accident, although it was evening when we got there. We were lodged in a Maori *wharry*, or house, close to Te Tarata, or The White Terraces, and we had a glimpse of the terraces through the indistinctness of the evening. There were steam and water jets all

A MUD CRATER.

around, and the potatoes for our supper were boiled in one of the natural caldrons, free of charge. To boil vegetables in one of these springs all you have to do is to enclose them in a net of hemp or flax and lower them into the water. When they have been there long enough take them out, and that's all there is about it. What a nice thing it would be to have a natural hot spring at your door, provided you could escape the other inconveniences connected with it!

"We bathed in a pool and also in the lake, the latter, though warm, being less so than the pool. The ground was warm, and made the atmosphere of the house too hot for comfort; and altogether we passed an uncomfortable night. Next morning we were up bright and early, to look at the terraces; and of all the wonderful things in the world, there are few that can surpass them.

"The White Terraces are on this side of the little lake, and the Pink Terraces on the other. Imagine, if you can, a series of irregular steps of silver or alabaster, or polished marble, about three hundred feet from side to side, and rising about two hundred feet from the shore of the lake. These steps or terraces have been formed by the crystallization of the silica contained in the hot water in the boiling lake above; the hot water holds it in solution, and as its temperature falls the silica is released and deposited.

"In the sunlight the terraces glistened and sparkled like a collection of all the precious stones in the world, and the picture was fascinating in the extreme. We ascended from the base to the edge of the boiling lake, where the terraces begin. Our guides cautioned us that we must expect to walk continually in the water which flowed over the terraces, but as the surface is soft and smooth we doffed our boots and encased our feet in moccasins, or shoes of untanned skin. The water at the bottom of the terraces is tepid; but each successive stage finds it hotter, and at last it is too much so for comfort. On one terrace after the other you find delightful tubs suitable for bathing; we should have bathed in them, but had been told to wait for the Pink Terraces, on the other side of the lake, where the baths are finer. There is just enough softness to the surface formed by the silica to make it pleasant to the touch and entirely safe to walk on without danger of slipping.

"Not only are the terraces beautiful, but the ornamentation which has been made by the hand of Nature, busily working here through many centuries, is beautiful in the extreme. The hanging ornaments and cornices at the outer edges of the terraces and on the rims of the baths surpass the work of the most gifted designer or the most vivid

THE WHITE TERRACES, SEEN FROM ABOVE,

imagination. Description by words is out of the question, and I must fall back on the picture which I send with this.

"The boiling lake at the top of the White Terraces is a pool perhaps a hundred feet in diameter, and varying in height from time to time. Curiously enough, it changes with the wind, though why the wind should affect it I am unable to guess. It is boiling, boiling, boiling all the while, though more furiously at some times than at others. The water is a beautiful turquoise blue, and so intense is the blue that it reflects upon the cloud of steam that rises from the lake. In fact, nearly all the hot springs in this region are blue, and the color is perceptible at very slight depths.

"We wanted to spend a whole day here; but time pressed, and we descended to the lake again and crossed to the Pink Terraces. The lake is a tiny one, only a mile in length by half a mile in width.

"The Pink Terraces are smaller and lower than the White Terraces, and the spaces between the pools, or bathing-tubs, are not so finely wrought. The Pink Terraces are really not pink at all, but salmon-colored; the White Terraces have a tint of salmon, but it is less pronounced than in the other. The formation is the same in both, and having described one, it is hardly necessary that I should describe the other. We were eager for the promised bath, and were not long in getting at it. And such a bath!

"We undressed on the rocks a short distance from the foot of the terrace, and then entered one of the pools. The water was tepid, almost too warm for thorough enjoyment, but we did not pay much attention to it. The tub, or pool, was large enough for six or eight persons to bathe in and have plenty of room, and we splashed and played there like dolphins—at least as far as our limited abilities would allow us. What surprised us most was the wonderful smoothness of the rock. It was soft to the foot when we stood upon it, and soft to the hands when we pressed them on the sides of the bath. We dashed our bodies with no light force against the rock, and somehow it seemed to yield, or at all events it did not hurt us. We went from one bath to another, and kept ascending till the warmth was more than we could endure. We sat on the edges of some of these great shell-like baths, and looked down upon the little lake and over to the White Terraces on the other side. It was a remarkable sight, and I certainly never heard of any other bathing-tub where there was so much scenery and so much enjoyment.

"At the top of the Pink Terraces there is a lake similar to the one

THE PINK TERRACES, SEEN FROM BELOW.

that feeds the White Terraces. It is about a quarter of a mile around it, the water in the lake is all the time boiling, and it has the same blue color that I have already mentioned. A cloud of steam rose continually from the surface, and it was only when we got on the windward side of the lake that we could see the water at all, and then only as the wind blew the steam away. All around the lake the rocks were incrusted with sulphur, and the incrustation continued for a good part of the way down the slope.

"We brought away some interesting souvenirs of our visit in the shape of leaves and flowers incrusted with silica, the substance out of which the terraces have been formed. Leaves, flowers, feathers, sticks, any small things placed in the water, become incrusted with the silica in a short time, and are easily preserved by wrapping them in cotton or other soft substances. A bird dropping in the water becomes, as it were, petrified, feathers and all: some of the Maoris who live in the neighborhood have adopted the plan of killing small birds, and after stuffing them with sand or other heavy substance, immersing them in the water long enough to allow the feathers to be incrusted with silica. We have bought some of these petrified birds, and find them very pretty and interesting.

"From the little lake we descended by a small and swift stream to Lake Tarawera, which is about seven miles long by four or five in width. We were in the ordinary canoe of the country, hollowed from the trunk of a tree, and very ticklish to sit in, as you cannot make the least inclination to one side or the other without risk of overturning. The canoe which carried us had eight rowers, so that with ourselves and guide we were twelve in all. The stream connecting the lakes is narrow and crooked, and so swift that it threatened to dash us on the shore and smash things generally; but we got through without accident, and then crossed the lake to the village of Wairoa. On our way we passed near the foot of Mount Tarawera, a truncated cone about two thousand feet high, which is considered sacred by the Maoris. They will neither ascend it nor allow any one else to do so; it is the burial-place of the Arawa tribe of Maoris and the dwelling-place of one of their tutelary gods, and for these double reasons it is held in rigid tabu.

"There's another tabu here, and that is on the ducks and other water-fowl that inhabit the lakes; and as no one is allowed to shoot them, they are in great numbers. The tabu was removed when the Duke of Edinburgh came here, and probably any one who would pay a high price could get it suspended long enough to allow him to satisfy

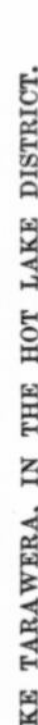

LAKE TARAWERA, IN THE HOT LAKE DISTRICT.

his desires for shooting. But the tabu does not include trapping or netting, and we had roast ducks for dinner and luncheon on payment of a few shillings. There is a grand slaughtering festivity in December of each year, and this is the real reason of enforcing the tabu at other times.

"Sight-seeing places the world over are the cause of great demoralization to the people that live near them, and the Hot Lake district of New Zealand is no exception. The Maoris here are as rapacious as the hackmen at Niagara Falls, the guides and hotel-keepers at Rome, Naples, and hundreds of other places on the Continent, or the custodians of the Taj Mahal at Agra, or the Mammoth Cave of Kentucky. Every step we take has a fee of some kind attached to it, and they have even established a charge of five pounds (twenty-five dollars) for the privilege of taking photographs in the Hot Lake district. Miss Cumming, who wrote "At Home in Fiji" and other interesting books, tells how they

THE TABU REMOVED.

tried to make her pay the photograph fee for taking sketches of the White Terraces and other curiosities during her visit. She resisted on the ground that a sketch was not a photograph; but they refused to listen to her excuses, and threatened to destroy her sketches unless she paid the sum demanded. She managed, however, to smuggle them away by concealing the sketches among some rugs, and leaving the district under the escort of a large party of English tourists.

"Wairoa is a pretty village with some two or three hundred inhabitants, most of them Maoris, and has a church, a school-house, and two

MAORI VILLAGE OF WAIROA, IN THE HOT LAKE DISTRICT.

hotels for the accommodation of tourists. The church and school are less prosperous than they used to be, as the natives are not as zealous in Christianity as when they were first converted. Soon after the Maori war broke out they hanged one of their pastors, and compelled another to flee to avoid the same fate.*

"We were comfortably lodged at one of the hotels, and the next morning took the coach for Tauranga, rejecting the advice of several

---

* Shortly after the visit described above, the famous terraces were destroyed by an eruption of Mount Tarawera. Soon after midnight of June 10, 1886, loud explosions were heard and violent earthquakes felt; in a few minutes Mount Tarawera broke out as an active volcano, hurling ashes, dust, and red-hot stones to a great height, and the whole sky in all directions seemed to be aflame. The ashes, dust, and mud were distributed over a wide area of country, some of the dust and ashes falling fifty miles away. The outbreak of Tarawera was followed almost immediately by a terrific outburst at Lake Rotomahana; the water of the lake, with its clay bed and the material of the Pink and White Terraces, was suddenly blown into the air in the shape of an immense mud-cloud followed by steam and smoke. The mud-cloud in its descent buried the surrounding country to various depths, ranging as high as thirty feet. The native villages of Wairoa and Te Ariki were completely covered, and the village of Mourea was bodily thrown into Lake Tarawera and swallowed out of sight. Over one hundred persons perished, the most of them natives. Mr. Hazard, the master of the native school at Wairoa, and four of his children were among the killed.

It was estimated that fifty square miles of country were covered to a depth of three feet and more by the mud, ashes, and stones, and sixteen hundred square miles more or less affected by the eruption or the deposits from it. Stones weighing half a ton and upwards were found nine miles from the scene of the explosion, and some within a mile or less weighed several tons. The explosions were heard eighty miles away, and are described as resembling heavy guns at sea. They continued about three hours, ceasing before daylight; and the night is well described as a night of terror.

persons who told us we should not fail to see Lake Taupo and Mount Tongariro. The country is desolate, and the most that can be said of it, so far as we could learn, is that it contains larger geysers and hot springs than are to be found around Lake Tarawera. There is a hot river which is fed from boiling springs below it, and Lake Taupo is a pretty sheet of water twenty-five miles long by twenty in width. Tongariro is an active volcano, much larger than Tarawera, and has been ascended by very few people. The ascent is attended with so many difficulties that we did not care to undertake it, and, as we had seen the most interesting part of the volcanic region of New Zealand, we concluded to return.

A MAORI PROPHET IN THE KING COUNTRY.

"The road from Wairoa to Tauranga was rough, but the strong coach endured it without injury, and the team of six horses carried us along at a good pace. Tauranga has a melancholy history, as it was the scene of severe fighting in the Maori war. About four miles from the town is the celebrated Gate Pah, which was built by the Maoris as a defiance to the English, who had a fort at Tauranga. It was a fortification of double palisades such as the Maoris usually make, the inner line of palisades being much stronger than the outer one. Inside the inner line there is a ditch where the men can stand, with the earth breast-high in front of them; and they aim their guns through loop-holes notched in the logs of the palisades. The outer fence is expected to delay the assailants sufficiently long to enable the defenders to shoot them down. A Maori fort is constructed with much more military skill than one would expect of a people without any training in engineering work.

"An English officer says that the salients, angles, ditches, and parapets of the Maori pahs greatly astonished the generals who tried to capture them, and often led to disasters. The Tauranga Gate Pah was held by about three hundred Maoris, while the English had about sev-

BRITISH SOLDIERS ATTACKING A MAORI PAH.

enteen hundred men for the attack. They shelled the pah all day with heavy guns, and about 4 P. M. tried to carry it by assault. They got inside the pah, and there the soldiers were taken by panic, and retreated in disorder, leaving the Maoris in possession, though they evacuated the place in the night. The English lost twenty-seven killed and sixty-six wounded, and among the dead there were eleven officers.

"We went through the ruins of the pah, and could not understand how the Maoris were able to stay there in all the rain of shot and shell that was poured in before the assault. There is a monument at Tauranga to commemorate the event, and an English resident showed us the little cemetery where those who fell at the Gate Pah were buried. It is quite close to the sea, and, like English cemeteries generally, is carefully tended and kept in order.

"Perhaps you would like to know something of the Maori war, as we have had occasion to mention it two or three times. Well, there was trouble between the natives and the English a few years after the establishment of the Government at Auckland; it grew out of the imposition of customs duties and the purchase of land, and the natives thought they had not been treated properly. There was a good deal of fighting on a small scale; but after a while peace was established, and it lasted practically for ten or twelve years.

"But in March, 1860, there were fresh troubles, and from the same cause as before, or rather from one of the causes, the sale of land. The Government had bought some land, for which they paid the man who claimed to own it; after he had been paid the tribe claimed it, and because the Government would not pay a second time the tribe declared war. It was joined by other tribes, and in a very short time a considerable number of Maori tribes were in full insurrection against the military authority. Bishop Selwyn and others thought the natives had been unjustly treated, and there was much dissension among the Europeans as to the right and wrong of the matter.

"The war lasted through 1860, and down to March, 1861, when the natives, having been several times defeated, ended the trouble by surrendering. Soon after this the Maoris thought they would have a king of their own, and representatives of some of the tribes assembled and proclaimed a native sovereignty. Previously to this they had formed a league which opposed the sale of land to the white strangers, and this league was entered into by a good many tribes. The movement for a king was based on the belief that, as the English had a queen, the Maoris could have a similar ruler, and so in 1862 a king was chosen.

"War broke out again in May, 1863. Troops were sent from Australia and from England, and a vigorous attempt was made to suppress the insurrection. There were many opinions as to the proper policy to pursue, owing to the differences between English and Maori laws and customs, and whatever was done by the Governor or the military authorities was sure to receive severe criticism. Sometimes there were long periods of inaction in which there was much negotiation, which generally amounted to nothing. The Maoris refused to give up their lands or arbitrate the questions in dispute, and seemed determined to defend their homes. They not only repudiated English laws regarding land tenure, but they started a movement for reviving their old practices of paganism, or, rather, setting up a new religion in place of the Christianity which so many of them had adopted.

OUTWORKS OF A MAORI PAH.

"Several tribes joined in this movement, and the new religion spread. It was called the Pai Marire by its adherents, who are known as Hau-Haus, or How-Hows, for the reason that they pronounce that sound in loud tones during their ceremonial worship or when engaged in battle. Some of the tribes killed or drove out their former pastors and Christian teachers, and all among them who refused to adopt the new faith were relentlessly persecuted. On the other hand, many tribes and individual Maoris remained friendly, and materially aided the Government in prosecuting the war.

"The Hau-Haus were subdued in 1866, and the murderers of Rev. Mr. Volkner and other missionaries were captured and executed. Peace came, but it was temporary; hostilities were soon resumed, but the

IN THE HARBOR.

fighting that followed was not of a very serious character. Straggling bands and isolated tribes continued to give trouble, and there was one guerilla warrior, named Te Kooti, who was hunted for years without success.

"The King of the Maoris lived among his own people, and made no trouble as long as he was allowed to remain undisturbed. His territory was known as the King Country, and no Englishman was allowed to enter it except with a special permission from the King or some other Maori authority. Gradually his power melted away, and he is now a very shadowy king indeed. Finding that war was not made upon them, the natives became less and less exclusive regarding the King Country, and in 1883 the chiefs consented to have their lands surveyed, with a view to having the titles determined in the native land-courts. In 1884 the Minister for Public Works passed right through the King Country with the avowed object of selecting a suitable route for a railway; he was not opposed in any manner, but, on the contrary, was respectfully received by the chiefs. A law has been passed which reserves a large area of land for the sole use of the natives, and from present appearances there will be no further trouble with the Maoris.

"There you have the Maori war boiled down. It cost the Government a vast amount of money, caused the shedding of a great deal of blood, led to bitter quarrels between the civil and military authorities, and very often was a matter of much perplexity to the Home Govern-

IN NAPIER FOR HIS HEALTH.

ment of Great Britain; and practically it all came from the determination of two races of people, one native and the other foreign, to possess the rich soil of New Zealand."

From Tauranga our friends went by steamer to Napier, touching on the way at two or three ports of secondary importance. Napier is the chief town in the provincial district of Hawke's Bay, and is prettily situated in a position that in some of its features reminded Fred and Frank of Naples. The harbor is fairly good, but not as deep nor as well sheltered as that of Auckland. Important works are in progress for improving the harbor, and one of the leading citizens with whom our friends conversed assured them that before their words were in print Napier would be ready to accommodate the largest steamers in any of the regular lines between New Zealand and Europe.

Fred learned on inquiry that Napier was the outlet of a large area of grazing country, its exports consisting mainly of wool, frozen and canned meats, hides, and other products of regions whose chief industries were the raising of cattle and sheep. His informant told him that since the railway had reached the forest region they had done a fine business in lumber, and expected the lumber-trade to increase year by year. He further said that while Napier was an excellent place for a man in good health it was attractive to invalids, owing to the mildness of its climate. "It is," said he, "the resort of consumptive and asthmatic patients from various parts of New Zealand, and in time we expect to have them come here from Australia and India. A sanatorium has been established here in charge of our local medical men, and we also," he added, "have a fine cemetery, where anybody who fails to be cured can be sure of a comfortable and quiet place." After this, what more could a town claim in its behalf?

Hotels, churches, public buildings, and all the paraphernalia of a perfect and prosperous town were visible to the eyes of the strangers as they rode or walked through the streets. Manufactories of various kinds were busy, there was a goodly number of ships in port, and altogether Napier had an attractive appearance. That it was in the region of the Maoris was evident by the numbers of the natives on the streets, though they did not seem to be busily employed. While looking at a group of them engaged in rubbing noses with friends they had just met—this is the Maori form of salutation—Frank asked a gentleman to whom he had been introduced if the Maoris around Napier were as industrious as those of Auckland and its neighborhood.

"They are not," said the gentleman; "at least, such is my impression. The Maoris here were friendly during the war times, and consequently were allowed to retain their lands, those of the hostile tribes having been confiscated. There are about four thousand Maoris in the Hawke's Bay district, and they own large tracts of fertile lands. Some of them have farms which they cultivate, but the greater part of them prefer to lease their lands to European settlers and live in laziness on the rentals they receive. They are as a rule improvident, and show little desire to improve their condition, though the Government maintains native schools among them at its own expense.

"This district," he continued, "is much more pastoral than agricultural, and we think it is the best part of New Zealand for sheep and cattle. I wish you could be here at the time of our annual fair, so that you could see for yourself what we produce. The show of sheep is excellent, and the merinos, Lincolns, and Cotswolds exhibited cannot be excelled anywhere in the whole colony. Our horses are certainly good, and at the last show there was not an inferior animal in the cattle-pens. One class of eight heifers was so good that the judges commended all that did not take prizes. Then we had ploughs, horse-rakes, grain-sowers, wagons, pleasure carriages, and other things, all made in our own factories, together with jewellery and silver and gold work from New Zealand metals, various manufactured articles, such as farina, starch, glucose, and other products from the growth of our fields.

SCENE ON A SHEEP FARM.—OFF TO THE PASTURE.

"And here," said the gentleman, as he took up a curious lump that resembled a dried and shrivelled mushroom, "here is something that will puzzle you."

The youths looked wonderingly at it, and confessed their ignorance as to its character.

FARM SCENES IN THE OPEN COUNTRY.

"I thought it would be new to you," their informant continued. "It is a fungus that grows in considerable quantities on the decaying forest trees; it is sent exclusively to China, where it is highly prized both as a medicine and an article of food, and it is said to be the base of a valuable dye. The export of this fungus began about 1870 or '71; in 1873 we sent about ten thousand dollars' worth of it to China, and ten years later nearly ten times as much. There is an abundance of it, and as fast as one crop is taken from a log a new one starts; so that there seems to be no reasonable limit to the business which may grow out of it."

Frank asked if the stuff was good to eat.

"I never heard of any one trying to eat it here," was the reply, "except a Chinaman. No European would venture to put it into his mouth, but that's no reason why we shouldn't send it to China for consumption."

Doctor Bronson and his young friends remained a day at Napier, and then proceeded by railway, coach, and railway again to Wellington, the capital of the colony. Napier is distant from Auckland by sea about three hundred and seventy miles, and two hundred from Wellington. The railway carried them southward to Tahoraiti, a distance of eighty-three miles, where they took the coach for a ride of forty miles to Mauriceville. There they found the railway to carry them to Wellington, another ride of eighty-three miles. They were told that within a year or two the gap would be completed, and the whole distance between Napier and Wellington could then be made by train between sunrise and sunset.

The first part of the ride was through a broken country, and the flocks of sheep and herds of cattle scattered on the hills supported the statement of their Napier acquaintance that the country was an excellent one for grazing. After leaving the grazing country they entered a forest region, where there seemed to be an inexhaustible supply of lumber; and farther south they came to a comparatively level and open territory, admirably suited to farms. The whole region was sparsely settled, but is said to be rapidly filling up. Rabbits are numerous, and our friends were told that the Government and settlers had expended a great deal of money to get rid of them; but in spite of all efforts they are on the increase, and have already rendered worthless large areas of good pasture land.

We will have more to say of the rabbit pest in another place. For the present we will land our travellers at Wellington, and send them to one of its many hotels.

CHAPTER XI.

ADVANTAGES OF WELLINGTON AS THE CAPITAL.—ITS INDUSTRIES AND PROSPERITY.—A CITY OF EARTHQUAKES.—ITS PUBLIC BUILDINGS.—THE COLONIAL GOVERNMENT.—HOW THE COLONY IS RULED.—THE COLONIAL PARLIAMENT.—MAORIS AS OFFICE-HOLDERS.—A WALK IN THE BOTANICAL GARDENS.—DIVISION OF THE ISLANDS INTO COUNTIES AND DISTRICTS.—NO CONNECTION BETWEEN CHURCH AND STATE.—RELATIVE STRENGTH OF RELIGIOUS BODIES.—EDUCATIONAL FACILITIES.—THE COLONIAL DEBT: ITS ENORMOUS FIGURES.—OVERLAND TO NEW PLYMOUTH.—ALONG THE SEA-SHORE.—MAKING IRON FROM SEA-SAND.—RIDING THROUGH THE BUSH.—NELSON AND PICTON.—THE WAIRAU MASSACRE.—TO PORT LYTTELTON AND CHRISTCHURCH.—AN ENGLISH MODEL COLONY.—THE CANTERBURY DISTRICT.—THE "SERVANT-GIRL" QUESTION.

"YOU have only to look at the map to understand why the capital was removed from Auckland to Wellington," said Doctor Bronson to Frank and Fred as they were journeying towards the latter city.

ON THE COAST NEAR WELLINGTON.

"Its position is a central one, while Auckland is far to the north. There may have been other reasons for the change, but the geographical one is certainly apparent to everybody."

"Yes," answered Frank, as he studied the map, "and see what a fine harbor it has in addition to its position. Here it is at the head of a bay which ought to be a shelter from all the storms that blow."

"It is the safest and most commodious harbor in New Zealand," remarked a gentleman who had joined them in conversation, while the train was rolling through the forest and undulating land that lies to the north of the city. "The bay is six miles long by the same in width. It was originally named Port Nicholson, and is still called so on many of the maps. The first settlement of the New Zealand Company was made here in 1839, a year before Captain Hobson started the government at Auckland. You are probably aware that the Government was not friendly to the New Zealand Company and its enterprises at that time, and consequently Captain Hobson, the first governor, went elsewhere to establish his authority and found his capital city.

JUST DOWN FROM THE INTERIOR.

"Commercially, Wellington has a good future before it, and already it is in a condition of prosperity. It has a population of thirty thousand and more, the country behind it is excellent for farming and grazing, and our position on Cook Strait, which separates North and South Islands, is the very best we could have. You will see for yourselves that we have a good many industries, and nearly all of them are profitable ones."

In answer to a question by one of the youths, the gentleman enumerated tanneries, candle and soap factories, founderies, boot factories, coach and carriage shops, breweries, planing and other mills; in fact, all the establishments that might properly belong to a growing city. "Besides these," said he, "we have meat-preserving works, and steamers leave regularly, carrying our frozen and canned meats for consumption in the Old World. We have several clubs, half a dozen banks, wharves and dry docks for shipping, three daily papers, and several weeklies and monthlies; and as for public institutions, in the way of hospitals, asylums, and the like, you cannot name one that we are without."

In their walks and rides about Wellington our friends verified the correctness of the foregoing statement in all its essential features. They saw the factories, founderies, shops, and other industrial establishments the gentleman had mentioned; they called at one of the banks to obtain money on their letters of credit; they visited one of the newspaper offices, and saw the press turning out the huge sheets which are the glory of Wellington and the admiration of all New Zealand—except where personal or local preferences are otherwise—and the Doctor was made at home at half the clubs before he had been six hours in the place.

"It is an enterprising city," wrote Frank in his journal, after their first round of sight-seeing was ended. "It has a hospital with more than a hundred beds, a lunatic asylum, and a prison, and according to what we hear, all these institutions are well patronized. But what most surprises us are the public buildings, which ought to be sufficient for the wants of the city for many years to come. The Government Building is an immense structure in the Italian style; it covers an area of two acres, and is said to be the largest wooden edifice in the world. Then there are Government House, where the colonial governor lives and exercises the duties of ruler of New Zealand; the Houses of Legislature, which are lighted by electric light, the Provincial Buildings, the Supreme Court Buildings, and the offices of the city and of the provincial district. The telegraph and postal departments are in the largest brick building in the colony; and as for churches, they are, as the auctioneers say in their advertisements, 'too numerous to mention.'

"We have the choice of twenty or more hotels, and if we should want to go to the theatre we have three to choose from, though the number is just now reduced to two, as one is closed for repairs. They showed us the College, which has about one hundred and fifty students, who come mostly from Wellington and its vicinity, though there are representatives of every district in the colony. The streets are well paved and lighted with gas; they have street railways by which you can go quickly to all the principal suburbs; and if you prefer to ride by yourself, there are as many cabs as you could wish for.

"We have visited the colonial museum, where we saw much to interest us, particularly in regard to the Maoris. There is a fine collec-

MOUNTAIN AND LAKE IN NEW ZEALAND.

tion of Maori weapons and articles of manufacture, and one might almost make up a history of this interesting people by studying the Maori department of the museum. Of course they have a skeleton of the gigantic Dinornis, or Moa, which we have already described; and there is a beautiful display of the birds of New Zealand, which has been arranged by a skilled ornithologist.

JUST ARRIVED FROM ENGLAND.

"From the museum we went to the Botanical Gardens, which cover an area of perhaps a hundred acres and are finely laid out. They are a favorite resort of the public, and here in the early evening we had an opportunity to see of what a curious mixture the population of a New Zealand city is made up. There were men and women from all parts of the United Kingdom; Yorkshiremen jostled against Londoners, a Dubliner against a representative of Glasgow, and a Welshman against one who first saw the light at Dover or Brighton. English, Scotch, Irish, Catholic, Protestant, Gentile, and Israelite all met harmoniously, and if they brought to this country any of their old quarrels of race or religion they forgot them all, at least while in the Gardens.

"But if the assemblage at the Botanical Gardens was interesting, so was the collection of trees and ferns. The Botanical Gardens are rich in these things, and will be richer as the years go on. Not far from the Gardens is a specimen of the New Zealand forest; we saw it at various points along the railway, but did not try to walk through it, as we did here. Unless a path is previously cut it is absolutely impervious, so closely woven are the vines that interlace between the trees and climb to their very tops.

"It is this impenetrability of the forest that gave the Maoris such an advantage during the war, as it was impossible for the English troops to follow them half a dozen yards into the 'bush.' When Wellington was first settled, and down to a few years ago, the hills around the town were covered with this kind of forest. Most of it has been cut down now, partly for the sake of the wood, and more particularly for the purpose of clearing the ground and making it available for agriculture or building.

A PROMENADER.

"As we are in the capital of New Zealand, this is a good place to study the government of the colony.

"Well, then, New Zealand is an English colony, with a governor appointed by the Queen, and acting in accordance with the principles of responsible government. Legislative power is vested in the Governor and two chambers. One of these chambers is called the Legislative Council, and consists of fifty-four members nominated by the Governor for life; the other is called the House of Representatives, elected by the people for three years, and consisting at present of ninety-four members.

"Down to 1876 each of the nine provinces of the colony had an elective superintendent and a provincial council; in that year the provincial form of government was abolished, and the colony was divided into counties and road-board districts, and the local administration is now managed by the county councils and municipalities. The colonial legislature meets once a year, and has power generally to make laws for the government of New Zealand. The acts of the legislature may be disallowed by the Queen, and in some cases they require her assent, but the royal prerogative is very rarely exercised.

"Voters must be twenty-one years of age, either born or naturalized British subjects, and must have resided one year in the colony and six months in the electoral district. Every male Maori of the same age whose name is on a rate-payer's roll, or who has a freehold estate of the value

HOME OF A PROSPEROUS RESIDENT.

of twenty-five pounds, may also be enrolled as a voter. There are four Maori members of the House of Representatives, elected under a special law by the Maoris alone. Legislation concerning the sale and disposal of the public lands and the occupation of the gold-fields is exclusively vested in the colonial parliament. In general it may be said that the parliament and the county and local boards have the management of public affairs, just as the parliament of England and the local authorities there conduct the affairs of the nation at home.

"There is no connection between Church and State, otherwise than in all ministers being registered once a year, in order that they may legally perform the marriage ceremony. At the last reports there were 638 registered ministers, belonging to the following denominations: Church of England, 235; Presbyterian Church of New Zealand, 81; Roman Catholic, 86; Presbyterian Church of Otago and Southland, 57; Methodists, 95; Congregational Independent, 19; Baptist, 17; and ten other bodies with from one to seventeen ministers each. The Episcopalians of various kinds have over 200,000 adherents; the Presbyterians, 113,000; the Methodists, 50,000; and Catholics, 70,000.

"The whole country is divided into school districts for educational purposes; the education is secular and free, the common branches being taught on the same basis as in the schools of most of the United States. There are high-schools and academies in the cities and larger towns; there are colleges and universities in the principal cities, and there is the University of New Zealand, which is an examining body only, and has the power to confer the same degrees as the Universities of Oxford and Cambridge. All things considered, the educational system of the

SEWING-CLASS IN AN INDUSTRIAL SCHOOL.

colony seems to be an excellent one, and the people deserve credit for the attention they have given to it.

"We were invited to visit some of the schools in Auckland, and also in Napier and Wellington, and while travelling through the country we have had glimpses of some of the smaller schools. It was very much like visiting similar establishments in New England or New York, the branches of study as well as the form of instruction being practically the same. They tell us there are more than eleven hundred schools of all kinds in the colony, and nearly one hundred thousand scholars attending them. Seventy-three per cent. of the male, and sixty-eight per cent. of the female, population can read and write, and about five per cent. can read only. In the coming generation the proportion will be much greater.

"In another respect New Zealand resembles England in having an enormous public debt in proportion to her population. According to the published figures the debt amounts to £35,000,000, or $175,000,000, which is very nearly $350 for each inhabitant of the colony. The interest charge on this debt is about $13 annually for each inhabitant, so that the tax for this purpose alone is by no means light. And yet the colony seems quite unconcerned about it, and the authorities generally seem to think that there will be no trouble whatever in paying the interest promptly, and also in wiping out the principal in course of time. A sinking fund has been established for the reduction of the debt, and at the last report it exceeded $15,000,000.

"The money has been expended in various public works, especially in the construction of railways, of which there are nearly two thousand miles in both islands, South Island having the greater number. There are a few private lines, principally for the use of coal-mining companies, and not amounting in all to twenty miles; all the others are the property of the Government, and are operated on its account. The profit of operating the railways is about two per cent. of their cost; but the lines are greatly benefiting the country in aiding its development, and will doubtless pay much better before many years.

"There, I'm afraid I've given you a large dose of figures; but if you don't like them you can skip. They were interesting to Fred and myself, and therefore I thought others might like to see them. Population, railways, education, and public debt are interesting studies when they concern a country which has been colonized only since 1840, and is literally on the other side of the world from England and the United States."

While Frank was occupied with the foregoing story Fred was making further investigations about Wellington. One of his first queries was about the use of wood in the construction of so many of the public buildings, and nearly all the private residences.

RESIDENCE OF THE GOVERNOR, WELLINGTON.

He learned, in response to his interrogatories, that Wellington has suffered at different dates from earthquakes; and at one time they were so severe and so numerous that it was thought it would be necessary to abandon the site altogether. Buildings of wood endure earthquakes much better than do those of stone or brick; and then, too, wood is a cheaper material. All through New Zealand the proportion of wooden buildings to stone, concrete, or brick is very large, and it is larger in Wellington than in any other city.

Many of the buildings stand on ground reclaimed from the sea, and the work of reclamation is still going on. High hills come down close to the original shore, and while they are good enough as the sites of residences, they are unsuited to the requirements of commerce, which prefers level ground. Wellington is the centre of a considerable steamship business; the lines from Sydney and Melbourne centre there; it is the port of the lines running between England and the colony, and all the coasting lines include it in their itinerary.

A pressing invitation was given to our friends to visit New Plymouth, the principal town of the provincial district of Taranaki north of the provincial district of Wellington. They at first declined, but afterwards accepted when they found that their time and engagements would permit their doing so. The journey was by coach seventy miles to Foxton, and thence by rail one hundred and ninety miles to New Plymouth. A railway is in course of construction between Wellington and Foxton, and is completed for a short distance from Wellington. The coach-ride was more interesting than coach-rides usually are, and is thus described by Fred:

"The weather was delightful, and we had seats on the outside of the coach, so that our view of the scenery was unobstructed. For the first few miles the road follows the shore of the bay; then it turns into a pretty valley, which was once heavily wooded but is now cleared, and no doubt deprived of much of its former beauty. We crossed the ridge which separates the harbor of Wellington from the ocean on the west coast, and after winding among a series of hills found ourselves rolling along close to the shore of the ever restless Pacific.—[N.B. No joke is intended in the juxtaposition of the last three words of the foregoing sentence.]

"The villages we saw had native and foreign names strangely mingled. One village was Johnsonville, and the next was Porirua; one was Horokiwi, and another close to it was Smithtown, or something of the sort. We wound through the Horokiwi valley, ascending steadily, and suddenly reached the summit of a hill, which gave us a magnificent view. To the north was a great plain, which seemed almost as limitless as the ocean that filled the western horizon, and lay far below us at the base of an almost precipitous hill. Rising out of the sea was the island of Kapiti, its summit nearly two thousand feet high, and forming a striking feature in the picture before us.

"The driver called attention to something that resembled a white cloud on the horizon to the north-west, and told us it was Mount Egmont, nearly a hundred and fifty miles distant, and which we should see very closely as we approached New Plymouth. We used our eyes every minute of the time the horses were taking breath, and then started down a steep hill-side to the sea again.

DOWN THE SLOPE.

"As soon as we reached the sea we turned along the beach, and followed it for forty miles till we drew up in Foxton. In a year or two the railway from Wellington will be completed to Palmerston, where it will connect with the Foxton-New Plymouth line; when this happens it is probable that the old stage-road will be abandoned, and travellers deprived of a very interesting ride.

"Foxton is a flourishing little place, with perhaps a thousand inhabitants, on the bank of the Manawatu River, four miles from its mouth. We saw numerous fields of flax in the vicinity, and were told that flax was an important article of export. We had little time to look around, as our coach connected with the train, and in less than half an hour we were rolling up the valley of the Manawatu, which the railway follows for some distance.

"Ten miles out of Foxton we entered the forest, or 'bush,' as they call it here, though much of it has been cleared away. Lumber is an important product; we saw a goodly number of saw-mills at work, and met freight-trains laden with lumber on its way to the seaport. The gentleman who accompanied us pointed out some villages which he said

LOGGING IN "THE BUSH."

were settled by Scandinavians, who had proved themselves the very best of colonists.

"From bush to open country and from open country to bush our train went on, stopping occasionally at stations with little villages grouped around them, but very often with no other buildings visible than those belonging to the railway. Our host explained to us that the railway was built to develop the country, and for the greater part of the route it was in advance of civilization and settlement. 'I think,' said he, 'you have built a great many miles of railway in the United States in the same way, and in doing so your stations have been practically in the wilderness until settlements sprang up around them. Railways in New Zealand have done a great deal for the development of the country, and will do a great deal more as time goes on. They give the settlers the communication they want with the markets, and without such communication they cannot get along.'

"The passengers that boarded or left the train at the stations were principally settlers on the agricultural lands, laborers on farms or in

SETTLERS' CABINS IN THE OPEN COUNTRY.

saw-mills, wood-choppers going to their work or leaving it for a visit to one of the towns, merchants and travelling agents of various kinds, and occasional natives. The Maoris have not been slow to perceive the advantages of the railway; at first they were disinclined to travel by it, through fear of evil consequences; but their prejudice is steadily diminishing.

"Doctor Bronson says prejudice against railways is not confined to savages, as he has known fairly intelligent men in New England and other parts of the United States resolutely refuse to trust themselves inside a railway-carriage under any circumstances. Our host tells us that the Maoris were once under the impression that the Englishmen had a demon of some kind chained in the locomotive and compelled to move it by turning a crank. Their more intelligent men have learned the power of steam and explained it as far as possible to the rest, so that the demon theory exists no longer.

"We left behind us the provincial district of Wellington, and entered that of Taranaki. The district takes its name from the Taranaki mountain, which has been called Egmont by the English, and is so known on the maps. Mount Egmont is a cone eight thousand three hundred feet high, and volcanic. We wanted to ascend it, but had not the time to do so, and consoled ourselves with the reflection that we were saved from a great deal of fatiguing work. It is no easy matter to ascend this mountain; those who have undertaken it have never shown any anxiety to repeat the journey. The mountain lies close to the sea, as you will observe by a glance at the map, and serves as a magnificent landmark for sailors approaching this part of the coast.

"New Plymouth has a population of some four thousand or more, and is the port of a section of country which is said to be very fertile, as it can grow nearly every English fruit and cereal. It was settled in 1841, but suffered much during the Maori wars, as most of the natives in the district of Taranaki were hostile. They showed us several factories, saw-mills, and a large flouring-mill, and they called our attention to an establishment for making iron from the sands of the sea-shore.

"All along this coast of North Island there is a large quantity of iron in the sand, sometimes as high as seventy per cent. The people call it steel, but it is really iron; it is in fine particles, just like the iron-sands of the southern shore of Long Island, near New York. They said the iron-works at New Plymouth had never been prosperous, as they could not get the proper flux for the metal; if they could only do this their success would be enormous. Doctor Bronson told them that exactly the same thing had been tried near New York for utilizing the black sand of Long Island, and thus far it had been a failure. The large proportion of iron in the sand is noticeable, not only to the eye

MOUNT EGMONT AND RANGES.

but to the sense of touch; as you pick up a handful its unusual weight at once calls attention to it.

"We visited a farm near New Plymouth, where we spent a night and a day listening to stories of the troublous times of the Maori war, riding or walking through finely tilled fields, and looking at herds of cattle and flocks of sheep which were well calculated to excite the admiration of all who are interested in grazing or agricultural pursuits.

"One gentleman whom we met was an old settler who had fought the Maoris, and had twice seen his farm devastated and his fields ploughed up to destroy the growing crops. On the road near his farm a party of Europeans was waylaid and murdered one day by the Maoris, and it was only an accident which prevented his being one of the party. As long as the troubles with the Maoris continued the district of Taranaki was in a precarious state, as the lands could not be occupied; but with the establishment of peace there was every reason to believe their settlement would be a matter of steady progress.

"We returned to New Plymouth in time to take the semi-weekly coasting steamer for Wellington, where we stopped a few hours and then continued across Cook Strait to Nelson and Picton, taking steamer at the latter place for Port Lyttelton, on the east coast. The route is an interesting one, as the steamer is for most of the time close to the coast, which is bold and rugged and contains many little bays that remind us of the fiords of Norway or the inlets on the coast of Newfoundland or New Brunswick.

"Nelson is on a landlocked bay which is rather difficult of entrance, but forms a perfect anchorage for a ship that once gets inside. Picton has a situation very much like that of Nelson, and each is the centre of a farming and sheep-raising region. They had a great deal of trouble with the Maoris in the war times, and one of the sights of Picton is a hill a few miles from the town, which was the scene of the so-called Wairau massacre. Thirteen settlers were killed there in a fight with the natives, and after the affair was over nine other settlers who had been taken prisoners were murdered in cold blood."

At Port Lyttelton our friends left the steamer and proceeded to Christchurch, which is reached by a railway eight miles long, and largely tunnelled through the hills, one tunnel being nearly two miles in length. Before the days of the railway the means of communication was along a wagon-road which was known as the Zigzag, and occasionally at present the road is patronized by those who dislike railway travel or seek the picturesque. Lyttelton has a good harbor, which is principally due to the expenditure of a large amount of money for the construction of a breakwater and other purposes, and the place is picturesquely situated at the head of a bay.

Christchurch owes its existence to a movement in England, near the end of the first half of the century, for establishing a thoroughly English colony in New Zealand. Its projectors proposed to retain everything that was best in English life, government, habits, manners, and

HOME SCENE AT CHRISTCHURCH.

above all the Church of England. The direction of the colony was to be in the hands of the Canterbury Association at home, rather than in the control of the Government, though there was no intention of taking a position hostile to it.

One of the founders of the Canterbury colony had been instrumental in establishing a Scotch colony in another part of New Zealand, and being Scotch, it was naturally Presbyterian. There is a story about him that he once projected an Anglo-Hebrew colony, where the Hebrews should govern themselves according to their own laws, and have no Christians living among them. He proposed this to a wealthy

HARVEST-TIME IN CANTERBURY.

Israelite, and hoped the scheme would be received favorably. The gentleman listened patiently to his proposition, and then said, "I do not see how my people can thrive in such a community; most of them live by trade, and will want to be where there's somebody to trade with." The plan of the new colony was rejected at once.

The British Government gave the Canterbury scheme all the privileges it desired, except that of perfect self-government, which, of course, could not be permitted. Canterbury was established as a province of New Zealand, with Christchurch as its capital, and altogether it has been prosperous. Christchurch is quite English in appearance and surroundings, and boasts a cathedral (which is not yet finished); and it has a fine array of public buildings, several churches of the Church of England, and others of the Baptist, Catholic, Presbyterian, Methodist, and other faiths. The design of the founders of the Canterbury colony has not been strictly carried out, but on the whole has been quite successful. There is an excellent museum, which is especially rich in New Zealand matters; and there are parks, gardens, cricket-grounds, and other places of amusement and exercise. With its suburbs it has a population of nearly thirty thousand, and therefore is entitled to dignified respect as a city.

"It would not have been difficult for us to imagine ourselves in England," said Frank in his journal, after describing their arrival at Christchurch. "Here are English shade-trees along the streets, and in the gardens and parks; the houses are English in their mode of construction and furnishing, and the little river that runs through the town is called the Avon. There are tram-ways, or horse railways, along the broad and well-made streets, the lawns are velvety with English grasses, and along the banks of the winding river the weeping-willow droops almost to the surface of the water.

"We have been riding in all directions and in the suburbs, and everywhere we have seen signs of prosperity and comfort. As we went out on the principal road we were very soon in the midst of some fine farms, and were not at all surprised to learn that the country around Christchurch is very fertile and well adapted to farming. The fields have English grasses, and are surrounded by English hedges; and many of the farms looked for all the world as though they had been picked up in England and dropped down here. The city has its watering-place at Sumner, nine miles away, and there the inhabitants go to get rid of the summer's heat as New Yorkers go to Coney Island or Long Branch.

"A gentleman to whom we had letters of introduction invited us to dine at his house the day we arrived, but an hour before the time for us to start he came to the hotel and evidently had something serious on his mind. After a few preliminary words he came straight to the point, and said he was obliged to ask us to consider the engagement 'off' for the present.

"'The fact is,' said he, 'my wife's cook has just left to get married, and our other girl left last week, and we've not been able to fill her place. There's nobody in the house to cook the dinner; my wife can take care of the household, but we would hardly like to try to entertain visitors under such circumstances.'

"Of course we excused him, and tried to make his mortification as slight as possible. The incident led to a conversation about the 'servant question,' which has troublesome features in many other countries as well as in New Zealand.

"The gentleman who wanted to be our host, but just then couldn't, told us that there was a great scarcity of house-servants in the colony, and he thought Christchurch was a little worse off than any other city, though he was not at all sure about it. Very often it is impossible to get maid-servants at any price, and those that can be obtained demand high wages, and are independent to a degree that would not be tolerated in England. A discharge has no terrors for a cook or house-maid who knows that a dozen places are open to her; and when she consents to take a place she can be sure of four dollars a week and her board, with at least two evenings out in a week, and sometimes three. Many of the well-to-do colonists had tried the experiment of importing maid-servants from England, but found the speculation a bad one, as the girls generally left service in a few months to get married. Their passage had been paid to New Zealand, and with matrimony in view, they laughed at any idea of working out the time for which they had agreed.

MAID-SERVANT OFF DUTY.

"He further told us that in many houses the mistress was obliged to do all her own work with the aid of her daughters, if she had any; and this, too, where they were perfectly willing and able to hire servants.

"Doctor Bronson told him the story of the man in San Francisco who was trying to hire a maid-servant that declined the situation on account of his three children. 'I will not go into a family where there is more than one child,' was her ultimatum. Whereupon the gentleman said, 'We can easily fix that, I think.'

"'How so?' she asked.

"'I'll speak to my wife about it, and rather than lose the chance of engaging you, I've no doubt she would be willing to drown two of them.'

"Our New Zealand friend laughed heartily over the story, and before he left us he had evidently forgotten his annoyance at the circumstance that brought him to the hotel. He added that the story would not be inappropriate to Christchurch, but he feared all his neighbors would not appreciate the joke.

"All along this part of the coast water is obtained by artesian wells at about eighty feet from the surface. Christchurch has hundreds of such wells, and the supply of water never fails; they reminded us of the wells in the sands of Long Island, and along the Atlantic coast of the United States all the way to Florida."

GARDENING IN THE PARK.

CHAPTER XII.

CHARACTERISTICS OF THE CANTERBURY DISTRICT.—VISIT TO A SHEEP-STATION.—HOW THE SHEEP-BUSINESS IS CONDUCTED.—THE AGRICULTURAL COLLEGE.—IRRIGATION IN NEW ZEALAND.—SHEEP LOST IN SNOW-STORMS.—THE SHEEP-RAISER'S ENEMIES.—DESTRUCTION CAUSED BY PARROTS.—THE RABBIT PEST.—HOW RABBITS ARE EXTERMINATED.—VISIT TO A WHEAT-FARM.—WHEAT STATISTICS.—IMPROVED MACHINERY.—THE SPARROW PEST.—TROUBLESOME EXOTICS.—WATER-CRESS, DAISIES, AND SWEETBRIER.—AN INDUSTRIAL SCHOOL.—MOUNT COOK.—FIRST ASCENT.—PERILOUS CLIMBING.—GLACIERS AND LAKES.—THE SOUTHERN ALPS.—DUNEDIN.—OTAGO GOLD-FIELDS.—INVERCARGILL.—LAKE WAKATIPU.—MINING AT QUEENSTOWN.

THE provincial district of Canterbury is both an agricultural and a pastoral country, part of it being well adapted to grain-growing, and the rest to grazing. Its staple productions are grain and wool, and it ships large quantities of both to England and other countries. There are more than 5,000,000 sheep in the district, besides 200,000 cattle and horses; the annual product of wheat is nearly 7,000,000 bushels, and of oats half that amount. Evidently the Canterbury pilgrims did not choose unwisely when they came here to found their Utopia.

UNDER THE SHEARS.

Our friends were invited to visit a sheep-station and wheat-farm in the interior, and at once accepted. Mr. Abbott, the gentleman who gave the invitation, explained to them that the

A SHEEP-SHEARING SHED IN NEW ZEALAND.

plain of Canterbury, which extended to the foot of the outlying hills of the Southern Alps, was principally devoted to agriculture, while the hilly region was more adapted to sheep-raising. "We will go to the sheep-shearing region first," said he, "and on our return will have a look at a wheat-farm. We will go by railway to Springfield, forty-six miles, and from there the coach will carry us in a few hours to the sheep-station that I wish you to see. Be ready for the train at eight o'clock to-morrow morning."

The party was ready at the time appointed; in fact, it was ready some minutes before the time, in accordance with the promptness which characterized the movements of Doctor Bronson and his nephews. They found the railway-station large and commodious, and arranged after the plan of an English station in a community of much greater extent. "It was built for our future rather than for our present needs," said Mr. Abbott. "In time we hope to require all the space at our command, but just at present there is sometimes a suggestion of loneliness about it."

The country through which the train passed on its way to Springfield bore evidences of careful cultivation, and our friends found it difficult to believe that previous to 1850 this whole region was a wilderness. Certainly the Canterbury pilgrims were not inclined to idleness, and the condition of their fields indicated that they belonged to men of industry and intelligence. As the train moved westward the mountains became more and more distinct, and long before Springfield was reached they filled the whole of the western horizon with their towering peaks.

"We have an agricultural college at Lincoln," said Mr. Abbott, "where our young men can learn practical and scientific agriculture adapted to the colony. It is under the control of the Canterbury College Board of Governors, and has a farm of five hundred acres, and comfortable buildings for the students. Agriculture is taught practically, and we have every reason to expect excellent results from the college in the course of the next few years."

From Springfield a ride of a few hours carried the party to the sheep-station, where they were warmly welcomed. The sun was just setting when they arrived, and it was too late to examine the place and its surroundings. A supper consisting of mutton in cutlets and stew, accompanied by bread baked on hot stones, and washed down with tea, received careful and appreciative attention by the hungry travellers. The sleeping accommodations were limited but comfortable, and in the morning all were out in good season, and ready to consider the sheep-raising question.

Horses were brought, and though somewhat unruly at first, they proved very satisfactory to their riders; at any rate, nobody had any bones broken in the forenoon's ride, though there were some narrow escapes. Accompanied by their host, the party rode over the sheep-run for several miles, visiting the herders in charge of their flocks, and

A FLOCK OF SHEEP AMONG THE HILLS.

studying the peculiarities of the country. Frequently during their ride Mr. Abbott drew rein and called attention to the natural and other advantages or disadvantages of the business, and showed them wherein it differed from sheep-farming in America.

"Here, as everywhere else," said he, "we must make sure of a plentiful supply of water if we want to prosper. Some of the streams run dry at certain seasons of the year, and it is necessary that a man should know before he locates if a stream can be relied upon throughout the year. On some of our runs we have made trenches and brought water for long distances, as it is cheaper to have the water run where we want it than to drive the sheep several miles. There is an abundance of water flowing from the mountains, but it is not properly distributed by nature; therefore we have called science to our aid, and extensive irrigation-works have been made by the local and colonial governments, and in this way thousands upon thousands of sheep-pasturing and agricultural lands that were formerly almost worthless are now valuable. You probably observed some of the irrigating-ditches as we were coming along the railway.

"In the lower hills we do not suffer from snow-storms, but some of the sheep-farmers who have established themselves high up among the mountains have lost heavily from this cause. Sometimes there will be several years without a severe storm, and then will come one that kills off thousands and thousands of sheep in a very few days. This was the case a few years ago, when the losses were very heavy; one flock of more than a thousand sheep was shut up in the mountains, and perished with their herder, who was found dead by their side. Other flocks were buried and died in the snow, but the herders managed to save themselves.

"But the rabbits and parrots are our worst enemies, as you may have heard."

"Yes, I've heard so," replied Frank; "at least I've been told that the rabbits have been terribly destructive of grass, and ruined many thousand acres of pasturage."

"Rabbits were first introduced," said Mr. Abbott, "as a table luxury and to furnish hunting sport; and besides, it was thought they would be handsome ornaments on a place. But very soon it was found that they were a great pest; they increase very rapidly, and as the country was sparsely settled, the settlers were unable to keep them down. Men were hired to trap, shoot, or capture them in some way, and were paid at the rate of twopence for each rabbit-skin; but this plan was not effective, as it was not rapid enough, and after many experiments we took to poisoning the creatures by wholesale."

"How did you do it?"

"By means of grain saturated with phosphorus; we prepare barrels with closely fitting lids, and fill them half full with oats; then we pour boiling water on the oats, and when they are thoroughly soaked and swollen we pour in a quantity of phosphorus, quickly replacing the cover, so that the poisonous fumes cannot escape. This grain scattered over the ground is death to the rabbits, but the disadvantages of the plan are that sheep are often killed by the poisoned grain.

"To give you an idea of the slaughter of rabbits in New Zealand, let me say that ten millions of rabbit-skins are exported every year, but the value of these skins is very little compared with the damage which

SHEEP AND HERDER KILLED IN A SNOW-STORM.

the animals have caused. The latest official reports show that the nuisance is checked in some localities, but there are yet many millions of rabbits to be disposed of. In England and other countries foxes, wolves, weasels, and other noxious animals keep down the number of rabbits, but here, where they have no natural enemies, the country suffers terribly. Many a sheep-farmer has been ruined by the total destruction of his pasturage, and the loss to the colony may be reckoned by millions of dollars.

REDUCING THE RABBIT POPULATION.

"Australia and Tasmania are equally afflicted by rabbits," the gentleman continued, "which were introduced into those countries from New Zealand for the same reasons that they were introduced here. Millions of pounds sterling would not compensate for their ravages, and the public and private expenditure for their destruction has already mounted into those figures. Dogs, ferrets, poison, trapping, drowning, and every other known means have been tried to reduce them, but without success. Occasionally the whole population turns out for a rabbit 'battue,' in which many thousands of the animals are killed. The owners of sheep and cattle runs have built hundreds of miles of rabbit-fences, and the colonial governments have done likewise; the fences stop the progress of the vermin for a time, but after a while they manage to burrow beneath them and come up on the other side, and so the fences are not effective to prevent the spread of the pest."

"Haven't I read about their being killed by forcing noxious gases into their warrens?" one of the boys asked.

"Yes," was the reply, "that has been done, but the machines for making and using the gas are costly and cumbersome, and in rocky regions they do not work satisfactorily.

"Recently the Government of New South Wales has offered a reward of twenty-five thousand pounds to any one who will devise a successful system of destroying rabbits, provided it is not dangerous to live-stock and to human beings. The attention of the scientific world is directed to the subject, and perhaps the remedy may be found. Pasteur, the celebrated French scientist, has proposed to inoculate a few rabbits with chicken-cholera and allow them to run among their kindred, and thus introduce the disease. He says it is harmless to all animals, with the exception of rabbits and chickens, and believes that the whole rabbit population could in this way be killed off, though at the same time our domestic fowls would be killed too, unless they were carefully shut up. We could afford to lose every fowl in the southern hemisphere if we could only get rid of this great pest of rabbits; but it will be necessary to proceed very cautiously, lest our sheep and cattle should suffer."

The youths had a realizing sense of the extent of this pest in the Australasian colonies, when they saw on several occasions whole hill-sides and stretches of plain that seemed to be in motion, so thickly was the ground covered with rabbits. Mr. Abbott further told them that Dunedin and other cities had a regular exchange, or market, for rabbit-skins, where dealings were conducted as in the grain, wool, and other exchanges. The skins mostly find their way to London, Paris, Berlin, Vienna, and Naples, where they are made into "kid" gloves of the lower grades. They are also made into hats, and it is hoped that they may be found useful for other purposes, so as to make profitable the wholesale slaughter of the animals on whose backs they grow.*

---

* A recent writer on this subject says: "On the arid, barren Riverina plains (whereon naturally not even a mouse could exist) there are pastured at present some twenty or twenty-five millions of high-class merino sheep. These sheep are being gradually eaten out by rabbits. The following will serve as an illustration, and it must be borne in mind that it is only one of many which could be adduced.

"On the south bank of the river Murray, consequently in the colony of Victoria, there is a station named Kulkyne, which has about twenty miles frontage to that river. The holding extends far back into arid, naturally worthless, waterless country. On that station, by skilful management and by command of capital, there came to be pastured on it about 110,000 sheep. When I two or three years ago visited that station I found

"How about the parrots?" Fred asked, when the rabbit question was disposed of.

"That is a strange piece of history," replied Mr. Abbott. "When the sheep-farmers first established their stations among the mountains there were flocks of the *kea*, or green parrot, living in the glens and feeding entirely on fruit and leaves. They were beautiful birds, and nobody suspected any harm from them.

"After a time it was observed that many of the sheep, and they were invariably the finest and fattest of the flocks, had sores on their backs, and always in the same place, just over the kidneys. Some of the sores were so slight that the animals recovered, but the most of them died or had to be killed to end their sufferings.

"The cause of these sores was for some time a mystery, but at length a herdsman on one of the high ranges declared his belief that the green parrots were the murderers of the sheep. He was ridiculed and laughed at, but was soon proved to be right, as a parrot was seen perched on the back of a fat sheep and tearing away the flesh.

"Investigation showed that in the severe winters the parrots had come at night to the gallows, where the herdsmen hung the carcasses of slaughtered sheep. They picked off the fat from the mutton, and showed a partiality for that around the kidneys; how they ever connected the carcasses with the living sheep is a subject for the naturalists to puzzle over, and especially how they knew the exact location of the spot where the choicest fat was found in the living animal. It seems that the attacks on the sheep began within a few months after the parrots had first tasted mutton at the meat-gallows."

"Have they done much damage?" one of the youths asked.

"Yes, a great deal," was the reply; "but not so much of late years, as they are being exterminated. One man lost nineteen fine imported sheep out of a flock of twenty, killed by the parrots; and another lost in the same way two hundred in a flock of three hundred. Every flock in the mountains suffers some from this cause, probably not less than two per cent.

"A shilling a head is now paid for keas, and there is a class of men who hunt them for the sake of the reward; but the sagacious birds

---

that the stock depasturing it had shrunk to 1,200 sheep dying in the paddock at the homestead; 110,000 sheep to 1,200 sheep!

"The rabbits had to account for the deficiency. On that station they had eaten up and destroyed all the grass and herbage; they had barked all the edible shrubs and bushes, and had latterly themselves begun to perish in thousands."

that formerly came without fear into the presence of man now keep themselves carefully concealed in the daytime, and only venture out at night. Their depredations have always been made in the night, and hence it was some time before the cause of the wounds on the sheep was known."

PARROTS.

Frank and Fred asked about the profits of the sheep-raising business, but the information they obtained did not encourage them to become sheep-farmers in New Zealand. What with the rabbits and the parrots, with diseases among sheep, fluctuations in wool, the high price of labor, especially at shearing-time, when extra men must be engaged, with a full knowledge of their importance, the profits are not what they were in the early days of the industry.

From the sheep-station they returned to Springfield, and took train again in the direction of Christchurch. At the second or third station from Springfield they were met by a carriage, which took them to the wheat-farm, which was one of the objects of the journey. Time did not permit a lengthened stay here, but it was sufficient to enable them to see a good deal before their departure.

Here is a summary of what they learned about wheat-farming in New Zealand:

"About four hundred thousand acres of ground are utilized for wheat in the different counties of the colony. The farmers expect twenty-five bushels to the acre in most localities, but frequently this figure is exceeded, the average throughout the country for one year being in excess of twenty-six bushels. Consequently, the wheat crop may be set down at ten million bushels, of which by far the greater portion is available for exportation."

A NEW ZEALAND PEST.

Frank made a note here to the effect that half a million acres of land were devoted to raising oats, at an average of thirty-five bushels to the acre. Barley, hay, potatoes, and other things brought the amount of land under crop up to a million and a half acres, while there were five and a half million acres under grasses, including grass-sown land that had not been previously ploughed. The figures were about evenly divided between the two islands. The colony contains about fourteen million sheep, seven hundred thousand cattle, and one hundred and sixty thousand horses.

"Of late years the export of wheat has fallen off, owing to the competition of India and America in the markets of Europe; the wheat-farms of New Zealand are so unprofitable that the owners talk of putting much of their ground into grass, though they will continue the cultivation in order to supply enough for home consumption and to employ the machinery they have on hand.

A STEAM THRESHING-MACHINE.

"The open country of South Island is admirably adapted for wheat, and the soil is so easy to manipulate that double-furrow ploughs are used. The large farms are provided with all the latest improvements in machinery and implements; and we found the intelligent farmers thoroughly familiar with American reapers and mowers, steam threshing-machines, steam wagons, and other things, so that we felt quite at home. They asked us about the wheat-farms of America, and were inclined to shake their heads when we told them of fields so large that a plough could only turn a single furrow around one of them in a day's time.

"'Do you really mean it?' said one of them, with an emphasis of surprise.

"Doctor Bronson assured them of the correctness of the statement, and added that on the Dalrymple farm in Dakota, or rather on one of the Dalrymple farms, there was a single field of thirteen thousand acres. 'That makes,' said he, 'about twenty square miles, and I doubt if you have any team that could plough more than one furrow around such a field in a day.'

"They acknowledged that such was the case, and though they had fields containing hundreds of acres inside a single fence, they had nothing that approached the wheat-fields of Dakota. We were sorry afterwards that we mentioned our enormous wheat-fields, as we thought it set them to thinking of American competition, and the effect it might have on their own business in future; but of course we couldn't resist our national tendency to 'brag' a little.

"Afterwards, when we were visiting a dairy-farm, a matter-of-fact Scotchman who owned the place remarked that he presumed we had much larger dairy-farms in America, as he had heard of one where they had a saw-mill which was propelled by the whey that ran from the cheese-presses, and also a grist-mill operated by buttermilk!

"In the wheat-growing belt of South Island there is a scarcity of timber, the forests being mainly in the hilly and mountain region. The scarcity of timber has led to the planting of forests. Considerable attention is given to this both by the authorities and by individuals, and good results are predicted at no distant day. There is also a scarcity of water, and to meet it irrigation-works have been constructed, as already stated.

"Wheat-farmers are troubled by rabbits, and also by sparrows, which were introduced to kill off caterpillars and other insect pests. The sparrows increased in numbers almost as rapidly as the rabbits; they changed their habits, and from carnivorous taste turned to eating fruits and grains. The New Zealand sparrow shuns the caterpillars and worms he was imported to devour, and feeds on the products of the garden and the field. The same is the case in Australia, where the sparrows are now in countless millions, the descendants of fifty birds that were imported about 1860. The colonial governments have offered rewards for the heads and eggs of the sparrows, and though this has caused an extensive destruction it has not perceptibly diminished their numbers.

ENGLISH SPARROWS AT HOME.

"In an official investigation of the 'sparrow pest,' one man testified that he sowed his peas three times, and each time the sparrows devoured them. Another told how the birds destroyed a ton and a half of grapes, in fact cleared his vineyard, and others said they had been robbed of all the fruit in their gardens."

This is a good place to say something about the exotics that have been introduced into the Australasian colonies. Cattle, horses, sheep, and swine have been of unequivocal benefit, and so has been the stocking of the rivers with trout, carp, and other food fishes of Europe. Larks and a few other song-birds have thus far proved of no trouble, but even they may yet give cause to regret their introduction. In addition to the animal pests already mentioned, the Indian *mina*, or mino-bird, a member of the starling family, has become a great nuisance, almost equal to the sparrow.

We will now turn from the animal to the vegetable exotics.

Wheat, oats, and the other grains are of course in the same beneficial category as the domestic animals. The innocent water-cress, which is such a welcome addition to the breakfast and dinner table, has grown with such luxuriance as to choke the rivers, impede the navigation of those formerly navigable, and cause disastrous floods which have resulted in loss of life and immense destruction of property. In the Otago and Canterbury districts of New Zealand, the Government makes a large expenditure every year to check the growth of this vegetable pest.

The daisy was introduced to give the British settler a reminder of home, and already it has become so wide-spread as to root out valuable grasses. Years ago an enthusiastic Scotchman brought a thistle to Melbourne, and half the Scotchmen in the colony went there to see it. A grand dinner was given in honor of this thistle, and on the following day it was planted with much ceremony in the Public Garden of Melbourne. From that thistle and its immediate descendants the down was carried by the winds all over Victoria, and many thousands of acres of once excellent fields are now covered with tall purple thistles to the exclusion of everything else. Large amounts of money have been expended in the effort to eradicate the thistle, but all in vain.

The common sweetbrier is another vegetable exotic that has become a pest. It was introduced for the sake of its perfume, but has become strong and tenacious, spreading with great rapidity, and forming a dense scrub that utterly ruins pasture-lands. Money has been expended for its destruction, but it refuses to be destroyed.

The English sparrow is the subject of much discussion in the United States, and the opinion seems to be gaining ground that he is a pest to be put out of the way if possible. Those who are inclined to advocate his continued presence under the Stars and Stripes would do well to study his history in the Australasian colonies, where the damage he has caused is practically incalculable.

Our friends returned to Christchurch, and after another day in that city proceeded by railway in the direction of the South Pole. At the earnest solicitation of one of their acquaintances, they stopped a few hours at Burnham, eighteen miles from Christchurch and on the line of railway, to visit the industrial school for children whose parents have neglected to care for them properly. The object is to instruct the children in useful trades and occupations which can afford them an honorable support in later years. The school has extensive buildings and grounds, and has constantly about three hundred children under instruction. Nearly all the ordinary trades are taught there, and the manager said the children generally showed great proficiency in learning what was set for them to do.

"The main line of railway to Dunedin," wrote Frank in his journal, "has several branches which serve as feeders by developing the country through which they pass. Portions of the line are through rolling or hilly country, and there are other portions which stretch across plains resembling the prairies of the western United States. On the western horizon rises the line of snow-clad mountains, again reminding us of railway travelling over our own plains as we approach the range of 'The Rockies.'

"We crossed several fine bridges spanning the rivers Rakaia, Ashburton, Rangitoto, and Waitaki; these rivers flow through wide beds, and though ordinarily of no great volume become tremendous torrents in seasons of floods. In the early days many a traveller came to his death while seeking to ford one of these treacherous streams, and many sad memories are connected with their history.

"As we approached Timaru, one hundred miles from Christchurch, Mount Cook, the highest mountain of New Zealand, was pointed out to

CLASS IN THE INDUSTRIAL SCHOOL.

us. It is 12,349 feet high, and its top is covered with perpetual snow; it is the highest peak of the Southern Alps, which stretch along the west coast of New Zealand for nearly two hundred miles, very much as the Andes lie along the west coast of South America. Fred and I thought we would like to climb Mount Cook, and spoke to Doctor Bronson about it. The Doctor dampened our enthusiasm by saying that it was more difficult of ascent than Mont Blanc, and he was unaware that the feat had been accomplished since Rev. W. S. Green and two Swiss companions reached the top of the mountain in 1883.

"He added that Mr. Green was a member of the famous Alpine

A PERILOUS NIGHT-WATCH.

Club, and had brought the two Swiss mountain-climbers to assist him in making the ascent. They made several attempts before they succeeded, and when they finally reached the summit it was after several narrow escapes from death. They passed one night standing on a narrow ledge of rock, where a single misstep would have hurled them to instant death thousands of feet below. Frequently they toiled for hours up the side of a spur of the mountain, and then found that their labor was lost, as farther ascent was impossible, owing to the steepness of the rock."

"They had all the variety of adventures recorded in the history of Alpine climbing," said a gentleman who was in conversation with Doctor Bronson at the time the query was propounded, "except that of being swept into crevasses or down the slope of the mountain and losing their lives. Mr. Green has published a book, entitled 'The High Alps of New Zealand,' in which you will find a description of the ascent of Mount Cook. After you have read it I don't think you'll want to follow the example of that gentleman, unless you have more than the ordinary enthusiasm about mountain-climbing."

"As we looked at the peak of Mount Cook rising sharply into the sky," Frank continued, "we concluded that a view of the mountain from below would satisfy all our desires. The gentleman roused our curiosity, however, when he told us about the wonderful glaciers that lie on the lower slopes of the great mountain, some of them larger than any of the glaciers of Switzerland. Then on the way he pointed out several lakes that are fed by the glaciers on Mount Cook and other peaks of the Southern Alps just as the lakes of Switzerland and Italy are fed by the glaciers from the Alps of Europe. Some of these lakes are forty or fifty miles long, and of almost unknown depth; indeed, some of them are deeper than the level of the ocean, though their bottoms have been filling up for ages with the débris brought down by the glaciers.

"Look on the map and find Lake Tekapo; it is fifteen miles long and three wide, and is supplied by the great Godley glacier, which lies just above it. The Tasman glacier, eighteen miles long, is the largest in New Zealand, though this statement is disputed by some authorities. At any rate, there are a great many glaciers, and all have not been fully explored. They are on the western as well as on the eastern slope of the mountains; one of them descends from Mount Cook to within seven hundred feet of the sea-level, and for a long distance is bordered by magnificent vegetation in which tree-ferns and fuchsias are conspicuous. In this respect the glacier resembles that of Grisons, in Switzerland,

THE SUMMIT OF MOUNT COOK.

which comes down far below the snow-level, and is bordered with pine forests and almost by cornfields.

"Some of the moraines, or channels, cut by the glaciers are very deep, and most of the lakes lie in what were moraines ages and ages ago, when the ice extended much farther than it does now. Lake Pukaki is a fine example of this; it is shut in by an old terminal moraine which attains a height of one hundred and eighty-six feet above the surface of the lake. On the western side of the Alps there are deep channels which are called 'sounds,' and greatly resemble the fiords of Norway. Some of them are eighteen or twenty miles long, and vary from half a mile to two or three miles in width; their sides rise almost perpendicularly, sometimes for hundreds of feet, and they are nearly all too deep to permit ships to anchor. Sounding-lines a thousand feet long often fail to find bottom there. Perhaps they are called sounds because they can't be sounded.

ATTEMPT TO CLIMB THE EASTERN SPUR.

"These sounds are supposed to be ancient moraines, and during the ice period of the world they were the beds of glaciers coming from immense lakes, encircling the bases of the mountains and covering areas of thousands of miles. Altogether the scenery of the Southern Alps is said to be magnificent."

Doctor Bronson had decided to make no stop on the way until reaching Dunedin, and though earnestly urged to spend a day at Timaru, in order to see the harbor works there, the establishment for freezing meat, the barbed wire factory, and other enterprises, he did not swerve from his resolution. The party reached Dunedin late in the evening, and went to the hotel which had been recommended as one of the best. They had no occasion to complain of it, and in the morning were ready to "do" the sights of the place.

Dunedin has the reputation of being the largest, best built, and most important commercial city of New Zealand; it is the capital of the provincial district of Otago, and the commercial centre of a large area of country. The settlement of Otago was projected in 1846, and it was intended to be exclusively occupied by adherents of the Free Kirk of

Scotland, just as Canterbury at a later date was to be the monopoly of adherents of the Church of England. The colony was not especially prosperous under its exclusive system, though the thrifty settlers had not much to complain of except the scarcity of neighbors.

But gold changed the whole scene, and broke down the barrier which the projectors of the colony had erected. In 1861 rich gold-diggings were discovered about seventy miles from Dunedin; diggers flocked in from Australia and from other parts of the world, and from the beginning of the gold rush Dunedin dates its prosperity.

It has all the characteristics of a thriving city; gas, paved streets, horse-railways, race-course, theatres, schools, academies, churches, colleges, parks, gardens, museum, manufactories, and numerous other urban things and institutions, all are to be found here. There are three daily papers published in Dunedin, and a score of weeklies and monthlies,

RIVER ISSUING FROM A GLACIER.

and there is an excellent library, supported partly by the municipal authorities, and partly by contributions of enterprising citizens. With its immediate suburbs it has a population of fifty thousand, and is steadily increasing year by year. Its Scotch origin is apparent in the faces and accent of the great majority of the residents, and by the statue of the Scottish poet, Burns, which stands protected by a railing in front of the town-hall. Most of the streets are named after those of Edinburgh and Glasgow.

HYDRAULIC MINING.

Our friends spent two days at Dunedin, and so attentive were the gentlemen to whom they brought introductions that there were very few leisure moments. Drives in the city and the suburbs, visits to the manufactories of various kinds, the public buildings, and the harbor, luncheons and dinners at the houses of their friends, kept them as busy as bees. They had hardly a minute to themselves, until they finally shook the dust of Dunedin from their feet, and departed with their faces once more towards the South Pole. Frank and Fred declared that their journals were so far behind that it would be difficult for them to catch up, and they had not taken nearly as many notes of what they saw and heard in Dunedin as they desired.

"I wanted," said Frank, "to make a note of the things they manufacture in Otago, and especially at Dunedin, but the list was so long and time so scarce that I didn't try; but I'll remark particularly that they manufacture a good deal of woollen cloth, leather, cotton, and other fabrics, which is something very unusual for so young a colony. There is more manufacturing here than in any other part of New Zealand, and the Scotch settlers of Otago seem to have brought here the thrift and industry for which their native land is celebrated."

Doctor Bronson asked Fred if he had learned anything about the product of gold in Otago.

"I have the figures right here," was the reply. "From 1861, when the first discoveries were made, down to the end of March, 1884, the Otago gold-fields produced 4,319,544 ounces, which were valued at £17,026,320, or about $85,000,000. Most of the gold has been obtained from alluvial washings of various kinds, such as sluicing, tunnelling, and hydraulic washing; auriferous reefs have been successfully worked in several instances, and unsuccessfully in more. Gold-mining has become a regular industry of the country, and is less subject to fluctuations than in former times. Once in a while a new field is opened, and there is a rush to work it; but the excitement over such discoveries is not like that of the five or ten years following 1861.

"Coal-mining is also an important industry of Otago," continued Fred. "Where formerly a great deal of coal was imported, the impor-

A SQUATTER'S HOME.

tation has dwindled to nothing, and for several years New Zealand has not only produced its own coal, but has a surplus for export. At least that is what one authority says; another says that the exportation consists of coal sent to Australia for gas-making, and that the quantity imported for uses to which New Zealand coal is not adapted exceeds the export by nearly fifty thousand tons."

From Dunedin our friends proceeded by rail again to Invercargill, 139 miles from Dunedin, or 369 from Christchurch. Invercargill is a prosperous town of some eight or ten thousand inhabitants, and is near the southern end of South Island, a sort of jumping-off place, as Frank called it while looking at its location on the map. The real terminus of the island, though not its most southerly point, is The Bluffs, about seventeen miles below Invercargill, which stands on an estuary called New River Harbor.

A MOUNTAIN WATER-FALL.

The morning after their arrival the travelling trio took the train for Kingston, eighty-seven miles, at the southern end of Lake Wakatipu. The train carried them through a fine country of broad plains dotted here and there with tracts of forest. The region appeared to be well settled, as there were little villages scattered at irregular intervals, fields and pastures surrounded by fences, herds of cattle and flocks of sheep, isolated farms, saw-mills, and other evidences of settlement and prosperity. Several branch railways diverge from the main line and open up agricultural, pastoral, mining, lumber, and other districts of much present or prospective value.

"As we approached the lake," said Frank in his journal, "the country became more mountainous and picturesque. The train wound through a long defile, and then came out upon the 'Five Rivers Plains,' which take their name from five streams of water that pass through them. We passed through the Dome Gorge, and at Athol, sixty-nine miles from Invercargill, the conductor told us we were in the lake country. The hills and mountains were everywhere about us, and in the west the great range of the Alps rose into the sky. At Kingston the railway ends, and we stepped on board the steamboat, which carried us the whole length of the lake. The lake is sixty miles long, and reminded us of Lake Lucerne in Switzerland.

"We spent the night at Queenstown, a mining and agricultural town about twenty miles from Kingston, and on the next day completed our journey to the head of the lake. The scenery is magnificent, and I can no more describe it adequately in words than I can tell how a nightingale sings or a mangosteen tastes. All around us are the mountains, the highest peaks covered with perpetual snow that seems to flash back the rays of the sun, before whose heat it refuses to melt. In the distance, higher than all the rest, is Mount Earnslaw; we saw it clearly defined against the sky, but it is very often veiled by the fleecy clouds that sweep around it.

"I am not surprised that the mountains of New Zealand have been called the Southern Alps, for they certainly bear a close resemblance to the Alpine chain of Switzerland; but I do not think any single peaks

SHOTOVER GORGE BRIDGE.

are equal to the Matterhorn or the Jungfrau, though Mount Earnslaw can well be called the peer of Mont Blanc. On the whole, the scenery of the lake is not surpassed by that of any one of the Swiss lakes; and when New Zealand becomes the regular field for tourists there will be a good deal of travel to Lake Wakatipu. Most of the residents shorten the name of the lake to Wakatip.

"We were urged to stop at Queenstown and see the mining operations in the neighborhood, but time did not permit us to do so, and we returned to Invercargill as quickly as the railway and steamboat could carry us. Queenstown is one of the mining centres of the Otago gold-fields, which we have already mentioned, and has had the usual ups and downs of mining life. The Otago mines cover a wide extent of country, and as much of the region in which they lie is agricultural, living is cheaper here than in most other mining regions.

"A good many Chinese are engaged in mining in the New Zealand gold-fields, and we were told that in one place—Orepuki—there was a mining population of four hundred Chinese that subscribed £100 ($500) towards building a Presbyterian church, the total cost being less than a thousand dollars. And yet I presume there are white men in Orepuki who would call one of their Mongolian neighbors a 'heathen Chinee!' Near Dunedin and other places, as well as in the neighborhood of most of the Australian cities, the market-gardening is largely managed by the Chinese. They seem to have almost a monopoly of this business, and we were told that no European could successfully compete with them when they went at it in earnest."

ON THE SHORE OF THE LAKE.

CHAPTER XIII.

FROM NEW ZEALAND TO AUSTRALIA.—ARRIVAL AT SYDNEY.—HOW THE CITY WAS FOUNDED.—ITS APPEARANCE TO-DAY.—THE PRINCIPAL STREETS, PARKS, AND SUBURBS.—PUBLIC BUILDINGS.—SHOOTING SYDNEY DUCKS.—THE TRANSPORTATION SYSTEM.—HOW AUSTRALIA WAS COLONIZED.—LIFE AND TREATMENT OF CONVICTS IN AUSTRALIA.—THE END OF TRANSPORTATION.—POPULAR ERRORS OF INVOLUNTARY EMIGRANTS.—THE PAPER COMPASS.—TICKET-OF-LEAVE MEN.—EMANCIPISTS AND THEIR STATUS.—SYDNEY HARBOR.—STEAM LINES TO ALL PARTS OF THE WORLD.—CIRCULAR QUAY.—DRY-DOCKS.—EXCURSIONS TO PARAMATTA AND BOTANY BAY.—HOSPITALITIES OF SYDNEY.

STEAMERS of the Union Steamship Company run weekly between the principal ports of New Zealand and the Australian ports of Sydney and Melbourne. The Melbourne steamers usually come from that

BOUND FOR SYDNEY.

city direct to "The Bluffs," the port of Invercargill, or to Hokitika, and then make the circuit of South Island; while the steamers from Sydney run to Auckland, and make the circuit of North Island, both lines touching at Wellington as a common and central port. Our friends

ENTRANCE TO PORT JACKSON.

were fortunate in finding at The Bluffs a steamer which was going direct to Sydney, and in less than six hours after their return from Lake Wakatipu they were afloat and away for their destination, about fourteen hundred miles distant. Six days later the coast of New South Wales was in sight, and they entered the Australian continent through the famous Sydney Heads.

All the way across from New Zealand they had been listening to the praises of the beauty and advantages of Sydney Harbor, which were sounded by some of their fellow-passengers who lived in the capital of New South Wales. "I doubt if you ever saw anything that approaches it," said one; "not even the famous Bays of Lisbon, Rio Janeiro, and New York can compare with it—so everybody says who has seen them all. The navies of all the world could anchor there, and I wish they would come some time in a peaceful way and do so. It would bring a lot of business to Sydney, and send up the price of naval stores and supplies."

This blending of the practical with the boastful and poetical did not fail to amuse the listeners. It was overheard by a Melbourne man, who remarked that it was no more than you could expect of those fellows in Sydney, who were always on the lookout for something to bolster up the decaying village they lived in.

Frank and Fred agreed that the Sydney advocate, whatever might be his practical view of the anchorage of the navies of the world, was justified in his praise of the beauty of Port Jackson, while his claims as to its harbor facilities were not overdrawn. Certainly if there is any harbor in the world where the navies of the world might anchor, it is the one at Sydney; the entrance between the Heads is a mile wide, and vessels drawing twenty-seven feet of water can come in at any time. The bay extends inland about twenty miles, and is completely

GENERAL VIEW OF SYDNEY HARBOR.

landlocked; there is deep water in most parts of it, and in many places ships can lie quite close to the shore. The shores are generally bold and rocky, and some of the cliffs rise to a height of two hundred feet and more. The borders of the bay consist of a great many promontories jutting into it, and the spaces between these promontories form little bays or harbors by themselves. Islands in the bay add to its beauty, and it is no wonder that Frank and Fred were more than ordinarily enthusiastic over the harbor of Sydney.

The city stands on Sydney Cove, one of the numberless bays or harbors of Port Jackson, about four miles from the entrance from the ocean. We will further remark that fortifications have been erected at the Heads, and the authorities are confident that a hostile fleet or army coming to attack them could be successfully resisted. Doctor Bronson told the youths that the harbor which resembled Port Jackson more nearly than any other of which he knew, was Avatcha Bay, in Kamchatka. "It has," said he, "several little bays or harbors around it, just as Port Jackson has, and is fully as capacious and easy of access. I wish we had a diagram of it to show to our Australian friends."

"Before we left New Zealand," said Frank in his journal, "Doctor Bronson telegraphed to an old friend, Mr. Donald Manson, telling him by what steamer we expected to arrive. Mr. Manson was at the dock to meet us; he had secured rooms for us at the best hotel, and under his care we saw everything that was worth seeing in Sydney. Later, in Melbourne, where he was equally well acquainted, he was similarly attentive, and we hereby record our unanimous vote of thanks to him for his unvarying and unwearying politeness. If we tried his patience at any time he never allowed us to know it, and we found him a perfect encyclopædia in everything relating to Australia, where he has been a resident for a goodly number of years.

"One day when a proposition was made to go on a hunting excursion, Fred innocently suggested that he had read about Sydney ducks, and would like to shoot some, provided, of course, they were in season. Mr. Manson suppressed a smile as he answered that the shooting of those peculiar birds was no longer practised; he then explained that Sydney ducks can hardly be said to exist at present, the term having been applied to runaway convicts, ticket-of-leave men, and other waifs and strays, of the time when Australia was the receptacle of transported criminals from England and the other British Isles.

"Sydney seems to have been founded by or for these unfortunates. Mr. Manson told us that the settlement was made here in January, 1788, by Captain Phillip, who came here with a fleet of store and transport ships, for the purpose of founding a convict establishment. He had previously landed in Botany Bay, but finding it unsuitable, had abandoned it for the future site of Sydney. The name of the place was given in honor of Viscount Sydney, who first suggested the colonization of New South Wales, and the bay was called Port Jackson, after Sir George Jackson, who was then Secretary to the Lords of the Admiralty.

STATUE OF CAPTAIN COOK, SYDNEY.

"As soon as we had settled ourselves at the hotel, Mr. Manson accompanied us in a stroll and ride through the principal streets. 'Great changes have taken place here in the past twenty or even ten years,' said Mr. Manson, as he called our attention to new and magnificent buildings, which he said occupied the sites of wretched

GEORGE III.

structures that had only recently given way for the more modern architecture. Some of the old streets are still narrow and tortuous, but the new part of Sydney has wider and finer streets, and the old-fashioned appearance of the city is steadily disappearing. The principal streets are laid out to the cardinal points of the compass, and intersect one another at right angles. They are called George, Pitt, Market, King, and Hunter, the leading one being George Street, which starts from the water's edge and runs through the city and out into the country, where it becomes George Street West.

"George Street is named after George III., and Pitt Street after his Prime-minister. The other principal streets, Macquarie, King, Hunter, Bligh, and Phillip, bear the names of the early governors, and Mr. Manson said it was fortunate that the governors were changed often enough in those days to permit no scarcity of names for the streets. Here and there we saw some wooden buildings dating from the early days of the colony; and there is an old hospital, and also an ancient church which has pews such as we find in the churches of England one or two hundred years old.

"St. James's Church, the one just mentioned, is old and uncomfortable, but the cathedral is just the reverse. The public buildings of Sydney would take several or many pages for their description, and the account would run the risk of being tedious before reaching the end. When we remembered the age of the colony they surprised us by their magnificence. The Government buildings in Macquarie Street, the Post-office in George Street, the Town-hall, the University, the Crown Lands Office, and several other edifices would well adorn cities of much greater age than Sydney, and yet some of the residents complain that their buildings are not sufficiently grand for their wishes, and suggest the demolition of some of these structures to make way for finer ones. St. Andrew's Cathedral was begun in 1819, and has been three times pulled down and re-erected!

AVENUE IN THE BOTANICAL GARDENS.

"We can't say much in favor of the street-railways, or tramways, of Sydney, most of which have steam locomotives to draw the cars. Two cars are coupled together and drawn by a noisy, puffing engine, stopping at every other block to receive or discharge passengers. Accidents are said to be frequent, but of course the managers of the tram-ways always declare that the fault is due to the carelessness of the victims. They have flagmen at some of the more dangerous crossings, but in spite of them somebody is occasionally run over. Strangers are especially liable to injury from this cause, as they are often unaware that locomotives are allowed in the principal streets.

"Our ride was extended to the suburbs; and, without question, no city we have thus far seen in the Southern Hemisphere has suburbs at all approaching in attractiveness those of Sydney. First we come to Wooloomooloo—what a funny word that is to write!—and then we wind along the coasts of the little bays between the promontories; Elizabeth Bay, Rose Bay, Double Bay, Rushcutter's Bay, and I don't know how many other bays and coves, where the well-to-do residents have their villas. One hundred thousand people are said to live in Sydney proper, and one hundred and fifty thousand in the suburbs, so that the city, with its suburbs, has a population of a quarter of a million.

"Fred suggested that he would like to see the park or public garden. Mr. Manson asked, 'Which one?'

"Fred didn't know, and then our host explained that he had a considerable number to choose from. 'There is Albert Park,' said he, 'of forty acres, with a statue of Prince Albert, and opposite to it is Hyde Park Square, with a statue to Captain Cook, the discoverer of New South Wales. Then there is the Domain, of one hundred and twenty-eight acres, surrounding the little bay known as Farm Cove, the Botanical Gardens, of thirty-eight acres; and we have, in addition, Belmore Park, Prince Alfred Park, Callan Park, Moore Park, Wentworth Park, and the National Park; and a few years hence, if you come here again, there will doubtless be "more parks to hear from."'

"During our stay at Sydney we saw most of the parks named in the foregoing paragraph, and can testify to their beauty and the appreciation in which they are held by the inhabitants. The Domain and the Botanical Gardens were especially attractive; their sites are beautiful, and the Botanical Gardens contain every plant known in Australia, together with exotics from nearly every country in the world. For a student of botany these Gardens would furnish opportunities for months or years of study.

"In the Botanical Gardens our attention was called to three Norfolk pines that are said to have been planted here nearly seventy years ago; one of them is ninety-five feet high, and its circumference, three feet above the ground, is within a few inches of five yards. The other two of the cluster are taller than this one, but not so large in girth. Then they showed us a she-oak tree, which is said to give forth, when the air is perfectly still, a sound like the murmur of a sea-shell. Another curious growth is the Australian musk-tree, which constantly gives out an odor which is perceptible several yards away. Trees and plants from tropical and semi-arctic regions grow here side by side; the Canada fir almost touching the Indian bamboo, and the Siberian larch mingling its branches with those of the palm and the banyan.

"In the evening and on the following day, Mr. Manson introduced us to all the officials of prominence, and to many of the leading citizens. It was a severe brain-tax to remember all their names, but we shall try to do honor to our country in this particular. We have been invited to so many houses that if we should stay here a month we could not exhaust the list, and probably by the time the end was reached a new list would be formed. The Australians are certainly a hospitable people, and the stranger has a 'lovely time' among them."

At their first opportunity Frank and Fred informed themselves about the early history of the colony. Among other curious things Fred made the following note:

"It seems that the people of the United States are indirectly responsible for the settlement of Australia by convicts. Here is a paragraph from page 18 of 'The Official History of New South Wales,' by Thomas Richards, Government Printer, and Registrar of Copyright.

"'. . . Whilst America was subject to England, British offenders, political or otherwise, were transported to the southern colonies of that continent, or to the West Indies, where they were in the first instance employed chiefly in the production of tobacco. The consumption of tobacco was large, and the revenue derived therefrom considerable, Virginia and Maryland being the chief producers. The American colonies having revolted against British rule in 1776, and after a long and severe struggle gained their independence, England sought a new field for colonization, and first tried the coast of Africa, but found it unhealthy. Her attention was then turned to Australia, the eligibility of which for the purpose had been spreading since Cook's famous voyage thither in 1768. Accordingly, a fleet of eleven sail, carrying more than one thousand souls, was assembled at Portsmouth, in the month of March, 1787, to proceed to Australia.'"

CANDIDATES FOR TRANSPORTATION.

Fred read the foregoing extract to Frank. The latter listened earnestly, and then remarked:

"I don't see that times have greatly changed after all. England still sends us her convicts and paupers, the only difference being that she turns them loose upon us instead of deriving something for their forced labor. Her example is followed by most of the continental nations, and thus we get the human rubbish of the Old World, just as we did before the Revolutionary War."

Fred then went on to say that the colony by which Sydney was founded numbered one thousand and thirty persons, including seven hundred and fifty-seven convicts, among whom were one hundred and ninety-two women and eighteen children. Besides the officers, there were one hundred and sixty soldiers, with forty of their wives; the live-stock included cattle, sheep, horses, pigs, and goats; and there was a large stock of seeds from the tropic and temperate zones. The natives did not oppose the landing, as they supposed it was only temporary. When they found that the settlement was a permanent one they became hostile, and many murders resulted, caused, no doubt, in great measure by the outrages committed by the convicts. Ships from England followed steadily, each one bringing its quota of convicts, and in a few years Sydney had quite a city-like appearance.*

Free emigration began a few years after the establishment of the colony, as just described, the earliest of the free emigrants being principally men of capital, who came with the object of employing the convicts under contracts with the Government. Free emigrants of more

---

* On the 24th of January, 1888, the celebration of the centenary of New South Wales was begun, the occasion being the anniversary of the landing of the first governor of the colony. Lady Carrington, the wife of the Governor, unveiled a statue of Queen Victoria in the presence of the governors of all the Australian colonies, including New Zealand and Feejee. The festival extended over a week, and included the dedication of Centennial Park, the opening of the Agricultural Society's exhibition, and an international regatta and state banquets. On the 26th, the anniversary of Governor Phillip's proclaiming at Sydney Cove the founding of the colony, there was a general illumination. The city was crowded with visitors, and the gathering thoroughly represented Australia. Special thanksgiving services were held on the opening day in the Anglican and Catholic cathedrals. The ceremonies in the Catholic cathedral were attended by the archbishop and all the bishops of Australia. Centennial Hall is one of the largest halls in the world, and is on the site of the old burial-ground of one hundred years ago.

Melbourne celebrated the centennial year of the settlement of Australia by a World's Exhibition, to which all nations were invited. South Australia had an International Exhibition at Adelaide in 1887, similar to the exhibitions of Sydney and Melbourne a few years earlier.

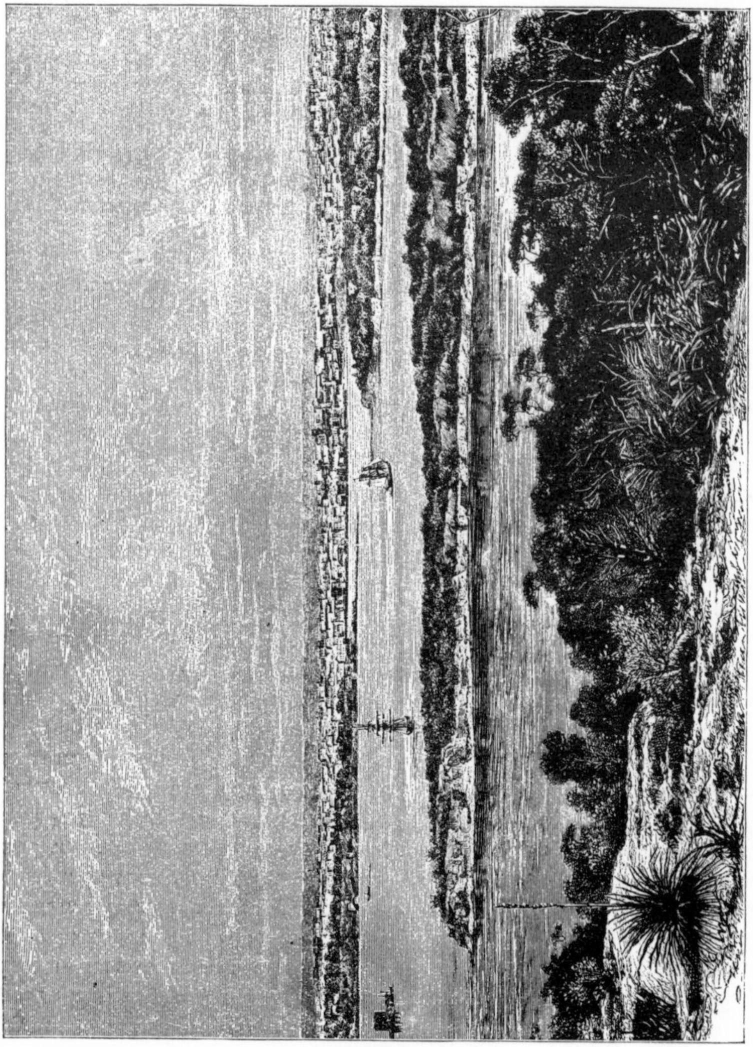

SYDNEY AND ITS HARBOR.

modest means naturally followed, and in course of time the free settlers were more numerous than the convicts and military combined. In 1831, out of 76,793 persons in the colony 27,831 were convicts.

In the early part of this century Australia had three classes of inhabitants—free settlers, convicts, and emancipists—the latter being convicts who had served out their sentences and become free men. The free settlers refused to associate with them, and they in turn would not associate with the convicts; the free settlers were inclined to be tyrannical, and wished to have the emancipists deprived of civil rights, and long and bitter quarrels were the result of their demands. The governors generally took the side of the emancipists as a matter of justice, and thus made themselves unpopular with the rest of the colony.

While studying the early history of the Australian colonies, Frank and Fred obtained considerable information from a gentleman who seemed to be thoroughly familiar with the subject. As he made no allusion in any way to his ancestry, the youths thought it just possible that he might be the son or grandson of one of the "involuntary emigrants" of early days. Desiring to respect his reserve as much as possible, they did not make any entry of his name in their note-books. Their suspicions were strengthened by a remark which he dropped, that it was not considered polite in Australian society to ask who and what a man's father was.

"The term 'convict' is of course odious," said he, "no matter what the circumstance that has caused it to be applied to a man. Many of the convicts who were sent to Australia owed their transportation to no worse offences than sympathizing with a rebellion, snaring a hare, or catching a fish out of somebody's preserved pond. I knew a man who was transported for seven years for nothing else than twisting the neck of a partridge, and his case was very far from being a solitary one. In the eye of the British law he was a criminal, a convict; but in the eye of common-sense and humanity his respectability was not greatly tarnished. The Irish rebellion of 1798 caused great numbers of Irishmen to be transported; they were treated as criminals, and all sorts of indignities were heaped upon them, but their only crime was that of seeking to free their country."

Frank asked how the convicts were treated on the voyage from England to Australia and after they arrived there.

"According to all accounts," was the reply, "they were very cruelly used. On the transport-ships they were closely herded together, poorly fed, and severely flogged for the least infraction of the rules. Many

THE TOWN-HALL, SYDNEY.

died on the voyage in consequence of the inhuman treatment they received; in some cases the deaths were a fourth of the entire number. On their arrival in Australia they were put at work in Government establishments, or on public roads and wharves, or were hired out to agricultural and other colonists. You must remember that those were the days of brute force, and no officer in charge of convicts ever thought of such a thing as moral suasion and kindness, however much combined with firmness. Flogging was of daily and almost hourly occurrence, and administered for trivial offences; a historian of the colony says that any man who failed to go to church on Sundays received twenty lashes on his bare back. Prisoners were put in irons often at the mere caprice of their keepers, their food was scanty, their clothing often insufficient for the weather, and if a man ventured to run away he was pursued by blood-hounds and bull-dogs and brought back, unless killed by the natives or dead from starvation.

"Settlements were formed at several places along the coast of Australia and in Van Dieman's Land (now Tasmania). The first convict settlement in Tasmania was on a peninsula, and a row of bull-dogs was chained across the narrow isthmus that connected the peninsula with the main-land, so close together that it was impossible for a man to pass between any two of them."

"I suppose the prisoners rarely managed to escape?" said Frank.

"Very rarely," said the gentleman. "There were many runaways, but they were generally brought back and punished, and if their escape was accompanied with violence they were hanged or shot. In the bush they were liable to starve, and many a convict's bones are whitening where he perished of hunger; the natives were hostile, and if a runaway escaped recapture and starvation, he was very likely to fall before the spear of a black man.

"Some of the Irish convicts of 1798 were so struck by the similarity between the Blue Mountains, about eighty miles from Sydney, and the Connaught Hills of Ireland that they rushed off expecting to reach their homes without difficulty. One man who had tried on the voyage out to fathom the mystery of the mariner's compass felt sure that he could find his way home if he only had the thing to steer by. He stole a copy of a work on navigation, and tore out the first leaf, which had the picture of a compass upon it. His theft was detected and punished, and he never had an opportunity to try his system of paper-compass navigation.

"A goodly portion of the emigrants thought China was only a little way overland from Sydney, and many tried to reach it. There used to be a story of a runaway who had wandered for days in the bush, and suddenly came to a hut in which was an acquaintance. He anxiously

SENTENCED TO HARD LABOR.

asked how his friend had got to China, and was much astonished to learn that he had reached a farm a few miles from Sydney, and his acquaintance had been hired there as a laborer.

"If you wish to learn how the convicts were brought from England to Australia," continued their informant to Frank and Fred, "how they lived when they got here, and how they were treated, read a story entitled 'His Natural Life,' by Marcus Clarke, an Australian journalist and littérateur. In the form of a novel he has preserved much of the history of the old convict days. It is not altogether agreeable reading, though it is instructive.

"All the colonists except the convicts themselves, and they had no voice in the matter, protested against Australia being peopled by these objectionable individuals, and protest after protest was made to the Home Government. These protests had their effect, and in 1840 transportation to New South Wales came to an end; an attempt was afterwards made to renew it, but was never carried out. It was continued later in Van Dieman's Land and other colonies, and in West Australia until 1868, when it was brought to an end, not so much at the wish of the people of West Australia as of those of the other colonies.

"And let me say in conclusion," he remarked, "that there are many prominent citizens of Australia whose fathers or grandfathers were transported, and nobody in his senses thinks any the worse of them in consequence. There are some gentlemen high in official position—of course it would not be polite for me to name them—who are thus descended, and so are some of the wealthiest and most prominent citizens in civil life. Everybody may be aware of it, but nobody talks of it in public.

"In our political contests the opposing candidates use as hard language about one another as the same class of men do in political contests in the United States; they may say anything they please except that the man they are denouncing is the descendant of a transported convict. Whenever this is done, although the statement may be perfectly true, the injured man can bring a suit for slander, and be certain of high damages. Only a few years ago an aspirant for office was compelled to pay ten thousand pounds for saying in a public speech that the man against whom he was contending was the son of an 'involuntary emigrant' from England."

The gentleman paused, and Fred took the opportunity to ask what a ticket-of-leave man was in the days of transportation.

"As to that," was the reply, "tickets-of-leave are in use to-day in other countries as well as in England, though they are not known by that name. In the United States you have a system of remitting part of a sentence in case of good conduct, and we do the same in England.

VIEW OF SYDNEY FROM PYRMOND, DARLING HARBOR.

Well, this is what the ticket-of-leave was in Australia: a man received a conditional pardon consequent upon good conduct up to the time it was granted, and also conditioned upon continued good conduct during the time it was in force. In Australia a ticket-of-leave man was required to remain in a certain prescribed district, where his conduct could be observed; in practice it often happened that the man ran away

HOME OF AN EMANCIPIST.

and sought a home elsewhere than under the British flag. A good many ticket-of-leave men found their way to the Feejee, Samoa, Society, and other islands of the Pacific, where they led lives that often were not in accordance with civilized rules. In consequence of their violation of the permit granted them, they were always greatly alarmed when a British ship appeared in the offing.

"Many ticket-of-leave men became good citizens; some of them obtained grants of land, and established farms where they supported themselves, and not a few of this class became prosperous and wealthy. The mechanics found plenty of occupation in the cities and towns, and thus there gradually grew up a population of emancipists, who have been mentioned already. In the disputes about the rights of the emancipists their cause was warmly espoused by Governor Macquarie, who earned the title of 'The Prisoner's Friend.' Some excesses followed the adoption of this policy, but the colony was benefited by it, and ultimately all classes of freemen were admitted to an equal footing, and the cessation of transportation in time caused a perfect commingling of classes and an extinction of the old feud."

The conversation terminated here, and the youths thanked their informant for what he had told them on this interesting subject. They closed their note-books as soon as the interview ended, and then went out for a stroll. Curious to see the shipping in the harbor, they directed their steps to the Circular Quay, the modern name of Sydney Cove, where the original expedition landed, in 1788. The founders of the settlement could hardly recognize the cove should they revisit it to-day.

"Circular Quay," said Fred, in his account of their walk, "is at the head of the cove, and has a length of one thousand three hundred feet, available for the largest vessels. It has piers and pavilions for the ferry-steamers, which are numerous and active, and the Government has made a liberal expenditure for extending the wharfage accommodations and erecting sheds for the storage of goods. The Australian Steam Navigation Company have their wharves here, and several of their vessels were loading or discharging at Circular Quay all at once.

"To give an idea of the commerce of Sydney with other parts of the world, let me mention the various steamship lines whose vessels were visible from this quay. One of the first to come within our line of vision was a great steamer of the Peninsular & Oriental Company, familiarly known as the 'P. & O.,' and not far from it was another equally large steamer belonging to the Orient line. Each of these companies has a fortnightly service each way between England and Australia, and the sharp competition between them has had the effect of reducing the price of passage and securing rapid voyages. A little farther away was a steamer flying the tricolor of France; it belonged to the 'Compagnie des Messageries Maritimes,' a rival of the P. & O. in Asiatic waters, and at the principal ports of Asiatic and Australasian lands. The Austrian flag was visible on a steamer of the Austrian Lloyds, and the German flag upon a magnificent vessel of the North German Lloyds, or 'Bremen Line.'

A TICKET-OF-LEAVE MAN.

"Australia has an abundance of steam communication with the rest of the world. The P. & O. line has a fortnightly service each way between London and Sydney *via* the Suez Canal, the other Australian ports included in its itinerary being Melbourne, Adelaide, and King George's Sound; the Orient line has a similar fortnightly service, also by the Suez Canal, but omits King George's Sound from its list of Australian ports. The North German Lloyds has a service each way every

JUST ARRIVED IN PORT.

four weeks between Sydney and Bremen, its Australian ports being Sydney, Melbourne, and Adelaide; the Messageries Maritimes—French mail-line—has a similar four-weekly service each way between Sydney, Melbourne, Adelaide, and Marseilles. Then there is a four-weekly service each way of the British India Steam Navigation Company, between Brisbane and Aden, connecting at Aden with the same company's line, to and from London, and touching at Batavia, Java, on every voyage. The New Zealand Shipping Company and the Shaw Savill & Albion Company have each a four-weekly service from London to New Zealand by way of the Cape of Good Hope and Hobart, Tasmania, and

SHIP-YARD SCENE.

their steamers return to London by way of the Strait of Magellan, Rio Janeiro, and the Canary Islands. Last, but by no means least, is the four-weekly service each way between Sydney and San Francisco, which has been already mentioned.

"All these steamship lines receive subsidies from the colonial governments, and all, with the exception of the American one, receive subsidies from their home governments. It is a curious circumstance, and a humiliating one, to Americans in Australia or having relations with the antipodes, that the American line between San Francisco and Australia is subsidized by the colonies, but receives nothing from the United States, under whose flag it sails. Our commerce with Australia and New Zealand now exceeds twelve millions of dollars annually, and could be greatly increased by the encouragement of regular and permanent steam communication with the colonies.

"An officer of one of the steamers running to San Francisco spoke to us, and remarked that he had met us in the last-named city just as we were taking passage for Honolulu. He told us we could start from Sydney for 'Greenland's icy mountains or India's coral strand,' or for any other mountains or strands on the globe. 'That wharf to the east,' said he, 'is called Wooloomooloo; it was built at a heavy cost, but the water near it is too shallow for sea-going vessels of the deepest draught, and it is principally used for coasting-vessels, of which you see there are a great many.'

"Then he told us that Darling Harbor, on the western side of the city, had its entire frontage covered with wharves and quays. Grafton Wharf, with its building, covers an area of more than three acres. As for dry-dock accommodations, he pronounced Sydney one of the best ports he had ever seen. There are two or three docks that were good enough for the ships of twenty years ago, but are of less importance to-day. A few years ago the Government built a dock four hundred and fifty feet long, and wide in proportion, and it was thought sufficient for all necessities for years to come; but hardly was it completed before it was found too short for the largest modern steamships, and so another has been built that is six hundred and eighty feet long, one hundred and eight feet wide between the walls, and eighty-five feet in the entrance-gate. How long will it be before they will find this dock too small for the wants of commerce?

ON THE PARAMATTA RIVER.

"In one year (1885) the number of British and foreign ships that entered Port Jackson was 2601, with an aggregate tonnage of 2,088,307 tons. There are several ship building and repairing establishments here; that of the Australian Steam Navigation Company alone covers more than six acres, and employs nearly five hundred persons. A hundred years ago this was a howling wilderness; that is, if the Australian savages were accustomed to howl, and I presume they were.

"We could give figures about Sydney that would make your head 'an ant-hill of units and tens,' as Doctor Holmes says; but perhaps you've had enough to convince you of the importance of the city. It has six daily papers, weeklies so numerous that the list would be monotonous, and as for schools, churches, hospitals, clubs, hotels, and other institutions of a great city, there are all that could be reasonably expected. As to manufacturing industries, it has a great many factories, founderies, and engineering establishments;

IRRIGATING AN ORANGE-GROVE.

for clothing alone there are more than fifty factories, employing from fifty to four hundred hands each, and the other manufacturing concerns are in similar proportion."

Our friends went on a steamboat excursion to Paramatta, which lies up the river of the same name, about fifteen miles from Sydney. Next to Sydney, it is the oldest town in the colony, having been founded in November, 1788; it was originally called Rosehill, but the name was afterwards changed to the aboriginal one of Par-a-mat-ta. The first grain raised in the colony was grown at Paramatta, and here the earliest grants of land were made to convicts who had served their time at hard labor and were entitled to become colonists. It is now a prosperous town with from eight to ten thousand inhabitants, and has a considerable business in manufacturing. Along the banks of the river and in the neighborhood of Paramatta, there are many flower-gardens, from which Sydney is abundantly supplied with boutonnières, bouquets, and huge baskets of flowers at all seasons of the year.

"Our chief interest in Paramatta," said Fred, "was to see the orange-groves, which have made the place famous throughout Australia. We were accompanied by a gentleman who was well known both in Paramatta and in Sydney, and he took us at once to the orangery of the late Mr. Pye, who devoted the greater part of his life to the introduction and cultivation of this excellent fruit. They told us that more than ten thousand oranges had been gathered in one season from a single tree! We have never eaten finer oranges in any part of the world than at Paramatta, and the other fruits grown in the orchards of the place are said to be equally good in their season. The oranges are best in December, but they are gathered ripe during every month of the year. Of course they wanted us to inspect some of the factories, hospitals, and other public buildings, but our time was too limited, and were returned to Sydney by railway instead of taking the steamboat back again."

Other excursions were made in the suburbs of Sydney, and Doctor Bronson and his nephews received invitations to visit some of the interior towns of the colony. One of their excursions was to Botany Bay, which lies five miles from Sydney by land, the distance by sea being fully fifteen miles. A horse-railway connects the village with Sydney, and the ride is quite a pretty one. The chief object of interest is the monument which marks the spot where Captain Cook landed in 1770, and took possession of the place in the name of the British Crown.

The consideration of the up-country invitations was postponed until the return of the party from Queensland, whither they went as soon as the sights of Sydney were exhausted. How they went and what they saw will be told in the next chapter.

CHAPTER XIV.

FROM SYDNEY TO BRISBANE.—POLITICAL DIVISIONS OF AUSTRALIA.—ORDER IN WHICH THE COLONIES WERE FOUNDED.—EXPLORATIONS AND THEIR EXTENT.—DOCTOR BASS AND CAPTAIN FLINDERS.—ABSENCE OF WATER IN THE INTERIOR OF AUSTRALIA.—A COUNTRY OF STRANGE CHARACTERISTICS.—NATURE'S REVERSES.—HOW THE COLONIES ARE GOVERNED.—RELIGION AND EDUCATION.—JEALOUSY OF THE COLONIES TOWARDS EACH OTHER.—NEWCASTLE AND ITS COAL.—RAILWAY TRAVELLING IN NEW SOUTH WALES.—TENTERFIELD AND STANTHORPE.—COBB'S COACHES.—AUSTRALIAN SCENERY.—THE EUCALYPTUS, OR GUM-TREE.—THE TALLEST TREES IN THE WORLD.—SILVER STEMS AND MALLEE SCRUB.—BRISBANE.—RELICS OF THE CONVICT SYSTEM.—QUEEN STREET AND THE BOTANICAL GARDENS.

A COASTING steamer carried Doctor Bronson and his young companions to Newcastle, a town which resembles the English one of the same name in being an important centre of the coal-trade. The distance from Sydney is about seventy-five miles, and consequently the

INTERIOR OF A COAL-BREAKER.

voyage was of only a few hours' duration; even this limited time was utilized by a conversation about the political divisions of Australia and the relations between the colonies.

The conversation began with a question from Doctor Bronson as to what the youths had learned on the subject since their arrival at Sydney or on the voyage from New Zealand. Frank was the first to reply.

"We have read to you our notes," said he, "about the settlement of New South Wales by the fleet of ships that came out from England by order of the Government. New South Wales was thus the parent colony, and the others, with one exception, are offshoots from it. In 1790 New South Wales established a penal colony on Norfolk Island, which has since been given up to the Pitcairn Islanders, descendants of the mutineers of the *Bounty*. Van Dieman's Land, or Tasmania, was settled as a penal colony in 1803, by Lieutenant Bowen, who was sent from Sydney with a few convicts and their guards, and formed a settlement near the spot where the city of Hobart now stands. Queensland, under the name of Moreton Bay District, was settled in 1825 from Sydney, and became a separate colony in 1859. Victoria, then known as Port Phillip, and forming part of New South Wales, was colonized in 1803, and afterwards abandoned; it was permanently settled from Tasmania in 1835, and on July 1, 1851, the colony was separated from New South Wales and became independent.

"South Australia was colonized by emigrants from Great Britain in 1836, and West Australia by a detachment of soldiers and convicts from Sydney in 1826. New South Wales can thus claim the parentage of all the colonies of the continent and its adjacent island, Tasmania, with the single exception of South Australia.

"West, or Western, Australia is described by its name, as it occupies the entire western part of the continent. South Australia is a misnomer; the parent colony is in the southern part of the continent, but its jurisdiction extends from ocean to ocean to the northern shore, and includes the so-called Northern Territory, or Alexandra Land, which will one day, no doubt, form an independent government. To the eastward of the Northern Territory and South Australia is Queensland, and south of Queensland and eastward of South Australia is the parent colony of New South Wales. Then comes the colony of Victoria, south of New South Wales; territorially it is the smallest of all the colonies, but it isn't small in any other way. Tasmania is a hundred and fifty miles south of Victoria, from which it is separated by Bass's Strait, which preserves, the name of its discoverer, Dr. George Bass of the Royal Navy." *

Frank paused a moment and gave Fred an opportunity to speak of something he had just read about Doctor Bass. "He made his first expedition," said Fred, "in 1796, in an open boat eight feet long, in company with Midshipman (afterwards Captain) Flinders and a crew of one

---

* See map at the end of this volume.

GOLD-FIELDS OF MOUNT ALEXANDER, AUSTRALIA.

boy. They narrowly escaped being drowned in the sea, and later in being killed by the natives when the wind drove them ashore. In the following year Doctor Bass went in a whale-boat, with a crew of six men and provisions for six weeks, and found that the coast trended so far to the west as to indicate the separation of Tasmania from the mainland, and in the next year (1798) he obtained a sloop, and in company with Captain Flinders actually sailed through the strait and determined the question."

"I see you have been reading to advantage," the Doctor remarked. "And please add to your notes that this same Doctor Bass is supposed to have died a slave in the mines of Chili. He was arrested at Valparaiso in consequence of a dispute with the authorities, and was never again seen or heard of by his friends. There was a rumor that he had been sent to the mines, and that was all."

"If the Australian continent were divided into one hundred equal parts," said Frank, "Victoria would include three, New South Wales ten, Queensland twenty-three, South Australia thirty, and West Australia thirty-four. The greatest length of Australia is about 2400 miles, and its greatest width, between Cape York on the north and Wilson's Promontory on the south, is 1971 miles. It has about 7750 miles of coast-line, and an area of 2,944,628 square miles. A good idea of the extent of Australia may be had by comparing it with other countries. It is about twenty-six times the area of Great Britain and Ireland, fifteen times the size of France, about one-sixth smaller than the whole of the United States of America, and only about one-fifth smaller than the whole of Europe."

Fred asked who gave it the appellation of Australia.

"The name was given by Captain Flinders, of whom we were speaking a few moments ago," replied the Doctor. "His memory is preserved in a river and a mountain-range of the continent whose coast he explored. On his return to Europe he was captured by the French, and was held a prisoner from 1806 to 1810. He died in England in 1814, shortly after publishing his book, 'A Voyage to Terra Australis.'"

"There is a great part of the country not yet explored," said Frank, as the Doctor paused. "A writer on this subject says that the unexplored region of the present day is almost entirely confined to Western Australia and a large part of the northern territory of South Australia. New South Wales and Victoria have an area of four hundred thousand square miles, almost every mile of which is fairly known; Queensland may still have a small extent of unknown land in the far northern peninsula; South Australia has at least two hundred and fifty thousand miles unexplored or but little known; and West Australia has fully half a million square miles that have been crossed at intervals by the tracks of a few explorers. In round figures, the extent of unexplored or partially known country in Australia is more than double that of the thoroughly known portion. The continent is almost fairly bisected by the overland telegraph line, which follows closely the track of Macdouall Stuart, the explorer, and the telegraph may be considered a line of demarcation between the explored and unexplored portions."

"And have you ascertained why the continent has not yet been thoroughly examined?" Doctor Bronson queried.

CLEARING IN AN AUSTRALIAN FOREST.

"I have," Fred replied, with alacrity, "and I presume Frank has done so too. It is because there is no water in the interior of the continent, or but very little. If you look on the map you will see very few rivers, and none of those that exist is of great size. Australia is nearly as large as Europe, and see the difference in the rivers. Europe has the Danube, Rhine, Volga, Don, Vistula, Seine, Rhone—all large rivers—together with more than twice as many of lesser note, but all of them important; while Australia has only a single river of consequence, the Murray. There are hundreds of miles of coast-line together where not a single stream, great or small, flows into the sea, and some of the interior rivers dry up and disappear in the hot season."

"I read about that too," said Frank; "the Murray and its tributaries, the Lachlan and Murrumbidgee, are lasting streams; but the Darling, a river of considerable size, flowing into the Murray from the north, has the Australian peculiarity of disappearing into quicksands and marshes. With the exception of the Murray, all the other permanent streams of Australia are short, and of little consequence; and, like the rivers of New Zealand, they have been clogged with water-cress, which was introduced from England in the expectation that it would be a great luxury."

A WATERLESS REGION.

"You have hit exactly upon the obstacle which has baffled Australian explorers," said the Doctor. "All who have sought to penetrate the interior have suffered terribly from thirst, and some expeditions that have never been heard from are supposed to have perished from the same cause. The rainfall in the interior of the continent is slight, the heat in summer is intense, and even in winter the thermometer sometimes runs to a high figure."

"Then it is fair to suppose that the interior of Australia is practically of no use," Frank remarked.

"It is fair to suppose so," was the reply; "but some scientists believe that good pasture-land and habitable country will yet be found in the interior, where the few explorers who have been there report only a desert unfit to sustain human life and impracticable for settlement. Artesian wells have been bored in many places, and a fair proportion of them have succeeded in finding water. There is so much territory in Australia that it is not likely the capabilities or disadvantages of all parts of it will be thoroughly known for many years to come.

"And now," he continued, as he glanced at a book he held in his hand, "let us read what an English author has written concerning this strange country :

"'Almost everything in nature is, in Australia, the reverse of what it is in England. When we have winter they have summer; when we have day they have night; we have our feet pressing nearly opposite to their feet. There the compass points to the south, the sun travels along the northern heavens, the barometer rises with a southerly and falls with a northerly wind. The animals are disproportionately large in their lower extremities, and carry their young in a pouch; the plumage of the birds is beautiful, their notes are harsh and strange; the swans are black, the owls screech and hoot only in the daytime; the cuckoo's song is heard only in the night. The valleys are cool, the mountain-tops are

AUSTRALIAN LYRE-BIRDS.

warm; the north winds are hot, the south winds are cold, the east winds are healthy. The bees are without sting; the cherries grow with the stone outside; one of the birds has a broom in its mouth instead of a tongue. Many of the beautiful flowers are without smell; most of the trees are without shade, and shed their bark instead of their leaves; some, indeed, are without leaves; in others the leaves are vertical. And even the geological formation of the country, as far as ascertained, is most singular. In other parts of the world coal is black, but in Australia they have bituminous coal as white as chalk.

"'Taken as a whole, the country, as far as explored, exhibits less hill and dale, with less compact vegetation, than in most other parts of the world. In the interior there is a bare, barren, stony desert, totally unfit for man or beast. A more or less broken chain of mountains extends from Spencer Gulf, round the south coast, all along the eastern coast, and round the northern coast, nearly to Limming's Bight. The rivers are few in number; the watercourses are very low in summer, and frequently dried up; no dense forest exists, as in America; the herbage generally is thin, the grasses, although highly nutritious, growing in patches. The highest peak is Mount Kosciusko, 6510 feet above sea, at the head of the Murray, which is the largest Australian river, 2500 miles long.

"'Australia contains no antiquities, and the tourist who expects to find the ruins of temples, palaces, and pagodas is doomed to disappointment. It was discovered by the Portuguese about 1530, and visited by the Spaniards in 1605, and by several navigators down to Captain Cook in 1770, and settled in 1788. All its cities are of modern foundation and growth; and Australia may be compared, in a general way, to that part of the United States west of the Mississippi River.'

"We shall have an opportunity to verify many of these statements," said the Doctor, "when we travel in the interior." Then, turning to Frank, he asked that youth what he had learned concerning the government of the colonies.

"I learned that they are wholly independent of each other," was the reply, "and furthermore, that there is great jealousy between them. Each of the colonies must be considered in many respects a distinct province, having its own government, local laws, and customs regulations. With the exception of West Australia, they all enjoy responsible government, and that colony will no doubt have the same constitutional privileges as the others before many years. The form of government is a modification of the British Constitution, the sovereign being represented by the Governor, who is appointed by the Crown; the House of Lords by the legislative council, nominated or elected; and the House of Commons by the legislative assembly, elected by the people.

"The imperial laws are in force unless superseded by local enactments, and all acts passed by the colonial legislatures must receive the assent of the sovereign before they can become laws. In each of the colonies the qualifications for exercising the franchise are placed very low, and manhood suffrage is practically the rule. An effort has been made to league the Australian colonies into one great confederation;

the friends of the movement are confident of its success in course of time, but local jealousies have thus far prevented it."

"It doesn't take long to find out that the colonies are very jealous of one another," Fred remarked. "It's a pity that this state of affairs exists; but after all, it has done a great deal towards the development

A MEMBER OF THE LEGISLATURE.

and population of the country. Jealousy between communities and colonies is the basis of enterprise, and many things have been done here in consequence of competition that without it would never have been done at all. When one colony sends out an exploring expedition another does the same; when one establishes a system of cheap emigration the rest will not be left behind. And so it goes through all their enterprises. It is exactly like the rivalry that existed between our Western States and cities twenty years ago, and still exists to some extent."

"Spoken like a statesman," said the Doctor, as he nodded approvingly towards his nephew. "Put your remarks on paper and send them home; they may be beneficial to some of our friends in St. Louis and Chicago."

Fred promised to do so, and when some time later he wrote out his views he added the following:

"It's very funny to hear the people of one city or colony talk about those of another. Each decries all the rest, and represents his own region as the only perfect one. Talking about the climate, a Sydney man will tell you that the capital of New South Wales is quite exempt from the cold winds that make life unbearable in Melbourne and Adelaide. The Melbourne man tells how you suffer from 'brickfielders' (hot and dusty winds from the interior) at Sydney, and how the poor wretches in Adelaide are perspiring at every pore with a temperature and humidity like those of a Russian bath.

"Each colony has its own postal regulations, its own postage-stamps, and its own rates for letters and other mail matter. New South Wales is a land of free-trade, while Victoria, its neighbor, is a land of protective tariffs; each can demonstrate the advantages of its particular system, and on the other hand each has a minority party that wants its laws patterned after those of its rival. The gauges of the railways are different, so that there is a break at every frontier; consequently passengers are obliged to change trains, and all freights bound across the line must be transshipped. The enactments of the colonial legislatures are often hostile to one another, and sometimes the rivalry expresses itself so strongly that it seems unfortunate that the colonies have a common language.

"None of the colonies has any State Church, and all religions are placed on the same footing. The Episcopalians are the dominant body so far as numbers are concerned, the Roman Catholics are next, and then come the Presbyterians, and after them the Methodists. These are the four great denominations; far below them in numbers and in their order of strength are the Lutherans and German-Protestants, Baptists, Congregationalists, Jews, Bible Christians, Church of Christ, Unitarians, and Free Presbyterians. The Asiatic proportion of the population adds Moslems, Confucians, and Pagans to the list of religionists. Considering the recent settlement of the colonies, the proportion of places of worship to the population will compare favorably with other countries.

"There is a tendency to exclude religious teaching from the public schools, and in place of this there is a wide-spread interest in Sunday-schools, which abound all over the continent wherever it has been settled. In the matter of education the colonies are happily actuated by the same impulse, all believing that it is one of the vital principles

INFANT CLASS IN AN INDUSTRIAL SCHOOL.

of good government. The children are taught either wholly or partially by the aid of the State funds of each province, and in nearly all the colonies a separate department, under a minister of the Crown, controls the machinery of education.

"The leading principles of education in Australia are that it is free, or very nearly so. It is compulsory, and it is secular, though not in all cases, to the absolute exclusion of Bible-reading. The latest reports at hand show that there are 5844 State schools in Australia, with 553,191 pupils and 11,890 teachers. There are numerous high-schools, academies, and denominational schools in the cities and larger towns, and there are colleges and universities at Sydney, Melbourne, and Adelaide."

We will now drop the journals and statistics of Frank and Fred, and attend to what they saw and heard on their journey.

We left them on their way to Newcastle, which they reached without mishap. A fellow-passenger told them that several disastrous wrecks had occurred at the entrance of Newcastle Harbor, which was formerly very dangerous when the wind blew heavily from the south-east. A breakwater has been constructed that greatly diminishes the danger, as it protects the bar from the heavy seas which formerly swept over it. Newcastle is the outlet of a considerable extent of country, but its principal business is in coal, of which it ships more than two million tons annually. The town has many evidences of prosperity, and its appliances for handling coal are extensive and excellent.

One of the citizens volunteered to show our friends the coal-mines. While they were making the round of the place he said that a careful estimate showed that the coal-seams now being worked contained enough coal to keep up the present rate of production for five hundred and twelve years. There are thirty-five seams of coal, varying from five to twelve feet in thickness, and one seam—the Greta—is twenty-one feet thick. Nearly five thousand miners are employed underground, and one thousand at the mouths of the mines. The deepest workings are those of the Greta, four hundred and fifty feet, and the Stockton, three hundred and eighty feet. The authorities of Newcastle believe they have the finest appliances for handling coal that are to be found anywhere, and Doctor Bronson said he certainly did not know of any that surpassed them.

Since the visit of our friends we are told that the railway from Sydney to Newcastle has been completed, and also the line which connects with the one from Brisbane, at the frontier between New South Wales and Queensland. From Newcastle they went by land to Brisbane; near Tenterfield they left the railway for a coach-ride of forty miles, which brought them to Stanthorpe, where they found a train to carry them to their destination. At several points on their coach-ride they saw the working-parties making cuttings and fillings along the route for the railway that now completes the connection between the capitals of the colonies of Queensland and New South Wales. There is now continuous railway communication from Brisbane to Adelaide, a distance of very nearly eighteen hundred miles.

The train left Newcastle at 7.15 in the morning, and brought them to Tenterfield at a little past midnight, the distance being three hundred and eighty-one miles. It carried them through a country of varied characteristics — hill, valley, plain, mountain, forest, and open country presenting themselves in succession. "It can be briefly described," said Frank, "as an agricultural, pastoral, and mining region, some of it being of great value, and other parts quite forbidding in aspect, owing to the scarcity of water. We passed through some of the gold-fields of New South Wales, but did not stop to visit them. We were told that considerable quantities of diamonds had been obtained near Bingera, one hundred and ten miles north from Tamworth, an important town on the railway, about half-way between Newcastle and Tenterfield.

"The names of stations on the line of railway are a curious mixture of native and foreign words; the foreign ones including English, Scotch, Irish, and American, together with some that were difficult to classify. For example, there were Murrurundi, Boggabri, Currabubula,

COMPLETING THE RAILWAY.

and Moonbi, all of Australian origin; and then we found Hamilton, Lochinvar, Dundee, Stonehenge, Emerald Hill, Kentucky, and other familiar words. Then followed Doughboy Hollow, Honeysuckle Point, Kelly's Plains, and Willow Tree, which reminded us of names that we had heard in the Pacific States of America.

"Occasionally we saw herds of cattle and flocks of sheep, and were not surprised to learn that the country is considered an excellent region for raising those animals. We passed through forests of gum-trees, as they are called here, the ordinary appellation of the Eucalyptus, of which there are many varieties. Compared with the trees of England and America, the gum-tree is not beautiful, and no one would think of growing it for ornament alone, but on the whole it is by no means ill-looking. The leaves do not spread out horizontally, but depend

A FALLEN GIANT.

vertically from the boughs. Consequently the tree gives little shade in the daytime, but the traveller who passes through a gum forest at night blesses this peculiarity of the tree, as it admits the light of the moon and stars, to the great advantage of the wayfarer. Compared with European trees, the verdure of the Eucalyptus is scanty, and its green is rather sombre. Some of the varieties of this tree are far more attractive than others, the handsomest of all being the Banksia, named after Sir Joseph Banks.

"The *Eucalyptus amygdalina*, or giant gum, has the reputation of being the tallest tree in the world, and the Australians are greatly pleased to mention this fact. There are reports of giant gum-trees that exceed five hundred feet in height, but the highest one with an official record is on Mount Baw-Baw, Gippsland; it was measured by Mr. Hodgkinson, a civil engineer, who certifies to its height of four hundred and seventy-one feet. This is considerably more than the height of the tallest of the Big Trees of California, according to the authorities we have consulted. New groups and forests are discovered from time to time, and perhaps one of these days we shall hear of a giant that exceeds five hundred feet.

"The Eucalyptus has been carried to other countries, and it seems to do well all over the world where the climate is not too cold for it. It grows rapidly, and is said to prevent malaria and fevers; we asked Doctor Bronson about the latter statement, and he said he was greatly inclined to believe it. The French introduced it into Algeria, and found that fevers diminished rapidly or disappeared altogether where it grew, and they are so thoroughly convinced of its utility that they have planted great numbers of Eucalypti. Mr. Bosisto, commissioner for Victoria at the colonial exhibition in London, 1886, discusses this subject thoroughly, and says that malarious diseases are not native to Australia, and imported fevers diminish in violence. He thinks this effect is caused by the Eucalyptus, which is evergreen and constantly exhausting humidity from the earth, and throwing off oil and acid from its leaf. A small quantity of Eucalyptus-oil sprinkled in a sick-room improves the air at once and renders breathing easier. Mr. Bosisto contends that the volatile oil thrown off by the leaf absorbs atmospheric oxygen and transforms it into ozone.

"The giant gums are sometimes called 'silver stems,' for the reason that after they have annually shed their bark—they shed their bark and not their leaves—the new skin is of the whiteness of silver. As the trunk is perfectly round, and the lowest limbs are often two hundred feet and more from the ground, the sight of a group of these enormous trees is a very fine one. The giant gums are more slender than the Big Trees of California; the former are the tallest in the world, but the latter have the greater diameter in proportion to their height.

"Next to the giant gum is the red gum, or *Eucalyptus rostrata*, and next to that is the blue gum, or *Eucalyptus globus*. The former is the finest timber-tree, while the latter is the most favored for its anti-fever qualities and is the tree most frequently carried to foreign lands. Don't expect me to go through the whole catalogue of Eucalypti, as there are fully two hundred of them, according to the botanists; the lowest and most wide-spread is the *Eucalyptus dumosa*, or mallee scrub, and you may judge of its extent when I tell you that a single tract of mallee scrub shared between South Australia and Victoria covers an area of nearly nine thousand square miles. 'And it isn't the largest area of scrub, either,' says an Australian at my elbow.

"Well, the mallee is a strange-looking plant, and I can compare it to nothing better than the frame of an umbrella turned bottom up and without any handle in the centre. It has a globular mass at its base, with a few horizontal roots, and then a long tap-root that goes down to a great depth till it reaches moisture. Above-ground there are a lot of shoots, or stalks, from a foot up to twenty feet long, each of them having a tuft of leaves at the top.

"No surface water can be found in the districts where it grows, and the scrub is just a little more than high enough to hide a man on horseback. To be lost in the scrub is very dangerous; you cannot see in any direction, there are no trees you can climb to find your bearings, water or food is not to be found, and the victim is very likely to lose his reason and die of thirst, starvation, and insanity. Terrible stories have been told us of the death of people lost in the scrub; men have gone there to search for missing friends, and both searchers and sought have never been heard of again."

SILVER-STEM EUCALYPTI.

It was after midnight when our friends reached Tenterfield, and at nine o'clock the next morning they were on the coach and dashing away towards Stanthorpe. Over the plains and hills they went at good speed, and were reminded of previous rides in the newly opened regions of the Rocky Mountains and in California. Coaching in Australia is less famous than formerly, owing to the rapid extension of the railway, but there are still many interior lines where the old system is maintained. Coaching in Australia owes its development to some enterprising Americans—Cobb & Company—who went there in the times of the gold discoveries, and established lines over all the principal roads, from the coast ports to the auriferous districts. The wonderful tales of coaching west of the Missouri River a quarter of a century ago might be repeated concerning the same business in Australia.

Doctor Bronson and his companions had no time to examine the mineral and other attractions of Tenterfield, though they were invited to do so. Gold, silver, tin, antimony, plumbago, and other minerals are found in the region round about the town, at distances varying from

FROM TENTERFIELD TO STANTHORPE.

five up to forty miles. Some mining localities were pointed out along the coach-road, and rich specimens of gold-bearing quartz were shown by the fortunate possessors.

Cobb's coach carried them safely to Stanthorpe, sometimes called the Border Town, owing to its position on the frontier, and the Sanatorium of Queensland, in consequence of the salubrity of its climate. It is celebrated for its tin-mines, which are scattered around the neighborhood; the product varies considerably from one year to another, being affected by the scarcity or the abundance of water.

They spent the night at Stanthorpe in a fairly comfortable hotel, and at nine o'clock on the following morning left by train for Brisbane —two hundred and seven miles—where they arrived at half-past ten in the evening.

Frank and Fred were out the next morning at an early hour to see the sights of the capital of Queensland. They found it smaller than Sydney, the total population within a radius of five miles of the centre of the city being less than a hundred thousand. It is on the river Brisbane; river and city were named after Sir Thomas Brisbane, the governor of the colony of New South Wales in 1825, the year when the city was founded as a penal settlement. The river surrounds it on two sides, and gives it an excellent water frontage; from the city to the debouchement of the river into Moreton Bay is about twenty-five miles by the course of the stream, though not more than half that distance overland.

Their walk took them along Queen Street, the principal avenue, to Victoria Bridge, a fine structure of iron which spans the river between North and South Brisbane. The bridge is more than one thousand feet in length, and divided into thirteen spans, with a swing in the centre to permit the passage of vessels. Like most works of the kind, it is said to have cost more than double the original estimates of the engineers who planned it.

The youths were not favorably impressed with the streets of Brisbane, on account of their narrowness, Queen Street being little more than sixty feet wide, and the others in the same proportion. They asked why the streets were made so narrow, when there was such an abundance of land in Australia at the time the place was founded, and were told that it was due to the orders of one of the early governors, Sir George Gipps, who wished to be economical with the land of the Government. But if Queen Street is narrow it is by no means unattractive, as it can boast of many fine shops and substantial buildings, including several belonging to the Government. Frank called Fred's attention to the verandas that on one side of the street ran almost from one end to the other, and extended quite across the sidewalk. Fred rightly conjectured that they were intended to screen pedestrians and goods from the heat and glare of the sun, Brisbane being blessed with a climate of tropical character.

A policeman of whom they made inquiry pointed out the post-office, town-hall, and exchange, the two last-named being in one building, which also contains the chamber of commerce and the council-chamber, and also the court-house and other public edifices. They were all fine buildings with the exception of the court-house, which is a low, solid-looking structure of stone, two stories in height, and of unattractive appearance. Fred asked the policeman the reason of the difference in these buildings.

"The court-house is one of the old prisons of the days of the convict system," was the reply; "it was the female penitentiary and workshop, and at one time was crowded with women who had been transported from England to spend the rest of their lives in Australia. It will probably be torn down before many years, as the people want to get rid of everything that can remind them of the convict system."

A BALCONY.

Turning to the right at the end of Queen Street, and close to Victoria Bridge, they walked along William Street, past the museum, and the Houses of Parliament, till they came to the Government Domain, which contains the residence of the colonial governor. Close by are Queen's Park and the Botanical Gardens, and here they lingered until it was time to return to the hotel and meet Doctor Bronson, who had announced his intention of sleeping till a late hour.

The river makes a sharp bend around Brisbane, and the Government Domain, Botanical Gardens, and Queen's Park are prettily situated at the end of the point of land enclosed in the bend. In colonial parlance it is called a "pocket," and Queen Street may be said to run across the top of the pocket, as it extends from the river to the river again, just as the numbered streets of New York go from the water on one side of Manhattan Island to the water on the other.

Frank and Fred thought they had nowhere seen more attractive Botanical Gardens than those at Brisbane. They were particularly impressed with the row of trees that lined the river-bank; they resembled pines, and were of a sugar-loaf shape, and the custodian of the place

PALM-TREES IN THE BOTANICAL GARDENS.

said they were known as bunya-bunya trees. All the shrubs and plants indigenous to the colony are to be found in the Gardens, together with exotics from all parts of the world whose climate in any way resembles that of Queensland. Our friends were told that the Gardens had been of great practical value to the colony in facilitating the introduction of plants which could be cultivated to advantage. Indigo, madder, coffee, and tea plants were introduced into Queensland by means of the Botanical Gardens, which first developed them, and then sent seeds and cuttings to those who made appli cation. Sugar and cotton were also developed from the same source, and at present the sugar and cotton interests of the colony are of very great importance.

On their way back to the hotel the youths again encountered the communicative policeman. Pointing in the direction of a round building similar to a windmill and supporting a signal-mast, he said,

"That is what we call the Observatory, and it is used for signalling vessels coming into the harbor. It's one of the relics of the convict time; there was once a windmill there where they ground the grain for the convicts to eat, and when the wind didn't blow the prisoners had to work a treadmill in the lower part of the building. I used to know an old fellow who had often done his 'trick at the wheel;' he said he used to have to go it four hours on a stretch, and when through with his trick he was ready to lie down and take a rest. There isn't any part of the treadmill there now, as it was quietly stolen away by the boys, who sold the old iron for a good price."

"NO MORE TRICKS AT THE WHEEL."

CHAPTER XV.

LEAVING BRISBANE.—THE REGIONS AROUND THE CITY.—QUEENSLAND SCRUB AND FOREST LAND.—FRUITS AND GARDEN PRODUCE.—TROUBLES OF THE EARLY SETTLERS.—IPSWICH AND ITS COAL-MINES.—WINE-MAKING IN AUSTRALIA.—CHARACTER OF AUSTRALIAN WINES.—THE LABOR QUESTION.—POLYNESIAN AND CHINESE LABORERS.—POPULATION OF QUEENSLAND.—NATIVES AND ABORIGINES.—PECULIARITIES OF THE BLACK RACE.—CATTLE-TRACKERS AND THEIR ABILITIES.—HOW THE ABORIGINALS LIVE.—THEIR HOMES, WEAPONS, AND MODE OF LIFE.—AUSTRALIAN MYTHS AND SUPERSTITIONS.—CURIOUS THEORIES OF RESURRECTION.—SMOKE AND FIRE SIGNALS.—HOW A WANDERING WHITE MAN SAVED HIS LIFE.—RELIGIOUS IDEAS.—HOW THE EEL MADE THE FROG LAUGH.—THE BUN-YIP AND HIS WONDERFUL ATTRIBUTES.

THE sights of Brisbane were soon exhausted, and our friends arranged to make a journey to the interior, in spite of the efforts of hospitable residents to detain them for several days in the capital. The

A RELIC OF OLD COLONIAL TIMES.

trio agreed that nowhere else in the world was there a more hospitable population than in Australia, and in no other country was the stranger made more heartily welcome. They had already recorded this impression, and it was renewed at every place they visited during their journey through the continent. Frank thought that the name of Australia Felix, which was originally applied to the Port Phillip district, should be given to the entire country, in view of the general amiability of the inhabitants and their courtesy to strangers.

Doctor Bronson and his nephews desired to make a study of "bush life," and an excellent opportunity was offered in an invitation to spend as long a time as they chose at an interior station in Queensland. Rising at an early hour one day, they took the train of the Southern & Western Railway at 5.40 A.M., and rode straight through to Roma, three hundred and seventeen miles, which they reached at ten o'clock at night. The railway continues to Morven, one hundred and ten miles distant, and from that point it will be extended in the near future—at least such is the promise—two or three hundred miles farther. The original scheme was to carry it to Point Parker, on the Gulf of Carpentaria, a distance of one thousand miles from Brisbane; but in consequence of the great expense of the undertaking, the completion of the line has been indefinitely postponed.

The railways of Queensland are on the special narrow-gauge principle, the rails being only three feet six inches apart. The gauge of New South Wales is four feet eight and a half inches, and that of Victoria five feet three inches. In South Australia the Port, North, and Southern lines, are of five feet three inches gauge, and other lines are three feet six inches or like the Queensland railways. For sparsely settled regions the narrow gauge has been found serviceable and economical, and thus far there has been no occasion for express trains at a high rate of speed. As on many of the smaller lines of the United States and other countries, the so-called "express" trains stop at all stations, and are not famous for their rapid progress.

The country through which our friends travelled was not unlike that between Newcastle and Brisbane, as already described. For some distance the railway lay along the valley of the Brisbane River, which contains some excellent farming country, with fine stretches of woodland and occasional swamps. The dividing range of mountains filled the western horizon, and the labored puffing of the locomotive at frequent intervals told that the grade was an ascending one. In the immediate vicinity of Brisbane the land is of poor quality, except in the neighborhood of the streams, and in the early days of the colony a great many settlers were ruined by attempting to establish farms where the soil was not suitable. But in spite of these early discouragements the capabilities of the region have been developed by the perseverance of the settlers; at present the visitor to the district around Brisbane will see prosperous farms, vineyards, orchards, and gardens, though he will still find a great deal of land that is practically unoccupied.

AMONG THE FOOT-HILLS.

At a station a few miles out from the city the train halted for several minutes, and gave Frank and Fred an opportunity to glance at one of these suburban farms. The house of the owner was embowered in vineyards, and close by was a field or plantation of pineapples, which grow here in great profusion, and are of delicious quality. Frank asked the name of a vine that had crept over the roof of the house and almost concealed it from sight; he learned that it was known as the passion-fruit, and was a native plant, producing a very pleasant tart fruit, which unfortunately was not then in season. There was a garden at one side of the house, and in it were all the vegetables of an English garden, including several kinds of melons, besides ginger, arrow-root, sweet-potatoes, and other tropical and semi-tropical productions. Farther back was an extensive field of sugar-cane, which was flanked on one side by a field of oats, and on the other by rows upon rows of luxuriant maize, or Indian corn.

"This is a wonderful region," said a gentleman who accompanied our friends, as the train moved on. "Probably there is no other place in the world where the products of the tropics and temperate zones grow so well together, and certainly there is none where they grow any better. Apples, peaches, pears, cherries, and other northern fruits are side by side with the lemon, orange, citron, pomegranate, fig, and guava. It took us a long while to find out exactly what was wanted, and during that time living was very dear in Brisbane. Now the city has a plentiful supply of fruit at very low prices, coming from the numerous gardens in its vicinity. Irrigate the soil abundantly, and it will produce almost anything in the world that you want. We send great numbers of pineapples and bananas to Sydney and Melbourne, and also to the higher country west of us.

"You already know," he continued, "that Australia is a land of contradictions, when considered from the stand-point of England or the

PICKING FIGS.

United States. In your country the land with the heaviest timber is the best for agriculture after the wood is cleared away, but here it is often just the reverse. The largest trees which cost most money to remove are quite likely found on soil that refuses to produce grass when the land has been cleared, or if it produces grass or grain at all it is not enough to pay the cost of clearing. It is in this particular that so many of the earlier settlers ruined themselves, by expending time and money in clearing up ground that afterwards proved worthless."

A CLEARING IN THE SCRUB.

In the course of the conversation that followed, the gentleman spoke frequently of "scrub" and "forest" land, as though they were distinct from each other. Fred politely asked what was the difference between them.

"Scrub land," replied the gentleman, "is distinct from forest land in several features, but particularly in that of undergrowth. Scrub in Queensland means the low land on the banks of the rivers; it is covered with a dense growth of trees intermingled with a denser growth of vines and creepers, which in many places render it impossible to proceed without cutting one's way through with a tomahawk or large knife. The vines run to the tops of the highest trees, and frequently cross from tree to tree, so that the whole area seems bound together with festoons of green cordage.

"There is a genuine bit of Queensland scrub," said he, pointing to what seemed an almost solid mass of verdure several acres in extent. "It contains cabbage and other palms, fig-trees which tower above most of their fellows, but are overtopped by the bunya, pine, and red cedar, though the latter are not very numerous. An agile sailor might climb from one side to the other of that scrub without once going to the ground; and as for a group of monkeys or squirrels, it would be no effort at all for them to make the journey.

"Of course we're too far off to hear any sounds there, but if you could be under the shade of those trees you would find that the scrub is full of life. I speak only of sunrise and sunset; at noon the place is as quiet as a cemetery, but in the morning and evening quite the re-

SUBURBAN RESIDENCE ON THE RIVER'S BANK.

GATHERING THE GRAPES.

verse. Flocks of pigeons, cockatoos, and parrots fly around and coo and chatter; cat-birds, bell-birds, whip-birds, laughing-jackasses, and a host of others dart about and make the air resound with their notes; and if you watch the ground you will quite likely get a glimpse of wild turkeys and other birds that make their home there and shun the limbs of the trees. Keep a sharp eye out, too, as you may come across snakes, and some of them are poisonous."

Fred was about to ask concerning the snakes of Australia, but their loquacious friend did not give him a chance to do so. He pointed to the opposite side of the train, and told the youths to observe what was there visible.

"That shows you the difference between scrub and forest," said he; "the forest land has heavier timber, but no underbrush; you can ride on horseback through it, while you cannot get along on foot in the scrub without a hatchet. I'm speaking now of the vine scrub along the coast," he continued; "in the interior we have myall, brigelow, mallee, and other scrubs of a totally different character. The forest land is monotonous; you may travel hundreds of miles through it, and find every mile so nearly like every other one that it is very hard to see any change. An experienced bushman knows the difference, but to a novice it is all the same."

The train ascended the slopes of the hills leading to the Dividing Range, having left the river at Ipswich, the head of navigation, and twenty-three miles from Brisbane. The Dividing Range presents a precipitous front, and great engineering skill was required to carry the road over it, the chain being passed at an elevation of two thousand six hundred feet. The scenery, as the range is mounted, is magnificent. The line vies with the Union Pacific Railroad in the United States in tall, spider-like bridges spanning fearful gorges, and in tracks passing round the precipitous spurs of the mountains. Cuttings and tunnelling are met with from the moment the ascent commences. The steepest gradient is one in fifty. Notwithstanding the apparent danger attending a journey on this portion of the line, no accident involving loss of life or serious injury to rolling stock has occurred here since the first engine ran on it.

Ipswich is in a mining and agricultural district, several rich seams of coal having been opened in its neighborhood, and the country around it being well adapted to farms. At Toowoomba, one hundred miles from Brisbane, their guide told the youths they were at the principal town of the rich pastoral district called the Darling Downs; the region was discovered and settled in 1827, and named after Sir Ralph Darling, who was then governor. Agriculture and the raising of cattle and sheep are the principal industries, and the town bears every evidence of prosperity.

"There are many Germans settled in this neighborhood," said Mr. Watson, the gentleman who accompanied our friends, "and they are largely interested in grape-growing and the manufacture of wines. Many thousand gallons of wine are made here every year; the grapes are ripe in January, and I have seen single bunches weighing fifteen pounds and over."

Frank asked how the wines of Queensland and Australia in general compared with those of other countries.

"Of course our wine-making is in its infancy," was the reply; "and thus far our products will hardly bear favorable comparison with the wines of Europe, where the industry has been prosecuted for centuries; but we think they are fully equal to the wines of the United States,

CELLARS FOR STORING WINE.

where the business is only a little older than it is with us. All the colonies are giving much attention to grape-growing; the yield is very large; but in the last few years the vines have suffered considerably from *phylloxera*, though fortunately all parts of the colonies have not been affected by it.

"We make so much wine, and it is so cheap and good," the gentleman continued, "that it ought to be the drink of the people, just as in France, Spain, Italy, and the other countries of Southern Europe. Very little wine is used by the laboring classes; some do not drink at all, others drink occasionally, and others daily and hourly if they have the opportunity, but nearly all prefer spirits to wine. What makes the matter worse is that the spirits are very bad in quality, and their consumption leads to much wretchedness and degradation, just as in Europe and America. Some of the working people drink beer, as in England, and in all the cities and large towns there are extensive breweries that do a good business.

"Competent and conscientious judges say that the ordinary Australian wines are better than the same grades sold in Paris and other French cities. They are the pure juice of the grape, the juice being so abundant and cheap that it does not pay to adulterate it. In Sydney, Melbourne, Adelaide, and Brisbane a man can buy for threepence a glass of as fine an ordinary wine as was ever made; it is nutritious and wholesome, but unfortunately the great majority of the laboring classes prefer to swallow the vile decoctions that are sold under the names of spirits. Our capabilities in wine-making are absolutely unlimited; we are shipping some of our products to Europe, where they take the place of the ordinary wines of France and Spain, and quite possibly you get many casks of them in New York and other American cities, where they are sold as Bordeaux wines."

"There's a great deal in a name," said Doctor Bronson, "especially when wines are to be considered. No doubt we have your Australian common wines in America under the name of Bordeaux or Burgundy, just as we have our own products. Thousands of casks of California wines are sold every year on the Atlantic seaboard, but not under their own name. Offered as California wines they would not find a market, but as Bordeaux wines they have a ready sale."

"And I have been told," said Mr. Watson, "that the Californian, although very enthusiastic about his own State, will not drink its wine. Am I right?"

"According to my observation, you are," the Doctor replied. "I do not think I ever saw a bottle of native wine on the table of a resident of California. Hotel-keepers in San Francisco have told me that

CHINESE LABORERS IN A VINEYARD.

those who order California wines at dinner are invariably strangers; a Californian would almost consider himself disgraced if he should do so."

"Well, it is pretty much the same in Australia," said Mr. Watson. "We are proud of our country and what it produces, but we prefer French champagne to our own sparkling wines, and Spanish sherry to what comes from our vineyards and wine cellars. And not altogether without reason, I must confess, as we have not yet reached perfection with our fine wines."

From wine-culture the conversation naturally turned to the labor question, which Mr. Watson said was one of the perplexities of Queensland. The climate is too hot to permit the white man to work in the fields and other places where severe manual exertion is required, with the exception of the elevated regions of the Darling Downs and some other comparatively cool places. Consequently there has been a necessity for imported labor, and in endeavoring to secure it Queensland has had a great deal of trouble.

ABORIGINAL AUSTRALIAN.

In previous chapters we have alluded to the Polynesian labor-trade, much of which was carried on in the interest of the sugar-planters of Queensland. There were many abuses in its early days, but at present the trade is under so many restrictions that the laborers have little cause for complaint. The natives are brought to the colony for three years; the master is bound to give them food and lodging, thirty dollars a year wages, and then pay their passage home in addition to the outward passage which he has paid to the ship-master who brings the laborers from their islands.

By the last census there were about six thousand Polynesians in Queensland, ten thousand five hundred Chinese, and about two thousand inhabitants of the Malay Archipelago. The Chinese, like the Polynesians, are mostly employed in out-door work, though a considerable number of them are utilized as house-servants, and in other domestic employments. They go to Australia to earn a certain amount of money, and then return home, just as they come to the United States. Of more than ten thousand Chinese in Queensland, all but forty-nine were men; and no matter how prosperous a Chinese may be in Australia, he rarely thinks of taking his family there.

Frank asked what was the total population of the colony.

"Not far from three hundred and fifty thousand," was the reply.

"There is an excess of males in the population, as is always the case in a new country, the proportions of men to women being about three to two. About one-half the population were born in the Australian colonies, and of the remainder fully three-fourths came from Great Britain. The colony encourages immigration by means of assisted or free passage, grants of land, and other inducements, and maintains constantly an agent in London who forwards the interests of Queensland in every way in his power."

"How many natives are there in the colony?" queried Fred.

"I am afraid if I answered your question without an explanation," said Mr. Watson, with a smile, "I should give you a wrong impression. By natives I suppose you mean the aboriginal inhabitants of the country?"

"Certainly," replied Fred.

"In Australia, when we speak of natives," Mr. Watson answered, "we mean white people who were born in the country, in contrast to those who have migrated from England and other lands. When referring to the aborigines we call them so, and we also call them 'blacks' or 'blackfellows.' At the last census there were 148,162 natives, or whites, born in the colonies, living in Queensland, and about 20,000 aborigines. The latter number is an estimate only, as it is impossible to take the census of the black population."

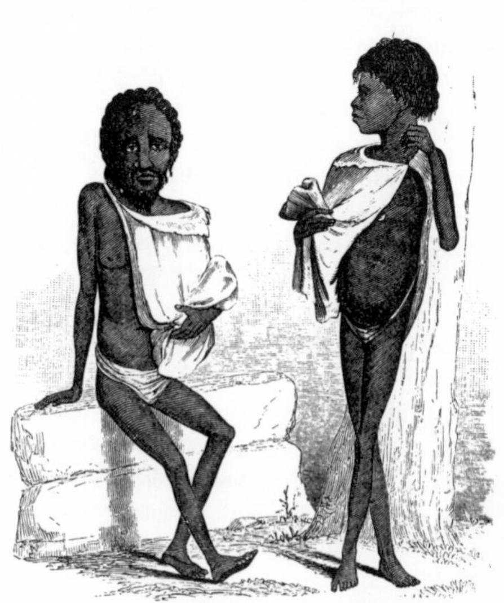
WEST COAST AUSTRALIANS.

"If you want to see the difference between a native and an aboriginal," said the gentleman, "look where I am pointing."

The youths followed with their eyes the direction of his finger, and saw a white man and a black one standing near each other, close to the little station where the train was halted, some miles beyond Toowoomba. The black man was in civilized garb and had a muscular frame, quite like that of an able-bodied negro in the southern part of the United States. His garments were coarse and rough, his hair was black and bushy, and his chin was covered with a beard that seemed to more than rival his hair in its swarthiness.

"The white man is probably a sheep or cattle raiser," said Mr. Watson, "and the black is one of his assistants."

"From that I suppose the blacks are employed about the farms and pastoral stations," Fred remarked.

"Certainly," responded Mr. Watson. "Nearly every station in Queensland has one or two blackfellows employed on it as stock-riders, a capacity in which they are very useful. They are good riders, and quite equal to your American Indians in following a trail. They will track lost cattle and sheep when a white man would be utterly unable to do so; and we have a police force of blacks, commanded by Europeans, who perform excellent service in hunting down highwaymen and other rascals who have taken to the bush."

Frank asked what was the reputation of the blacks for honesty and in other ways.

"I'm sorry to say it is not of the best," was the reply. "Like most savages, they show great readiness for acquiring the vices of civilization, but great reluctance for adopting its virtues. They are adepts at lying and stealing, though they are generally faithful to those who employ them as long as they are employed. They are like all other savages in their fondness for intoxicating liquors, and rarely miss an opportunity for drinking. Most of those employed about the cattle and sheep stations do not remain there long. As soon as they become fairly useful they demand higher wages, and in a little while their demands are so exorbitant that they must be sent away.

"When they are out of work they take to stealing cattle, and generally from the station where they were formerly engaged, and with which they are familiar. Many of them loaf around the towns, doing small jobs of work, and generally dying of drink."

"Why don't they return to their tribes?" one of the youths inquired.

"For the very simple reason that they would be put to death by their own people. A black who has been employed by a white man is forever after an outcast from his own tribe; at least such is the case with nearly all the tribes I ever heard of."

Frank asked Mr. Watson if he had been among the blacks and seen them at home. The gentleman replied in the affirmative, and then both the youths asked him to tell more about them and their ways of living. Mr. Watson kindly assented, and at once began his story.

"At starting let me say," he remarked, "that the aborigines of Australia are about the lowest type of the human race that can be found, with the possible exception of the natives of Terra del Fuego. They belong distinctively to the black race, though their hair while curly has not the woolly crispness of that of the African negro. In the interior, away from settlements, they go entirely naked, and when white men first came to Australia the natives had no knowledge of the uses of clothing. Around the settlements they have adopted civilized customs in the matter of dress, but only upon compulsion. I have known the

CIVILIZED ABORIGINES.

blacks who were employed at a sheep-station to go naked when away from the dwelling of their employer, and only resume their clothing on returning to the house."

"What kind of houses do they live in when by themselves?" Frank asked.

"They had not learned to build houses until the Europeans instructed them," was the reply, "and the wild tribes of the interior still continue to live as they did of yore. They occasionally build rude huts of bark by inclining two or three strips against each other in the form of a cone, but more frequently their only protection against the weather is a single strip of bark, or a large bough of a tree, inclined towards the wind, and held in place by an upright stick.

"In my younger days I owned a station in a region where the blacks were numerous, and though they occasionally stole some of my sheep and cattle, and committed other depredations, our relations were, on the whole, of a friendly character. I allowed them to visit my house, but only on condition that they were properly dressed, the dress consisting of a skin or piece of cloth around the waist. As a single garment lasted them a long time, it was evident that they wore it only when coming to my house, laying it aside as soon as they were out of sight. When going into battle they paint their bodies with red earth, to give them a hideous appearance, and if they can obtain European paints of different colors they are especially happy; they imagine that the more hideously they are decorated the more likely are they to be victorious in fights with other tribes.

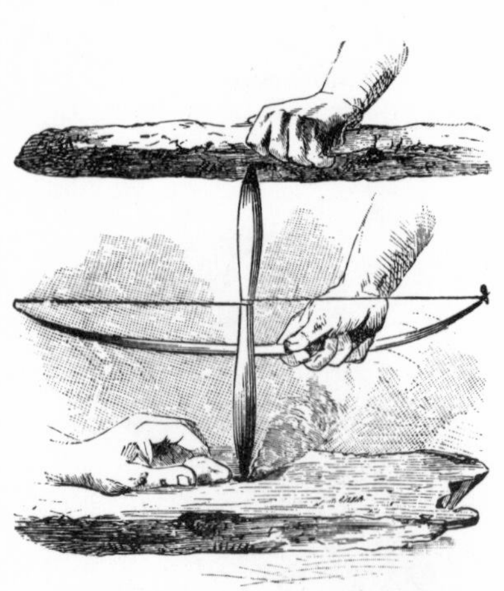

ABORIGINAL METHOD OF MAKING FIRE.

"Like most other savage people, they obtain fire by rubbing two sticks together; but the operation requires so much exertion that they take great care to preserve fire when once they have obtained it. A tribe will wander about for days and weeks carrying fire in coals carefully protected by strips of bark; some of the old women are designated as fire-carriers, and are generally exempt from other work. When they build fires at night they surround them with shields of bark, so that their locality will not be revealed by the glare of light.

"They use columns of smoke by day, and fires by night, for conveying intelligence. They have a very good telegraphic code by columns of smoke, which can be made to indicate warnings, the position of game, ships or whales in sight along the coast, and various other things. They can make smoke signals that will be understood by their own or friendly tribes, but be unintelligible to hostile ones. In former times they used this smoke signal occasionally to the injury of the white settlers, who had at first no idea that the thin column of smoke rising through the trees was a signal for the warriors to make a simultaneous attack upon half a dozen places at once."

Fred asked what kind of weapons they used in fighting with one another or attacking the Europeans.

"Their principal weapon for close work," said Mr. Watson, "is the waddy, or club. It is a heavy club made of hard-wood, and has a knob at the end of the handle for greater security of grasp. Etiquette requires that blows with the waddy should be aimed only at the head; to strike any other part of the body with it would not be fair. The form of the weapon differs with different tribes, so that it is possible sometimes to learn to what tribe a party belongs by looking at their clubs. Some tribes have wooden swords about three feet long, which they handle very skilfully.

AUSTRALIAN WARRIORS WATCHING A BOAT.

"They are expert in throwing spears, which they launch very accurately for distances of thirty or forty yards. Sometimes their spears are a single piece of hard-wood tipped with bone, iron, or sharp stone; other spears have heads of hard-wood, while the shaft is a light reed which grows abundantly on the banks of most of the rivers of Australia. The spears vary from six to eleven feet in length; I have seen spears fifteen feet long, but they were intended for fishing, and not for war, though they were often used for fighting purposes.

BATTLE BETWEEN HOSTILE TRIBES OF AUSTRALIANS.

"A black in his wild state is rarely seen without a spear in his hand, and this reminds me of one of my early experiences. I went out in the bush one day with some of the friendly blacks, and had walked a short distance in front of them when one of the party stopped me. He motioned for me to step to the rear, and then said,

"'When you walk in bush along a blackfellow, you make him blackfellow walk first time (in front).'

"When I asked what for, he replied, 'I den know. I believe debil debil jump up; want him blackfellow spear whitefellow.' You can be sure I took the hint, and ever afterwards allowed the blacks to take the lead. Several times since then friendly natives have told me that when a white man is walking in front of them there is an almost irresistible inclination to spear him.

"They have a superstition which they express in these words: 'Blackfellow die, jump up whitefellow;' which means that when a black man dies he reappears as a white one. In the early days of the settlement at Sydney, the convicts who ran away into the bush were almost certain to be killed by the blacks if they escaped death by starvation before the blacks found them. One convict who thus escaped wandered about for several days, and finally became so weak that he could hardly stand. In this dilemma he took a staff which he found sticking in a mound of earth, and used it as a support. A few hours afterwards he fell in with a party of natives, who treated him with the greatest respect. They fed him bountifully, and nursed him as well as their limited means permitted, and in course of time restored him to health and strength. Every man indicated a desire to obey him. He remained for years with the tribe, and as soon as he had acquired enough of their language to communicate with them, they made him understand that he was their chief.

"It turned out that the mound of earth where he found the staff was the grave of their chief, who had recently died and been buried

ABORIGINAL AUSTRALIANS AND THEIR HUTS.

there. The stick which he took from the mound was the shaft of the chief's favorite spear, which was stuck into his grave according to their custom. When he appeared leaning on the stick, the superstitions of the natives told them that he was their chief returned in the shape of a white man. To this accidental circumstance he owed his life, as the tribe was in the habit of spearing every white man who came in their way."

Fred asked what were their burial customs, and if they had any belief in a future existence.

"The dead are buried in the spots where they die, and these places are never inhabited again by members of the dead man's tribe, nor are they even visited except on rare occasions or from necessity. The names of the dead are never pronounced, and those having the same names are obliged to change them. My partner at the sheep-station died of fever; he had been kind to the blacks, and was evidently liked by them, but I could never get them to listen to any reference to him after his death, and they did not like to look at his photograph, which hung in the house.

"They have very crude ideas on religious matters. They believe in good and bad spirits; and some tribes have a belief in a supreme being, while others have none. They have many myths and superstitions, and some of these myths display a vivid imagination on the part of those who invented them. Shall I tell you some of them?"

The youths said they would greatly like to hear some of the Australian myths, whereupon Mr. Watson continued:

"The aboriginal theory about the creation is that Pund-jel, or Bunjil, created two men out of the clay of the earth, but he did not create women. That honor was reserved for Pal-ly-yan, the son of Pund-jel, who made a woman for each of the men. Pund-jel gave each man a spear, and told him to kill the kangaroo with it; and to the women he gave a digging-stick for digging roots from the ground. The men and women were ordered to live together, and thus the world was peopled. By-and-by people became very numerous, and then Pund-jel caused storms to arise, and winds to blow so severely as to scatter the people over the earth, and thus the human race was dispersed.

"The first man and woman were told not to go near a certain tree in which a bat lived, as he was not to be disturbed. One day the woman, in gathering firewood, went near the tree; the bat flew away, and after that came death."

"How closely it resembles the Biblical account of the fall of man!" Fred remarked.

"The resemblance has been noticed by writers on the subject," said Mr. Watson, "and some believe that the tradition is not genuine. Mr. Brough Smyth, author of an exhaustive work on the Aborigines of Victoria, accepts it as genuine, and so do other prominent writers. I have given some thought to the subject, and notwithstanding the similarity, I agree with them.

"The blacks say there is a very wicked man who has a very long tail living under the ground. He has many wives and children, and laughs at the blacks because they have no tails. They have another tradition that at one time there was no water anywhere on the earth, all the waters being contained in the body of a huge frog, where men and women could not get it. There was a grand council on the subject, and it was ascertained that if the frog could be made to laugh, the waters would run out of his mouth and the drought would be ended.

ABORIGINAL CHILDREN PLAYING IN THE WATER.

"Several animals danced and capered before the frog to induce him to laugh, but without success. Then the eel began to wriggle, and at that the frog laughed outright; the waters ran from his mouth, and there was a great flood, in which many people were drowned. The pelican took it upon himself to save the black people. He cut an immense canoe, and went with it among the islands which appeared here and there above the waters, and with this canoe he saved a great many men and women."

"A distinct tradition of the flood," remarked Fred to Frank, as Mr. Watson paused a few moments to consider what he would next say.

"There is a myth about the sun that is quite interesting," Mr. Watson continued. "They say that because the sun gives heat it needs fuel, and when it descends below the horizon it goes down to a great depth, where it is supplied with fuel. They have some knowledge of astronomy, and have names for and traditions concerning the principal

THE HAUNT OF THE BUN-YIP.

planets and fixed stars. They have mythical snakes and other animals possessing supernatural powers, and can tell you stories upon stories of the wonderful things these creatures have done. The monster most widely believed in is the bun-yip; he is of dreadful aspect, devours great numbers of human beings, and altogether bears a close resemblance to the dragons which were believed in in other parts of the world at different times since the history of man began. He can cause death, illness, disease, and other misfortunes, and is supposed to haunt lakes, rivers, and water-holes all over the continent. Many natives claim to have seen him, and a considerable number of white men confirm their accounts of the creature."

"And do you think such an animal exists?" Frank asked, with an expression of astonishment.

"Of course not with the attributes the blacks give him," was the reply, "but it is quite possible that Australia possesses an amphibious animal which we have not yet been able to examine. As described by those who claim to have seen the bun-yip, he resembles a seal or large water-dog. The seal abounds in Australian waters; I presume that he is the bun-yip of the natives, and that their imaginations have supplied his wonderful powers."

CHAPTER XVI.

RIDING THROUGH THE BUSH.—AUSTRALIAN HOSPITALITY.—ARRIVAL AT THE STATION.—THE BUILDINGS AND THEIR SURROUNDINGS.—A SNAKE IN FRED'S BED.—SNAKES IN AUSTRALIA.—UNDERWOOD'S REMEDY FOR SNAKE-BITES, AND WHAT CAME OF IT.—CENTIPEDES AND SCORPIONS.—A VENOMOUS SPIDER.—NOCTURNAL NOISES AT A CATTLE-STATION.—HORSES AND THEIR TRAITS.—BUCK-JUMPING AND ROUGH-RIDING.—HOW A "NEW CHUM" CATCHES A HORSE.—ENDURANCE OF HORSES.—AMONG THE HERDS OF CATTLE.—RIDE TO A CATTLE-CAMP.—DAILY LIFE OF THE STOCKMEN.—CASTE IN AUSTRALIA.—SQUATTERS AND FREE SELECTORS.—HORRIBLE ACCIDENTS IN THE BUSH.—A MAN EATEN ALIVE BY ANTS.—BURNED TO DEATH UNDER A FALLEN TREE.—CHASING AN EMU.—ROUSING A FLOCK OF WILD TURKEYS.

ON their arrival at Roma, Doctor Bronson and his young companions spent the night, or what remained of it, in a hotel that was anything but comfortable by comparison with the spacious caravanseries of the city, but fully as good as they had expected to find in an

THE TEAM.

interior town. After an early breakfast they were taken in a light but strong wagon, drawn by two powerful horses, to the station of their host.

The road lay through an undulating country in which there was an agreeable diversity of open areas interspersed with gum forest and occasional scrub. The road was good for a track in the bush, but was

PETS AT THE STATION.

cut up with numerous gullies, ruts, and holes, which gave a liberal amount of exercise to the occupants of the vehicle. Mr. Watson said it was an excellent road in the dry season, but anything but agreeable after heavy rains had converted it into a long stretch of mud. "One of my neighbors used to say," he continued, "that the road between our houses was ten miles long, twenty feet wide, and two feet deep; and he was not far from the mark."

We will let Frank tell the story of what they saw and heard at the station; and we may add that where he found his memory at fault while writing his account of the sheep and cattle raising business, he refreshed it by glancing at several books on the subject, and particularly at "Advance Australia!" by the Hon. Harold Finch-Hatton.

"We stopped several times on our way from Roma," said Frank in his narrative, "as our host seemed to know everybody in the country, and wished us to meet as many of his acquaintances as we could. Every one was hospitable, and it was not easy to get away; partly for this reason and partly in consequence of the distance, it was almost sundown when we reached the station, which was quite a village of houses.

The principal house, where the owner and his family lived, was in an enclosure perhaps two hundred feet square. There were several trees in the enclosure, and a perfect wilderness of vines and creepers of many kinds. The vine most abundant was the scarlet geranium, which is supposed to keep away snakes; but if half the stories we heard are true, its virtue is not absolute in this respect.

"The house was a two-story building of wood, about fifty feet by thirty, and stood upon posts, or piles, seven feet high, each post having a geranium vine growing around it. There was a wide veranda all around the house; the space on the ground was occupied with dining-room, pantry, store-room, office, and bath-room, and was easily accessible on all sides. There was a huge fireplace in the dining-room, and also one in the large sitting-room directly above it. On the same floor with the sitting-room there were four good bedrooms. One of these was given to Doctor Bronson; the others being occupied by the family, Fred and I were shown to a small house just outside the yard, where were two very good rooms, plainly but comfortably furnished. After arranging our toilets we returned to the big house, and were ready for dinner, which was shortly announced.

"We dined substantially on roast mutton, preceded by a soup of kangaroo tail, and followed by a plum-pudding which had been put up in London and sent to Australia in a tin can. We spent an hour or two in the sitting-room listening to tales of Australian bush life, and then started for bed; and thereby hangs a tale.

THE TIGER SNAKE.

"Fred's room was separated from mine by a thin partition. When Mr. Watson left us Fred remarked that he was quite ready for a good sleep, as he was very tired. As he spoke he turned down the bedclothes, and then shouted for me to come quick.

"'Here's a big snake in my bed!' said he. 'Come and help me kill him.'

"Mr. Watson heard the remark, and hastened back before I could get to where the snake was.

"'Don't harm that snake,' said he; 'it's a pet, and belongs to my brother. It's nothing but a carpet snake.'

"With that Fred cooled down, but said he didn't want any such pet in his bed, even if it was nothing but a carpet snake. The serpent, which was fully ten feet long, raised his head lazily, and then put it down again, as if he was quite satisfied with the situation and did not wish to be disturbed.

"Mr. Watson explained that the snake had no business there, and without more ado he picked the creature up by the neck and dragged it off to a barrel which he said was its proper place. After he had gone Fred and I put a board over the top of the barrel to make sure that the reptile did not give us a call during the night. Poverty is said to make one acquainted with strange bedfellows, but poverty can't surpass Australian bush life where a man finds a snake in his bed altogether too often for comfort.

"While we are on this subject," Frank continued, "we will have a word about the snakes of Australia. The carpet snake, to which we were so unceremoniously introduced, is the largest of the family, and is really harmless, so far as its bite is concerned, though it has powers of constriction that are not to be despised. It lives upon small game which it can easily swallow, and occasionally ventures upon a young wallaby or kangaroo. It may be kept as a pet, as you have seen; but as it can't sing, doesn't learn tricks, never undertakes to talk, and does nothing for the amusement or entertainment of its owner, I don't understand why anybody should want to pet it. But there's no accounting for tastes. It catches a few rats and other vermin, and occasionally creates havoc in the chicken-yard.

"There are five deadly serpents in Australia—the black snake, the brown snake, the tiger snake, the diamond snake, and the death-adder. The black and brown are most common, and the brown snake frequently reaches a length of nine feet. The most vicious and dangerous is the tiger snake, which seems to be allied to the *cobra-de-capello* of India, as, when irritated, it flattens and extends its neck to twice its ordinary size. It secretes its maximum amount of poison in the summer, and its bite is speedily fatal. The bite of any of the snakes here enumerated will cause death in a few hours unless the proper antidotes are applied.

"The death-adder is unlike the other snakes in one respect; it never attempts to get out of any one's way, but lies quite still until it is touched, when it instantly strikes at its victim. The best-known remedies for snake-bites are hypodermic injections of ammonia, cutting out the wound, and swallowing large quantities of brandy or other spirits.

CAMPING-OUT ON A CATTLE-RUN.

"Mr. Watson says there was once a man named Underwood, who discovered a perfectly efficacious antidote to the bite of a poisonous snake. He gave several performances in which he allowed himself to be bitten by snakes that were undoubtedly healthy and in full possession of their venomous powers. Dogs and rabbits that were bitten by the same snakes after they had tried their fangs on Underwood died very soon afterwards; and it must be remembered that the second bite of a snake is always less poisonous than the first. After being bitten by the snakes, Underwood applied a remedy which was known only to himself, and soon recovered from the effects of the bite.

"The manner of his death is a very convincing proof of the perfection of his remedy. One day, while under the influence of liquor, he allowed himself to be bitten by a snake; in consequence of his intoxication he was unable to find his antidote, and so he died of the bite. His secret perished with him; he had demanded £10,000 ($50,000) for it, which the Government refused to pay, as they thought the price exorbitant.

"Every new chum—freshly arrived men in the colonies are known as 'new chums'—has a nervous apprehension about snakes when he first sets foot in the bush, and has quite likely provided himself with a pair of long boots as a protection against venomous reptiles. Within a week or so this feeling wears off, and after a while a man thinks no more about snakes than in England or the United States. Most of the deaths from snake-bites occur among the laborers in the fields, and altogether they are by no means uncommon. In some localities one might go about for years without seeing a snake, while in others the deadly reptiles are so numerous that caution must be exercised. The worst regions are said to be the cane-fields of the Mackay district and the reed-beds on the Murray River.

"There are centipedes and scorpions in Australia whose bite is poisonous, and there is a black spider about the size of a large pea, with a brilliant crimson mark on its back. It lives in old timber, and frequently takes up its abode in a house, where it does not wait to be disturbed before attacking one. Its bite is very painful; death not infrequently follows it, but more probably the victim becomes hopelessly insane or paralyzed. Mr. Finch-Hatton tells how he was bitten by one of these spiders, and within ten seconds he had cut out the flesh and rubbed the wound with ammonia, which he always kept about him. But his leg got very bad; the pain for days was intense, and afterwards the whole leg swelled and became

THE POISONOUS SPIDER (MAGNIFIED).

soft, like dough. The wound turned into a running sore, which did not heal for months.

"We thought we were going to sleep well at the station, but soon found our mistake. We were not far from a pen where a dozen weanling calves were shut to separate them from their mothers. The calves kept up a steady bleating, and their mothers in the paddock close by plaintively answered them. About the same distance off on the other side was the chicken-house, and we had the benefit of the voices of the chanticleers. Cocks in Australia begin to crow at midnight and stop at sunrise. They must have had a clock to look at, as the first of them crowed exactly at twelve, and the others followed without a minute's delay. Then a flock of ducks added their clamor; and the fun was liveliest when a dingo, or wild dog, set up a howl in the bush. This started all the canines on the place, and as Mr. Watson and his brother were the owners of four bull-dogs, six fox-terriers, three cattle-dogs, four kangaroo-dogs, and two wolf-hounds, I leave you to imagine the sounds that greeted our ears.

THE PROSPEROUS SQUATTER.

"One gets used to this sort of thing, like everything else, and on the second night on the place we slept without much interruption; but on that first morning we were glad when daylight came, so that we could get up; and when we saw the beauty of the breaking day we were very glad we had risen so early. There was a peculiar freshness about the air, and the scent of the gum-trees was clearly perceptible. Over the low ground there lay a thin mist, which the rising sun dispelled, and then as the sunlight came breaking over the landscape it bathed the whole scene in an atmosphere of gold. Ducks flapped their wings over the surface of a pond a few hundred yards away; crows sailed around in the air or perched on trees not far from the dwelling-house, and two or three other birds added their notes to the chorus. Chickens, pigeons, and other domestic birds gathered in front of the storehouse, waiting for their morning meal; cows were low-

"I'M WAITING FOR YOU."

ing and horses neighing in the yards, and everything betokened activity.

"We went in the direction of the yards, and as we did so a black boy came dashing up behind a drove of thirty or forty horses which he had brought in from the great paddock. They were intended for the day's riding, and one of the men about the place told us that it is the custom on an Australian station to bring up the horses every morning in this way, and turn them out again after the selections for the day have been made.

"The stock-keepers were on hand to pick out their horses, and we watched the work with a good deal of interest. Australian horses have a bad reputation, and as we saw the men going into the yard we felt sure there would be a lively time; but, contrary to our expectations, the animals quietly submitted, and were saddled and bridled without the least resistance. The horses are cunning creatures and know their masters, so that when an old hand approaches them they thoroughly understand the folly of resistance, as it is sure to bring punishment.

"It was very different the next morning when a new chum went in to catch a horse. With the aid of a black boy he cornered it off in the yard, and then, with the bridle over his arm, approached it slowly and with soothing words, which might as well have been addressed to a grisly bear. Australian horses are cruelly treated all their lives, and consequently they nearly all have vicious tempers, on which kindness is wholly thrown away. The horse immediately understood the man to be a stranger in the

PERFORMANCE OF A BUCKER.

country, and proceeded to act accordingly. The expression of his eye and the droop of his quarters were not to be misunderstood; and just as the man put out his hand with the bridle, the horse gave a snort and a rush, knocking down his would-be captor, and then galloped round and round the yard with his tail in the air.

"Again the man got the horse in a corner, and just as he was about getting the bridle into place the brute put his head over the fence, where it could not possibly be reached, and at the same time spitefully threw his heels in the air in a way that made the new chum look out for his safety. Three or four other attempts were made, to the great delight of the old hands, who always sit on the fence and watch the performance until they grow weary of laughing; then they come to the relief of the novice, and saddle and bridle the horse for him at once.

THE MILKING-YARD.

"After the horse had been saddled the new chum tried to mount him. He got safely into the saddle, but hardly was he seated before the beast began to 'buck,' as we call it in America, or 'buck-jump,' as it is designated here. The horse brought his head and all his feet together, arched his back till it resembled a section of the dome of a church, and then jumped up, down, sidewise, forward, backward, and in every other direction in very rapid succession. The man was a good rider, and managed to stick until the horse lay down and tried to roll over him, when he slid out of the saddle and gave up.

"Then one of the old hands tried the horse, which repeated the performance, but not so successfully, as the rider suddenly pulled the

COMING IN FROM PASTURE.

animal's head up and prevented his falling to the ground. Practised riders sometimes show their skill by putting a silver coin the size of a half-dollar between each thigh and the saddle, and retaining it there in spite of all the plunging and bucking of the animal.* One of the men gravely told us he had seen a man thrown twenty feet into the air by a bucking horse, and then come down astride the saddle in exactly the right position. Another said he had seen a horse swell himself suddenly, so as to burst the girths of the saddle; the saddle and the man on it then went fully ten feet into the air, and came down on the horse all right and in order. We had intended to tell them about the remarkable riding of Buffalo Bill and his cow-boys, but after these two stories we had nothing to say.

* In an article on "Ranch Life in the Far West," in *The Century Magazine* for February, 1888, Hon. Theodore Roosevelt says: "The flash-riders, or horse-breakers, always called 'broncho-busters,' can perform really marvellous feats, riding with ease the most vicious and unbroken beasts, that no ordinary cow-boy would dare to tackle. Although sitting seemingly so loose in the saddle, such a rider cannot be jarred out of it by the wildest plunger, it being a favorite feat to sit out the antics of a bucking horse, with a silver half-dollar under each knee or in the stirrups under each foot."

"Australian horses are credited with remarkable endurance. A ride of a hundred miles between sunrise and sundown is not a wonderful performance. There is a story of a man who rode a pony a hundred miles in a day, and then carried it a hundred yards; but it is proper to add that the pony died from his rough usage. One horse carried his rider, a Mr. Lord, two hundred and sixty-three miles in three days, and suffered no ill effects from doing so. The distances made were eighty-eight miles the first day, eighty-three the second, and ninety-two on the third. Mr. Lord weighed one hundred and ninety-nine pounds, so that the horse had no feather-weight to carry.

"We were called away to breakfast before the men had finished their work with the horses, as some were to be reserved for the use of the strangers. Mr. Watson had given orders that the best horses

AN AUSTRALIAN STOCK-RIDER.

were to be turned over to us; not the best from the stockman's point of view, but those of the kindest disposition and least addicted to tricks. A horse without any bad tricks is not easy to find on an Australian station; if what we were told about their breaking is true, it is no wonder.

"There are men who go about breaking horses for eight or ten dollars a head. They are regular cow-boys, who cannot be thrown out of a saddle by any motions the horse may make short of lying down and rolling over them. A lot of young horses which have never been in a yard twice in their lives are driven up into an enclosure; a horse is selected, separated from the herd, and driven into a small yard by himself. He is lassoed or secured in some way, and a saddle and bridle are put on him. While the animal is held by his assistants, the horse-breaker mounts, and then sticks his spurs into the poor beast and sets him to bucking till he is tired out and gives in; then the horse is left for a few hours with the saddle on. After two or three days of this kind of treatment he is turned over to his owner as 'broken.'

AN UNSTEADY SEAT.

"The Australian saddle is very much like the Mexican, or like that used in the Western States of North America and on the frontier. It has a high pommel and cantle, weighs not far from twenty pounds, and is used with a saddle-cloth beneath it, the same as the Whitman and other well-known saddles of American make. Some riders prefer English saddles, but they are useless for bucking horses. A gentleman who has had a great deal of experience in Australia says he has seen men ride very bad buck-jumpers barebacked, and has often *heard* of men who could ride them in an English saddle, but he never saw it done, and does not believe such a thing possible.

"For breakfast we had broiled steak, with fried eggs and bacon, plenty of good bread, some pickles and jam, washed down with strong tea. Coffee is not often used in the Australian bush, the greater convenience of tea having made it much more popular. Living in the bush is not luxurious, and on many stations the unvarying round of tea, damper, and beef or mutton soon becomes monotonous. These are the staples of food; vegetables of any kind are rarely seen; and as for pickles, jam, and the like, they are luxuries which only the prosperous can afford. 'Damper' is dough baked in hot ashes or on a hot stone; when you are hungry and the damper is fresh, it is by no means unpalatable; but cold damper requires an excellent appetite to get it down.

A NEW CHUM'S FIRST RIDE.

"Soon after breakfast the horses were brought up, and we started, under the guidance of Mr. Watson, for a ride among the cattle. The run, as a cattle or sheep range is called (the word corresponding in usage to the American 'ranch'), was about twenty miles square, and was said to be an excellent one, as the grass was good and there was plenty of water. Cattle and sheep runs are frequently much larger than this; I heard of some that covered areas of more than six hundred square miles, and were capable of carrying thirty thousand head of cattle; but such runs are becoming more and more rare every year.

"The large runs have two or three, and sometimes more, stations, or residences, with yards and buildings; one of them is the 'head station,' where the owner or manager lives, and from which orders are sent out.

A STAMPEDE.

Each station has from one to three or four stockmen, with as many black assistants; this force is sufficient for managing the cattle; and each station has its herd of horses, which are driven up every morning, as already described. The horses are in a paddock, or fenced pasture, but the cattle roam at large and are generally about half wild. Some of the runs have boundary fences; but this is by no means the rule, and the consequence is that cattle of different owners are constantly mixed up and require separating.

"All over the runs there are cattle-camps at intervals of a few miles; these are level places, free from stones, and with plenty of water, and it is part of the stockman's work to accustom the cattle to run to these camps whenever they hear the crack of his whip. Driving into camp is called tailing, or mustering, and we were bound on a mustering expedition to a camp five or six miles away. The object of the muster was to draft some bullocks to sell to a cattle-dealer who arrived at the station about the time we did.

"Two of the stockmen had been sent off very early in the morning to work the other side of the camp; we jogged on at an easy pace through alternating forest and open ground, where sometimes we could not see half a mile in any direction, and again coming out to ridges where we had an extensive view. We had gone about three miles when

A FREE SELECTOR AT HOME.

suddenly we came upon a mob of some fifty or sixty cattle that went off in the right direction as soon as they heard the cracking of the whips. Mr. Watson said they would go straight to the camp, and Fred and I might follow them, which we did. Sure enough, they took us right where we wished to go; and when we reached the camp we saw fully five hundred cattle gathered there in charge of the two stockmen from the other side.

ARRIVAL OF THE WEEKLY MAIL.

"The rest of the party had turned off to the right as soon as our mob of cattle started, and didn't come up to us until we had been fully half an hour on the ground. They were preceded by three or four mobs of cattle that came dashing in with tails in the air, and acting as though they enjoyed the sport.

"The camp was a picturesque sight. The stockmen and the black boys were riding constantly around the herd, to keep the animals from straying or breaking away; the cattle were moving restlessly about, the cows lowing for their missing calves, the bullocks indulging in an occasional fight, in which none of them was hurt, and the whole herd separating occasionally into little groups composed of those that had been accustomed to run together on the pastures. The camp was partially covered with a very thin forest of iron-bark trees, and the white, red, and roan colors of the animals made a very pretty contrast against the black tinge of the wood and the green of the grass.

"We dismounted, and sat down on a log, while the stockmen and the cattle-dealer proceeded to draft out the animals that were wanted. I may as well explain some of the terms used here, as they will doubtless seem strange in America.

"A 'mob' is a bunch or group of cattle that have assembled for grazing purposes. A herd consists of several or many mobs.

"'Tailing' is the assembling of one or a few mobs at the stock-yards or cattle-camps; tailing is sometimes called mustering, but the latter term applies more particularly to the annual or semi-annual assemblage of all the cattle belonging to a run for the purpose of counting, branding, and other operations to which cattle are devoted. The muster is exactly analogous to the American 'round-up.'

"Unruly cattle in Australia are termed 'rowdy;' 'drafting' is the process of selecting animals from the herds, and when they are rowdy, as they generally are, the performance is by no means free from danger. Not infrequently drafting is called 'cutting out.'

"CUTTING OUT."

"The word 'squatter' in Australia has a meaning almost the reverse of its American one. In America a squatter is the occupant of a small area of land on which he has 'squatted,' or settled, with a view to acquiring title under the homestead laws, or perhaps to being bought off by somebody else. In Australia the squatter is the holder of a run which he obtains by lease from the Government for a term of years, paying an annual rental of ten shillings per square mile, with a privilege of renewal, and also with the right of pre-emption or actual purchase.

"What we call a squatter in America is here a 'free selector;' he has the privilege of selecting land not already occupied for agricultural purposes, and between the squatters and the free selectors there is a feeling of great hostility. The laws of the colony have been subject to a great deal of change in the last twenty years; the squatters feel that they have been unfairly treated, and we heard many stories of downright hardship.

"Into this question of the rights of land-owners in Australia we will not enter, as the discussion would be an interminable one. More interesting to the boys at home will be the performance of drafting cattle from the herd.

"A small mob of cattle was separated from the herd and driven away a little distance to serve as the nucleus of the draft-mob. Then the cattle-dealer and two of the stockmen rode into the herd and selected the animals they wanted; each man was mounted on a good 'camp-horse,' one used to cutting out cattle, and it was interesting to see the intelligence of the horses in their work. The men selected the bullocks they wanted, and then edged them out in the direction of the draft-mob; most of the bullocks were rowdy, and gave the men a lively chase before they submitted to be separated from their fellows.

"The horse followed the bullock wherever he went, as though the latter was leading him. Over rocks, fallen trees, and among upright ones went the bullocks, with men and horses after them, and it was a wonder that none of the men had their necks broken in the chase. Accidents do happen, however, and sometimes they are fatal; one occurred at this very place a few months ago, a stockman being killed by his horse falling and then rolling over him. He was a graduate of Cambridge College, in England, the son of a gentleman of good position but small fortune, and had come to Australia to make his way in the world.

"In speaking of this incident Mr. Watson said that a considerable proportion of the stockmen in Australia were men of education and of good families, who had come to the new country because it afforded better means of advancement than they could hope for at home. It is no disgrace in Australia for a man to work with his hands for an honest living, any more than it is in the new States and Territories of the

United States. I heard a story of an ex-officer of a crack regiment of dragoons who cut wood near Brisbane, loaded it on a wagon with his own hands, unloaded it at the house of a Government official, and received his pay for it just as any other wood-dealer might have received it. In the evening of the same day he dined at a formal dinner at the very house where he had delivered the wood, and in consequence of his former rank in the army he escorted the hostess to the table.

MUSTERING CATTLE.

"The Premier of one of the colonies—the Premier is equivalent to our Secretary of State—worked on the public roads when he first came to Australia, and nobody thinks the worse of him for it; the Minister of Public Instruction in another colony drove a coal-cart in Sydney, and there are dozens of men of prominence who have been shepherds, cattle-drivers, carpenters, bricklayers, and the like. Australia seems to have taken a leaf out of the history of the United States, and been greatly

BRANDING A CALF.

benefited by so doing. It appears to be the antipodes of England in many social customs, just as it is in geographical position and many of its natural features.

"While we were seated on the log, watching the drafting operations, Fred asked Mr. Watson about the daily life of the stockmen on a cattle-run.

"Mr. Watson answered that it was active enough, and no man who engaged in the business need have a bad digestion. The stockman gets his breakfast early in the morning, and immediately after breakfast the horses are brought up. Then he starts out over that part of the run which is assigned to him; he jogs along about five miles an hour, accustoming the cattle to the sight of men, keeping his own mobs inside the boundaries and driving back those of his neighbors, hunting up stray calves, and bringing them home and branding them, and occasionally driving the cattle to the camps, so that they will know what is expected of them when they hear the cracking of the whip.

"Sometimes the man is accompanied by a black boy, but quite as frequently he goes alone. 'Really it ought to be the rule for a stockman never to go out alone,' said Mr. Watson, 'as there are so many dangers connected with bush-riding, and on my run I insist upon it.

"'Many accidents have happened, and the history of the colonies is full of melancholy stories about men who fell and were crippled away from home, and died in consequence. Many a man has disappeared, and no trace of him has ever been found; in other cases bleaching skeletons have been discovered years later, and the few who have not forgotten the missing men will connect these skeletons with their fate.

DIED ALONE IN "THE BUSH."

"'There was a horrible case,' said Mr. Watson, 'that is fresh in the memory of many men. A man was riding alone in the bush, when his horse threw him and injured his spine in such a way that he could not move. Close to where he fell was an enormous ants' nest, and when the man was found, three days after the accident, he was still alive and conscious, but unable to speak, his body having been half devoured by the ants. He died a few hours after, and it is awful to think of what his sufferings must have been.

THE EMU.

"'A parallel to this terrible story is found in the fate of a woodman who was felling trees in the forest several miles from any one else. A burning tree fell on him and pinned him to the ground, but without doing him any serious injury. He was unable to extricate himself, and for the day and a half it took for the fire to smoulder slowly to him he was fully aware of his impending fate. He scratched an account of the occurrence on a tin dish that lay within his reach; when he was found his body was so charred and blackened that it would not have been recognized as the remains of a man had it not been for the tin dish that told the horrible story. The tree which fell on him was of a kind that has the peculiarity of smouldering slowly and leaving nothing but a track of white ashes on the ground.'

"Each of us had brought his dinner, tied at the back of his saddle; and after looking on a while at the drafting, we went to a spring near by and heartily enjoyed our meal. It consisted simply of beef and bread, and was eaten from the fingers in a very primitive way. Soon after dinner we rode back to the station, leaving the stockmen and their assistants to bring up the drafted animals, while the rest were let loose again.

"On our return we saw a young emu, the famous bird that is sometimes called the Australian ostrich. Fred and I started after him, but we might as well have tried to run down a railway-train; he left us out of sight in less than ten minutes, although we were on fairly good horses. Mr. Watson said the speed and endurance of these birds was really wonderful; he had often tried to run them down, but had only succeeded in a single instance, and that by a sudden spurt when the bird was frightened. Hunters on fleet horses sometimes run down these birds, and they can also be overtaken by swift-footed dogs.

"He said the funny thing was that the emu struggles along as though just ready to drop dead with exhaustion, keeping not far from ten yards in front of the horse, and regulating his speed according to that of his pursuer. Doctor Bronson said he was like the jack-rabbit of our Western plains, that will keep about the same distance in front of a dog, no matter how fast the latter may run.

"The bones of the emu contain an oil which is used by the natives for curing sprained sinews and swollen joints. It has remarkable qualities, as it is said to sweat through the side of a glass bottle; the natives believe that if applied to the joints of a person who has not reached maturity, it will soften the bones and render them brittle.

"Soon after losing sight of the emu we roused up a flock of wild turkeys; one of the stockmen carried a gun, and by circling in the direction of the birds he got near enough to bring down two of them. They are very shy of persons on foot, but can be approached on horseback with comparative ease."

CHAPTER XVII.

CATTLE AND SHEEP RAISING IN QUEENSLAND.—GRASS THAT KILLS SHEEP.—PROFITS OF RAISING CATTLE.—RELATIVE ADVANTAGES OF THE TWO ENTERPRISES. —INCREASE OF FLOCKS AND HERDS.—STATISTICS.—LIVE-STOCK IN QUEENSLAND. —VISITING A SHEEP-STATION.—DUTIES OF A GOOD SHEPHERD.—INSANE TENDENCIES OF SHEPHERDS.—MONOTONY OF THEIR LIVES.—DISAGREEABLE WORK FOR NOVICES.—SHEEP-SHEARING, AND HOW IT IS PERFORMED.—PACKING AND SHIPPING WOOL.—AMUSING STORY OF A STOLEN HORSE.—THE MINER WHO HID HIS GOLD IN A HORSE-COLLAR.—BUSH-RANGERS AND THEIR PERFORMANCES.— "STICKING UP."—"OLIVER, THE TERROR OF THE NORTH."—HELD BY A WOODEN LEG. — TRICK OF A DISHONEST GENIUS. — PEARL-FISHING IN AUSTRALIAN WATERS: HOW THE BUSINESS IS CONDUCTED.—ALLIGATORS.—THE "CARDWELL PET."—SUNDOWNERS.

IN their search for knowledge Frank and Fred made many inquiries relative to the profits of cattle-raising in Australia, and the chances of making a fortune at it in a given number of years. Here is a summary of what they ascertained:

THE PRIDE OF THE STATION.

The part of Queensland bordering the coast is not suited for sheep, owing to a peculiar grass which grows there. It has a seed with a barb at the end, and this barb enables it to work its way into any soft substance; the wool of the sheep becomes so full of this seed that it is absolutely worthless, and after a time the seeds work their way into the flesh of the unfortunate animal until they kill him. A man riding or walking in this grass when it is ripe gets his clothing full of the seed, and is very apt to lose his temper, from the continual pricking of the sharp points. Sheep cannot live in this region, but the seeds do not affect cattle, which thrive on the grass. In the interior the obnoxious grass does not exist, and consequently it may be roundly stated that all parts of Queensland are suitable for grazing cattle, but only the interior is adapted to sheep.

Cattle-raising is less profitable than raising sheep, but it does not require as much capital, and is less risky. A cattle-run may be made to pay from the start, while a sheep-station requires a heavy outlay before any returns can be received.

Mr. Watson said that five thousand cattle could be put on an unimproved run for about one hundred thousand dollars; the necessary buildings, yards, weaning-paddock, horse-paddock, and other enclosures would cost three thousand dollars, while two thousand dollars would pay all the wages of employés, and for the food and equipment of everybody attached to the place, for a year. For the first five years only fat cattle should be sold, and these would be enough to pay working expenses, in addition to improvements in the way of boundary and other fences.

THE SQUATTER'S PET.

At the end of five years there would be ten thousand cattle on the run, and after making liberal allowances for expenses from that time, the annual increase would be two thousand five hundred, of which fully eight hundred would be fat cattle. The sale of the increase would return from twenty-eight to thirty thousand dollars annually; and after deducting liberally for working expenses, the yearly profit could be put

CATTLE GOING TO WATER.

down at twenty thousand dollars. Meantime the run has doubled in value, and the investment is paying handsomely.

This is the bright side of the picture. The dark side contains epidemics of pleuro-pneumonia, which has been the ruin of squatters on more than one occasion; added to this is the danger of a severe drought, in which thousands of cattle die of thirst and the inability to get food in consequence of the drying up of the grass. In some years millions of cattle and sheep have perished in this way, and hundreds of owners were ruined.

"Compared with sheep-raising," said Mr. Watson, "the cattle business will return a high interest on the capital invested if properly managed and fairly successful, but does not afford the rapid road to wealth that many have travelled by a few successful years with sheep. Cattle require few men to manage them, and entail no great expense before they are sold and the money is obtained for them. A cattle-station has rarely an occasion to ask the banks for loans, while the sheep-raiser constantly requires money to pay for shepherds, shearers, and other laborers, and is under heavy expense for the carriage of his wool to the seaports.

"It is safe to say," he continued, "that the palmy days of sheep and cattle raising are gone forever. There is very little country suitable for grazing purposes that is not already taken up, and the holders want

A HOME IN THE BUSH.

high prices for their titles and improvements. Formerly a man could go into the interior, find a good location for a run, enter it for lease, and then obtain a partner with the capital necessary for stocking it with a few thousand sheep. With half a dozen good seasons they would make their fortunes, partly from the sale of wool and the increase of stock, and partly from the rise in the value of the lease; but at the same time they might be ruined by two bad seasons of drought, disease among the sheep, or by the low price of wool."

Frank asked what was the nature of the droughts of which Mr. Watson had spoken.

"In a general way, they are like droughts anywhere else," was the reply; "but they have some features peculiar to Australia. In 1883 and 1884 we had two successive years of drought, a thing never known before. Very little rain fell in all that time, and in some localities not a drop; the grass withered, water-holes, springs, and creeks that for years had been unfailing sources of supply dried up, and the whole country was desolate. There were single areas hundreds of miles in extent where not a drop of natural water could be found, and the sheep and cattle perished in great numbers. Experience has shown that every part of Australia capable of producing sheep is subject to occasional periods of unusual drought, and nobody can foretell them. There is only one way of guarding against their effects."

"What is that?"

"Build reservoirs, and store water in sufficient quantities to last through the severest droughts. Of course this will cost money, but it will be a profitable investment in the long run. Many squatters are now doing this, and they are also putting down driven wells after the system invented in America about 1860. It is probable that the next long-continued drought will not cause the death of so many sheep as did that of 1883 and 1884. The loss of sheep in Queensland in those two years was nearly three millions."

Fred asked how many sheep, cattle, and horses there were in the colony.

"According to the official figures," Mr. Watson replied, "we had at the last reports (December, 1885), 260,207 horses, 4,162,652 cattle, and 8,994,322 sheep. Compare these figures with those of 1844, when we had 660 horses, 13,295 cattle, and 184,651 sheep. We had more than 12,000,000 sheep in Queensland at the end of 1882, and will doubtless reach that number again with a single prosperous season. Sheep increase more rapidly than cattle, as you are doubtless aware, provided the flocks do not suffer from distemper, drought, severe storms, or other drawbacks. According to the official figures, we have 75,000,000 sheep in Australia, or more than twice as many as you have in the United States."

At the end of the visit to the cattle-station Doctor Bronson and the youths returned to the railway, and proceeded to a sheep-station in which their polite and hospitable entertainer was interested. We have already described sheep-farming in New Zealand, and as the business is

HERD OF MIXED CATTLE ON A STATION.

much the same in Australia, the visit was not altogether full of novelty.

But our friends ascertained that one important difference between sheep-farming in the two countries was in the matter of snow-storms. We have seen how the New Zealand flocks suffer from heavy falls of snow; in Queensland there is no such hinderance, the sheep remaining out-of-doors the entire year, and needing no protection other than the yards into which they are driven at night or when wanted for shearing or selection.

A SHEPHERD'S DOG.

An Australian sheep-station consists of two yards built of logs, brush-wood, or small saplings. Each yard must be large enough to contain fifteen hundred sheep; and there is a small hut for two men to sleep in at night. These stations are scattered over the run at distances of two or three miles from one another, and there is a head, or central, station, where the squatter or his manager lives, and whence the supplies for the men are sent out. According to the size of the run and the number of sheep upon it will the stations be multiplied. The run our friends were visiting had twelve stations altogether, the nearest being one mile from the head station, and the farthest fourteen miles.

In reply to his inquiry as to the duties of a shepherd, Frank learned the following, which he carefully noted:

"A good shepherd will let his flock out of the yard soon after sunrise and before the heat is uncomfortable, and allow them to spread out as far as can be done with safety. With the aid of his dogs he heads them towards water, and allows them to feed so as to reach the drinking-place about noon; then he turns them around and feeds them slowly back again, so as to get to the yards just at sunset. This is the routine day after day, with slight variations when the sheep are mustered for selection, which is not very often. Sunday is the same as any other day on a sheep-station, as the animals must be pastured exactly as on week-days, and there is no relay of shepherds."

"It must be a terribly monotonous life," Frank remarked.

"It is indeed," was the reply. "The two men at a station are sep-

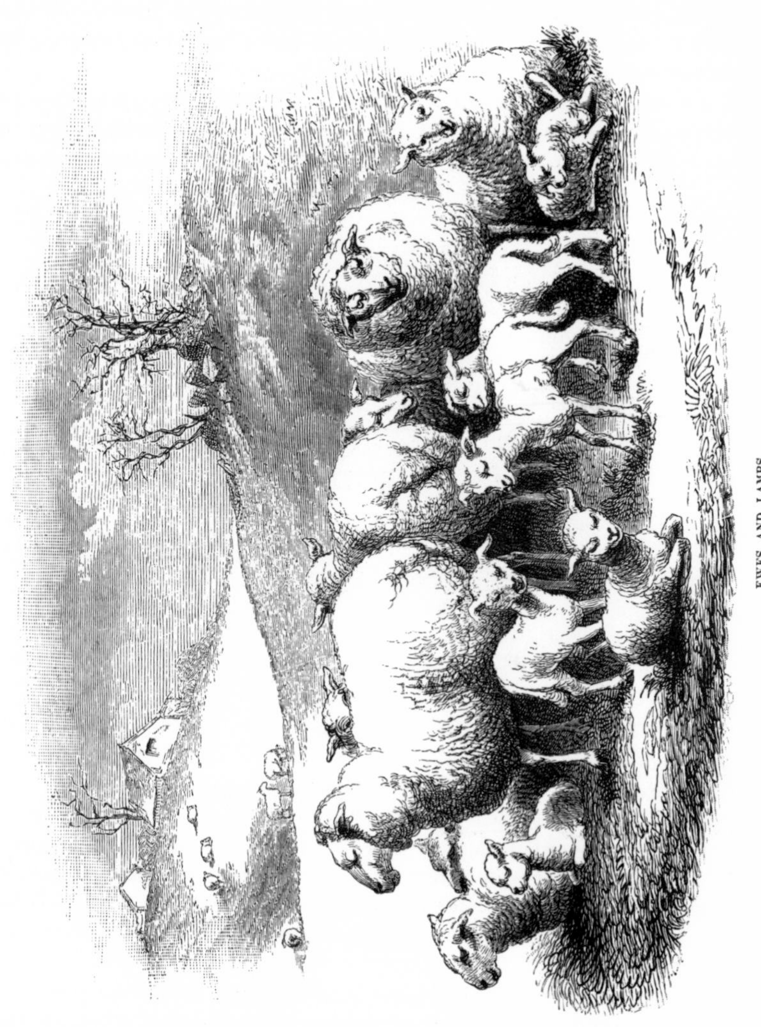

EWES AND LAMBS.

arated during the day, as they feed their flocks in different directions, and at night they are too tired to do much talking, and very often are not on speaking terms. They become moody and taciturn; and it is a sad fact that three-fourths of the occupants of insane asylums in Australia are shepherds.

"Every shepherd should go armed, as he never knows when he may be attacked by the blacks. Many a poor fellow has been speared by the aboriginals; they watch for months until they see him without his

MOTHER OF A FAMILY.

gun, and then rush upon and spear him. Many of the shepherds seem indifferent to life; and it is not to be wondered at, as they are cut off from society, have no friends or friendships, and no encouraging prospects for the future. I have often wondered how it was possible for us to procure shepherds, when the future has so few inducements for them; but somehow we always manage to find enough of them. Many men come here with bright hopes, but they soon tire of the work; if they have money enough to get away, they generally do so at the end of a few months.

"The new chums that engage as shepherds are always put at the most disagreeable work, that of looking after diseased sheep, if there are any on the station. If you want to see what it is, read Mr. Eden's book, 'My Wife and I in Queensland,' and learn what he went through when he came to the colony. He engaged as a shepherd, and was as-

SHEEP-SHEARING IN AUSTRALIA.

signed to look after sheep affected with the foot-rot. Every morning each animal had to be caught, its hoofs pared, and a dressing applied of a peculiar ointment that burned a hole in the operator's clothing if any fell upon it. He and another man had seven hundred sheep to look after, and each animal had to be lifted bodily over a fence, and held down by main force during the operation. When this was completed the flock had to be fed; and if any sheep died while they were out in pasture the men brought in the skins, or the value of the animals was deducted from their wages. No wonder he left the place at the end of two months, and walked back to Brisbane."

Fred remarked that they must have a very busy time of it at the sheep-stations during the shearing season.

"It is the busiest time of the year," said Mr. Watson, "and one that taxes all our abilities. The sheep are driven to the wool-shed, which is a large quadrangular building, varying in size according to the capabilities of the station and the extent of its working force. Walk out with me and look at ours, which is accounted a good one."

The boys were interested in the building, and especially so as Mr. Watson explained its peculiarities and uses.

"You observe," said he, "that there is a bulkhead running across the middle of the building, dividing it into two parts, one of which is intended for sheep, and when full holds about five hundred. This smaller enclosure opens out from the larger one, and is always kept full, so that a shearer can lay his hands on a sheep at once without the necessity of chasing it. This plank floor on each side of the small enclosure is for the shearers, and there is a small door abreast of where each man stands. He lets his sheep out of that door after they have been sheared; and there is a small yard outside each door, where they remain, so that they can be counted by the manager, and thus all disputes avoided.

"The shearer drags a sheep from the pen, and places it between his knees with its head uppermost; he always stands when at work, and for a novice it is very wearying till he gets used to it. He shears from the throat downward, leaving the back to the last, when the fleece falls off in one piece."

"Do the men ever cut the sheep while shearing?" Fred asked.

"Yes, very often," was the response; "and some men 'tomahawk' a great deal worse than others, and never seem to improve. When this happens the shearer does not stop an instant; he calls out 'tar!' and the man or boy whose duty it is to gather up the fleeces rushes to the spot with a tar-bucket and brush, and covers the wound with tar to keep away the flies. The sheep do not struggle, no matter how badly they are hurt, and are literally 'dumb before the shearers.'"

"How many sheep can a good operator shear in a day?"

"The number varies according to skill and experience," said Mr. Watson. "The men are paid an agreed price per score — usually five shillings, or four sheep for a shilling. I have known men who could shear sixscore, or one hundred and twenty sheep, in a day, but under ordinary circumstances it takes a good shearer to do fourscore. In addition to their pay, the squatter must feed them; in rainy weather all work ceases, as the wool cannot be packed when wet."

"Where do the shearers come from?"

"That's a hard question to answer. They follow other occupations except at shearing-time, when they form themselves into gangs and travel about the country; they are usually well mounted, and generally

SHEDS AND CHICKEN-YARD OF A STATION.

a gang carries its own cook, and is very particular about its way of living. The squatters find it to their advantage to feed the shearers liberally, and I have known one who hired a fiddler to play all day in the shed, to keep the men in good-humor. Most of these fellows are gamblers, and generally by the end of their season a few skilful players among them have all the money earned by the entire gang.

"After the wool is sheared it is packed into bales and pressed hard by means of machinery almost identical with a cotton-press. In this condition it is sent to the coast, and shipped to England or whatever market is open for it. High prices for wool make good profits for the squatters, and low prices the reverse, just as is the case in business generally. Many squatters have their entire crop of wool mortgaged to the bankers who have made advances upon it; in this respect sheep-stations are more desirable than cattle-stations, as money can always be had in advance upon the crop of wool."

Some of the large establishments have adopted improved methods of washing sheep; our friends had an opportunity to inspect one of them; during the inspection Frank made a drawing of the washing apparatus, to which he appended the following description:

"*A* represents a twenty-horse-power engine working a sixteen-inch pump, *B*, which raises water from the river alongside, discharging about three thousand gallons per minute into spouting tank, *C* (half of which is cut off in the drawing to show the work behind). The tank is of iron, four feet deep, furnished with a spout four feet six inches deep, terminating in a narrow opening three feet long and three-sixteenths or one-quarter inch wide, the width being regulated by screws.

"Through this aperture the water, under the pressure of eight feet six inches, rushes with great force. *E e e* is an iron tub in which the 'spouter' stands while holding the sheep under the spout. *F* is an inclined plane, up which the sheep walk after emerging from the water, passing on to large batten yards, one hundred and fifty feet by one hundred feet, where they remain till partially dry. These yards are not shown in the drawing. *G* is another ten-horse-power engine, used for cutting firewood at the circular-saw bench, *h*, and to furnish steam to heat water in the soaking tank, *i*, and the ten square tanks, *k*, ranged along either side of the soaking tank.

"To each of these tanks is fitted a branch steam-pipe, *m*, communicating with the main steam-pipe, *n n*, leading from the boilers of both engines, *A* and *G*, so that both are available for heating water, of which a very large quantity, varying from seven thousand to ten thousand gallons, is required for a single day's work. *O o o* are water-pipes leading from the spouting tank, *C*, to supply the square tanks, *k*, the soap-tubs, *P* and *Q*, and spare-water tub, *R*. The soap-tubs are also fitted with steam-pipes, for the purpose of boiling their contents. *S* is a donkey-engine placed over a well, from whence, driven by a continuation of steam-pipes from both boilers, it draws water for showering through a flexible hose the dirty sheep in the receiving yard, *t*, for transmission through the pipe *n* of water to drinking-troughs for the washed sheep in the batten yards, filling up the pump by branch pipes, which is often necessary, and for various other purposes.

"The receiving yards having been filled with sheep, the water in, and the tanks brought up to the required temperature by means of the steam-pipes, and the soaking-tank charged with the prescribed proportion of dissolved soap, etc., the pump is set to work to fill the spouting tank and reservoirs underneath into which the spouts discharge. The portcullis gate, *W*, is then lifted, and from eight to ten sheep are sent down the inclined

SHEEP-WASHING ON THE MODERN PLAN.

shoot, *X*, into the soaking-tank, when they are manipulated by men on either side, and allowed to swim for four or five minutes. Hence they pass on to the rinsing stage, *Y;* again down a short incline to the stage, *Z;* from thence, lastly, they are handed to the spouters. By these they are rolled and turned under the knife-like jet of water for two minutes, when they swim out to the inclined landing-stage as white as snow.

"When the water in the soaking-tank becomes overcharged with dirt, by a simple arrangement it can be emptied and refilled with clean hot water from the square tank, in which a constant supply is kept up, in eight or ten minutes. From twelve hundred to two thousand sheep are washed daily."

Frank and Fred learned many other things about sheep-farming in Australia, but they made no further notes on the subject, and therefore we will drop it. At any rate, they did not conclude to go into the business when they learned of its hazards and discomforts, and ascertained from the newspapers that the price of wool was at that time quite low.

Frank made a memorandum of a good story that he heard during the evening, while they sat in front of the fire in the sitting-room of the head station. It was told by the manager of the place, and was as follows:

"When I first came to Australia," said the manager, "I was employed on a cattle-station in Victoria; while I was there gold was discovered about ten miles away from us. The rush to the mines caused a demand for our cattle, and the owner did a fine business in supplying the miners with beef; but, on the other hand, there was a great deal of stealing, so that he was obliged to hire more men than usual. The favorite objects of the thieves were our saddle-horses, and every few days a horse would be missing from the paddock, and the chances of his recovery were doubtful.

"But we had one horse that was a treasure. He was perfectly docile in harness, and would stand quietly while being saddled, but anybody who mounted him was thrown at once. He was kept as a carriage-horse, and was a favorite of the manager, and was so docile that he could be caught at any time with a handful of oats.

"Once or twice a month he would be missed from the paddock. In a day or two he reappeared, and almost always with a saddle and somebody's 'swag,' or baggage, strapped to it. Once he came back with a new saddle and a swag containing, among other things, thirty ounces of gold-dust, and nobody ever appeared to claim it. Another time he brought in twenty ounces and three gold watches. Altogether, in the course of a year, he was stolen about twenty times, and must have brought home two or three thousand dollars' worth of gold-dust, to say nothing of the saddles. He kept the place supplied with saddles all the time I was there."

"A very profitable horse," remarked Doctor Bronson. "I suppose the owner was not willing to sell him?"

"Not by any means," was the reply. "He used to say that he had only to 'set' that horse in the paddock as he would any other trap, and the thieves walked in at once."

"That reminds me of a Melbourne horse story," said one of the listeners. Being pressed to give it, he did so.

THE RUSH FOR THE GOLD-MINES.

"In the days of the gold rush in 1851," said he, "there were two men in Melbourne who made a fortune in horse-trading. They had two or three horses trained for their business, and when a party was fitting out for the mines, one of these horses would be offered for sale. Of course the would-be purchasers wanted to try the animal first, and the dealer would point to a steep hill on Bourke Street, and suggest that the horse be tried with a load up that hill.

"The animal was attached to a loaded dray, and straightway pulled it to the top of the hill without hesitation or pause. Of course that settled the question of his usefulness, and he would be sold at a good price; but when attached to a load and started for the mines, he balked and refused to pull at all. Silent partners of the dealer were watching on the road, with other horses for sale, and they soon made a trade in which the balky beast was thrown in for almost nothing.

BUSH-RANGER OUT OF LUCK.

"The fact was, the trick-horses were fed at the top of the hill, and only after they had drawn up a heavy load. Sometimes the same horse was sold two or three times in one day; and it was afterwards said that a single horse had been disposed of for fifty pounds and bought in for five pounds at least a hundred times."

"I can't tell a horse story," said another of the party, "but I've one that comes close to it, and that's a horse-collar story."

Of course everybody wanted to hear it, and he complied with the general wish.

"You all know that soon after the discovery of gold in Victoria the country was infested with bush-rangers, or highwaymen, who made it very unsafe to travel with gold-dust or other valuable property. A man was liable to hear the order to 'bail up!' at any moment, and find a gun or pistol levelled at him. Unless he obeyed with alacrity and threw his hands in the air, he was in great danger of having a bullet through him. Very often it happened that an armed man would be taken unawares, and though he had a rifle in his hand or a pistol at his belt, there was no chance to make use of the weapon. Sometimes two or three bush-rangers would 'stick up' a stage-coach; while one watched the passengers, ranged along the road-side, and kept them within range of a revolver, and perhaps two revolvers, another searched them and took possession of their valuables.

"Gold was sent down from the mines under a Government escort to protect it from the bush-rangers, and of course a heavy charge was made for the service. Various devices were adopted to foil the rascals by those who undertook to transport their own treasure.

"Men concealed their gold in their clothing or about their wagons, and one smart fellow put nearly a hundred ounces inside a horse-collar, which was worn by the single horse drawing a dray containing a few bundles of clothing and other insignificant things.

"He got along all right for the first two days, and on the third began to feel entirely safe. While he was jogging along the road he was overtaken by a man who said the police were after him on account

BUSH-RANGERS AT WORK.

of a fight with a drunken fellow at a way-side inn. He said his horse was much jaded, and he would give the stranger ten sovereigns to exchange.

"The bargain was quickly made, as the animals appeared to be of about equal value. The miner unfastened his horse from the dray, and began to unharness it. As he did so the stranger, quick as a flash, seized the collar, threw it around the neck of his own steed, sprung on its back, where the saddle still remained, and was off like the wind.

"'That's all I wanted, mate,' said he, as he rode away. He had somehow learned the miner's scheme for carrying his gold, and played this elaborate game to rob him."

"Speaking of bush-rangers," said another, "did you ever hear of Oliver, 'the Terror of the North?'"

Some had heard of him and others had not, so the story was called for.

"There was once a bush-ranger of that name in the north of Queensland," said the narrator, "and he had been 'sticking up' people in the country back of Robinson. He had a wooden leg, but in spite of this defect he was a bold robber and a very slippery one to hold. He got away from the police several times after they had fairly caught him; and catching him was no small matter.

"One time when he'd been at his tricks, the police got him and brought him to Robinson. The jail there was in a very bad condition, and the police magistrate was at a loss how to keep Oliver, until a happy thought struck him. What do you suppose it was?"

Nobody could guess, and the story-teller continued:

"Well, he locked Oliver up in the jail, but took his leg to his own house, and locked *that* in a trunk. Oliver stayed that time, and didn't even try to break jail."

"We were speaking of horses just now," said one of the party, "and that reminds me of a clever trick which was played on a rich squatter by a man in his employ. He had sent the man on an errand, and mounted him on a valuable white horse. It was at the rainy season of the year, and all the creeks were flooded. On the bank of a creek which he had to cross the man spied a white horse lying dead at the water's side.

"A brilliant idea occurred to him, an inspiration of rascally genius. He dismounted, skinned the dead horse, concealed the skin in the bushes, and rode away, and sold the animal he was riding for a good price. Then he returned to where he had concealed the skin; and after soaking his saddle and bridle in the river for an hour, he went back to the station, carrying saddle, bridle, and skin, and covered from head to foot with mud. There he told how in attempting to cross a creek the horse was overcome by the waters, and had just strength to reach the bank, where he died. As for himself, he had a narrow escape with his life; and to prove the truth of his story, he had brought home the skin of the once valuable beast.

"The squatter believed the story, blamed himself for sending the man on such a dangerous mission, and gave him ten sovereigns as a reward for his fidelity and compensation for his wetting. The man left the place soon afterwards for another part of the colony; months later the squatter saw his horse advertised for sale, and on inquiry found how he had been imposed upon."

LEADING CITIZENS OF SOMERSET.

From anecdotes about horses and bush-rangers the conversation turned upon the pearl-fishery on the northern coast of Queensland.

"It is quite an extensive industry," said Mr. Watson, "and employs a considerable number of men. The exports of pearl-shell from Queensland for the year 1885 were 13,189 hundred-weight, valued at £87,110, or $400,000; and in some years the product has exceeded that amount. Other parts of Australia produce pearl-shell and pearls, and altogether the fishery is a very important one."

Doctor Bronson asked if it was profitable.

"Very much so," was the reply. "At one time pearl-shell was worth £250 a ton; the pearls were reckoned to pay the cost of the work, so that the money obtained for the shell was clear profit. Even when shell fell to half that price the profits were heavy; and certainly they ought to be, to induce a man to endure the privations of the work.

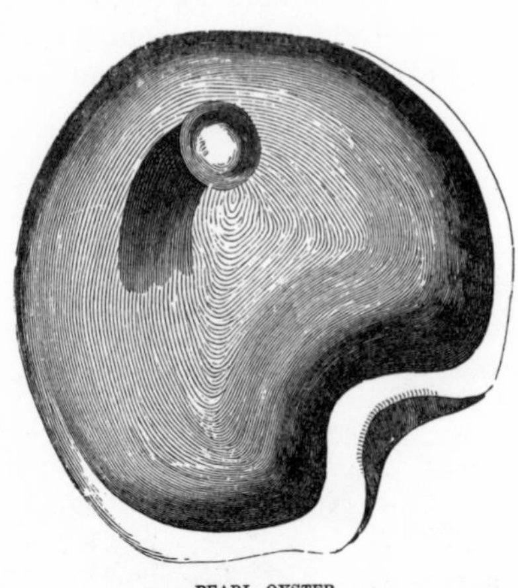

PEARL OYSTER.

"The best pearls are from the west coast of Australia; they are not equal to Oriental pearls in color, but they are very large, and are eagerly sought. One was sold in London for £1500, or $7500; and frequently single pearls bring as high as $2000.

"I stopped a short time at Somerset, which is the most northerly town in Australia, and entirely devoted to the pearl-fishery. The men living there are a rough lot, wearing very little superfluous clothing, and quite careless about appearances. They go out with sloops and schooners, and send down divers in just the same way that pearl-diving is carried on in Ceylon and the Persian Gulf. Their divers are all black men, and in fact many of them come from the Persian Gulf, being attracted to Australia by the higher wages paid there. The shells are shaped like oyster-shells, and are from twelve to fifteen inches across. The lining of the shell, technically known as *nacre*, or mother-of-pearl, is the article sought; but the oyster is carefully examined to see that no pearls are missed."

AUSTRALIAN PEARLS (FULL SIZE).

"Didn't I read not long ago about the drowning of many pearl-fishers on the coast of West Australia?" said one of the youths.

"Quite probably," was the reply, "and you are liable to hear of such a calamity at any time. The West Australian fisheries are subject to terrific hurricanes. The signs of these hurricanes are well known, and every fishing-boat has ample time to reach a place of safety; but the fishers are too reckless to take any precautions, and every few months a lot of their boats are sent to the bottom or driven high and dry on the shore. The few that escape death on such occasions immediately get new boats, and start off on another expedition as if such a thing as a hurricane had never been heard of.

"Alligators abound in all the rivers of the northern part of Australia; they grow to a great size and are dangerous, and not a year passes that we do not hear of somebody being killed by them while taking a swim or attempting to cross a swollen stream. They are great nuisances at cattle and sheep stations located on the rivers where they abound, as they make a clean sweep of calves, dogs, sheep, and other small animals while drinking, and have been known to attack full-grown bullocks."

"Did you ever know an adult alligator to be treated as a pet?" said the man who had told the horse-collar story, addressing his query to Mr. Watson.

Mr. Watson shook his head, whereupon the story-teller said he had known such a case. The saurian was not only an individual but a public pet.

Frank and Fred were curious to learn about it. Their curiosity was gratified as follows:

"Years ago," said the man, "I was at the town of Cardwell, in North Queensland. It is on a pretty bay, which is full of fish and oysters, and was then the home of a monster alligator which was known as the 'Cardwell Pet.' Every morning something resembling a huge log was seen floating under the trees near the shore; it was not a log, but the back of the pet, and he was on the lookout for a stray dog coming down to the water.

"He ate up most of the dogs in town soon after he appeared, and whenever a new dog happened along with a stranger he usually became a *bonne bouche* for the pet. But there were two dogs in Cardwell that knew his ways; when ordered to do so, they would go down on the beach, where they barked and played with each other, apparently heedless of the alligator, but all the time keeping out of range of his jaws. In this way he was often enticed out upon the sand, the dogs seeming to enjoy the fun. He became the lion of the place, and was always the first sight shown to strangers. When the town was first established, shots were fired at him; but as soon as his importance as a curiosity became known, he enjoyed immunity, and at the time I was there any one who ventured to harm him would have been roughly handled by the inhabitants, as he was literally the pet of the town."

Frank asked the narrator if he knew how large the Cardwell Pet was.

"I do not," was the reply, "and circumstances did not permit accurate measurement. I have seen many alligators in Queensland that exceeded nineteen feet in length, several that were more than twenty, and there was one taken on the Fitzroy and called Big Ben that measured

BIG BEN AND HIS FRIENDS.

twenty-three feet six inches. When I last heard of him he was owned by Jamrach, in London. I think the Cardwell Pet was quite equal to Big Ben, and possibly larger; you know it is always the largest fish that is not weighed or measured. Anyway, the pet was said to have made a meal of a sundowner, though I don't believe he really did, as that class of game is too cautious."

Fred asked what a sundowner was. He had heard the term several times, but thus far it had not been explained to him.

"He is the equivalent of the American 'tramp,'" said Mr. Watson, "and abounds freely in Australia. He is fed and lodged at the stations, where he is careful to arrive at sundown or a little later, and hence his name. If he gets there before sunset he is requested to move on to the next stopping-place, or else he is asked to make himself useful at some kind of work during the remaining hours or minutes of the day. He abhors work, and therefore times his arrival to avoid it. Sometimes a group of these fellows will rest by the way-side a mile or so from a station, waiting for the sun to disappear.

"Many a vagabond makes an easy living by wandering from one station to another, pretending that he wants employment but carefully avoiding it. The sundowner is as insolent as the American tramp; by Australian custom he is welcome to supper, lodging, and breakfast, the food consisting of tea, sugar, bread, and beef or mutton, and the lodging being in his own blankets on the floor of the men's hut or the wool-shed. I have had a dozen or more of these 'travellers' on a single night, and my monthly average is not less than one hundred and twenty. Sometimes a party of them has been so unruly and so threatening in their demands that I have been compelled to send for the local police to carry them away.

WAITING FOR SUNSET.

"On one occasion," the gentleman continued, "a ruffianly traveller drew a knife and threatened to stab my cook, because the latter refused to give him a mutton-pie that had been prepared for the men, the travellers' table being filled with cold beef as the only viand. I had him handcuffed and taken to the police-station, where he was recognized as a man who was 'wanted' for a robbery somewhere up country.

EVENING SCENE AT AN UP-COUNTRY STATION.

"As a general thing, the squatters hesitate to quarrel with the sundowners, preferring to suffer their impositions rather than run the risk of having their buildings and fences burned, and other depredations committed. Of late years the number of vagrants seems to have diminished, but the supply is yet far in excess of the country's needs."

NOTE.—Since this book was put in type the laboring classes in Australia have united in a popular agitation against the Mongolians, and have compelled the leading governments to adopt stringent measures. The poll-tax on these immigrants has been increased in New South Wales from fifty dollars to five hundred dollars; their naturalization has been prohibited altogether; rigid restrictions are imposed as to residence and trading; and vessels are allowed to land only one Chinaman for every three hundred tons. Chinese merchants are allowed to trade in certain districts of the provinces, but the number for each district is limited to five. These restrictions were authorized by a government bill which was passed by the Colonial Assembly without a dissenting voice. The resident Chinese have been attacked by mobs at Brisbane, and immigrants and cargoes have not been permitted to land at Sydney and Melbourne. The Colonial authorities of Queensland and Victoria favor a policy of complete exclusion, and in New Zealand the Premier has publicly announced his conversion to the same views.

CHAPTER XVIII.

THE PLAGUE OF FLIES IN AUSTRALIA.—OTHER CREEPING AND FLYING THINGS.—LAUGHING-JACKASSES, BOWER-BIRDS, LYRE-BIRDS, PARROTS, ETC.—TRICKS OF THE LYRE-BIRD.—ORIGIN OF THE BOWER-BIRD'S NAME.—BLACK SWANS AND WILD-DUCKS.—SNIPE, QUAIL, AND OTHER BIRDS.—AUSTRALIAN RIVERS AND THEIR PECULIARITIES.—RETURN TO THE COAST.—GYMPIE AND THE GOLD-MINES OF QUEENSLAND.—AN AUSTRALIAN GOLD RUSH.—DOWN THE COAST TO SYDNEY.—THE GREAT BARRIER REEF: ITS EXTENT AND PECULIARITIES.—SPORT IN NORTHERN QUEENSLAND.—GOING UP-COUNTRY IN NEW SOUTH WALES.—A KANGAROO HUNT.—DIFFERENCE BETWEEN A HUNT AND A DRIVE.—AUSTRALIAN MARSUPIALS.—SHOOTING WILD HORSES.—KILLING AN "OLD MAN" KANGAROO.—DINGOES.—STORIES OF KANGAROO HUNTS.

SEVERAL days were passed agreeably in the pastoral and agricultural region of the Darling Downs, and our friends were overwhelmed with invitations from the hospitable squatters who inhabit that region. Fred said the invitations would have enabled them to spend a year there, and even then he was confident their welcome would not be worn out. Wherever they went they were comfortably lodged and well cared for, and they were unanimous in declaring that the world contained many worse places than the Darling Downs, even among those that were classed as highly attractive.

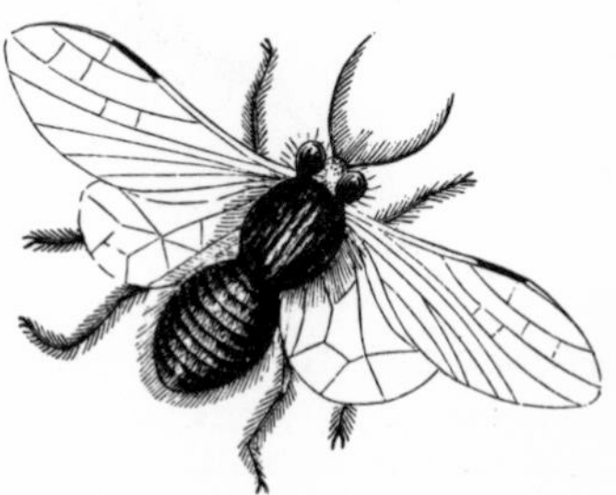
AN AUSTRALIAN PEST.

Frank considered the flies and other creeping and winged things a great drawback to existence in that region. "They have mosquitoes and sand-flies in certain localities," said he, "while others are entirely free from them; but as for the common fly, he is everywhere and is a first-class nuisance. On the coast the flies are said to be troublesome only for a few months in the year, but in the interior they are perennial, and sometimes almost make life a burden. They are worse at some periods than at others, but bad enough at all times. In the worst 'fly-time' nobody ventures to ride about without wearing a veil; and men have taxed their ingenuity to keep the pests out of their houses, but practically without success.

"Fleas are also abundant, though not as much so as flies; neither are they seen as much in public. They abound most in sandy places, and the sundowners transport them from one station to another free of charge. A more welcome insect is the common honey-bee; it has long been acclimatized in Australia, and owing to the great number of honey-bearing flowers, it has become very abundant. Bee-farming is an important industry in New South Wales, and is carried on to quite an extent in the other colonies.

"They tell us that in the north of Queensland white ants are very

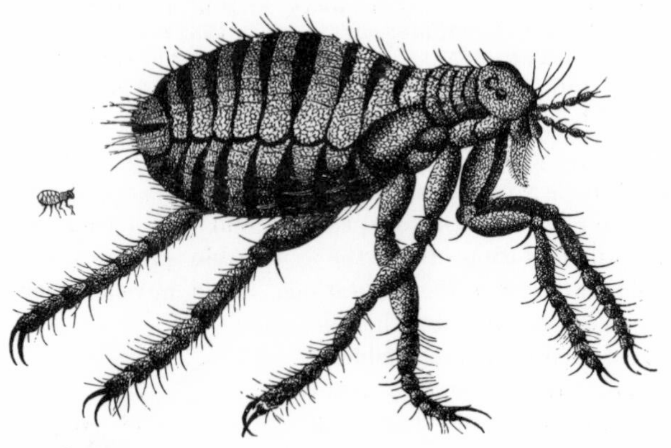

THE SAND-FLEA (NATURAL SIZE AND MAGNIFIED).

destructive, as they eat nearly every textile fabric, and have a voracious appetite for all kinds of wood. They have even been charged with devouring window-glass, iron bars, and similar substances usually considered inedible. I heard a man say with the utmost gravity that they had eaten up two cross-cut saws and a boxful of American axes, handles and all; but I don't believe it, and I doubt his veracity in several other statements he made, and therefore won't repeat them."

One day while the youths were strolling in the bush not far from the station, they were startled by the sound of immoderate laughter that seemed to come from among the limbs of a low tree. The sound was repeated after a short interval, and, curious to know the cause, they went in its direction. As they neared the tree, two or three birds flew from it and settled in another tree a short distance away. They did not seem at all alarmed at the presence of Frank and Fred, and the latter remarked that the creatures were evidently allowed to go about unharmed. On their return to the station they told what they had seen and heard, and asked what were the birds that had so surprised them.

THE AUSTRALIAN BOWER-BIRD.

"Those were laughing-jackasses," was the reply; "or if you want another name for them, you may choose between 'giant kingfisher,' 'piping crow,' 'musical magpie,' or 'settler's clock.' The bird under consideration belongs to the kingfisher family, and is called by all these names, the last being given on account of the uproar he makes at noon, and thus tells the settler who does not carry a watch when the middle of the day is reached. Many people believe he destroys snakes; some of us are skeptical on this point, which has never been satisfactorily decided; but at any rate he is useful, as he often indicates the locality of fresh water, and so has saved many persons from suffering, or perhaps perishing of thirst. He is never shot, and consequently is not fearful of the presence of man.

"I wonder you have not heard the bird before this," he continued, "as he abounds near the cities and towns as well as in the bush." Then the boys remembered that they had heard the same sound on several occasions, but always supposed it was somebody laughing, and did not consider it any business of theirs to investigate.

"There's another curious bird in Australia," said their informant, "which we call the satin, or bower, bird. He builds a bower, or walk, and decorates it with any gaudy feathers or other things he can find, and also with shells, bleached bones, and similar small objects. So well is his propensity known that when we drop a pipe-bowl or a penknife in the bush, we search for it in the bowers or runs of these birds, and very often find it there. As the bower-bird feeds entirely on seeds and fruits, it is evident that he secures these small things for the sake of ornament."

Fred suggested that perhaps the bower-bird had been infected with the bric-à-brac craze which pervades society in other countries. The ambition to gather a cabinet of curiosities was a fashionable one, and why shouldn't a bird have it as well as any one else.

Frank asked if it was possible to see a lyre-bird in that region, and was disappointed when told that it was rarely seen outside of the fern country of South-eastern Australia. Their authority on birds told them that this winged emblem of Australia was about the size of a pheasant, and had a tail three feet long; the outer feathers of the tail are beautifully marked, and form the lyre from which the bird takes its name. The male bird forms a mound of earth on which he promenades, displaying his beautiful tail to its utmost advantage, in the same way that the peacock exhibits his feathered ornaments. The female is as plain as an ordinary hen, and presents a very mean appearance by the side of her lord.

The youths were further informed that the lyre-bird is an excellent mocking-bird, and could imitate with exactness the notes of all the other feathered denizens of the forest. "He can also," said their authority, "reproduce nearly every sound made by man. Settlers in the region inhabited by these birds are often deceived by them, and many amusing stories are told. Sometimes a man working on his clearing hears somebody chopping wood a short distance away, and a dog barking at his

WALLACE'S STANDARD-WING BIRDS-OF-PARADISE, MALE AND FEMALE.

heels. He goes in search of the intruder, and finds after a long walk that the 'pheasant' has been making game of him. A man using a cross-cut saw hears somebody doing the same thing, and after searching unsuccessfully for him, discovers that it is the pheasant's performance."

Frank summed up the rest of the ornithology of Australia as follows:

"The great southern continent has many varieties of the parrot family; it possesses the king parrot, the bird-of-paradise, the blue mountain-parrot, the cockatoo—blue, white, and crested—lories, parroquets, and love-birds. It has the wild turkey, which we have already mentioned, and a bird closely allied to it, called by the singular name of 'native companion.' Wild-ducks are found all over the country, the 'mountain duck' being the finest; then in their order come the black duck, wood-duck, and the Australian teal, followed by five or six other varieties less known and less liked by sportsmen."

"Don't forget the black swan among the water-birds," said Fred, as Frank paused after reading the foregoing paragraph.

"I was not forgetting him," replied Frank; "what would be our picture of Australia without the black swan? He is found in all the lakes and swamps of the southern coast; in the Gippsland lakes thousands of black swans may sometimes be seen in a single flock, and the sound of their feet and wings striking the water as they rise for a flight may be heard for miles when the air is still. The black swan is not strictly a game-bird; his flesh is rather rank, but this taste can be removed in cooking, and then he isn't at all bad to eat.

HEAD OF THE VALLEY QUAIL.

"Going from large birds to small," continued the youth, "I learn that snipe are abundant in many localities, but they do not seem to be appreciated as in England and America. The Argus snipe is the prettiest of the family, and also the most difficult to find; he is beautifully marked on the back and wings, and is a valuable addition to an ornithological collection.

"There are at least a dozen varieties of quail in Australia, and as articles of food they are abundant and cheap. With very little effort a settler in most parts of the country could have quail on toast every day in the year; at least the quail would be easily forthcoming though the toast might not. Cold roast quail and damper are not to be despised for lunch after a long ride in the bush."

While Frank was busy with the study of the birds of Australia, Fred contemplated with great care the map of the country. He observed that all the mountain ranges were near the coast, so that the course of the larger rivers was towards the interior. "There is not," said he in his note-book, "a single large river flowing into the ocean from all this great continent, with the exception of the Murray. Every other stream is short and insignificant; and even the Murray and its tributaries do not form a first-class river.

"Here we are," said Fred, "on the head streams of the Darling, one of the rivers that unite with the Murray to pour into the sea through

A QUAIL FAMILY.

Lake Alexandria, between Melbourne and Adelaide. On looking at the map I thought we should be able to descend in a boat to the ocean, but Mr. Watson tells us we can do nothing of the sort. Some of the rivers on the maps are at this season simply dry beds, though at times they have water enough to float a first-class boat from the Mississippi.

"Steamboats have ascended the Darling to Walgett, 2345 miles from the sea, but they can only do so at certain, or rather uncertain, times, and therefore no dependence can be placed on the navigation of the Murray and its tributaries. The Darling depends on flood-waters; sometimes they will fill the stream to its junction with the Murray, and thence to the sea, and again they fail before going half way. The river can never be navigated throughout the year, and in some years boats are not able to run at all.

"So my scheme of going down by water to the ocean is not practicable, and we return to the coast the way we came."

And return they did, taking the railway to Brisbane, and thence going by coach and rail to Gympie, the centre of the Queensland gold-mining region, or rather one of its centres, as the colony possesses several auriferous fields. There is a standing offer of a reward of £1000, or $5000,

OUT PROSPECTING.

to any one who discovers paying gold-deposits in a new locality upon which there shall be upwards of two hundred men at work six months after the fields are opened. Consequently a great many prospectors are constantly at work, through the double hope of the reward and of making a fortune out of the discovery.

The gold-fields of Gympie were discovered in 1868 by Mr. James Nash, and the settlement which rose there was at first called Nashville. The existence of the precious metal in the colony was known for at least a decade before that date, but none of the mines had proved remunerative. At present there are upwards of twenty gold-fields in Queensland, and the aggregate annual yield exceeds $5,000,000. From 1867 to 1885 inclusive the mines of Queensland yielded 4,840,221 ounces of gold, valued at not far from $80,000,000.

But we are forgetting Frank and Fred in our contemplation of these dry statistics. Here is what Frank wrote concerning their visit to Gympie:

"We came here partly by rail and partly by coach, the railway from Brisbane to Gympie not being completed, though perhaps it will be by the time this is in print, if it should ever have such good-fortune. It is one hundred and sixteen miles from Brisbane to Gympie, and sixty-one from here to Maryborough. The town is prettily situated on the side of a range of hills on the river Mary; it has handsome public buildings, and bears every evidence of prosperity. It has a School of Arts, a public library, and other institutions not always to be found in mining towns, and altogether deserves the good name that it bears. It has a population of nearly eight thousand in the municipality alone, and there are four thousand more in the immediate neighborhood.

QUARTZ-MILL IN THE GOLD-MINES.

"There are the usual paraphernalia of the mining industry, which we have already described in other places. In every direction there are mining-shafts and reduction-works, and for miles and miles around the country is full of prospecting holes, where gold has been sought but not found, at least in paying quantities. The first rush here was for the alluvial diggings, and large amounts of gold were taken out by the early comers.

"We were much interested in hearing about the adventures of Mr.

Nash, the discoverer of the gold-diggings here. He had been an unsuccessful prospector for twenty years, had gone through all kinds of privations, narrowly escaped death at the hands of the blacks on many occasions, and was almost killed by the earth caving in on him while working a prospect hole. He always went by himself, and worked alone. When he found gold here he managed to work away for three months without interruption; then he was discovered by a stockman, who took a claim next to his and spread the news abroad. Nash became a rich man at last, but his health was ruined, and he had little real enjoyment of his wealth.

AUSTRALIAN GOLD-HUNTERS.

"The alluvial diggings at Gympie were soon worked out, and reef, or quartz, mining followed. In fact, the reef mining began while placer mining was at its height and the alluvial diggers were in the full tide of success. The placers were, and the reefs are, very rich, and many of the workings have paid enormously to their owners. Of course where there have been so many prizes there has been a proportionate number of blanks, and there is no telling how many thousands of men have left Gympie poorer than when they came here.

"The town consists practically of a single street which straggles up and down for more than a mile, with here and there an attempt to run

A GOLD-MINER'S HOME.

a lateral street in the direction of a mine or a crushing-mill. Most of the houses are of wood, and scattered over the hills are the huts of the miners, in order that they may be near the places where they are employed. This does not prevent their coming into the town in the evening, and occasionally making it a very lively place. In the early days there were the usual disorderly scenes of the centre of a 'gold rush;' and one of the old inhabitants told us that a few months after the discovery became known, it seemed as though half the bad characters in Australia had congregated there.

"When the alluvial diggings had been exhausted, the wandering miners disappeared and wended their way to newly reported fields. The place became more orderly, and then the abandoned claims were occupied by the Chinese, the most patient workers the world ever saw.

They are contented to take up what white men consider unprofitable, and, considering all their disadvantages, they have done wonderfully well. They are not allowed to enter any gold-field until it has been open for two years; and there is a poll-tax of £10 a head upon every Chinese who enters the colony. They are generally peaceable, but occasionally they quarrel among themselves over the right to work a certain spot, and then the noise they make is something tremendous."

A CHINESE DISCUSSION.

From Gympie our friends went by rail to Maryborough, a seaport town on the Mary River, twenty-five miles above its mouth, and one hundred and eighty from Brisbane. The railway carried them past many sugar plantations, and they learned that Maryborough is the outlet of a considerable district devoted to sugar cultivation, the annual product being not far from five thousand tons. Large quantities of lumber are exported from Maryborough, and there is also a considerable business in wool and hides from the cattle and sheep stations in the country towards the interior.

Here they took steamer for Sydney, touching at Brisbane, Newcastle, and several other ports of lesser consequence. During their voyage they became acquainted with a resident of one of the northern ports, who had much to say about the advantages of his part of the colony, and greatly regretted that they had not been able to visit it.

"It's a pity," said he, "that you missed the Great Barrier Reef, which is one of the most remarkable geographical and geological phenomena to be found anywhere on the globe. It stretches along the whole eastern coast from opposite Port Bowen, in latitude 23°, to Torres Strait, at the extreme north of Queensland, and is one thousand two hundred miles long. Its greatest width, which is near its southern end, is about seventy miles, and it is from five to one hundred miles from the shore of the continent. All along its whole length there are sunken reefs, which make navigation in its vicinity very dangerous. Many a ship has been lost on this reef, and scores or hundreds of persons have found a watery grave by its side."

Fred asked if a ship inside the reef was obliged to go its entire length before finding an opening to the ocean.

"Not at all," was the reply. "There are many openings to the ocean through the reef, some of them very narrow and others several miles in width; and the reef contains specimens of all kinds of coral formation—atolls, fringing reefs, and others. The portion of the reef above water, and the numerous coral islands near it, are thought to have an aggregate surface of thirty thousand miles."

"What is supposed to have caused the formation of this reef?" Frank inquired.

"The outer margin of the Great Barrier Reef probably indicates the former coast-line of this part of Australia," was the reply. "This was fringed with coral reefs; but as the land sank, the coral animals continued to build upward to the level of the sea, and thus a great ridge was formed which was broken and heaped up by the waves of the Pacific. Fresh water prevents the formation of coral, and the openings in the Great Barrier Reef are thus formed by the fresh-water streams. The largest is opposite the mouth of the Burdekin River, which drains a considerable area of country.

"The reef is a good place for sport, just as are the reefs of the Feejee, Samoan, and Society Islands, which you tell me you have visited. Vessels go there in search of beche-de-mer, for which they have a good market in China. The fishery for this curious article of food is practically just the same as in the island groups of the Pacific, and therefore I need not describe it to you.

"Very good sport can be had in Northern Queensland in hunting the dugong, or sea-cow. This animal abounds along the coast of that

WRECKED ON THE REEF.

region; its flesh is not bad eating, and its oil was formerly in demand as a substitute for cod-liver oil, but some of the fishermen got to mixing it with shark-oil and other abominations, so that its good name was ruined. If you have a taste for turtle-catching, it can be accommodated. We supply the Sydney and Melbourne markets with green turtle, and also put the soup and meat into tin cans and send it to England. There are numerous fishes, some good to eat, and others worthless as articles of food but with all the colors of the rainbow. We have sharks of the largest size, and the stranger should be careful about venturing into the water for a bath."

Their new acquaintance had a great deal to say about the northern part of Queensland, whose praises he was never weary of sounding. He declared that within a very few years Queensland would consist of two colonies instead of one, as the north was inclined to cut loose from the south and set up a government of its own. He thought it did not receive its fair share of the public money, and having paid its proportion of the taxes, it had a right to grumble when the south received all the appropriations for railways and other costly improvements.

On his arrival in Sydney Doctor Bronson called at once on the gentleman who had invited the party to see the interior of New South Wales. Arrangements were made for immediate departure, and at nine o'clock on the following morning they were off for the upper country.

So far as their experiences of cattle and sheep stations were concerned, they were practically a repetition of what they had gone through in Queensland. A new feature of the trip was a kangaroo hunt to which they were invited, and of which Fred gives the following account:

"You must know that this is the land of marsupials, or animals which carry their young in a pouch until they are able to take care of themselves. Nearly all the animals of this country belong to this family; and geological researches show that there were once some marsupials here that equalled if they did not exceed in size the rhinoceros and

THE MANATEE, OR DUGONG.

hippopotamus. But these big fellows are all extinct; there are one hundred and ten species now, and the largest of them does not exceed two hundred pounds in weight.

"The largest of the marsupials is the kangaroo, and the next in size is the wallaby. There are eight species of large kangaroo, inhabiting different parts of the country, the prince of them all being the red kangaroo of South Australia. Then come seventeen species of small kangaroos (*Halmaturus*), weighing from ten to fifteen pounds; and then three species of silky-haired kangaroos (*Onychogalea*), inhabiting the interior of the continent. They weigh eight or ten pounds, and are about the size of a common rabbit; then come five species of hare-kangaroos, five of jerboa-kangaroos, and then the rat-kangaroos, the bandi-

EVENING AT HOME ON THE NORTH COAST.

coots, opossums, 'rabbit-rats,' and numerous other small animals. We'll go back to the large kangaroos, where we began.

"In former times, when the only human inhabitants of Australia were the savage blacks, the kangaroo was kept from increasing too rapidly, through the combined efforts of the dingoes and the natives. The dingo is the Australian wild dog, and closely allied to the wolf and jackal, of which he is certainly the first-cousin. He is carnivorous, and fond of sheep, and was therefore poisoned and otherwise killed off by the settlers, to prevent his depredations upon the flocks. A bounty was placed on his scalp, and he has been greatly reduced in numbers. The natives have likewise died off since the settlement of the country; and with their natural enemies removed, the kangaroos, which live wholly on grass, have increased till they have become a nuisance. A kangaroo eats as much as a sheep, and when a drove is undisturbed its numbers multiply with a rapidity that dismays the squatter on whose land it has made its home.

"Our host gave us the foregoing information while we were riding to the place where we were to enjoy the sensation of hunting the kangaroo. He furthermore told us that it was no uncommon thing for them to kill several hundred kangaroos in a single drive, but it could not be called sport. He said a drive wasn't a hunt, and I asked him to explain the difference, which he did.

"The necessity of killing off the kangaroos to prevent their utter destruction of all the grass in the country was forced upon the settlers by the rapid increase of the animals. The Government passed a law giving a bounty for the scalps of kangaroos; and none too soon, as in some parts of the country the droves fairly blackened the plains for

DINGOES, OR AUSTRALIAN WILD DOGS.

many miles, and literally starved the sheep out of the country. The bounty on the scalps, added to the value of the meat and skins, partly paid for the trouble, which required a muster of all the squatters and their employés for a considerable distance around.

"A drive, or battue, is managed in this way: A yard with a high fence is built in one of the scrubs on the plains, and from this yard two fences run out on the plain for a long distance, widening like the sides of the letter V. All the men, boys, and blacks in the neighborhood are mounted on horseback, and scour the country for many miles around; they move in the direction of the jaws of the V, and when the herd is once inside it, the animals are doomed. They go straight towards the scrub which conceals the yard, and do not discover where they are till they are inside the enclosure. Then the rails are put up, the blacks enter with clubs, and the slaughtering begins. A kangaroo can jump clean over a horse, and therefore the fence must be not less than seven feet high to prevent his escape when frightened.

AUSTRALIAN WILD HORSES.

"We were not bent on any such performance, which is nothing but slaughter, though made necessary by the conditions of the country. I may add here that in some parts of the colony it is often necessary to make a drive of wild horses exactly as they drive the kangaroo. It is no uncommon matter for a squatter to make a drive of four or five hundred wild horses, which are killed for their hides, but more especially to prevent their eating the grass, destroying the fences, and enticing tame horses out of the paddocks. We have seen several droves of wild horses, and they look very pretty as they gallop over the plain. We wished we had some of them under the saddle, but were told that the value of the animal rarely pays for the trouble and cost of breaking him. Occasionally horses with brands on them are found in the wild herds; they are impounded and advertised; at least such is the theory, but quite as often they are killed with the rest to save trouble.

"A black boy mounted on a swift horse came riding back to us, and said the kangaroos were in a part of the plain that was concealed from us by a patch of scrub. We moved in their direction, keeping the scrub between us and them, so as to get as close as possible before they discovered us.

"Our manœuvre worked very well. There were ten or twelve of the animals feeding quietly, and we were within a few hundred yards of them before they were aware of it. At the first alarm they rose on their hind-legs and took a look all around, and a second later they were away. How they did jump! They seemed to go thirty or forty feet at a time, but our host says it was little if any more than fifteen feet. Even that is a tremendous jump; if you don't think so, just try it.

A KANGAROO BATTUE, OR DRIVE.

"We let loose the dogs, which up to this time had been kept behind us, and they went away without any urging. The dogs are kept for this purpose, just as fox-hounds are kept in England and France, or deer-hounds in Scotland. The dogs soon overtook and pulled down a young kangaroo; this caused some delay, but not much, and they were speedily put on the track of an 'old man' kangaroo, as a full-grown male is called.

"The 'old man' led the dogs a lively chase. He made directly for water, several miles away, which is always the custom of the kangaroo;

RED KANGAROO.

if he cannot reach water he takes his stand with his back against a tree, and in that position he is a dangerous creature to approach. We followed the dogs as closely as we could, but did not come up to them until the kangaroo was at bay in a pool where the water just left his fore-legs clear as he stood upright.

"The dogs were all experienced in kangaroo-hunting, and knew enough to keep out of reach of his legs. Had they come within grasping distance he would have held them under water till they were drowned, or else have ripped them open with a blow from his powerful hind-leg, which has a claw in the middle capable of inflicting a fatal wound upon man or dog.

"The dogs swam around him, or stood on the shore of the pool, when we came up. The pool was a small one, and the creature realized that it was his safest retreat, and he was evidently determined to die game. A shot from a rifle in the hands of one of the men finished him, and he was quickly dragged to the shore. Fortunately, not a dog was killed or injured; rarely does a hunt terminate without some one or more of the dogs receiving a scratch, and nearly every kangaroo-dog in the country has a scar or two to show as evidence of his experience and prowess.

SHORT-EARED KANGAROO.

"After this exploit we dismounted, and took our lunch.

Then we made a circuitous journey homeward, and roused up another 'old man,' which we despatched as he stood fighting with his back to a tree, but not till he had wounded one of the dogs. Another full-grown kangaroo was killed by one of the stockmen the same day, in another part of the run, and the three skins will be properly cured and sent to Doctor Bronson and ourselves as souvenirs of the day's experience.

"We supped on steaks from a young kangaroo; the meat of the old and full-grown animals is too rank to be enjoyable, and is usually fed to the dogs. We had soup made from kangaroo tail, and it was delicious; kangaroo soup has become an article of export, and some epicures are said to prefer it to ox-tail, or even to turtle soup, though I very much doubt the latter statement.

"Our host says the natives in former times were very skilful in killing the kangaroo with the boomerang; when a native armed with this weapon was within reach of a kangaroo, the aim rarely missed. Another way of killing the creature was by stalking The blackfellow dressed himself with twigs and brush to look like a small tree. In this disguise, and carrying his spear between two toes of his foot, he advanced slowly, taking care to keep to leeward, so that the animal could not get the scent. Slowly he closed up, remaining motionless when the kangaroo looked up, and moving again when it began to graze. Once within spearing distance, he speedily settled the question of dinner or no dinner from the flesh of that identical beast."

Frank asked what became of the skins of the kangaroos when they were slaughtered by wholesale, as already described.

"They are pegged out on the ground and dried," said their host, "and then are shipped to market. Many of them go to America, where they are made into leather for boots and shoes and other purposes. The leather is very tenacious, and almost impervious to water, and the demand for it is said to be increasing. Previous to 1869 very few of the skins were tanned, as the merits of the leather had not become known. The first that were sent to America were sold at a loss, and then in a few years, when their qualities were known, the American tanners could not get enough of them. One firm in Newark, New Jersey, is said to receive six thousand skins every week, and even with that number cannot meet the demand for kangaroo leather."

During the evening, stories of kangaroo hunts were naturally in order, and a goodly number were told; but as all were of the same general character it is hardly necessary to give them. Frank made note of the fact that there is one kind of kangaroo which climbs trees and jumps, like a squirrel, from limb to limb. He is called the tree-kangaroo, and has curved claws on his fore-paws to enable him to cling to the branches. He is not a bad pet to have about a park, but his numbers should be judiciously kept down, or he may become a nuisance, like the larger kangaroos that live on the ground.

KANGAROOS IN CAPTIVITY.

CHAPTER XIX.

A NATIVE ENCAMPMENT AND A CORROBOREE.—RIDING ACROSS-COUNTRY.—AMONG THE BLACKS.—NATIVE DANCES.—A WEIRD SCENE.—ABORIGINAL MUSIC.—STORIES ABOUT CORROBOREES.—CURIOUS CUSTOMS.—HOW THE BLACK MEN OBTAIN THEIR WIVES.—TESTING THE STOICISM OF YOUTHS.—AN ALARM AT NIGHT.—RETURN TO SYDNEY.—A BRICKFIELDER.—HOT WINDS FROM THE DESERT.—HOW A PICNIC WAS BROKEN UP.—OVER THE BLUE MOUNTAINS.—RAILWAYS IN NEW SOUTH WALES.—SALUBRITY OF THE MOUNTAIN CLIMATE.—GOULBURN.—THEATRICAL GOSSIP.—FIRST THEATRE IN AUSTRALIA.—A CONVICT'S PROLOGUE.—THE DRAMA UNDER DISADVANTAGES.—THE RIVERINA.—ALBURY AND THE VICTORIAN FRONTIER.—PROTECTION AND FREE-TRADE.—FISHING IN THE MURRAY RIVER.—AUSTRALIAN FISHES.—FROM ALBURY TO MELBOURNE.

BEFORE returning to the coast our friends had an opportunity to visit a native encampment and see a corroboree. The reader naturally asks what a corroboree is; we will see presently.

Arrangements were made by their host, and early one morning the party was off for the native encampment, which was nearly thirty miles away. A tent and provisions had been sent along the previous evening, so that the travellers had nothing to carry on their horses beyond a lunch, which they ate in a shepherd's hut at one of the out stations. Early in the afternoon they reached their tent, which had been pitched on the bank of a brook about half a mile from the village they intended to visit.

Taking an early dinner, they set out on foot for the encampment, being guided by a native who had come to escort them. We will let Frank tell the story of the entertainment.

"The village was merely a collection of huts of bark, open at one side, and forming a shelter against the wind, though it would have been hardly equal to keeping out a severe storm. To construct these huts the bark had been stripped from several trees in the vicinity. Fires were burning in front of most of the huts, and care was taken that they did not extend to the trees, and thus get a start through the forest.

"There was an odor of singed wool and burning meat, but no food was in sight. The blacks are supposed to live upon kangaroo meat as their principal viand, but a good many cattle and sheep disappear whenever a tribe of them is in the neighborhood of the herds and flocks. In addition to kangaroo, they eat the meat of the wallaby, opossum, wombat, native bear, and other animals, and are fond of eels and any kind of fish that come to their hands, or rather to their nets and spears. Emus, ducks, turkeys—in fact, pretty nearly everything that lives and moves, including ants and their eggs, grubs, earth-worms, moths, beetles, and other insects—are welcome additions to the aboriginal larder. All the fruits of trees and bushes, together with many roots and edible grasses and other plants, are included in their bill of fare.

"There were twenty or more dirty and repulsive men and women in the village, some squatted or seated around the fires, and others walking or standing carelessly in the immediate vicinity. A dozen thin and vicious-looking dogs growled at us as we approached, but were speedily silenced by their owners. These dogs were simply the native dingoes, either born in captivity or caught when very young and domesticated. They are poorly fed, and the squatters say they can generally distinguish a wild dog from one belonging to the blacks, by the latter being thin and the former in good condition.

"More women than men were visible, and it was explained that the men who were to take part in the corroboree were away making their preparations. The corroboree is a dance which was formerly quite common among the tribes, but has latterly gone a good deal out of fashion. At present it is not often given, except when, as in the present instance, strangers are willing to pay something in order to see it. Our host had arranged it for us, and the camping party that preceded us with the pack-horses had brought the stipulated amount of cloth, sugar, and other things that were to constitute the payment for the entertainment.

"We tried to make friends with some of the children, but they were decidedly shy, and we soon gave it up. In a little while the men who were to dance came out from the forest, and as they did so the women formed in a semicircle at one side of the cleared space in the middle of the encampment; and some of the men brought fresh supplies of wood, and heaped it on the central fire. The women sat on the ground, and each had an opossum rug stretched tightly across her knees and forming a sort of drum.

"The dancers assembled in the centre near the fire; they wore only their opossum rugs around the loins, and the exposed parts of their bodies were streaked with paint in the most fantastic manner imaginable.

A CORROBOREE

Faces and bodies were adorned with white and red paint, and altogether the aspect was a combination of the ludicrous and the hideous. The leader, holding a stick in each hand, took his place midway between the women and the fire, and at a signal from him the women began a chant, and kept time by beating with their hands upon the opossum-skins.

"Suddenly the leader struck the two sticks together, and the dancers formed in line. When the line was completed he struck them again, in unison with the chant and the time beaten on the drums. The dancers regulated their movements by the music, throwing themselves into all sorts of positions, moving to the right or the left, advancing or retreating, standing straight in line, circling around each other, and in a general way forming figures not altogether unlike those of civilized dancers in other lands.

SOMETHING FOR BREAKFAST.

"As the dance went on, the leader quickened the time; the chant and drumming quickened likewise, and so did the exertions of the performers. They grew hot, and perspired at every pore; faster and faster went the music; faster and faster were the movements of the bodies, till it seemed as though they would drop from exhaustion.

"Suddenly the men, as if by a prearranged plan, jumped higher than ever into the air, and as they did so each gave a sort of shrill shout. The drumming and chanting ceased immediately, and the men fled to rest in the shelter of the bushes. There they remained for perhaps a quarter of an hour, and then they returned and resumed the dance. The second part was much like the first, except that some of the figures were different; the whole performance showed that it was the result of practice, as the time was well kept and all the movements were based upon a system of no insignificant character. At the end the leader gave two heavy strokes with his sticks, the men retreated, the women followed them, and the dance was at an end.

"We are told that the natives have various dances, and in this particular they resemble the savage tribes of most other lands. They have their war-dances before and after fights, dances for the time when the youths are 'made men'—*i.e.*, when they attain their majority, and are no longer to be classed as boys—dances in which only the women take part, dances in which the movements of the kangaroo and other animals are imitated, and a variety of religious and mystical dances to which Europeans are never admitted. In some dances an entire tribe—men, women, and children—participate; in others only the men, or only the women; and there are certain dances in which several tribes may join. All the people of the tribe are instructed in these dances, and the rules concerning them must be observed with most scrupulous care.

"Nearly all the dances are performed at night, and quite often by the light of the moon added to that of the fire. I have heard some amusing descriptions of dances where there was a mimic battle between white men and aboriginals, the fictitious white men biting their cartridges and going through the motions of loading and firing a gun with great exactness. There was a representation of a herd of cattle feeding, of some of the animals being speared by the blacks, who then went through the motions of skinning and cutting up the slaughtered beasts. The movements of the kangaroo, emu, and other animals were imitated, and so were those of the pig, the bear, and the opossum.

NEAR THE CAMP.

"At the end of the dance we went to our camp accompanied by the natives, who were to receive payment for the performance. After their departure we sat around the fire for a while listening to corrorobee stories, and then retired to our blankets and to sleep. Our dreams were filled with pictures of yelling and gyrating natives, and altogether neither Fred nor myself felt much refreshed when we rose in the morning; but we were all right in an hour or so, and shall always remember our adventure among the Australian blacks.

"We heard some curious stories about their customs, particularly of the way the men get their wives. Marriage as understood among civilized people is unknown among the Australian blacks. Fathers dispose of their daughters as they would of sheep or cattle; and if the father be dead, the right falls to the nearest male relative. A man with a daughter of marriageable age arranges to dispose of her, and when the price is agreed upon she is called forward and told that her husband wants her. She may never have seen him before, or seen him only to detest him; if she cries and protests, the father exercises his authority by prodding her with a spear or striking her with a club, and he often winds up

AN AUSTRALIAN COURTSHIP.

by seizing her by the hair and dragging her to the hut of the man who has bought her. If she attempts to run away she is clubbed into obedience, and sometimes her father spears her through the leg or foot, so that she cannot run.

"Among some of the tribes brothers exchange their sisters with other men, so that a marriage is generally a double affair. There is no ceremony, as we understand it, any more than in a horse-trade with us.

"If a man has no sister, he steals a wife from another tribe than his own; he lies in wait in the neighborhood of the other tribe, and when a young woman passes near him he rushes out and knocks her down with a waddy, or club. Then he drags her to his hut and pounds her into submission. Such a proceeding is perfectly proper, though it almost invariably leads to a fight between the two tribes, no matter how friendly they may have been before the occurrence. It is the duty of the woman's tribe to avenge her abduction, and that of the man's to protect the newly wedded couple.

"The ceremonies for celebrating the coming of age of a young man vary a good deal among the tribes, but in none of them is the performance a pleasing one for the subject thereof. In one tribe he is shut up in a tent for a whole month, and nearly starved; in another he is shaved, painted with mud and pigments, and compelled to sit in a pool of dirty water for a whole day, while the rest of the tribe pelt him with mud; in another he has two of his front teeth knocked out; and in another the young beard on his chin is plucked out by the roots. In every case pain is inflicted, so that the valor of the youth can be tested; and he is expected to endure everything without flinching.

"During the night we had an alarm which roused us from sleep, and for a few moments it looked as though we were to have serious business. There was a yell in the forest near us, and as we sprang out

THE NIGHT ALARM.

of our blankets and went to the front of the tent, we saw a crowd of natives in war-paint brandishing their spears and waddies, and acting as though they intended to attack us. Some of them were hideously painted, and altogether the spectacle was not a pleasing one. After a few demonstrations they retired, and our host told us it was a part of our entertainment, to show how a night attack was made by the aboriginals.

"The mimic attack was quite sufficient for our purposes, and we were quite willing not to pass through the experience of a real one. We were told that had the attack been actual, the first warning of it would have been the hurling of spears. Very often it happens that a camping party of white men has no knowledge that natives are within many miles of them until the spears begin dropping in their midst. Our host was once in a party of this sort; they were eight in all; five of them were killed or wounded by the spears; but the remaining three with their rifles and revolvers beat back the assailants, and thus saved their lives."

Our friends returned to the station without further adventure, and a few days later were once more in Sydney, preparing to leave for Melbourne. Up to the last moment of their stay they were busily occupied with the attentions of the numerous acquaintances they had made, so much so that they had barely time to write up their journals and preserve a record of what they had seen and heard.

But there was one attention which was as unexpected as it was interesting, though it could hardly be said to have been bestowed by an inhabitant of the city. It was a visit from a "brickfielder," and is thus described by Fred:

"Mention has been made already of the tendency of an Australian to speak exultingly of the climate of his own city or section, and to disparage that of other localities. All parts of the country suffer from the hot winds of the interior, but the inhabitants of each place declare that it is worse anywhere else than with them. Be that as it may, our first experience of the hot wind here in Sydney is quite bad enough, and if Melbourne or Adelaide can surpass it we pity them.

"They call this wind a 'brickfielder,' probably because it brings a vast quantity of dust such as might be blown from a field where bricks are made or brick-dust has been thickly strewn; and this was what we saw and felt:

"There was a period of calm and ominous silence, and we observed that the sky was changing from blue to a sort of fiery tinge. Puffs of heated air came now and then, like blasts from a furnace; they grew in force and frequency, and in an hour or so became a steady wind with increasing force. It was hot and dry and scorching, and we seemed to be withering under its effects. 'It's a brickfielder, sure enough,' said a friend, and he cautioned us to get back to our hotel as soon as we could. We took his advice, and went there.

"In a little while there was a driving volume of dark clouds like a London fog; the wind increased almost to a gale, and then came the dust. It was not a fine, impalpable sand, like that brought to Cairo by the *khamseen* in April, but a perceptible and gritty dust that sifted into every crevice and cranny, blinded our eyes, filled our ears, and made its way inside our clothing, till we could feel that it was all over our skins.

RECEPTION OF A BRICKFIELDER.

Nothing is sacred to it, and it invades the most stately mansions as well as the humblest cottages. The air was filled with dust gathered up from the streets, in addition to what the wind brought from the interior; the dustiest and most disagreeable March day of New York was the perfection of mildness compared to it.

"Windows and doors were closed, and it is the rule to keep them so as long as a brickfielder lasts. The hot gale will make its way inside if it can find the least opening, and then the entire house and all its contents will be thickly sprinkled with dust. The heat was intolerable, but there was no help for it, as an open door or window would only bring more heat and the dust in addition. We looked out of the windows, but the dust-cloud was so thick that we couldn't see across the street. A few luckless wayfarers were clinging to posts or struggling to keep their feet, and those who were trying to go against the wind made very slow progress.

A BRICKFIELDER PUTTING IN ITS WORK.

"The brickfielder lasted all day and far into the night, and then it suddenly stopped. With its cessation there was a heavy fall of rain, which converted the dust into mud and made pedestrianism anything but comfortable. They tell us that these winds sometimes last two or three days, or even longer; they are always followed by rain and a cool wind from the south, and never was cool wind more acceptable than at such a time. Nobody can predict when the wind will come, whether in a day, a week, or a month; and when it does come everybody prepares to stay in-doors, if he can possibly do so, and wait till it is over. Every man, woman, and child has a dust-cloak or dust-coat to be worn when necessity compels going out-of-doors in a brickfielder.

"One gentleman says these winds prefer to put in their appearance on Sunday morning, just as the congregations are assembling in church. The dates of large picnic parties are also favorite times for their appearance, and when they come the picnic ceases to be a delight. He says that some years ago, in one of the Australian cities, arrangements had been made for a grand banquet out-of-doors, the finest that had ever been known in the colony. The date had long been fixed and extensive arrangements made, invited guests came from afar, the best speakers of the antipodes were present, and all was going finely, when suddenly, just as the early courses of the banquet had been served, a brickfielder came, and the scene was as disorderly as a political meeting in one of the lower wards of New York. The feast came to a sudden end and not a speaker opened his mouth, lest it might be filled with dust.

"One swallow may not make a summer, but one brickfielder is enough for a whole year."

Consulting the railway time-table, Doctor Bronson found that the express train for Melbourne left at 5.15 P.M., and ran through in nineteen hours, thus making the greater part of its journey in the night. As our friends wished to see as much of the country as possible during their tour through Australia, they decided to take a slower train at 9 A.M., which would bring them to Goulburn, one hundred and thirty-four miles, at 4 P.M. Another train at 10.35 the following morning would reach the frontier at Albury, three hundred and eighty-six miles from Sydney, at eight o'clock in the evening. In this way they would get a good view of the country, and be able to say far more about its features than if whizzed through on an express train at night.

BUILDING A RAILWAY ON THE PLAINS.

The first railway in the colony of New South Wales was projected in 1846, and within two years the surveys for the line to Goulburn were completed. Ground was broken in July, 1850, the first turf being turned by the Hon. Mrs. Keith Stewart, in the presence of her father, Governor Fitzroy, and a large assemblage of people. The first railway-line in the colony, from Sydney to Paramatta, was opened in 1855.

The engineering difficulties and the high rate of interest upon loans retarded the work of railway building, so that in twenty years after the opening of the first line only four hundred and six miles had been completed; but in more recent times the enterprise has been rapidly pushed, the mountains having been passed, and the construction upon the great plains of the interior being comparatively easy. In September, 1886, no less than 1831 miles of railway were in operation in New South Wales, and the Colonial Parliament had authorized 1590 miles in addition, of which a part is now under construction.

The railways of New South Wales are divided into the Southern, Western, and Northern systems. The Southern stretches from Sydney to Albury, on the frontier of Victoria, three hundred and eighty-six miles; at Junee the South-western line branches from the Southern, and runs to Hay, four hundred and fifty-four miles from Sydney, on the Murrumbidgee River, and one of the most important towns in the Riverina district. The Western line runs in the direction indicated by its name, and terminates at Bourke, on the Darling River, five hundred and three miles from Sydney. These are the longest railway-lines now in operation in any part of Australia, though not equal to some that are projected in Queensland and South Australia. The Northern line extends to the frontier of Queensland, as already described.

In round figures, Australia has at present about ten thousand miles of railway in operation, with another ten thousand miles—and perhaps more—in contemplation. The completed lines have cost not less than two hundred millions of dollars, and there are about thirty thousand miles of telegraph in working order.

The up-country journey of our friends, in which they took part in a kangaroo hunt and witnessed a corroboree, was made over the Western line. "We have rarely seen finer engineering work on a railway anywhere else in the world than on this line," said Frank in his journal. "It reminds us of the Brenner line over the Alps, the Central Pacific in the Sierra Nevada mountains, and the ride from Colombo to Kandy, in Ceylon. It was an uninterrupted succession of magnificent views of mountain scenery, with deep gorges and snowy water-falls at frequent intervals. We advise those who may follow us to note particularly the Katoomba and Wentworth Falls and Govett's Leap; and if they have an interest in engineering, they will be much attracted by the Lapstone Hill and Lithgow Valley Zigzags, where the railway climbs the steep sides of the mountains. There is a fine bridge over the Nepean River at Penrith, and a tunnel, called the Clarence, three thousand seven hundred feet above sea-level, and five hundred and thirty-eight yards in length."

There is also some fine engineering on the Southern line; and for a long time, when the railway was first proposed, many doubters predicted that it would never be able to pass the Blue Mountains to the plains beyond. The longest tunnel in Australia—five hundred and seventy-two yards—is near Picton, on the Southern line; and the zigzags, bridges, cuts, and fillings are well calculated to excite the admiration of the professional railway man. As for the scenery, it fully justifies the praises which Australians bestow upon it, and the ride over the Blue Mountains is one that everybody who visits the country should take in the daytime.

The engineers of this line claim to have succeeded in solving a problem which has been pronounced impossible by many experienced men, and has been tried elsewhere occasionally, and always with disastrous

ZIGZAG RAILWAY IN THE BLUE MOUNTAINS.

results—that of having two trains pass each other on a single-track railway. It is done in this way: At the end of each zigzag there is a piece of level track sufficiently long to hold two trains. The engineer of a descending train sees an ascending one on the zigzag below; he runs his train out to the end of a level, and there waits until the ascending one has entered the same level, reversed its course, and gone on its way upward. One of the railway managers said to Doctor Bronson, "There isn't any double track here at all, and yet, you see, two trains can pass each other without the least difficulty. The ends of our zigzags serve as switches, that's all."

"You have no idea what a salubrious region this is," said one of the passengers to whom they had been introduced by a friend who came to see them off. "The air is wonderfully bracing, so much so that it is a

THE BLUE MOUNTAINS.

common saying, 'Nobody ever dies in the Blue Mountains unless he is killed by accident or blown away.' Many people live to more than a hundred years old; there is an authentic account of a man who celebrated his one hundred and tenth birthday six months before he died, and another who was cut off by intemperate habits when he was only one hundred and one. This man used to speak of a neighbor who lived to be one hundred and eight years old and hadn't an unsound tooth in his head, when he was killed by the kick of a vicious horse."

The Blue Mountains are a part of the great dividing range already described in our account of the visit to Queensland. Of late years they have rapidly grown in favor as a pleasure resort, and thousands of the inhabitants of Sydney go there to escape the heat of summer. The mountains increase in height as they approach the boundary between New South Wales and Victoria, where they are known as the Australian Alps. The highest peak of all, Mount Kosciusko, is 7308 feet high, and its summit is covered with snow throughout the year.

Frank and Fred were at once seized with a desire to visit Mount Kosciusko, but were restrained by the Doctor, who did not share their enthusiasm for mountain-climbing. So the youths contented themselves with a distant view of the snowy tops of the high peaks of the range, and allowed Mount Kosciusko to rest undisturbed. The country is wild and picturesque, but the facilities for travel are not extensive, and only those travellers who are accustomed to fatigue should undertake the

ON THE HEAD-WATERS OF THE MURRAY RIVER.

journey. The starting-point for the excursion is the little town of Tumberumba, from which the mountains are about forty miles away. A coach runs between Tumberumba and Calcairn, seventy-four miles, the nearest point on the railway, and the town is said to be pleasantly situated at an elevation of two thousand feet above the sea.

The Murray River, which is sometimes called the Hume in the upper part of its course, takes its rise at the foot of Mount Kosciusko and its companion mountains. The scenery is quite Alpine in all its characteristics, and well justifies the name which has been applied to this part of the great chain. Deep gorges and precipitous cliffs enclose the head streams of the Murray, and the forest extends far up the sides of the mountains wherever there is sufficient soil for trees to find a place to grow. Lower down there are considerable areas of open or cleared country that have proved well adapted to agriculture. Wheat and oats are profitably grown in the vicinity of Tumberumba; and in some parts of the Albury district, in which Tumberumba is situated, tobacco is an extensive crop. (See *Frontispiece.*)

At Goulburn, where they halted for the night, as previously arranged, our friends found a well-built city of about eight thousand inhabitants, and owing its prosperity to the large amount of inland trade which it controls. Frank and Fred asked for the gold-mines of Goulburn, but asked in vain; they were told that there were no gold-fields in the immediate vicinity, and that the city depended upon its commercial position and the agricultural advantages of the surrounding region. They were invited to visit some lime-burning establishments, and learned that there were extensive quarries of limestone in the neighborhood, with promising indications of silver, copper, and other metals, which as yet are hardly developed.

In the evening the party witnessed a theatrical performance by a strolling company, which was making the rounds of the interior towns of Australia in the same way that American companies go "on the road" during the dramatic season. The acting was good, and the company included several players who were not unknown in New York and other American cities.

The youths had already noted the fact that Australia is a favorite resort of members of the dramatic profession of England and the United States; a considerable number of the men and women well known to the foot-lights of English-speaking countries have at one time or another appeared on the boards of Melbourne and Sydney. Australians are fond of the drama, and there are few cities in the world that can be counted on for a more liberal patronage of good plays and good players, in proportion to their population, than the principal cities of the great southern continent.

From one of the books in his possession Frank drew the following interesting bit of theatrical history:

GALLERY OF A THEATRE DURING A PERFORMANCE.

"The first theatrical representation ever given in Australia was at Sydney, in 1796. The play was 'The Ranger,' performed by a company of amateurs, all of whom were convicts. The manager was also a convict. An admission fee of one shilling was demanded, and the Governor and his staff were graciously invited to free seats. Coin being scarce in the colony, a shilling's worth of flour or rum was accepted in lieu of money. The convict who played Filch recited the prologue, and was probably its author. It ran as follows:

"'From distant lands, o'er wide-spread seas we come,
But not with much eclat or beat of drum.
True patriots all, for, be it understood,
We left our country for our country's good!
No private views disgraced our generous zeal;
What urged our travels was our country's weal,
And none can doubt but that our emigration
Has proved most useful to the British nation.
He who to midnight ladders is no stranger,
You'll own will make an admirable Ranger;
To seek Macheath we have not far to roam,
And sure in Filch I shall be quite at home.

Here light and easy Columbines are found,
And well-trained Harlequins with us abound;
From durance vile our precious selves to keep
We've often had to make a flying leap;
To a black face have sometimes owed escape,
And Hounslow Heath has proved the worth of crape.
But how, you ask, can we e'er hope to soar
Above these scenes, and rise to tragic lore?
For oft, alas! we've forced th' unwilling tear,
And petrified the heart with real fear.
Macbeth a harvest of applause will reap,
For some of us, I fear, have murdered sleep.
His Lady, too, with grace and ease will talk—
Her blushes hiding 'neath a mine of chalk.
Sometimes, indeed, so various is our art,
An actor may improve and mend his part.
"Give me a horse!" bawls Richard, like a drone;
We'll show a man who'd help himself to one.
Grant us your favors, put us to the test;
To gain your smiles we'll do our very best;
And, without dread of future turnkey Lockits,
Thus, in an honest way, still pick your pockets.'"

The principal theatres of Melbourne, Sydney, and Adelaide will compare favorably with those of any other city on the globe, and there is hardly a town of any consequence at all that does not possess a minor theatre or a hall where entertainments are given occasionally. During the days of the gold rushes the mining regions proved more remunerative to the strolling actors who visited them than to the majority of the men who were digging for the precious metal.

The theatres of those days were often the rudest structures imaginable, and not infrequently performances were given in tents, and sometimes in enclosures that were open to the sun and rain. It is said that a performance of "Hamlet" was once given on an open-air stage in a pouring rain. Ophelia wore a water-proof cloak, and in the last scene in which she appeared she carried an umbrella. Polonius, being an old man, was permitted to wear an India-rubber coat; but Hamlet's youth did not permit such a protection from the weather, and when the play ended he bore a close resemblance to the survivor of an inundation of the Ohio valley, or a man rescued from a shipwreck on the Atlantic coast.

Beyond Goulbourn the railway carried our friends through the district of Riverina, famous for its pastoral and agricultural attractions. At Albury they crossed the Murray River and entered the colony of

Victoria; a change of gauge rendered a change of train necessary, and Fred remarked that it seemed like crossing a frontier in Europe, the resemblance being increased by the presence of the custom-house officials, who seek to prevent the admission of foreign goods into Victoria until they have paid the duties assessed by law.

As before stated, Victoria has a protective tariff, while New South Wales is a free-trade colony. Consequently, Victoria is obliged to guard her frontier to prevent smuggling, and the work of doing so effectively is by no means inexpensive. But she derives a large revenue from the duty on imports, and the statesmen and others who favor a protective tariff can demonstrate by argument and illustration that

SCENE IN THE RIVERINA.

it is the principal cause of the prosperity of the colony. There is, of course, a goodly number of free-traders in the colony, and the war between free-traders and protectionists is as vigorous and unrelenting as in the United States or England.

The federation of all the Australian colonies, and their union under a single government, on the same general plan as that which was adopted for the British-American provinces, has been for some time under discussion; doubtless it might have been accomplished before this had it not been for the opposition of New South Wales, which holds aloof from the movement mainly on account of the tariff question. Federation will probably come before long; many Australians say it will be a step in the direction of independence, and they argue that a country so far away from England can hardly be expected to retain its allegiance to the mother-country forever, in view of its growing power and population, its diversity of interests, and the perils to which it would be subject in case of a European war in which England should be concerned.

The railway from Melbourne reached Wodonga, opposite Albury, in 1873, but the line from Sydney was not completed till 1881. From that time till 1884 there was a break of three miles which passengers traversed by coach or on foot; in the year last named the connection was completed by the construction of an iron bridge over the Murray, and the closing of the gap with tracks adapted to the gauges of both the colonies. There are now commodious stations on both sides of the river. The New South Wales trains cross the river to Wodonga, while those from Victoria cross it to Albury.

It was evening when the party arrived at the frontier, and as soon as the formalities of the custom-house were over, the Doctor and his young companions went to a hotel near the station. The custom-house was not rigorous, as none of their baggage was opened, the officials being contented with the declaration that they had nothing dutiable in their possession. Next morning the youths were up early to have a look at the great river of Australia; they were somewhat disappointed with the Murray, their fancies having made the river much larger than it proved to be. Compared with the Mississippi, the Hudson, the Rhine, or the Thames, it was insignificant, but it was nevertheless a river navigable from Albury to the ocean, one thousand eight hundred miles away.

A steamboat lay at the bank of the river a short distance below the railway-bridge; it was not much of a boat in the way of luxury, but was well adapted to the work for which it was intended, and had a barge fastened behind it by a strong tow-rope. Fred learned that there were several boats engaged in the navigation of the Murray and its tributaries, but they were unable to run at all seasons of the year. In ordinary stages of water boats can reach Albury, but there are certain periods of the year when they cannot do so.

Some boys were sitting on the bank farther down the river, engaged in fishing with pole and line. Frank and Fred made their acquaintance, and examined the fish they had taken; the oldest of the boys, evidently much more intelligent than his companions, enlightened the strangers as to the piscatorial possessions of Australia.

STEAMBOAT ON THE MURRAY RIVER.

FISH-HATCHING BOXES ON A SMALL STREAM.

"That is the 'Murray cod,' or 'cod-perch,'" said he, as he pointed to one of the results of the morning's work.

"What a splendid fish!" Fred exclaimed.

"What?—that!" said the Australian youth, with an air of contempt. "That's only a little one, and doesn't weigh more'n two pounds."

"How large do these fish grow?" queried Frank.

"Oh! we catch 'em weighing thirty or forty pounds," was the reply. "We bait with tree-frogs, and have to use strong lines, or they'd get away from us."

"They're pretty good eating," he continued, "but not so good as bream and trout; the trout were brought here from your country, and we're getting 'em all through the rivers of Australia, so folks tell me. They sent us the eggs, and the fish were hatched out here; and several kinds of European and American fishes have been introduced that way. We've a good many kinds of perch; how many I don't know, but the best is the golden perch of the Murray and the rivers running into it. We've got a black-fish, as we call him; he's black outside, but his flesh is white as snow, and he's splendid for eating.

"If you want to go trout-fishing, you can do so twenty miles from Melbourne and find all you want; they've been trying to raise salmon in Australia, but the rivers are too warm for 'em. Sometimes we read in the newspapers about somebody's catching a salmon, but it never amounts to much."

Frank presented his informant with a shilling, partly in return for his information and partly to secure the fish, which he carried to the hotel and requested that it be cooked for breakfast. It was cooked accordingly, and when, accompanied by the Doctor, the youths sat down to their repast, the fish was pronounced a toothsome morsel.

Soon after ten o'clock they were in the railway-train for Melbourne. They traversed a varied country, passing through a rich pastoral and agricultural region, through widely extended wheat-fields, and in sight of numerous flocks of sheep and herds of cattle, through stretches of forest more or less luxuriant, over plains and among hills, along winding valleys, and occasionally in sight of the mountains which lie between the Dividing Range and some portions of the coast. In due time the crest of the range was passed, and the train descended gently to Melbourne and deposited the travellers safe and sound at the railway terminus.

IMMIGRANT'S CAMP IN THE FOOT-HILLS OF THE RANGE.

CHAPTER XX.

THE FOUNDING OF MELBOURNE. — BATMAN AND FAWKNER. — GROWTH OF MELBOURNE, CHICAGO, AND SAN FRANCISCO COMPARED.—SIGHTS AND SCENES IN THE AUSTRALIAN METROPOLIS.—COLLINS STREET, BOURKE STREET, AND OTHER THOROUGHFARES.— A GENERAL DESCRIPTION.— THE YARRA RIVER.— BOTANICAL GARDENS.—DINING AT A SUBURBAN RESIDENCE.—THE SUBURBS OF MELBOURNE. — HOW ONE HUNDRED DOLLARS BECAME ONE MILLION IN FIFTY YEARS.—SANDRIDGE (PORT MELBOURNE).—SCENES IN THE HARBOR.—REMINISCENCES OF THE GOLD RUSH OF 1851.—BUSH-RANGERS AND THEIR PERFORMANCES.—PLUNDERING A SHIP IN PORT.—HOBSON'S BAY AND PORT PHILLIP BAY. —WILLIAMSTOWN AND ST. KILDA.— SHARK FENCES.— QUEENSCLIFF.—CURIOUS ROCKS ON THE COAST.—GEELONG.—MELBOURNE NEWSPAPERS.

FRANK and Fred were impatient to see Melbourne, the city of which they had heard so much, and whose praises are loudly chanted by every resident of the colony of Victoria. As they rode from the railway-station to their hotel they could hardly believe that they were in a city where half a century ago there was little more than a clearing in the forest on the banks of the Yarra.

Yet so it was. On June 2, 1835, John Batman ascended the Yarra and Salt-water rivers, and made a bargain with the native chiefs of the locality to purchase a large area of ground, more than one thousand two hundred square miles, for which he paid a few shirts and blankets, some sugar, flour, and other trifles—probably not a hundred dollars' worth altogether. The Government afterwards set aside his purchase, but paid to Batman and his partners the sum of £7000 for the relinquishment of their claim.

Batman returned immediately to Tasmania to procure a fresh supply of provisions, and near the end of August, 1835, during his absence, another adventurer, John Fawkner, landed on the banks of the Yarra from the schooner *Enterprise*, and made his camp in the forest on the bank of the stream. He brought five men, two horses, two pigs, one cat, and three kangaroo-dogs; and this was the colony that founded the present city of Melbourne. Fawkner may be fairly considered the founder of Melbourne, as the permanent occupation of the site dates

THE FOUNDING OF MELBOURNE, AUGUST, 1835.

from the day he landed from his schooner. But Batman's part of the affair should not be forgotten; he returned in the following April, and settled on what is now a part of the city. As might be expected, there was a bitter quarrel between Batman and Fawkner as long as both survived, and it was continued by their descendants.

The inhabitants of Melbourne have duly honored Batman by erecting in the old cemetery of that city an appropriate monument to his memory. He died in 1839, before the city had grown to much importance though it was giving good promise for the future. At the time of Batman's death there were four hundred and fifty houses, seventy shops, and three thousand inhabitants in Melbourne, and the first ship had sailed for London with a cargo of four hundred bales of wool.

Frank and Fred learned all this before taking their first stroll along the streets of Melbourne on the morning after their arrival. They also learned that the city took its name in honor of Lord Melbourne, who was then Premier of Great Britain. Frank suggested that perhaps Shakespeare had Melbourne in mind as the "bourne whence no traveller returns," since a great many deaths occurred there during the gold rush. Fred reproved his cousin for using this antiquated "chestnut," and the topic was indefinitely postponed.

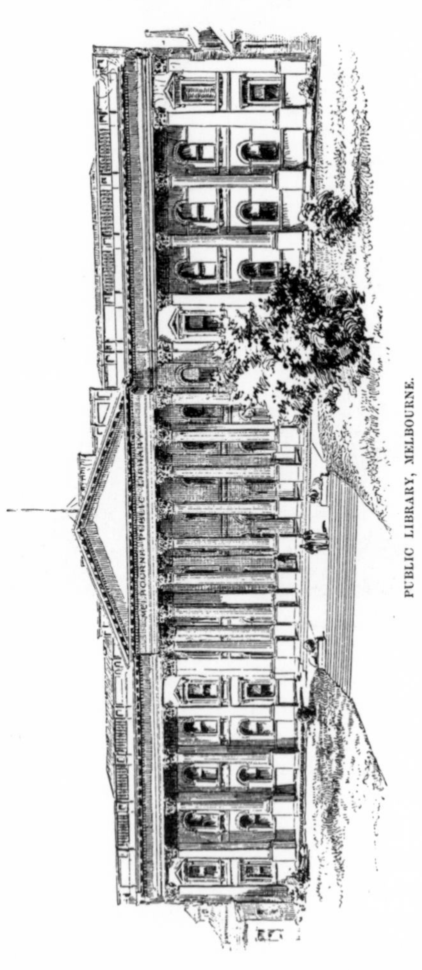

PUBLIC LIBRARY, MELBOURNE.

The first thing to attract the attention of the youths was the width of the streets (ninety-nine feet, or a chain and a half) in contrast with the narrow streets of Sydney. Then the situation is pleasing, as it is on some rolling hills something like those on which Moscow, the ancient capital of Russia, stands. The hills afford good drainage to the central part of the city, and as one goes about he finds himself occasionally upon an elevation from which he can look away for a considerable distance. The city itself is about a mile and a half square, and is regularly laid out; it is surrounded by parks and gardens, and its suburbs include a radius of not far from ten miles, and are steadily extending. Within this radius it is claimed that there are fully 360,000 inhabitants, and the number is increasing year by year.

"Three hundred and sixty thousand people in a city which was first settled in 1835!" said Fred. "Chicago and San Francisco must look sharp for their laurels."

"They may look, but they won't find them," replied Frank.

"Are you not mistaken?" queried his cousin. "Did not each of them have as many inhabitants as Melbourne within fifty years after its settlement?"

"We will see," was the reply. "Chicago was practically founded in 1816, when Fort Dearborn, which had been destroyed in 1812, was rebuilt. In 1870, fifty-four years later, it had, according to the census, 298,997 inhabitants.

MELBOURNE POST-OFFICE.

"San Francisco was begun in 1776, when the Mission of San Francisco de Asis, more commonly called the Mission Dolores, was established there; but some people claim that the city was not really founded until 1835, when the village of Yerba Buena was built, and to please them we'll start from that date, which is the year in which Melbourne was founded. By the census of 1880, forty-five years from its foundation, it had 233,959 inhabitants, and at its fiftieth anniversary was doubtless considerably behind Melbourne. But Chicago has gone ahead of both of the other cities in question, as it contained more than half a million people in 1880, and was still growing as fast as the extensions on the prairie would permit. Perhaps in time it will cover the whole State of Illinois."

"Melbourne, Chicago, and San Francisco are the marvels of the world in their growth," responded Fred, "and they've no reason to be jealous of one another." Frank echoed this opinion, and then the figures of populations were dropped from discussion.

GOVERNMENT HOUSE, MELBOURNE.

Their walk took them along Collins Street, which is the Broadway or the Regent Street of the city; they traversed its entire length from west to east, and then turned their attention to Bourke Street, which runs parallel to Collins Street. To enumerate all the fine buildings they saw in their promenade would make a list altogether too tedious for anything less than a guide-book. As they took no notes of what they saw, it is safe to say that neither of the youths could at this moment write a connected account of the sights of the morning.

"If we had been skeptical about the wealth and prosperity of Melbourne," wrote Fred in his journal, "all our doubts were removed by what we saw during our first tour through the city. One after another magnificent piles of buildings came before us, the banks and other private edifices rivalling the public ones for extent and solidity. The highest structure in Melbourne is known as Robb's Buildings, and was built by a wealthy speculator, on the same general plan as the Mills, Field, and similar buildings in New York. There are many banks, office buildings, stores, warehouses, and other private edifices that would do honor to London, Paris, or New York; and the same is the case with the Post-office, Houses of Parliament, Law Courts, Public Library, National Gallery, Government House, Ormond College, and other public structures.

"We turned down Swanston Street in the direction of the river, the Yarra, or, to speak more properly, the Yarra-Yarra, as it was originally known, though few now call it by the double name. Anybody who comes here expecting a great river will be disappointed, as the Yarra isn't much of a stream on which to build a city like Melbourne. It answers well enough for people to row upon with pleasure-boats and for occasionally drowning somebody, but is altogether too small and shallow for large vessels. Steamers and sailing-craft drawing not more than sixteen feet can come up to the city, but large vessels must stop at Sandridge, or Port Melbourne, two and a half miles away. The Yarra supplies water for the Botanical Gardens, but not for the city generally.

COLLINS STREET IN 1870.

"We reached the river at Prince's Bridge, where a fine viaduct of three arches replaces the former one of a single arch. There are several bridges across the Yarra, which separates Melbourne proper from South Melbourne and other suburbs, and we were told that new bridges are under consideration, and will be built as the necessity for them becomes more pressing. A great deal of money has been expended in deepening and straightening the river, and it is certainly vastly improved upon the stream which Batman and Fawkner ascended in 1835, when they made the settlements from which Melbourne has grown. Since 1877 the river has been deepened three feet, and the minimum low-water depth is said to be fourteen feet six inches at spring-tides.

PUBLIC OFFICES AND TREASURY GARDENS.

"Street-cars, or 'trams,' some drawn by horses and others by cables, run in every direction; and there are omnibuses, cabs, and other conveyances; so that one can go pretty nearly anywhere he chooses for a small amount of money. Some of the omnibuses remind us of the new ones in Paris, as they have three horses abreast, and dash along in fine style. Hansom and other cabs are numerous, and the fares are about a third more than in London; this is a great change from the days of the gold rush, when the most ordinary carriage could not be hired for less than £3 a day, and very often the drivers obtained twice or three times that amount. We have been told of a gold-digger just down from the mines of whom £12 was demanded one day for an afternoon's drive; he handed the driver a ten-pound note, and told him he would have to be satisfied with that—and he was.

"We went into three or four arcades, which form pleasant lounging and shopping places, like the famous 'passages' of Paris and the arcades of London. One of them is called the 'Book Arcade,' and is principally devoted to the sale of books; and if we may judge by the number of volumes we saw there, the people of Melbourne are liberal patrons of

TOWN-HALL, MELBOURNE.

literature. No matter what the taste of a person might be in books, whether he desired a work of fiction or a treatise on science, a volume of travels or an exposition of Hindoo philosophy, he could be accommodated without delay. They have a public library here containing nearly one hundred and fifty thousand volumes, all of which can be read without charge.

"When we got back to the hotel and met the Doctor, it was time to sit down to breakfast. He had already received two invitations to dinner from gentlemen to whom he brought letters; they had heard of our arrival, and knowing we had been hospitably received in Sydney, were determined that we should be initiated at once into the courtesies of Melbourne, and start off with a favorable impression of the place.

VIEW FROM SOUTH MELBOURNE, 1868.

"A few minutes after we were through with breakfast a gentleman called for us and gave us a carriage-drive, in which we saw more than we can begin to describe. We visited the Botanical Gardens, which are about a mile from the city, and on the south bank of the Yarra; they cover an area of not far from a hundred acres, and do great credit to the gentlemen who designed and perfected them. The collection of plants and trees is very large, and everything is labelled, so that the scientific student can know at once its history and character. We strolled along a winding walk among the ferns, and could easily imagine ourselves in the heart of a tropical forest. We also visited the Fitzroy, Carlton, Treasury, and other gardens and parks, of which Melbourne has an abundant supply.

"On many of the streets trees have been planted, and they add much to the attractions of the city. The water-supply of Melbourne comes from an artificial lake nineteen miles from the city, and is brought in by the Yan Yean Water-works, which are not altogether unlike the Croton works of New York or the Cochituate of Boston. Water seems to be abundant in all the houses, and we are told that there are more bath-tubs in Melbourne than in any other city of its size in the world.

"We can't begin to name all the churches we have seen in our rides and walks along the streets. Suffice it to say there are no finer modern churches anywhere than here, and the inhabitants of Melbourne have shown great liberality in their contributions for building these religious edifices. There is no State Church in the colony, but the Church of England is the fashionable one, and has a greater number of adherents than any other church.

"In their order, and omitting the smaller figures, there were by the last census of the colony 311,000 Episcopalians, 203,000 Catholics, 132,000 Presbyterians, 108,000 Methodists, 20,000 Independents, or Congregationalists, 20,000 Baptists, and 11,000 Lutherans and German Protestants.

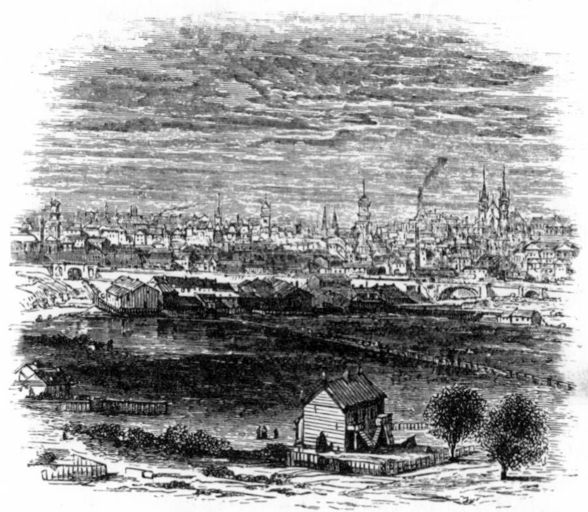

PART OF MELBOURNE IN 1838.

On the first of January, 1886, there were 2150 churches and chapels in Victoria, and about the same number of public buildings and dwellings used for public worship, or more than 4000 in all.

"While we were riding about the city we asked our host whence came the names of the streets.

"'The principal ones commemorate men who were connected with the early history of the colony,' was his reply. 'Collins Street is named for Colonel Collins, who established a convict settlement on the shores of Port Phillip Bay in 1803, but soon gave it up and removed the settlement to Tasmania. Bourke Street is named after the governor of New South Wales in 1836; Flinders Street after Captain Flinders, of whose explorations you are doubtless aware; Lonsdale Street after Captain Lonsdale, who was in command here about that time; and Swanston Street after one of Batman's companions. King, Queen, William, and Elizabeth Streets are tokens of our loyalty to the royal family of Great Britain, the same as are the streets of like names in Sydney and Brisbane.'

"I should have said, in speaking of the streets, that between every two wide streets there are narrow ones which were originally intended as back entrances, and were known by the prefix of 'little.' Thus we have Little Collins Street between Collins and Bourke Streets; Little Bourke Street between Bourke and Latrobe, and so on through the list. Most of these 'little' streets have become known as lanes, and are spoken of as Collins Lane, Bourke Lane, etc. Bourke Lane is largely occupied by Chinese, and Flinders Lane, between Flinders and Collins Streets, is generally known as 'The Lane,' especially among the dealers in clothing throughout Australia, as it is the peculiar haunt of the importers of wearing apparel, or 'soft goods.'

"Elizabeth Street runs in the valley between the two principal hills on which the city is built, and divides it into East and West, just as Fifth Avenue divides the numbered streets of New York. As Melbourne is on the other side of the world from New York, it is quite in the nature of things that the custom of designating the portions of a street should be the reverse of ours. In New York we say 'East Fourteenth Street,' or 'West Twenty-third Street.' Here they say 'Collins Street East,' or 'Bourke Street West,' according as the designated locality is east or west from Elizabeth Street.

"We returned to the hotel in good season to dress for dinner," continued Fred, "and at the appointed time went to the place where we were to dine. It was several miles out of town, and our journey thither was by railway, our host sending a carriage to meet us at the station. Melbourne resembles London in having a net-work of suburban railways, and resembles it further in having a great rush of people to the city in the morning, and out of it in the afternoon. Ordinarily the facilities of travel are fairly equal to the demand, but if a heavy shower of rain falls about 6 P.M., the supply of vehicles is insufficient.

"The house of our host is well built and well furnished, and has plenty of ground surrounding it for garden, lawn, and shrubbery. English trees grow in the grounds. Much of the furniture came from the old country, but the portion of it that was made in Melbourne is by no means inferior to the imported part. Prosperous people in Melbourne know how to live well, and some of the wealthier inhabitants spend a great deal of money on the support of their establishments.

A SUBURBAN RESIDENCE.

We dined as well as we could have dined in London or New York, the local luxuries of those cities that were wanting here being fully atoned for by the products of the colony.

"It was late in the evening when we got back to our hotel in the city, after listening to stories of colonial life in general, and of life in Melbourne in particular, until our heads were nearly giddy with what had been poured into them. Anthony Trollope intimates that the Melbournites are given to 'blowing' about the wonders of their city, and he excuses them on the ground that they have something worth 'blowing' about. If we were to make any remark on this subject, it would be to agree with him on both points. But as one hears the same kind of talk in Chicago, St. Louis, San Francisco, and other American cities, and also in the other colonial centres of Australasia, we have ceased to wonder at it, and set it down as a matter of course."

In the next day or two our friends visited some of the suburbs of Melbourne, including Notham, Carlton, Fitzroy, Collingwood, and Brunswick on the north, and Richmond, Prahran, Windsor, Malvern, and Caulfield on the south. Frank noted that some of these suburbs were prosperous and well populated, while others were much less so, and seemed to base a goodly part of their hopes on the future. There is a great deal of speculation in suburban land, just as in the neighborhood of all large cities the world over; fortunes have been made in suburban speculation, and still larger fortunes hoped for but not yet realized.

Melbourne was originally laid out in half-acre lots, but nearly all of them have long since been divided and subdivided. One of the few that have not been divided, but are held by the families of the purchasers, is in a good part of Collins Street. The colonist who bought it paid £20 for the lot in 1837; it is now worth £100,000, and since the time of the original purchase the holders have received at least £100,000 in rents. One million dollars in fifty years from an investment of one hundred dollars may be considered a fairly good return for one's money.

Doctor Bronson and his nephews were not neglectful of the harbor of Melbourne any more than they had been of Sydney Cove when at the capital of New South Wales. There are trains at short intervals from Melbourne to Sandridge (Port Melbourne), and cars and omnibuses every fifteen minutes. The fare is threepence, or six cents. This is a great reduction from the days of the gold rush in 1851, when the omnibus charge between Sandridge and Melbourne was two shillings and sixpence (sixty-two and one-half cents) for each passenger, and a carriage for four persons cost from five to twenty dollars for the single trip.

Mr. Manson, who was so attentive to our friends in Sydney, was equally well acquainted with Melbourne; he called upon them shortly after their arrival in the latter city, and proposed to accompany them in their visit to the port. His offer was at once accepted. During the ride to Sandridge the conversation turned upon the days of the gold rush, and the incidents that long since passed into history.

"It was before I came to Australia," said he, "so that I cannot speak from personal knowledge; but I have heard the stories from so many old residents that I have no doubt of their correctness. The expense of getting goods from Sandridge to Melbourne, three miles, was often as much as to bring them from London to the harbor. William Howitt tells, in his 'Two Years in Victoria,' that the cost of carrying his baggage from the ship to his lodgings in Melbourne was more than that of bringing them the previous thirteen thousand miles, including what he paid for conveyance from his house to the London docks.

HARBOR SCENE IN THE MOONLIGHT.

"When a ship arrived with passengers, the charge for taking them from the anchorage to the beach was three shillings, and then came the omnibus charge already mentioned. If a man was alone, the boatmen charged him ten or perhaps twenty shillings; and if a person was obliged to go out to a ship, and they knew his journey was important, they would charge any price they pleased. A gentleman having occasion to visit a ship that was about to sail, and manifesting some anxiety to do so, was obliged to pay £12, or sixty dollars.

"After goods were landed they were loaded into carts for transportation to Melbourne. A clerk looked at a load, and then said, glibly, 'These things will be £3;' and if anybody demurred at the price, the gate-keeper was ordered not to let the cart pass out of the yard till the sum demanded was paid. People grumbled and denounced the charges as outrageous, but they generally paid them and went on.

"In the city the same high scale of prices prevailed. In the shops the prices were about three hundred per cent. above the cost of goods.

BOARDING-HOUSE OF 1851.

Lodgings were in great demand; the meanest kind of an unfurnished room was worth ten dollars a week, and two poorly furnished ones were from twenty to thirty dollars a week. Hotel-keepers turned their stables into sleeping-places, and a man paid five shillings a night for a third of a horse's stall, good straw, a blanket, and a rug. One landlord had seventy of these five-shilling lodgers in his stable nightly, in addition to the occupants of the rooms in the legitimate portion of his house."

"I wonder the people didn't live in tents till they could arrange to go up country," one of the youths remarked.

"They did so," was the reply, "and so many tents were spread on the waste ground outside the city that the place became known as Canvas Town. The Government charged five shillings weekly for the privilege of putting up tents on this waste ground, or at the rate of sixty dollars a year. Of course all were anxious to get away as soon as possible, but they were often detained three or four weeks, or even longer, waiting to obtain their goods from the ships."

"Was there much security for life and property in those days?" Frank asked.

"According to all accounts there was a great deal of disorder," Mr. Manson responded. "There were many runaway convicts here from Tasmania and New South Wales, together with other bad characters. Robberies along the road were very common. One Saturday afternoon in broad daylight four fellows armed with guns and pistols stopped some twenty or more people, one after the other, tied them up to trees, and robbed them, on the road from Melbourne to St. Kilda. The bush-rangers carried on their performances up to the very edge of Melbourne, and sometimes they rode through the streets and out again before they could be stopped.

"The coolest piece of robbery was performed in the harbor one night. A ship was to sail for England at daylight, and she had several thousand ounces of gold on board. About midnight a party of eight or ten went out in a boat pretending to have business on board, and were admitted without suspicion. Their real business was to plunder the ship, and they succeeded; they 'stuck up' the officers and crew, bound them hand and foot, loaded the gold into their boat, and escaped. No alarm was given until some one went on board the next morning, as all the officers and crew had been gagged and locked in below. The robbers got clean away; nothing was ever learned about them, but it was suspected that they were ex-convicts from Tasmania."

A GOOD LOCATION FOR BUSINESS.

The carriage had by this time brought our friends to Sandridge, and they alighted at the head of one of the piers. There are two piers at Sandridge (to use its former name in place of its more modern appellation of Port Melbourne). These piers run far out into the bay, and ships of almost any tonnage may lie alongside to discharge or receive cargoes. One is known as the town pier, and the other as the railway pier; on the railway pier trains of cars may load or discharge at the side of the ships, and thus effect a great saving in the handling of freight.

It was a busy scene from one end of the pier to the other, and as the strangers walked about they were obliged to be cautious lest they were run over by moving cars or stumbled among the piles of goods that lay about. Vessels from all parts of the world were lying at the piers; at anchor in the bay were other vessels, steamers and sailing craft, likewise hailing from the four quarters of the globe. All the great companies known in the East, the "P. and O.," North German Lloyds, Messageries Maritimes, Orient, and others, were represented, and the ubiquitous "tramp" steamers were there in goodly numbers. Then there were numerous "intercolonial" steamers engaged in the trade between Melbourne and the ports of the Australian coast, and also with Tasmania, New Zealand, Feejee, and other islands.

LOADING A SHIP FROM A LIGHTER.

Some of the steamships have their docks at Williamstown, which is on the other side of Hobson's Bay, directly opposite Sandridge, and connected with Melbourne by railway. The business of Williamstown, like that of Sandridge, is mostly connected with the shipping; a steam ferry carried our friends across the bay, and they spent an hour or two in Williamstown, the time being principally devoted to an inspection of the ship-building yards and the graving dock, which has accommodations for the largest ships engaged in the Australian trade.

Hobson's Bay may be called the enlarging of the Yarra at its mouth, or the narrowing of Port Phillip Bay at its head. But by whatever description it is known it is an excellent harbor for Melbourne, as it has good anchorage and abundance of space for the ships that congregate there. Port Phillip Bay is about thirty-five miles long and the same in width; its entrance is nearly two miles across, and, like Sydney harbor, it has space for all the navies of the civilized world. No doubt the Melbourne people would not object to such a visitation, provided it were peaceful, for the same reason that the Sydneyite gave to Frank and Fred, "that it would be a good thing for business."

On their return from Williamstown to Sandridge the party drove to St. Kilda, the Coney Island of Melbourne, and a great resort for those who are fond of salt-water bathing. Farther down the bay is Brighton Beach, a familiar name whether the visitor be from New York or London, and if he looks further he will find other names that will not be altogether strange. All around the bay there are pleasure resorts, private residences, business establishments, factories, and other evidences that the region has long since been reclaimed from the possession of the savage and become the permanent home of the white man.

Fred observed that there were fences far out in the water enclosing areas where bathers were splashing and, to all appearances, having a good time. He immediately asked what was the use of the fences.

"They are for protection against sharks," replied Mr. Manson, "which are abundant in these waters and all along the Australian coast. You have doubtless heard of them at other points."

The youth remembered the sharks at Queensland and New South Wales, and the stories he had heard about them. He remarked that if the creatures were as bad as they were farther north, he should not venture into the water at St. Kilda until satisfied that the fence was thoroughly shark-proof.

The carriage was sent back from St. Kilda, and on assurance that the fence was strong the whole party indulged in the luxury of a sea-bath. Then they strolled on the beach, dined at one of the restaurants for which St. Kilda is famous, and returned in the evening by railway to Melbourne. Frank and Fred thought it was very like an excursion to Coney Island, and Doctor Bronson fully agreed with them, except that he missed the broad ocean which spreads before the popular watering-place of New York.

"There's a fine watering-place at Queenscliff, at the entrance of Port Phillip Bay," said Mr. Manson, "where you can look out on the Pacific and can see and hear the surf breaking on the shore. There's a fort there to guard the entrance in case of war, and all ships are signalled from that point on their arrival. As St. Kilda is the Coney Island of Melbourne, Queenscliff may be called its Long Branch, as its distance is about thirty-two miles, and it can be reached both by railway and steamboat.

"Farther down the coast," said he, "there are other watering-places, and what with the mountains and the sea Melbourneites are well provided with retreats. Here is something interesting."

As he spoke he took from his pocket a photograph, which Doctor Bronson examined attentively, and then passed it over to the youths. It represented some rocks which resembled pieces of artillery, and were overlooked by a head that reminded Frank of "The Old Man of the Mountain," in Franconia, New Hampshire.

"The height to the crown of the head," said Mr. Manson, "is twenty-four feet, and the tuft of coast scrub that has found sufficient soil to cling to it in the cleft of the rock increases the resemblance to a head by representing hair. The guns are more realistic when viewed from another angle; near them are some spherical blocks of sandstone that might almost serve as cannon-balls. The head has been named the 'Sentinel,' and is also called the Sphinx; it is on the southern coast of Victoria, and about eight miles from Lorne, which has a growing popularity as a watering-place. The rocks resembling cannon are known as 'The Artillery Rocks.'"

Frank and Fred hoped they would have an opportunity to visit this natural curiosity, but circumstances did not favor them, as Lorne was too far away from the route of travel to justify the detour.

The day after their visit to St. Kilda they were taken on a steamboat excursion to Geelong, a pretty and well-built city on the shores of an arm of Port Phillip Bay, and about forty-five miles from Melbourne. It is famous for its woollen mills, tanneries, and other manufactories, and at one time its inhabitants firmly believed that it would be a successful rival of Melbourne on account of the superior advantages of its harbor and its greater nearness to the ocean.

It is said that the Geelong people caused a railway to be built between that city and Melbourne in the expectation that all the wool shipped at Melbourne would be brought to their city, which would also be the landing-place of all the goods destined for Melbourne. The result was exactly the reverse, the railway serving to take from Geelong most of the foreign trade it already possessed and carry it to Melbourne. Cargoes of wool are shipped from there still, but they are few in number when compared with those from Melbourne.

THE ARTILLERY ROCKS, NEAR LORNE, ON THE COAST OF VICTORIA.

Before the mail closed for America, Frank and Fred busied themselves with a large number of papers, which they sent to friends at home. They included the *Age* and the *Argus*, dailies which reminded them of *The London Times* or *Daily News*, *The Illustrated Australian News* and *The Illustrated Sketcher*, pictorials making their appearance monthly, a dozen or more weekly and monthly papers, some of them of Brobdingnagian proportions, and representing all shades of religious, social, and political feeling, and a quarterly called *The Imperial Review*. In a letter to his mother Frank said they had visited the office of *The Melbourne Age* at the invitation of one of its proprietors, and had

WAITING TO SEE THE EDITOR.

come away with the belief that few people in the northern hemisphere had a just appreciation of the journalistic skill and enterprise of the antipodes.

"The weekly edition of the *Age* is called the *Leader*," said Frank, in his letter, "and there isn't a daily paper in the United States that has a weekly edition to rival it in size, quantity, and variety of matter; and the same may be said of the *Australasian*, which is the weekly edition of the *Argus*. The *Leader* for this week, of which I send you a copy, contains forty-eight pages, and they tell me this is the regulation number. The pages are the size of those of HARPER'S WEEKLY, and are filled with whatever is considered of greatest interest to their readers in the country districts.

"It is evident," continued Frank, "that there are many waifs and strays in the population of Australia, if we are to judge by the advertising columns of the newspapers. All the leading dailies have advertisements headed 'Missing Friends,' and sometimes there will be a whole column of these inquiries for persons about whom information is desired by their friends. Here is one of them:

"'Robert Wiffen, arrived at Melbourne by ship *Covenanter* on Christmas Day, 1852, and was last heard of in 1867. Any information respecting him will greatly oblige.' . . .

"What volumes might be written by the novelist if he knew all the inside history covered by the 'Missing Friends' column of *The Melbourne Age* or *The Sydney Herald* for a single twelvemonth!"

DISTRIBUTING PAPERS TO NEWSBOYS.

CHAPTER XXI.

THE RACE FOR THE MELBOURNE CUP.—POPULARITY OF HORSE-RACING IN AUSTRALIA.—CRICKET AND OTHER SPORTS.—SUMMER RETREATS AMONG THE MOUNTAINS OVERLOOKING MELBOURNE.—"A SOUTHERLY BURSTER."—ITS PECULIARITIES.—RAPID FALL OF THE THERMOMETER.—FLOODING THE STREETS OF MELBOURNE.—CHILDREN DROWNED IN THE GUTTERS.—BALLARAT AND THE GOLD-MINES.—HISTORY OF THE DISCOVERY OF GOLD IN AUSTRALIA.—THE RUSH TO BALLARAT AND BENDIGO.—SANDHURST.—ITS PRESENT APPEARANCE.—REMARKABLE YIELD OF THE BALLARAT MINES.—"THE WELCOME NUGGET."—WESTERN DISTRICT OF VICTORIA.—LAKE SCENERY.—AUSTRALIA'S POTATO FIELD.—GIPPSLAND.—FROM MELBOURNE TO TASMANIA.—LAUNCESTON.—A CHAPTER OF TASMANIAN HISTORY.—MEMORIES OF CONVICT DAYS.—CORRA LINN AND OTHER SHOW PLACES.

"WE'RE sorry you are not to be here for the Cup Race," was remarked to our friends by half the acquaintances they made in Melbourne. "It's the greatest day in the southern hemisphere," said one of them, "and is to Australia what the Derby Day is to England. Banks, stores, courts, legislative councils, and all other places of business are closed on that occasion, and the whole population takes a holiday."

The race for the Melbourne Cup is the sporting sensation of Australia, and it is said that nearly two hundred thousand people assemble to witness it. The city and suburbs furnish a large part of the attendance, and the rest is made up from the country regions, from the other colonies of the continent, and not a few visitors from New Zealand and Tasmania. For weeks—and, one may say, for months—preceding the event it is the principal topic of conversation, and the stranger is often surprised at the prevalence of "horse talk" in the best social circles. For a week before the memorable day the city is crowded with strangers, and the oft-repeated question, "Which horse will win the cup?" is heard everywhere and from every lip.

The first Tuesday of November is Cup Day, and the race may be considered one of the harbingers of spring. Every available conveyance is in requisition, vehicles of all kinds rent for high prices, the railways run frequent trains, and many thousands of spectators go and

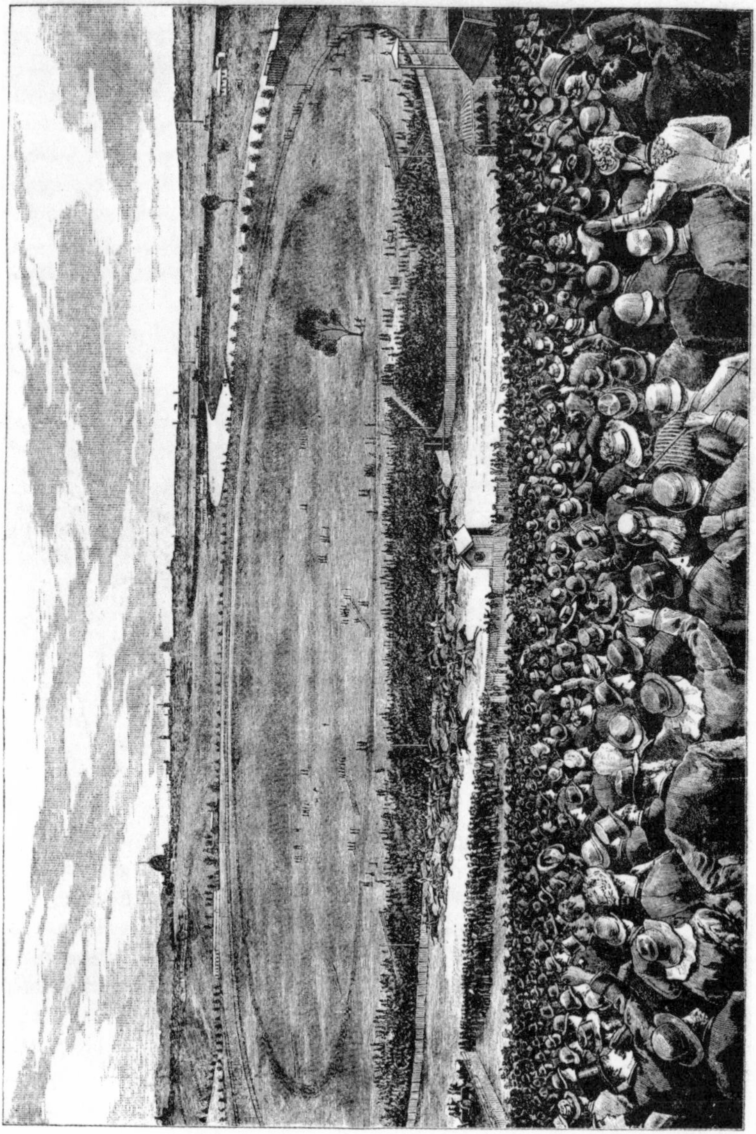

THE RACE FOR THE MELBOURNE CUP.

return on foot. The race-course is at Flemington, three miles from Melbourne; it covers three hundred and sixteen acres of ground, and is considered one of the finest racing-tracks in the world. From the grand-stand the towers and spires of Melbourne are distinctly visible; the whole track lies directly in front, and altogether the scene, as the horses come in at the finish, is one long to be remembered.

Horses from all the colonies may compete for the cup. It is a curious circumstance that of all the competitors for the Melbourne Cup in 1887 not one was bred in the colony of Victoria.

Though Doctor Bronson and the youths were not in Melbourne at the right time for the cup race, they had abundant opportunity to witness games of cricket, the sport for which the Victorians are famous. The

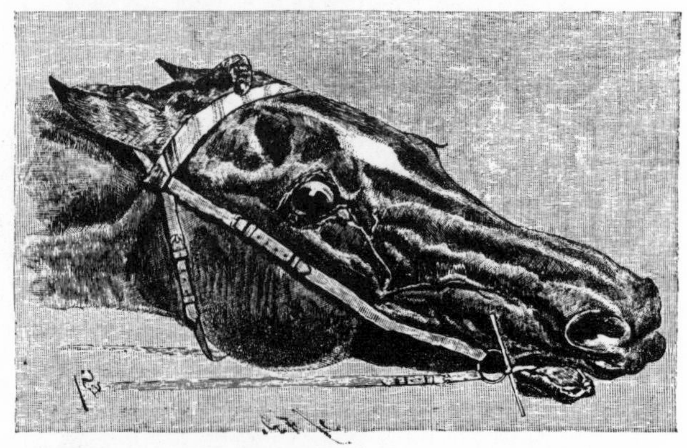

HEAD OF A WINNER.

game is universally popular in the colony; in and near Melbourne there are two or three cricket-grounds splendidly equipped with everything that players or spectators could desire, and when notable games are played they are sure to draw large crowds. The interior cities and towns have their cricket-grounds, and every vacant lot in Melbourne large enough for a game is the resort of "larrikins" and other youths, from seven years old and upwards, all intent upon cricket. In fact, the game is to Australia what base-ball is to America.

The "Australian Eleven," and its successful competition with the "All-England Eleven" and other British clubs, is too well-known to cricket-players to require more than passing mention. It is no more

A CRICKET MATCH.

than justice to say that the Australians are the champion cricket-players of the world.

The "larrikin" of Australia, mentioned in the preceding paragraph, is the equivalent for the "street arab" of New York and the "young hoodlum" of San Francisco—a youth who is subject to no parental restraint, and all too often is without any place he can call home. Under these circumstances he is very apt to drift into vicious ways, and gives the police a good deal of trouble. When Frank first heard the word "larrikin," and heard its meaning, he naturally asked for its origin.

"Nobody knows positively," was the reply. "The story goes that years ago a policeman arrested a boy whom he had caught in some violation of the law. When called to testify against the young culprit the policeman, who was a native of Dublin, gravely said,

"'I caught him, yer honor, a larrikin (larking) around and making a dale of noise.'

"From that time to this, so the story goes, the turbulent youth of Australian cities and towns have been known as 'larrikins.' Sydney, Melbourne, Adelaide, and all other large places in the colonies are plentifully supplied with them."

"Melbourne was determined, as I've said before," wrote Frank, "not to be outdone by Sydney in hospitality, and it certainly wasn't. We have had invitations that would require weeks and months to accept them. Everybody has made us welcome, not only to their houses here but at the sea-side and up-country. Doctor Bronson received cards for all the clubs, and in a good many ways we have had 'the freedom of the city.' There are several fine clubs here—among them the Athenæum, the Australian, the Melbourne, and the Yorick, the last being semi-professional in its character, like the Lotos of New York. In fact, it has an exchange with the Lotos, members of either club having the privileges of the other without charge for a period of three months.

"Many of the private houses have ball-rooms attached, and dancing-parties are very common in fashionable life. A favorite social amusement is lawn-tennis, and I don't think there is any place in the world where it has greater popularity. It is played by old and young of both sexes, and many of the young ladies in society devote three or four hours daily to the sport. We were invited one day to accompany a gentleman on a round of afternoon calls. The calls amounted to visiting six or eight tennis-courts in succession, and in each court we found a goodly-sized party, some of the ladies and gentlemen playing as though their lives depended on winning, and the rest drinking tea, chatting, and looking on.

"When the heat of summer comes on those who have country-houses, either by the sea or on the mountains, retire there, just as New Yorkers run away to Long Branch, Newport, or the White Mountains. Some of the owners of country-houses keep them open throughout the year, and are never contented unless they have a party of guests to accept their hospitality. We were invited to several of these houses, but time prevented our accepting all the invitations. We ran up for a few days to a rural retreat on the southern slope of one of the mountains that looks upon Melbourne from a distance of forty or fifty miles. The place and all its appointments were delightful.

"The house stands in a broad clearing in the gum forest, and in a position commanding an extensive view. To the rear and on each side the wood-covered slopes rise above it, but in front there is a view along the gently descending plains to Melbourne and the ocean beyond. Though the city is nearly fifty miles away we can clearly make out its position on a fine day, so great is the purity of the atmosphere. When the air is a trifle murky we see in place of Melbourne a cloud of smoke, which the winds bear away, sometimes to the north and sometimes to

SUMMER RETREAT IN THE MOUNTAINS.

the south or east. Port Phillip Bay shines between the city and the ocean, and with a glass we can trace the course of the steamers as they enter or leave the great haven or creep along the coast.

"Immediately in front of the house the lawn sweeps down to a pretty pond or tiny lake, and around it is a garden in which all the flowers of two hemispheres seem to have made their home. We have been reminded over and over again, and on nearly every day of our stay in Australia, of the welcome which the climate gives to the flowers of other lands, and nowhere is the reminder more forcible than in the gardens of these country-houses near Melbourne. Every description of ornamental tree and flowering shrub is to be found there, and exotics vie with the native flowers of Australia in covering the ground with all the colors known to the artist. Not only is the ground carpeted with them, but the trunks of the trees, the posts that support the houses, and even the fronts and roofs of the buildings themselves, are so covered with creeping and flowering plants that scarcely any of the original wood or other material is visible.

"Evidently Melbourne knew that we had been treated to a brickfielder in Sydney, and was therefore determined to give us a taste of its climatic peculiarities before our departure. To offset the hot wind of Sydney we had a 'southerly burster' in Melbourne, and also two or three showers of rain that came down with such vigor as to fill the gutters of the lower streets to a depth of two or three feet. Most of the crossings are bridged, so that one can walk over the temporary rivers in safety, but in former times accidents were not infrequent. 'Another Child Drowned in the Gutters Yesterday' was by no means an unusual heading in the Melbourne papers, and sometimes full-grown men fell victims to the streams that flowed like mill-races while they lasted.

"A gentleman says that quite recently he saw a man try to jump across a gutter, but he made a miscalculation and fell into it. Instantly the stream took him off his feet and carried him partly under a low bridge, where he would have been drowned had not the spectators pulled him out by the heels. Melbourne streets are very muddy in wet weather and very dusty in dry times. The mud in winter is said to be something almost surpassing belief, unless one has actually seen and tested it. Most of the streets are macadamized with a basaltic rock which breaks up into a very irritating and disagreeable dust that is said to be trying to the eyes of a good many people.

"But about the burster, which I had forgotten for the moment. The weather was fine and warm, with a north-east breeze and not a cloud in the sky. In the morning Doctor Bronson remarked that the barometer was falling, and during the forenoon it continued to go down with considerable rapidity.

"We were going on an excursion, but the gentleman who had invited us came around to suggest a postponement, as we were about to have a burster. 'We always expect it,' said he, 'when the barometer falls rapidly in the forenoon, as it is doing now.'

"So we stayed in and watched for the storm. There was an appearance as if a thin sheet of cloud was being rolled up before the advancing wind; in fact it was not unlike the beginning of the brickfielder in Sydney. Then came a high wind which brought clouds of dust, and then the breeze chopped suddenly to the south and blew with great violence. It was thirty miles an hour at the start, but before it got through with its performance it was sixty or seventy miles. It has been known to go to ninety or a hundred miles, and on one occasion it reached one hundred and fifty miles an hour, and did a great deal of damage.

CAUGHT IN A "BURSTER" ON THE AUSTRALIAN COAST.

"The thermometer fell more rapidly than the barometer had done. In the morning about nine o'clock the mercury was at 89° Fahrenheit, and it remained about that figure until the wind went around to the south a little past noon. In less than an hour it had fallen twenty degrees, and in another hour twenty more. These sudden changes are the trying features of the Australian climate, but the people say nobody suffers from them except in discomfort.

"They tell us that the mercury has been known to drop thirty degrees in half an hour, and the readings of the thermometer at noon and midnight sometimes show a variation of ninety-nine degrees. William Howitt mentions experiencing a temperature of 139° in the shade, and it is no uncommon thing for the mercury to mount to 130°. There is an official record of 179° in the sun and 111° in the shade in South Melbourne, and at the inland town of Deniliquin of 121° in the shade.

"The burster ended towards evening with a heavy fall of rain that filled all the gutters to their fullest capacity, and but for the bridges at the crossings would have made them navigable for small boats. Thunder and lightning accompanied the rain, and while it lasted the shower was as tropical as one could have wished. Nowhere else in the world have we seen heavier or more drenching rain than in Australia.

SEEKING SHELTER.

"If you want to know how fast rain can fall here, look at these figures:

"On February 25, 1873, nearly nine inches of rain fell in as many hours. At Newcastle, March 18, 1871, they had the heaviest rainfall ever recorded in Australia; ten and a half inches fell in two and a half hours, accompanied by a terrific squall of thunder and lightning. During the whole storm, which lasted twenty-two hours, more than twenty inches of rain fell."

Our friends went to Ballarat, one hundred miles from Melbourne, and once an important gold-mining centre. It is still heavily interested in gold-mining, but the alluvial diggings in its neighborhood were exhausted long ago, and the operations at present are confined to the reefs or ledges of rock. The mines are in the suburbs, and as our friends entered the city and passed along the wide avenue called Sturt Street, with shade-trees along its centre, they could hardly believe they were in a mining town. There is hardly a trace of the usual features of a mining region; the public buildings are substantial, there are numerous churches, the streets are wide, well shaded with trees, and the town boasts of a botanical garden on the shores of a lake where there are numerous pleasure-boats! Who would dream of finding these things in a town devoted to taking gold from the earth?

This was the scene of the great rush in 1851, after the discovery of gold became known. Some of the earlier diggers obtained from twenty to fifty pounds of gold daily; the precious metal lay almost on the surface, and in several instances large nuggets were turned up by the wheels of bullock-carts, or were found shining in the sun after a heavy shower.

"They told us," said Frank in giving the account of his visit to the gold-mines, "that a man one day sat down to rest at the foot of a tree in the scrub. Wishing to sharpen his knife, he proceeded to rub it upon a large stone that lay half imbedded between the roots. As he rubbed away on the supposed stone, what was his surprise to see it turn to gold! With his knife he dug around it, gashed it in several places, and found he had unearthed a nugget larger than he could carry. Here was a fortune, and all gained by accident!

"What to do he did not know. He could not carry the nugget, and he dared not go away to obtain aid, lest it might be discovered in his absence, and also for fear he might not find his way back to it. If he dug a hole and concealed it, some one might observe him, and would know at once what he was about; and he could not wait where he was, as he might be there for days without being seen, and he had no provisions with him. Besides, his first visitors might be bush-rangers, who would appropriate his treasure to their own use, and quite likely knock him in the head to get rid of a disagreeable witness against them.

PIONEER GOLD-HUNTERS.

"He did the best thing he could under the circumstances. He covered his treasure with earth and leaves, then tied his shirt to a neighboring tree to mark the spot, and, half naked, went as quickly as possible to the Gold Commissioner of the district and obtained an escort to

MAP OF THE GOLD-FIELDS OF VICTORIA TWENTY YEARS AGO.

accompany him to the place and secure the prize. Luckily no one had been there in his absence, and the great nugget was borne safely to the commissioner's tent.

"According to Australian history, gold was discovered at Lewis Pond Creek, in New South Wales, in February, 1851, by Edward Hargreaves; and at Clunes, sixteen miles from Ballarat, Victoria, in July of the same year, by a miner named Esmond. Both Hargreaves and Esmond were rewarded by the Government for their discoveries; they had been gold-miners in California, and were led to search where they did through the similarity of the ground. There is a report that gold was really found by a shepherd near Clunes at least two years before the discovery by Esmond; and there is another report that gold was found in 1814 by convicts who were building a road over the Blue Mountains, but the Government kept the discovery secret.

"No gold-mining region in the world ever gave up so much of the precious metal in the same time as did Ballarat in the early days. Claims eight feet square and the same in depth yielded from fifty thousand to sixty thousand dollars each; at the Prince Regent mine men made eighty thousand dollars each in a few months' time; at one claim a tubful of earth washed out nearly ten thousand dollars; one nugget, the 'Welcome,' was sold for fifty-two thousand five hundred dollars; and a claim that had been abandoned on the supposition that it was worked out, gave to the fortunate two men who then took possession no less than forty thousand dollars in less than two weeks. I could fill a volume with stories such as these and then shouldn't be at the end. The total yield of the Australian gold-mines up to the present time is said to be very nearly one billion seven hundred million dollars.

EDWARD HARGREAVES, THE GOLD DISCOVERER.

"Just before gold was discovered in Victoria the colony had seventy-seven thousand inhabitants; in a single year eighty thousand were added to the population, and three years after the gold discovery there were two hundred and thirty-six thousand inhabitants there. The number has increased ever since with more or less steadiness, and now exceeds a million. In 1854 there were fifty-one females to every one hundred males; now the proportions are eighty-eight to one hundred."

"We went from Ballarat to Sandhurst, another mining city," said Fred in his journal. "It was formerly known as Bendigo, and in old times was the scene of a rush much like that to Ballarat. It has had about the same history as Ballarat, having been wonderfully rich in alluvial diggings, then almost deserted, and finally doing a fine business

THE RUSH TO BALLARAT.

in quartz mining. In one respect, to-day, it differs from Ballarat; at the latter place the mines are in the suburbs, while here they are right in the city. There is a mine in nearly every backyard; gold is sometimes—so they say—picked up in the street, and is even in the bricks of the houses. The first brick house built in Sandhurst was pulled down and crushed, and the crushing yielded three ounces of gold to the ton; at any rate, that's what they tell us, and they're very earnest about it too.

LAKE SCENERY.

"Then we came back by railway through Ballarat as far as Geelong, where we turned off to Colac and Camperdown to see the famous Lake district of Victoria. At Colac we climbed a hill, and from its summit counted fifteen lakes varying in size from tiny ponds to that of the Dead Sea of Korangamite, with an area of forty-nine thousand acres, and a circuit of more than ninety miles. It is so salt that no fish can live in its waters—salter a good deal than the sea.

"A strange feature of the lakes of this region is that they are alternately salt and fresh. Almost at our feet, as we sat on the summit of the hill, were five lakes, two fresh and three salt, and they were separated by very narrow strips of land. The salt is said to come from the drainage of the rocks, the water being evaporated faster than it flows in. In summer the lakes fall below their winter level, and leave great quantities of salt on the banks, where it is gathered by the people.

"We all agree that we have never seen prettier lake scenery anywhere in the world than in this famous western district of Victoria. The lakes are at various levels, the larger ones studded with islands, and the shores of the salt lakes glistening with snowy crystals. In the landscape are plains, undulating areas, and mountains. The plains are dotted with trees, there are flocks of sheep and herds of cattle scattered over them, and here and there we can make out the houses of the prosperous farmers, and trace the fences that enclose fields of grain. Most of the smaller lakes are in the craters of extinct volcanoes, and there is abundant evidence that this region was once the scene of great convulsions of nature.

"Warnambool and Belfast are the ports of this district, and they supply the markets of Sydney, Brisbane, and Adelaide, as well as the nearer one of Melbourne, with potatoes. The people claim that their potatoes are without competitors, quality and quantity being of the highest class. The maximum yields are from twenty to thirty tons an acre; land sells for four hundred dollars an acre for growing potatoes, and one happy land-owner lets out two square miles of ground for twenty-five dollars an acre annually! This is the part of the country that was originally named Australia Felix, and it certainly deserved the title."

"Where will we go next?" queried one of the youths, as the party was returning from Colac to Melbourne.

"Where do you wish to go?" said the Doctor, answering one question by asking another.

"According to what they tell us," responded the original questioner, "there is still a great deal to be seen—at least from a resident's point of view.

"We are urged to visit cattle and sheep stations in the interior, but there can hardly be anything especially new about them after what we have seen in New South Wales and Queensland; so I vote against any more pastoral visits."

The other members of the party assented to his opinion, and it was decided that time did not permit them to stay longer among sheep and cattle.

For a similar reason it was concluded to decline an invitation to spend a few days in Gippsland, which was named after one of the former governors and is famous for its mountain scenery, its lakes, rivers, and other natural features. Some portions of it are too rough for agriculture, but a considerable part is peculiarly rich and fertile, and produces abundantly when brought under cultivation. A large proportion of the cattle sold in the Melbourne market comes from Gippsland; and the region has great resources in minerals, which are as yet but slightly developed.

Tourists with a love for fishing and shooting generally find time to visit Gippsland, as these sports can be had there to the fullest extent. The forests of this region are very dense, and consequently the clearing of the land is attended with considerable expense. Frank thought, with a sigh, of the trout in the streams of this fertile district; he had hoped to be the captor of some of them, but his hopes were dashed when it was decided to give the go-by to Gippsland.

"And now," said the Doctor, "I'll tell you my plan." The youths listened attentively as he continued:

"To-day is Tuesday. There's a steamer twice a week (Monday and Thursday) for Launceston, in Tasmania. We are due at Melbourne at 3.41 this afternoon; we will devote this evening and to-morrow to saying good-by to our friends, and leave by the steamer on Thursday for Launceston. How will that do?"

A GIPPSLAND SETTLER.

The youths promptly assented, as they always did when the Doctor told them his plans, and it was at once agreed that the scheme would be carried out. Arrangements were made accordingly, the farewell calls were made in the time prescribed by social rules, and the steamer started at noon on the appointed day. She carried the party across Bass's Strait during the night, and on the next morning they were at the entrance of the Tamar River, on their way to Launceston, forty miles up the stream, and two hundred and sixty-seven from Melbourne.

Frank wondered why the name of the island was changed from Van Dieman's Land to Tasmania. He received the following explanation:

"It was discovered by the Dutch navigator Abel Jans Tasman, in 1642, and by him was named Van Dieman's Land, in honor of the then governor of the Dutch East Indies. Tasman was in love with the Governor's daughter, Maria, and gave her name to one of the smaller islands. Van Dieman's Land was first permanently occupied in 1803, when the British Government established a convict-station there, and soon followed it by other convict-stations. It was a penal colony from its settlement until 1853, when transportation was discontinued; during this half century many thousands of convicts were sent there, and the name of Van Dieman's Land was inseparably connected with the horrors of the system of English deportation and the crimes which led to it.

"Consequently many of the colonists sought a change of name for their country; and on the first of January, 1856, it was made, in reply to an address of the Legislative Council, in which it was represented that the 'letters patent of the bishop were for the diocese of Tasmania, that the colonists used the title generally, and it was preferred to Van Dieman's Land by the colonists and by this council.' It is to be hoped that the history of transportation will eventually be as much a thing of the past as is the former name of this beautiful island."

Our friends found the scenery of the Tamar interesting; and as the steamer slowly stemmed the current, they were treated to a constantly changing and never wearying panorama. The island is the smallest of the Australian colonies; it is about the size of Scotland, and resembles it in being full of fine scenery. It is a land of mountains, lakes, and rivers; its climate is a little warmer than that of England, and a little more dry, and everything that grows in the British Islands will grow in Tasmania. The banks of the Tamar reminded our friends of those of the Thames, save that they were not as well peopled, and the mountain ranges which formed the background on either side were lofty and picturesque.

As the vessel neared her destination, Frank and Fred were informed that they were at the head of the Tamar, or would be when they reached Launceston. "The North Esk and the South Esk," said their informant, "come together at Launceston, and their union forms the Tamar. The North Esk comes tumbling down from a rocky region, while the South Esk flows through a rich agricultural district closely resembling some of the best farming country of England."

And so they found it when on the following day they made an excursion into the region under consideration. The resemblance to England was heightened by the hedges that separated the fields from one another, and were a most agreeable change from the rail and wire fences to which they had become accustomed during their travels in Australia. The soil appeared to be of unusual fertility, and they readily accepted the statement of one of the residents that Tasmania was the garden of the world. "Everything that grows in England grows here," said he, "and grows better. The fruits are larger and of finer flavor; the yield of grain is more to the acre; and as to quality, there is nothing that can surpass that of our products. Our great drawbacks are distance from markets, the high price of labor, and the lack of suitable means for bringing the products of the farms to the seaports. We could supply the whole of Victoria with jam made from our fruits; but as she grows fruit herself, she has a protective tariff that practically excludes us."

They found Launceston a pretty little city of about seventeen thousand inhabitants, and picturesquely situated. It has the usual public buildings and parks, and in its vicinity are several show-places, which

THE PEACH HARVEST.

they visited in the afternoon. In a carriage they went to Corra Linn, six miles from Launceston, where the North Esk pours through a gateway of basaltic rock, and dashes over a bed of bowlders that break the water into a mass of foam; then it changes suddenly into a quiet stream which reflects the rocks and foliage bending over it; then changes again into tumbling rapids, and afterwards becomes the calm stream that unites with the South Esk to form the Tamar.

"After Corra Linn," said Frank, "we saw the Cataract Gorge and the Punch Bowl, which are favorite places of resort of the citizens, and are certainly very pretty and interesting. Then we walked in the Town Park, and saw the Garden Crescent, which is a popular recreation ground and much frequented. In the evening we had an interesting conversation with a gentleman whom we met at the hotel, or rather on

COTTAGE IN THE SUBURBS OF LAUNCESTON.

the steamer which brought us from Melbourne. We asked to be permitted to take notes of what he said; he readily consented, and here it is as Fred and I jotted it down:

"'We have about one hundred and thirty thousand inhabitants in the island, which is divided into eighteen counties, and these are again subdivided into parishes, for administrative purposes. We have self-government on the same general plan as the other Australian colonies, and have been self-governing since 1856. Our climate is remarkable for its mildness, being removed from the extremes of heat and cold; the summers are never unpleasantly hot, and woollen clothing may be worn throughout the year; while the winters are not severe enough, even in the table-lands of the interior, to stop work in the fields. Snow covers the tops of the mountains in winter, but rarely falls on the lowlands; and when it does come it doesn't stay long.

"'We love England, and have named most of our counties after those of the old country; and in religion we are English. Out of our whole population more than half are adherents of the English Church; then come the Catholics with 30,000, Methodists 10,000, Church of Scotland

AN OLD SETTLER.

9000, and Independents 5000. Other religions are not numerous in their following, but we have a good deal of variety, as we have Mohammedans and Pagans in addition to Israelites and several smaller sects of Christians. We are a law-abiding people generally; and when you remember that the country was for so long the receptacle of convicts, you will admit that our proportion of crime is very small.

"'The people of Australia sometimes call us Van Demonians in derision; but we don't mind it, though we would like to have the name of Van Dieman's Land forgotten, as it has so many unpleasant associations. But however glad we are that we ceased to be a convict colony, there is no getting over the fact that the most prosperous days of the island were when transportation was in existence.'

AT BAY IN THE BUSH.

"Doctor Bronson asked him to explain this, which he did.

"'The prosperity,' he continued, 'was due to several causes. In the first place, the Government sent its convicts here, and it maintained a large military and police force to take care of them. This meant an expenditure of money; the annual outlay of the Government in Tasmania was £350,000, and of course we lost this when transportation stopped. Then, too, the free colonists that came out here received grants of land, and also assignments of convicts to work the land, the size of the grants being proportioned to the number of convicts that a colonist would receive.

"'It was a good thing for the squatter, and he was not slow to take advantage of it. It was like negro slavery, with the addition that the slaves cost nothing to the owner. If a man died, the squatter could get another for nothing; if a man ran away, he was generally recaptured at once if he did not starve in the bush; and if he misbehaved himself in any way, the squatter sent him to the nearest magistrate to be flogged.'

"'Were the squatters not allowed to administer punishment?' queried Doctor Bronson.

"'No, they were not,' was the reply; 'but the magistrate usually applied the lash without taking the trouble to inquire into the case. It was no uncommon thing for a convict employed on a squatter's station to be sent with a note to the magistrate, in which the latter was requested to give the man two or three dozen lashes, as the case might be. He received them and was sent home; if he ran away, either before or after the flogging, notice was given at once, and the police were speedily after him. In the bush he could easily elude the police, but the necessity for food generally drove him to surrender or led to his capture. No one was allowed to give food to a runaway; and as the general safety depended on the suppression of bush-ranging, no one was inclined to do so.'

"'But didn't men sometimes make their escape and live in the bush?'

A CAMP IN THE BUSH.

"'Only in a few instances. One runaway managed to hide himself for seven years, building a hut and raising a few vegetables in a spot where he was not discovered. He kept a goat and a few sheep, and came occasionally in the night to the nearest station to steal a few articles that he needed. But at length the solitude was too much for him, and he came to the very station that he had plundered, and gave himself up. The squatter's wife was alone with her children when the man appeared, with his hair long and tangled, a few sheepskins stitched together for his clothing, and his whole appearance denoting destitution and despair.'

"'What was done with him?'

"'The squatter was a gentleman of influence; he realized that the convict could easily have murdered his wife and children, and in gratitude for his forbearance he became interested in the man's case, and obtained his pardon. The man afterwards became a prosperous farmer, and led a strictly honest life.

"'Not only were the convicts valuable as servants or laborers for the squatters and employers generally,' continued the gentleman, 'but they were also useful for the public works that are needed in a new country. There is a fine wagon-road from Launceston to Hobart, one hundred and twenty miles, which was built by gangs of convicts working under overseers and guards. There isn't a better road in Europe than this; and the same may be said of other roads that were built by convict labor in the early days of the colony. Before the railway was built, the stage-coaches used to run through from one place to the other in thirteen hours, or at the rate of nine miles an hour.

"'When you reach Hobart, the capital of Tasmania, you will find a handsome town of twenty thousand inhabitants, with good streets and substantial buildings, the Government House being one of the best belonging to a British colony anywhere. Hobart was largely built by convict labor; and so, you see, we have many things to remind us that transportation was not by any means a detriment to the country.'"

CHAPTER XXII.

EXCURSION TO DELORAINE.—THE CHUDLEIGH CAVES.—FROM LAUNCESTON TO HOBART.—ACROSS THE MOUNTAINS.—THE OLD WAGON-ROAD BUILT BY CONVICTS.—DEATH OF THE LAST TASMANIAN.—HOW THE ABORIGINES WERE DESTROYED.—A WONDERFUL TIN-MINE.—HOBART: ITS CLIMATE AND ATTRACTIONS.—LOVELINESS OF TASMANIAN LADIES.—PORT ARTHUR.—DOGS AT THE NECK.—FROM HOBART TO ADELAIDE.—ARRIVAL IN SOUTH AUSTRALIA.—ADELAIDE: ITS PRINCIPAL FEATURES.—A RIVER THAT IS NOT A RIVER.—CHURCHES AND RELIGIONS.—POPULATION OF THE CAPITAL AND COLONY.—EXTENSIVE WHEAT-FARMS.—PRODUCTS OF SOUTH AUSTRALIA.—FRUIT-GROWING.—GLENELG.—THE HISTORIC GUM-TREE.—PARKS AND GARDENS.—OVERLAND TO PORT DARWIN.—HOW THE TELEGRAPH WAS BUILT.—EXPLORATIONS OF STURT AND STUART.—CAMELS IN AUSTRALIA.—A SIDE-SADDLE CAMEL.—AN AFFECTING INCIDENT.—THE OVERLAND RAILWAY.

"THE forenoon of our second day in Tasmania," said Frank, "was devoted to an excursion on the Launceston and Formby Railway as far as Deloraine. We left Launceston at eight o'clock in the morn-

ENTRANCE TO CAVE.

ing, reached Deloraine, forty-five miles, at a quarter past ten, had an hour and three-quarters in and around the place, and started at noon on our return. They urged us to stay longer, and see more; and some of the acquaintances we had made seemed much disappointed that we declined to do so. The Tasmanians are as hospitable as their Australian neighbors, and do their utmost to make the stranger feel at home.

NEAR DELORAINE.

"They specially wished us to visit the Chudleigh Caves, which are about twenty miles from Deloraine, and are considered, by the Tasmanians at least, among the wonders of the world. We were told that we could walk five miles underground, and see the entire caves in about four hours; that the mud and water would nowhere be more than three feet deep, and there were many places in the caves where there was no mud at all. No doubt the caves are remarkable; but as we had seen the Mammoth and Luray Caves, we did not specially care for those of Chudleigh, much to the disappointment of the gentleman who urged us to see them.

"The railway between Launceston and Deloraine passes through a fertile country in which there are many fine farms, and a goodly number of pastoral stations devoted to the rearing of high-class sheep which are exported to Australia to improve the flocks of that country. The train rolled through glades and over plains, along the sides of mountains and across rippling streams, and as we approached Deloraine the conductor called our attention to a bold spur of a mountain called Quamby Bluff, which is the end of a long range that filled the horizon.

"On our return to Launceston we were just in time to catch the

3 P.M. train for Hobart, which we reached at eight o'clock in the evening. The Launceston and Western Railway is of broad gauge, but the line to Hobart is a narrow one (three feet six inches), on account of the heavy work in the mountains through which its route is laid. As long as the daylight lasted we had a beautiful panorama, the scene changing at every turn of the sinuous track. Occasionally we had glimpses of the old carriage-road built by the convicts, and were impressed with its solidity and the thoroughness of the work of which it is evidence. It is said that the road cost more than a railway would at present; and I have no doubt, after seeing it, that this was the case.

"We asked if any aboriginals could be seen along the route, and were told that the last Tasmanian aboriginal, Truganini, or Lalla Rookh, died in 1876, and the last Tasmanian man in 1869. When the island was first occupied by the English, there were four or five thousand natives upon it; there was incessant war between them and the whites until 1832, when the greater number of the blacks had been killed, only a few hundreds remaining. In 1854 there were only sixteen of them alive, and these gradually died off.

"It is said that when the English landed in Tasmania they mistook the friendly signs of the natives for hostile ones, and the mistake led the commanding officer to order his men to fire on the group that had assembled on the beach. Fifty natives were killed on this occasion, and thus a needless war was begun.

"Of course we have been invited to visit gold-mines and other places where valuable minerals are found; they tell us that Tasmania contains the most valuable tin-mine in the world, its annual yield being worth nearly a million dollars. It was discovered in 1872 by a man who was regarded by his neighbors as more than half a lunatic. For years he sought for tin among the mountains, suffering all sorts of hardships and privations; and when at last he found the desired deposit, his assertion that he had done so was not believed. He was nicknamed 'Philosopher Smith,' and had great difficulty in securing attention to his discovery and raising the necessary capital for working the mine. Like most discoverers, he did not reap the reward for what he found, as he was compelled to sell his shares in the mine while they were at a very low price. A share originally costing thirty shillings was worth £80 a few years later.

"A few miles before reaching Hobart we came to the banks of the Derwent, the river on which the capital stands. It is a beautiful stream flowing down from the interior mountains, and its valley is said to be exceedingly picturesque. Hobart justified the description which our friend at Launceston gave us; it stands on seven hills, with a larger hill, called Knocklofty, behind it; and behind this hill again is Mount Wellington, 4166 feet high. The harbor is deep and capacious, and the navigation is so easy that ships often come in without pilots.

"Until 1881 this place was called Hobart Town, or Hobarton; in that year the name was officially changed to Hobart.

"The day after our arrival we climbed to the top of Mount Wellington, and were well repaid for the fatigue of the ascent by the magnificent view it afforded. It was landscape and seascape together, and both extensive and picturesque. Water and land were spread below us as on a map, and we looked away towards the Southern Pole, and wondered what would be encountered if we journeyed in that direction.

AUSTRALIA AT THE FEET OF TASMANIA.

"Hobart is a famous resort of Australians, who come here to escape the heat of summer. Its climate is delightful, and if all that the inhabitants claim is true, the Australians who come here have no reason to complain. Doctor Bronson says he has been told that the ladies of Tasmania are so charming that the friends of an Australian bachelor tremble for him whenever he decides to spend the summer at Hobart. But the Doctor says the friends of a Tasmanian bachelor might be equally fearful when the latter goes to Melbourne or Sydney for an extended visit.

"New York boasts of its Franklin Square, where the Harpers have their great publishing house. Hobart has its Franklin Square, which is a pretty garden in memory of Sir John Franklin, who was governor here at one time; in the centre of the garden is a bronze statue of the

OLD CONVICT CHURCH, PORT ARTHUR, TASMANIA.

renowned navigator. There are other gardens and parks; there are the Royal Society's grounds and the Queen's Domain, which are much frequented; and there is a splendid cricket-ground, where games are played very often. We have witnessed a rowing match between the Hobart and the Mercantile rowing clubs, and are told that there is a grand regatta here every year that brings many visitors from Melbourne, Sydney, Adelaide, and other cities. Altogether, Hobart impresses us most agreeably, and the inhabitants are justly proud of it."

The stay of the party in Tasmania was somewhat shortened by reason of their haste to reach South Australia. They made a brief visit to Port Arthur, which is about three hours distant from Hobart by steamer, and lies in a landlocked bay enclosed between rugged hills, which completely shelter it from the wind. Here are the prisons where thousands of convicts were once confined under the most rigorous discipline, the least infraction of the rules being punished with the lash, and serious ones by death through hanging.

ONE OF THE WATCH-DOGS.

The story is that the latter punishment was so frequent that the jail chaplain at Hobart once made a protest, not against hanging in general or the number of men hanged, but at the pressure upon their facilities. He said that no more than thirteen men could be comfortably executed at once, and the crowding had been too great; he trusted that for the future the accommodations of the jail might not be overtaxed.

Our friends saw the prisons at Port Arthur, but the prisoners have been gone since 1876. The massive buildings remain without tenants, and are going to decay as fast as solid stone structures can go. Frank and Fred were specially interested in "The Neck," the narrow isthmus which connects the main-land with the peninsula, where the prisons stand. Across The Neck savage dogs were formerly chained at such close intervals that a man could not pass between them; the isthmus is not more than a hundred feet in width, and as there were fifteen dogs kept there, a man had no chance of passing them. If he attempted to swim around them at night, the dogs were expected to give warning by barking; and the waters are so infested with sharks that a person swimming has little chance of getting away with his life.

"LAND, HO!"

The dogs were also used for hunting down the few prisoners who managed to get past the line. The number of escapes was very small; but in spite of all precautions, escapes did occur. The most notable instance is that of three men, Martin Cash, Jones, and Cavanagh, who swam across the bay one night, reached a farm-house in the early morning, and there provided themselves with weapons and ammunition before their escape was discovered. Thus equipped for highway robbery and defence, they remained free for years, but were taken and

ON THE PIER.

hanged at last. Convicts at Port Arthur and other Tasmanian prisons were known as "yellow-birds," on account of the yellow uniform they wore.

"Rather suddenly," said Fred, "we left Hobart one day for South Australia, as we found that if we waited for the next steamer we should be detained longer than we cared to be in Tasmania. Three days carried us to our destination at Port Adelaide, where we again set foot on the Australian continent.

"We passed up the Gulf of St. Vincent, and entered Port Adelaide between two large shoals of sand which are marked by light-houses. The captain of the steamer told us that the port was formerly difficult of entrance and quite shallow, but it has been deepened within the past few years, and the channels have been widened, so that it is now accessible for very large ships. As its name implies, it is the port of Adelaide, the capital of South Australia, seven miles away, and easily accessible by a double-track railway.

"We landed at a long and handsome pier, and had time to observe, before leaving for the city, that a great deal of money has been expended in dock and pier facilities, and in making the harbor a suitable one for an ambitious colony. There are immense sheds for the storage of wool and grain, there are graving docks and repair shops, manufactories of several kinds, two or three hospitals, a home for sailors, churches, schools, public buildings of the usual kinds found at a well-arranged seaport, and hotels and restaurants sufficient for the entertainment of all who are likely to remain long enough to require them.

"The railway carried us to Adelaide in about twenty minutes, and we found ourselves in a city whose regularity reminded us of Philadelphia or Chicago. It was founded in 1837 by Colonel Light, who named it after the queen of William IV.; it originally contained one thousand and forty-two allotments of one acre each, and is built nearly in the form of a square, with the streets at right angles. The ground is almost a level plain, and the situation is about five miles from the Mount Lofty range of hills, whose highest point is two thousand three hundred feet above the sea-level.

"The streets of Adelaide are wide and generally handsome; the show one of all is King William Street, which runs from south to north and bisects the city. We drove along this street, and were all agreed that we would have to travel very far to find a handsomer avenue in a city no older than this. We passed the Government Offices, which is an extensive pile of buildings forming a solid block, and covering a large area. Close by the Government Buildings is the Town-hall, which is conspicuous for its high tower, and on the other side of the street is the Post-office, which accommodates both the post-office and the telegraph, and will do so until Adelaide is more than twice its present size. The white freestone of which the Town-hall and Post-office are built is said to have come from some extensive quarries near the city.

POST-OFFICE AND TOWN-HALL, ADELAIDE.

"In addition to the public edifices, King William Street contains banks, newspaper offices, and other private buildings that would be a credit to any city of Europe or America. As for churches, I don't know how many we have seen in our drive through the principal streets; they give the impression that Adelaide is a very religious city, and that her wealthy people have been very liberal in providing places of worship. All the prominent religions are represented, the Church of England taking the lead, as in the other colonies.

"At the last census of South Australia the Church of England had 76,000 adherents, Roman Catholics numbered 43,000, Methodists 42,000, Lutherans 20,000, Presbyterians 18,000, Baptists 14,000, and Congregationalists, Bible Christians, and Primitive Methodists about 10,000 each. No State aid is given to any of the churches, all of them being supported by voluntary contributions. There are nearly a thousand churches and chapels in the colony, exclusive of four hundred other buildings which are occasionally used for religious worship.

"We asked the driver of our carriage to show us some of the finest private residences; he did so, and we certainly commend the good taste of the leading citizens in their architecture. Our drive extended to North Adelaide, which is to 'the city' what South Melbourne is to Melbourne, being principally a place for residence. The river Torrens separates Adelaide from its northern suburb; we crossed it on one of three handsome bridges, and found it less worthy of the name of river than is the Yarra at Melbourne, its bed being little more than a dry waste of sand. Ten months in the year this is said to be its condition; for the other two months it is an impetuous flood.

"The river isn't as bad as it was, as a dam has been thrown across it near the jail, and the water held by it forms a narrow lake about two miles long, which furnishes a floating-place for steam-launches and row-boats in great number. We took a sail on one of the launches, and enjoyed it very much; the lake reminded us in some respects of the Ausser Alster at Hamburg, and seems to be much appreciated by the citizens. The water supply of the city comes from the Torrens; it is drawn into reservoirs a few miles above the city, and brought thence through covered mains into the city limits.

"The population of the city itself is about 50,000, and there are said to be 130,000 people living within a radius of ten miles from the Town-hall. The population of the whole territory of South Australia is not far from 350,000, including about 5000 aboriginals. The area of the colony, including the Northern Territory, is estimated at 903,690 square

ADELAIDE IN 1837.

miles; it covers twenty-seven degrees of latitude and twelve of longitude, and is more than fifteen times as large as England and Wales combined. Its greatest length is 1850 miles, and its greatest width 650 miles.

"We delivered some letters of introduction, and were hospitably received, our entertainers doing their best to give us a good opinion of the city and colony. One of them told us that Adelaide had been called the 'City of Churches,' on account of the number and beauty of its religious edifices; and also the 'Farinaceous City,' owing to its great shipments of wheat and flour. South Australia is largely devoted to wheat culture, and some of the farms will rival the great wheat-farms of the North-western States of America. They have all the improved machinery for raising wheat on a grand scale, and their owners are liberal buyers of American ploughs, mowers, reapers, and other apparatus intended for economy of labor in producing the 'staff of life.'

"We visited one of these large wheat-farms, and were greatly impressed with what we saw there. It employs ordinarily about seventy hands, and in the busy season the number often exceeds two hundred. Everything is reduced to a system, and the manager is autocratic in his power; there is a set of printed rules to govern the conduct of the men, and they are required to sign them when engaged. All hands are called when a bell rings at 5 A.M.; horses are cleaned and fed before 6 A.M., when breakfast is served; the teams are in the field by seven o'clock; an hour is allowed at noon for dinner, and then work continues till 6 P.M. in summer and 5 P.M. in winter. Supper is served at seven; horses are fed and watered at half-past eight, and the dining-room is cleared and locked up at ten o'clock.

"First-class hands receive twenty shillings (five dollars) weekly, second-class eighteen shillings, and third-class sixteen shillings. Any one in charge of horses who abuses them, or neglects to feed and care for them properly, is discharged at once, and forfeits all wages due him. Varying penalties are affixed for other offences, and the inducement is held out that any laborer can raise himself to a first-class position by good and industrious conduct.

"The product of wheat in the colony varies in different seasons; in 1884–85 it was nearly fifteen million bushels, but since then it has been much less, owing to severe droughts. There are nearly seven millions of sheep in South Australia, and the wool crop is the next in importance to the bread-stuffs. The colony produces great quantities of grapes, and the export of wine is steadily increasing. Grapes, peaches,

REAPING BRIGADE AT WORK.

apricots, oranges, and kindred fruits grow with very little attention, and in their season they are retailed in the market of Adelaide at a penny a pound; so that all tables are liberally supplied with them. We have eaten some very fine fruit since we came here, but the people tell us we are not in the time of year to see the orchards at their best.

"There are several pretty watering-places within a few miles of Adelaide, where the people go in summer to enjoy the cool breezes from the southern seas. One of the favorite spots of this sort is Glenelg, which is only a few miles distant, and easily reached by railway. We went there one afternoon, partly to see what it was like and partly because it is where the colony was founded. On the 28th of December, 1836, Captain Hindmarsh landed there, and in the presence of a few officials and some two hundred immigrants, who had been sent out from London, read his commission as the first governor of South Australia, and proclaimed the foundation of the colony.

"The ceremony took place under a venerable gum-tree, or Eucalyptus, which is known as "Proclamation Tree." We saw the tree, but it has fallen and is greatly decayed, and were it not for the board affixed to it, telling that on this spot the colony was founded, no one would consider it of any importance. The anniversary of this event is celebrated as a public holiday. All business is suspended on that day, and Glenelg is crowded with people who come to look at the Proclamation Tree, and enjoy the cool breeze that blows from the ocean.

PROCLAMATION TREE AT GLENELG, NEAR ADELAIDE.

"The long pier jutting into the bay at Glenelg is a favorite resort on pleasant evenings, and our experience there reminded us of an evening at Coney Island or Long Branch. The Orient and P. & O. steamers stop at Glenelg to land and receive the South Australian mails. The anchorage is somewhat exposed to heavy winds, and occasionally there is considerable delay in landing or embarking.

"The Adelaideans are very proud of their parks and gardens, and with good reason. They certainly compare well with those of Sydney

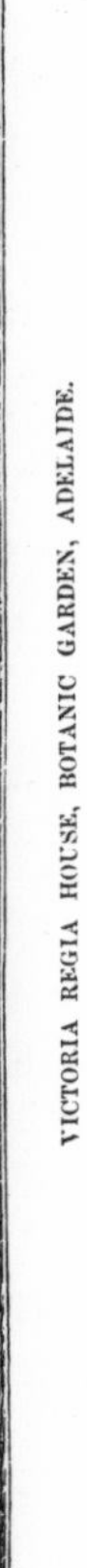

VICTORIA REGIA HOUSE, BOTANIC GARDEN, ADELAIDE.

and Melbourne, and that is saying that they are very fine indeed. All around the city there are reserved lands which vary in width but will average not far from half a mile. They are intended for parks for the public, and are planted with shade-trees and laid out into walks and drives. As the city grows they will be in the midst of houses, and not at such distances that a special journey will be required to reach them.

"Then they have squares of several acres in each quarter of the city, beautifully laid out and planted with shade-trees, and they have the Botanic Garden, of about forty acres, containing among other things several fern-houses, shade-houses, a Victoria Regia house, and a large and handsome palm-house, in which tropical plants are sheltered. We went repeatedly through the Botanic Garden, and constantly found something to interest us. A few years ago a Museum of Economic Botany was erected, and since it was opened to the public it has done much practical good. Plants are distributed to those who desire them, and many valuable or beautiful exotics have thus been acclimatized in Australia."

As usual, Frank and Fred studied the map of the country, and considered its capabilities in the way of travel. Frank thought it would be the best kind of fun to cross the continent from south to north, following the line of the overland telegraph from Adelaide to Port Darwin. Fred was of the same opinion, but suggested that before broaching the subject to the Doctor they should learn something about the route.

With this object in view they made inquiries, the replies to which quite discouraged their enterprise. What they learned can best be given in the words of their informant, a gentleman connected with the telegraph service.

"I have been over the whole line from Adelaide to Port Darwin," said he, "and will briefly tell you about it. The distance is about seventeen hundred miles, and more than half of it is uninhabited by white men, except at the telegraph stations. Some of it can never be occupied, as it is absolutely waterless; but in course of time, and with improved means of obtaining or storing water, the greater part can be made inhabitable.

"The first white man to cross the continent was John McDouall Stuart. Don't confound his name with that of Captain Sturt, a thing that's very likely to happen, as they were intimately associated."

"Won't you kindly tell us a little about Captain Sturt?" asked one of the youths. "We've heard his name frequently as that of one of Australia's heroes."

"Certainly," was the reply. "Captain Charles Sturt was sent out by the Sydney Government to make an exploration beyond the Blue Mountains in the direction of the interior of the continent. Between 1827 and 1830 he made two expeditions, in which he discovered the Darling and Murray rivers; on the second expedition he descended those streams in a whale-boat which he had taken along for the purpose of navigating any rivers or lakes into which the smaller streams already

EXPLORING EXPEDITION ON THE MARCH.

discovered took their course. The Macquarie, the Lachlan, and the Murrumbidgee flow westward from the Dividing Range, but their outlets were then unknown.

"On his voyage down the Murray to the sea Sturt had several fights with the natives, underwent many hardships and accidents, and found his men greatly reduced in strength. There he was obliged to turn back and propel his boat against the stream to the point whence it started.

"It was a toilsome journey. The natives opposed the explorers, and they fought their way from place to place, and it was only by the superiority of their fire-arms over the primitive weapons of the blacks that they escaped with their lives. For fifteen hundred miles they travelled in this way, and when they reached their old camp, on the twenty-seventh day of their upward voyage, Sturt was hardly able to stand.

Provisions were exhausted, and when aid reached them they were at the point of starvation.

"In 1843, this same Captain Sturt offered to lead an expedition from South Australia to the interior of the continent; his offer was accepted, and in 1844 the expedition started on its way. Unfortunately summer was approaching, and the party was destined to suffer terribly from heat and thirst. For six months it was encamped in one spot, unable to move; there was little or no water in the country, and four months passed without a drop of rain or even of dew. Sturt reported that the heat drew every screw and nail in their boxes; the horn handles of their instruments, as well as their combs, were split into fine laminæ; the lead dropped out of their pencils; their signal-rockets were entirely spoiled; their hair, as well as the wool of their sheep, ceased to grow; and their nails became as brittle as glass. Their flour lost more than eight per cent. of its original weight, and other provisions in greater proportion. The mean of the thermometer during December, January, and February was 101°, 104°, and 101° respectively in the shade, and in the sun it sometimes reached 160°.

"Sturt did everything that lay within human power to reach the centre of the continent, but was unable to get nearer than within one hundred and fifty miles of it. Some of his men died, and he turned back when at a point where it was absolutely certain that no water lay beyond.

"His draughtsman on that expedition was John McDouall Stuart, the man who was the first to cross the continent from south to north, and whom I asked you not to confound with Captain Sturt. Stuart tried three times before he succeeded; at last, on July 10, 1862, he reached the sea, at the mouth of the Adelaide River, in Van Dieman's Gulf, on the north coast.

"Very soon after the result of Stuart's expedition became known, it was proposed to build a telegraph line across the continent, following Stuart's track, to meet the cable from Singapore to Port Darwin, and thus connect the colonies with the rest of the telegraphic world. The work was planned and completed by Mr. Charles Todd, superintendent of telegraphs, and was begun in 1870. On August 22, 1872, the first message was sent over the completed line, and congratulations were exchanged between London and Adelaide."

"Didn't the blacks give you a great deal of trouble?" Frank asked.

"Less than was feared," was the reply. "We managed to give them a wholesome dread of the 'white fellow's devil,' as they called it, and

CAMP SCENE ON THE DESERT PLAINS OF SOUTH AUSTRALIA.

though they have raided the stations on several occasions and killed the officers, they have never disturbed the wires. While we were building the line we gave every native who visited us an electric shock, and it seriously affected their nerves, and also their imaginations. Once we had two of the most important chiefs at points more than a hundred miles apart; we carried on conversations for them for two or three hours, and then had them meet half way between the stations and compare notes. To say they were awe-struck would be expressing it mildly; they were fairly paralyzed with astonishment."

"How far apart are the stations?"

"The distances vary according to water and other conditions. Some of the stations are more than a hundred miles from their neighbors on either side, and at every station there are two operators and four line-repairers. When a break occurs a repair party starts from the station on each side, and travels along the line, testing it every twenty or thirty miles until the fault has been found and communication restored. Then the parties return to their own stations, generally without seeing each other."

"How do you carry supplies through this desert?" inquired Fred.

"We use camels, which were first introduced from Afghanistan by

Sir Thomas Elder, and have been found admirably adapted to the arid regions of Australia. A camel-breeding establishment has been in existence at Beltana for nearly twenty years, and more than a thousand camels have been supplied from it for hauling stores and doing other work that is usually performed by oxen or horses. They are broken to harness or the saddle; they draw drays or light pleasure-wagons, singly, and teams of six or eight camels are harnessed to heavy wagons, which they easily pull through the sand together with a load of two or three tons. The belle of Beltana, the daughter of the superintendent of the station, has a camel which she rides with a side-saddle just as a belle of New York rides her favorite saddle-horse. All the later exploring expeditions have been equipped with camels, and it was for exploration that these animals were first brought here.

"About three years after the line was opened, the men at the Barrow Creek station, a thousand miles from Adelaide, were attacked by the blacks. A line-repairer and an operator, Mr. Stapleton, were mortally wounded, and two others seriously. As Mr. Stapleton lay dying, the news was flashed to Adelaide by the other operator. The doctor and Mrs. Stapleton were summoned to a room in the Adelaide office, where they listened to the click of the instrument, which told how the husband's life was ebbing away in the far distant desert.

"An instrument was brought to his bedside and placed under his hand. He received the doctor's message that his wound was fatal, received the farewell of his wife, then telegraphed her an eternal good-by, and as he finished it his fingers clutched the key, and in a moment he lay dead. I was one of the group that stood in the Adelaide office that day, and you can easily believe that the scene moved everybody to tears."

The youths easily did believe it, for their own eyes were moist as they heard the sad story. The gentleman paused for one, two, in fact for several minutes, with his head turned away, and then resumed:

"The success of the telegraph has emboldened us, and we are now building a railway along the same line, and hope to have it done within the next ten years. Four hundred miles are completed northward from Adelaide, and on the other side of the continent half that distance is in the hands of contractors. Camels are employed to carry supplies, material, and water to the men in advance of the end of the track, and the work is being pushed forward very much as your builders in America constructed the Central and Union Pacific railways across the great plains east of the Rocky Mountains, and between those mountains and the Sierra Nevada range."

GOVERNMENT HOUSE AND GROUNDS, ADELAIDE.

CHAPTER XXIII.

AUSTRALIAN EXPLORATIONS.—THE BLUE MOUNTAINS FIRST TRAVERSED.—DISCOVERY OF THE LACHLAN, MACQUARIE, MURRUMBIDGEE, AND MURRAY RIVERS.—EXPLORATIONS OF STURT, MITCHELL, CUNNINGHAM, HUME, AND OTHERS.—EYRE'S JOURNEY ALONG THE SOUTHERN COAST.—SUFFERINGS AND PERILS.—BURKE AND WILLS: HOW THEY PERISHED IN THE WILDERNESS.—MONUMENT TO THEIR MEMORY.—COLONEL WARBURTON AND HIS CAMEL TRAIN.—STRAPPED TO A CAMEL'S BACK.—PRESENT KNOWLEDGE OF THE AUSTRALIAN DESERT.—ABORIGINALS OF SOUTH AUSTRALIA.—THROWING THE BOOMERANG.—A REMARKABLE EXHIBITION.—ORIGIN OF THE BOOMERANG.—DUCK-BILLED PLATYPUS: A PUZZLE FOR THE NATURALISTS.—VISITING A COPPER-MINE.—MINERAL RESOURCES OF THE COLONY.—WESTERN AUSTRALIA.—ALBANY, ON KING GEORGE SOUND.—DESCRIPTION OF THE COLONY.—CURIOUS POISON-PLANTS.—FAREWELL TO AUSTRALIA.—THE END.

THE mention of the explorations that preceded the construction of the Australian overland telegraph drew the attention of our young friends to the men whose names are famous in the history of Australian discovery. They had already thought of the subject when they saw in Melbourne the bronze statue in memory of the explorers, Burke and Wills; but at that time they were too busy to make any extended investigation concerning it.

The result of their reading and other study of Australian explorations they briefly summed up as follows:

"For the first twenty-five years after the settlement at Sydney, in 1788, exploration was confined to the strip of land between the Blue Mountains and the sea; it was not until 1813 that the mountains were passed and the valley of the Fish River and the Bathurst plains visited. The Lachlan River was discovered in 1815, and the Macquarie shortly afterwards; both these rivers were traced to a marsh, and were supposed to lose themselves in an inland sea.

"The Murrumbidgee River was discovered in 1815, and the Murray in 1824, by Mr. Hamilton Hume. Afterwards Mr. Hume accompanied Captain Sturt, when the latter discovered the Darling River; later (in 1831) occurred Captain Sturt's descent of the Murray, which has been already mentioned. Major Mitchell, Mr. Cunningham, and other explorers continued the work of investigating the interior of the great continent, and every year added something to the maps of the country.

"A most perilous journey was made in 1839 and 1840 by Mr. Eyre, who was afterwards governor of New Zealand and Jamaica. He explored a portion of the eastern shore of Spencer Gulf, and then turned to the westward along the shore of the Great Australian Bight, a distance of twelve hundred miles. Two hundred and fifty miles from the head of the gulf he had lost four of his best horses; and as he could not carry sufficient provisions for his party, he sent back his companion, Mr. Scott, and three others, and continued the journey with his overseer, two natives, and a native servant of his own.

READY FOR THE START.

"To make sure of water Mr. Eyre explored in advance of the party before moving the animals, and was sometimes gone five or six days without finding any. Most of the horses died of thirst, and the men only kept themselves alive by gathering dew with rags and a sponge.

"One night the two natives armed themselves with guns, killed the overseer, and ran away, leaving Mr. Eyre, with his servant, Wylie, two horses, and a very small stock of provisions; they had six hundred miles of unknown desert before them, and their whole supply of food was forty pounds of flour, four gallons of water, and part of a dead horse. They had to go one hundred and fifty miles before finding any more water, and after struggling on for a month, living on horse-flesh, fish, and occasional game, with a little flour paste, they were rescued by a whaling-ship just in time to save their lives. They remained two weeks on the ship, and then continued their journey, with more sufferings for twenty-three days, to King George Sound.

"The next great exploration was that of Captain Sturt towards the middle of the continent, mentioned in the previous chapter. About the same time Dr. Ludwig Leichhardt, a German naturalist, was fitted out by private subscription in Sydney, and explored Eastern Queensland from its southern border to the Gulf of Carpentaria. In less than five months he made a journey of three thousand miles, and was highly successful in every way.

EXPLORERS IN CAMP.

"Afterwards he started with another expedition to attempt to cross the continent from east to west, carrying provisions for two years; but after struggling for seven months he was forced to turn back. Later he set out again with the same object, but since April, 1848, nothing authentic has been heard from him or any member of his party. Several searching parties were sent out, but beyond a few trees with the letter 'L' carved upon them, nothing was ever found to show where he went, and nobody knows what was his fate; the general belief is that he and his companions perished of thirst. About the same time Sir Thomas Mitchell explored a part of what is now Queensland, and a year or so later Mr. Kennedy started on an expedition in which he, with most of his party, was killed.

MONUMENT TO BURKE AND WILLS, MELBOURNE.

"And now," continued Frank, "we come to Burke and Wills, the explorers whose monument we saw in Melbourne. The Victorian Government fitted out an expedition in 1860, with Mr. O'Hara Burke as chief, and Mr. W. J. Wills second in command. The party consisted of eighteen men, twenty-seven camels (which had been imported specially for the service), a great many pack-horses, and several wagons.

"They formed a camp on Cooper's Creek, and left a party in charge of it, under command of a man named Brahé; Burke and Wills, with two men, King and Gray, with one horse and six camels, then pushed on to the Gulf of Carpentaria, and thus made the journey across the continent. On their return they suffered great privations; Gray died, and the others were so weak that they hardly had strength to bury him; the horse was killed for food, four of the camels were abandoned, and on the evening of April 21, 1861, the three men crawled into the camp on Cooper's Creek.

"Imagine their despair when they found the camp deserted, and the word 'DIG' rudely cut on a tree. They did dig, and found a bottle containing a letter saying that the camp had been abandoned by Brahé that very morning. He had left a few articles of food, but no stimulants, tea, or clothing, of which they were in great need. They rested a few days, and then tried to reach a sheep-station one hundred and fifty miles away; but they were driven back by scarcity of water, and both the camels broke down and had to be shot. Brahé returned to the camp only two hours after Burke and Wills left it; but Burke had buried his despatches in the hole where the bottle was found, replaced the earth carefully, and left no sign to indicate that he had been there. Consequently Brahé supposed the explorers had not returned.

"The wanderers found some friendly natives who assisted them, but both Burke and Wills died of exhaustion within a few days of each other, about six weeks after their return to the camp. King joined a party of natives, and was eventually rescued and brought to Melbourne. He was found by one of four search expeditions that were sent out by the Victorian Government as soon as it was known that the depot on Cooper's Creek had been abandoned. Though only one of these expeditions was able to afford assistance to the missing explorers, all made interesting journeys, and added considerably to the stock of geographical information concerning the country.

"Since the unhappy termination of the expedition of Burke and Wills several expeditions have sought to explore Western Australia. The first man who succeeded in traversing the Great Desert from east to west was Colonel Egerton Warburton, who started from Alice Springs, on the overland telegraph route, in April, 1873, and reached the mouth of the Oakover River, in Western Australia, in the following December. He had seventeen camels when he started, but was obliged to kill or abandon all but three; the party nearly died of starvation, and for a part of the time Colonel Warburton was so ill that he was strapped at full length on the back of his camel. The country was a fearful desert, the heat was intense, and for hundreds of miles there was not a drop of water.

"Forrest, Giles, and other explorers have traversed various parts of Western Australia; and it may now be said that though there is a very large area of unexplored or little-known land, the character of the whole continent is sufficiently well known for all practical purposes. Not more than half of it is inhabitable by Europeans, or ever will be.

COLONEL WARBURTON STRAPPED TO HIS CAMEL.

Some few districts now considered sterile may be made useful by irrigation, but the western half of the continent is an arid waste, where even the native black man cannot make a living."

Frank paused as he read to Fred the foregoing paragraphs.

"Perhaps you'll have to change the last statement," said Fred.

"Why so?" queried his cousin.

"Because it does not harmonize with the opinions of some of the scientific men of Australia," was the reply. "Here is something I have just found in a late number of a Melbourne newspaper."

Frank listened with interest while Fred read the following:

"At a recent meeting of commercial and pastoral men in Sydney, an interesting paper on the Australian Desert was read by Mr. E. Favenc. Here are some passages from it: 'In looking back at the past history of Australia, the many disillusions that have taken place with regard to our knowledge of its geographical formation are very striking. In no particular is this more noticeable than in the gradual disappearance of the dreaded desert. Each successive adventurer has turned back with the tale that beyond his farthest point it was impossible to penetrate, only for after-generations to reverse his opinion and reclaim the waste land for habitation and settlement. In a pastoral community, from the earliest ages, the necessity of fresh grazing-lands for the increasing flocks and herds has existed; and the residents on the border-land of civilization soon found out that the herbs and shrubs of the interior possessed qualities hitherto unappreciated and unrecognized, and country looked upon as unfit to sustain animal life became eagerly sought after as first-class fattening country. That this has been the experience of New South Wales and Queensland has resulted in the shadowy desert being driven into the heart of South and Western Australia.

"'That immense areas of spinifex of the worst description exist in the interior, which may well be called desert, there is no doubt; but as yet we have no evidence to show that they are not belts. All through the alleged desert blacks are found all the year round. Although they can exist on a very small allowance of water, they cannot live without it, and this proves the existence of a permanent supply throughout the continent, although the springs that are the source of the supplies may be but scanty drainage and hard to find. Wherever large reservoirs are found—the standing waters of the interior—fish form one of the principal native dishes, and they are as a rule so fat as to be almost uneatable. On these waters, too, wild feathered game are in profusion, from the larger species—geese, pelicans, native companions, etc.—down to the smaller kinds, the little pigmy goose and the plover.

"'Country, then, which can sustain human and animal life throughout the year can scarcely be classed as an irreclaimable desert; and when we know from experience that even at their driest stages the edible grasses of this region can keep stock in good condition, and in the case of some of the grasses even fatten, the future occupation of the whole of the continent does not seem so very problematical. The wonderful success that has attended boring efforts to the northward of the Great Bight, long considered as the driest country in Australia, and stigmatized by Eyre as the most awful desert ever trodden by man, now being rapidly stocked with sheep, points out the way to the gradual reclamation of the desert. The knowledge we already have of some of the inland springs, slight as it is, proves the existence of these subterranean supplies throughout the continent. These springs are not what are known as surface springs—that is, the residue of a former exceptionally wet season, issuing from the foot of some well-soaked hill or ridge—but strong volumes of water that vary not in any season, totally unaffected by drought; in fact, running stronger during dry weather. I think, therefore, that in most cases a judicious selection of the site for boring will bring about a successful result; and in this country, so deficient in surface drainage, we shall find that Nature has provided a store that will render the settlers independent of variable seasons.'"

"That reminds me," said Frank, "of what Doctor Bronson was saying the other day when we were talking on this very subject. He said that when he was a boy the maps of the school geographies had a 'Great American Desert' between the Missouri River and the Rocky Mountains, and another desert between the Rocky Mountains and the Sierra Nevadas. But as civilization has pushed westward the desert disappeared, and all that region once supposed to be uninhabitable is now occupied as cattle-pastures, and thousands of farms have been established and are doing well where fifty years ago it was thought nothing could be made to grow. Quite likely it will be the same with the great Australian desert, but as my paragraph represents the present state of things we will let it remain as it is."

DESERT SCENERY.

The conversation then turned to the aboriginals who had been mentioned in Mr. Favenc's address. Fred asked Frank if he had ascertained how many there were at present in South Australia, and how they lived.

"Yes," was the reply, "and here is what I've learned. When the colony was settled, in 1836, there were estimated to be twelve thousand blacks within its borders. Now the number has diminished to about five thousand; they have died of diseases of various kinds, and the annual number of births is considerably less than that of the deaths. They are protected by the Government, an official being charged with their care, and the annual distribution of twenty-five thousand dollars' worth of food, clothing, and medical comforts from some fifty depots which have been established for that purpose. Five special reserves of land, about six hundred and seventy thousand acres in all, have been set apart for them, and they are being taught in the ways of civilization, just as our American Indians are being instructed on their reservations."

THE WAY OF CIVILIZATION.

"There's one thing we've forgotten to describe in our accounts of the Australian aboriginals," said Fred.

"What is that?"

"The boomerang," was the reply. "No account of Australia is complete without a description of the boomerang."

"That's so," responded Frank. "But first we ought to see it used."

Fred agreed to this, and in compliance with their desire one of their Australian friends arranged that they should see a performance with this remarkable weapon. Here is Fred's account of it:

"The performer was a half-wild aboriginal who had been promised a reward for displaying his skill. Our friend explained that there were

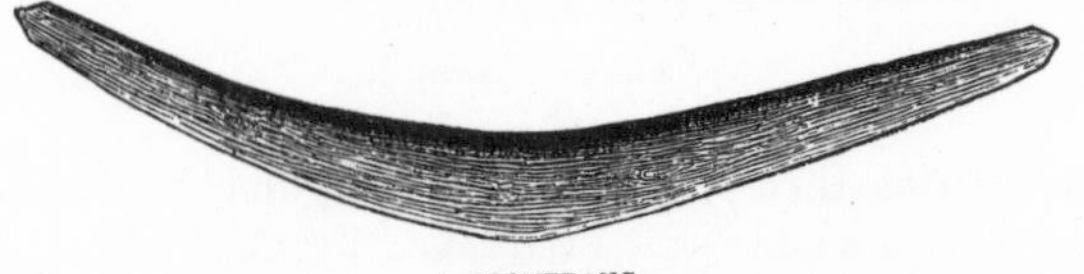

A BOOMERANG.

several kinds of boomerangs. The differences are in shape and weight; the variations in shape are hardly perceptible to the eye of a novice, though readily distinguished by those accustomed to them. The weight

A WAR-DANCE OF AUSTRALIAN BLACKS.

varies from four ounces to ten and a half ounces; the blacks of Western Australia used lighter ones than those of the eastern regions.

"Some of the boomerangs are intended for playthings, while others are for war or hunting purposes. The playthings can be made to return to the feet of the thrower, but the war boomerangs are not expected to return; you can readily understand that a boomerang would be deviated from its course or stopped altogether by hitting an object, and if it did not hit anything it would not be of much use as a warlike weapon.

"We examined the boomerang that the man was to perform with. It was about nineteen inches long from point to point, two and a half inches wide in its broadest part, half an inch thick, and weighed eight ounces and a half. Its shape was somewhat like that of a slightly bent sickle, the curve being about a quarter of a circle.

"When we had done looking at it the fellow took it and examined it carefully, and then he looked at the trees and the grass to note the direction of the wind. Our friend cautioned us to stand perfectly still, especially after the weapon had been launched; the performer selects beforehand the spot where he wishes the boomerang to fall on its return, and sometimes a spectator in his excitement moves to that very spot and is injured. We promised to obey, and we did.

"Two or three times the man made a motion to throw it but did not. Finally, when he felt that he could strike the wind at the proper angle, he launched the weapon almost straight into the air; it went up a few yards, then turned and seemed to glide along a little way above the ground, gyrated on its axis, made a wide sweep and returned with a fluttering motion to the man's feet. The farthest point of the curve was about a hundred yards away. We are told that skilful throwers can sometimes project the boomerang nearly two hundred yards before it starts on its return.

"We offered him a sixpence for every time he would bring it back to his feet and make it fall in a circle two yards in diameter which we drew on the ground. In ten throws he brought it within the circle four times, and in the six misses it dropped only a short distance outside.

"He did not throw it the same way every time. Once he made it skim along the ground for at least fifty yards, then rise into the air fully one hundred feet, and after making a great curve it returned. Next he threw it so that it made at least half a dozen great spirals above him as it came down, and another time it passed around a tree in its course.

"Frank paced off fifty yards from the performer, and placed a shilling in the end of a split stick four feet long, which was then stuck in the ground just far enough to hold it up. We offered the shilling to the man if he would knock out the coin without disturbing the stick, and he did it, but the boomerang did not return.

"Our friend told us that the powers of the return-boomerang had been greatly exaggerated. The non-returning one is the real weapon, and is greatly to be feared in the hands of a skilful thrower. It has been known to hit a man behind a tree or a rock, where he was quite safe from bullet, spear, or arrow; and if an expert in its use comes within throwing distance of a kangaroo or an emu, the creature's fate is sealed.

"He further said he had never known a white man to become expert in the use of the boomerang, though many had practised with it for years.

"We asked if the natives knew how long ago and by whom the boomerang was invented. He shook his head and said no one could give any account of it; but as all the tribes throughout the country are familiar with it, it must be of very ancient date. He said there was a theory that the natives derived the invention from observing the peculiar shape and turn of the leaf of the white gum-tree. As the leaves fall to the ground they gyrate, very much as does the boomerang, and if one of the leaves is thrown straight forward, it gyrates and comes back.

AMERICANS WHO USE THE BOOMERANG.

"Such an origin is certainly quite possible. Children might be playing with such leaves, and to please them a man might make a large leaf of wood, and from this the boomerang may have been developed. *Quien sabe?*

"And with this query of 'Who can tell?' we will drop the boomerang, or leave it in the hands of the aboriginals of Australia, who alone of all the people in the world know how to handle it."

"That is true as to the return-boomerang," said Doctor Bronson when Fred read the foregoing account, "but not of the non-returning one. According to those who have carefully studied the subject, such a weapon was used by the ancient Egyptians and by the Dravidian races of India. The Moqui Indians of Arizona and New Mexico have a form of boomerang for killing rabbits, and a similar weapon is said to be used by some of the tribes of California Indians. The Moqui boomerang resembles the Australian one in its general shape, but it is not a returning one. It gyrates along the surface of the ground and is fatal to a rabbit twenty-five or thirty yards away."

PLATYPUS, OR DUCK-BILLED MOLE.

"There's something else peculiar to Australia that you've forgotten," remarked the Doctor, after a slight pause.

"What is that?"

"It is the platypus, or duck-billed mole," said the Doctor, "the paradoxical animal of Australia."

"We had not forgotten him," Frank responded, "though we have not yet written a description of this singular creature. He seems to be the connecting link between bird and beast, as he has the body of the mole or rat and the bill and webbed feet of the duck. The female lays eggs like a bird, but it suckles its young, which no bird was ever known to do. The one we saw at Melbourne was larger than the largest water-rat; they told us that it lives in a hole which it digs for itself on the banks of the rivers, is very sensitive to sound, and hard to catch. Its fur is as fine as sealskin, and if it were larger it would be systematically hunted for its skin."

"When the first specimens were taken to Europe," said Doctor Bronson, "it was thought to be a hoax like the Feejee mermaid, and it was some time before the naturalists were convinced of its genuineness. When its existence was officially acknowledged, it received the name of *ornithorhynchus*."

"But isn't there a question as to whether the platypus lays eggs?" Fred asked.

"I believe there is," replied the Doctor, "but the latest student of the subject, Mr. W. H. Caldwell, of Cambridge College, England, who visited Australia in 1884–85 for the special purpose, says the creature is oviparous; so we will rest on his authority."

From Australia in general the conversation changed to South Australia in particular. It was directed to the mineral products of the colony, in consequence of an invitation that had just been received by the Doctor to visit a famous copper-mine. The Doctor explained to the youths that copper was the principal mineral resource of the colony: the exportations of mining products in the year 1885 amounted to £344,451, of which £322,983 were in refined copper or copper ore.

HOME OF THE DUCK-BILL.

"Gold has been found in several localities in the colony," he continued, "but never in such quantities as in Victoria or New South Wales, the annual export rarely exceeding £70,000, equal to $350,000. There are also deposits of silver, lead, bismuth, and tin, and many persons believe that the colony will ultimately prove very attractive as a mining region; but up to the present time copper is very far in advance of anything else."

They accepted the invitation, and went to the copper-mine which is known as the Burra-Burra, and is one hundred and one miles by railway from Adelaide. Starting at seven o'clock in the morning, they reached the station near the mine a little past noon, spent three hours at the works, and returned to Adelaide in the evening. It was a long day and a wearying one, but the ride and visit were greatly enjoyed.

The Burra-Burra mine was discovered by a shepherd name Pickitt, in

1844, and has proved highly profitable to its owners; for a good many years its annual product of ore was ten thousand tons, yielding two thousand five hundred tons of pure copper. More than twenty million dollars' worth of copper has been taken from this mine, and the supply is by no means exhausted.

ONE OF THE MINERS.

But our friends heard of even richer mines than the Burra-Burra. They were told of the Moonta mines, which paid from the very start; not a penny of capital was ever subscribed, but the mines have yielded large dividends, in some years as high as eight hundred thousand dollars, in addition to paying for costly buildings and machinery. It should be added that the success of these and other mines led to a great deal of mining speculation which was very disastrous for nearly all the investors.

Early one Thursday morning it was announced that the regular mail steamship of the Peninsular & Oriental Company was at Glenelg, and would leave in the evening for King George Sound, Western Australia. Doctor Bronson had taken passage for himself and his young companions; his first intention was to stop at King George Sound, but owing to the limited facilities of travel in Western Australia, the small population, and the slight development of the country compared to that of the eastern half of the continent, the idea of making an extended tour through the only remaining colony of Australasia was definitely abandoned.

The steamer left Glenelg in the evening of Thursday, and on the morning of the following Monday arrived at Albany, in King George Sound, one thousand and seven miles from Adelaide. She anchored about a mile from shore, and our friends were landed in a row-boat on payment of one shilling each, the same fare being charged for the return trip before the departure of the vessel in the evening. King George Sound is about five miles long and nearly the same in width, and forms a good anchorage for ships. Its advantages as a naval possession were long ago recognized, the British Government having secured it by establishing a colony there in 1826. There are two entrances on opposite sides of an island called Breaksea, a massive rock that reminded Frank and Fred of Alcatraz Island, in the harbor of San Francisco, or Capri, in the Bay of Naples.

VIEW OF PERTH, CAPITAL OF WESTERN AUSTRALIA.

The youths were disappointed with Albany, which they had imagined to be a place of some importance. It stands on rising ground on the north shore of the harbor, and has not far from one thousand two hundred inhabitants—hardly enough to give it the dignity of a city, which most of its residents claim for it.

Frank asked how they could get away from Albany in case they had decided to travel through Western Australia.

"There is a road from here to Perth, the capital of the colony," said the gentleman to whom the inquiry was addressed. "The distance is two hundred and sixty-one miles; and whenever the mails arrive here they are sent through to Perth by a coach, which makes the journey in about fifty-three hours. You may travel by the mail-coach, or you can take a coasting steamer once every fortnight, and touch at all the ports worth seeing, as well as some that do not pay for the trouble."

"How many railways have they in the colony?"

"Not many," was the reply. "The Northern Railway, thirty-five miles long, runs from Champion Bay, on the coast, to the town and mining district of Northampton. The Eastern Railway, ninety miles long, extends from the port of Freemantle, at the mouth of Swan River, to Perth, and thence to Beverley, whence it is to be extended to Albany. There are branches from both these lines, but none of great length, and there are some private railways belonging to timber companies. All the lines of the colony are of three feet six inches gauge; several new lines are projected on the land grant system, in the same way that many of your railways in the United States have been constructed, and on some of them work is now under way. But it will be several years yet before the country has an adequate system of railways."

"Western Australia is territorially the largest colony of Australia, but there are not yet fifty thousand inhabitants in its whole area," the gentleman continued. "The largest place is Perth, which has a population of about six thousand. Freemantle, its port, twelve miles lower down on the Swan River, has four thousand, and the other places of consequence are Guildford, Geraldton, and Roebourne, the latter the centre of the pearl-fishery."

Fred asked what were the products of the country, and how it happened that Western Australia, while nearer to Europe than any other colony of Australasia, had been so neglected.

"To your first question I will reply," said his informant, "that wool is our largest item of export, and then come sandal-wood, lumber, pearl-shell and pearls, horses, and sheep. We send many horses to India, Singapore, and Java, and our trade in this line promises to increase. Our annual exports of all kinds amount to £290,000, and our imports to something less than that figure. We have mines of gold, lead, copper, iron, and tin, but up to the present, though there have been a few gold rushes, very little attention has been given to our mineral resources, and we really know little about them.

"There is an abundance of fine country in Western Australia. There are splendid forests in the south-west, and excellent pasture lands in the west and north. An American visitor once said that Western Australia had been run through an hour-glass, alluding to the great number of sandy regions in the limits of the territory. Of course we have considerable areas of desert, but his remark is unfair as a general description. We could support a large population, and when our advantages become better known we shall have it too.

FOREST SCENE IN THE SOUTH-WEST.

"I ought to tell you that some of our most fertile land in the south-west is unfit for pasturing sheep and cattle, owing to the poison-plants that abound there. There are several of these plants, four of them being well known and easily recognized. The most common is the York-road plant, a low scrubby bush with narrow green leaves and a white stem. Sheep feed eagerly upon it, swell to a great size, and live only a few hours; at certain times when the plant is full of sap a single mouthful is sufficient to kill a full-grown sheep. The plant will also kill horned cattle, but does not affect horses, or only slightly. As you go to the north you cease to find this dangerous plant, and the pastures there are as good for sheep as those of Victoria or New South Wales.

"The latter half of your query," he continued, "compels me to speak of something which the most of us wish to forget. In the first place, when the colony was formed, in 1829, enormous grants of land were given to a few individuals of capital and influence who were to bring out colonists and otherwise develop the country. The grants were all the way from one hundred thousand to two hundred and fifty thousand acres, and the system proved a bad one. The capitalists came here to live on their estates, and not to work, and the colony was the reverse of prosperous. The stories of the old colonial days would be ludicrous if they were not saddening; of fine gentlemen and ladies, blooded horses, pianos, carriages, packs of hounds, and other belongings of old countries landed on this desolate coast, and nobody knowing where his allotment of land could be found. These kid-gloved colonists ate up all the provisions they had brought, came near starvation, and then returned to England, or went to Victoria and New South Wales to seek new homes.

A KID-GLOVED COLONIST.

"In the languishing condition of the colony it was sought to galvanize it into new life by allowing the Government to send convicts here under the stipulation that there should be an equal number of free colonists brought out at Government expense.

"The system was continued until 1868. It was stopped in that year, partly because no free emigration could be induced to come here as long as the colony received convicts, and partly because of the opposition of the other Australian colonies. One of the Governments of the eastern part of the continent proposed to exclude from its ports all ships that came from ours, through fear that our convicts would escape to their shores. Every free immigrant shunned us as he would shun the cholera or the plague, and if the system had been kept up to the present time our population would consist almost entirely of convicts and their guards. All our prosperity dates from the suspension of transportation, and we want to forget that there was ever anything of the kind."

A desultory conversation followed, in which Frank and Fred learned many things concerning the colony, but we have not a place for all of them in this narrative. Talking about the pearl-fishery, they were told that in 1883 a mass of nine pearls, forming a perfect cross, was found in Nicol Bay, each pearl being the size of a large pea, and perfect in form and color. About the same time a rich bank of pearl oysters fifteen miles long (the bank, not the oysters) was found in the vicinity of Beagle Bay, and a single pearl weighed two hundred and thirty-four grains.

They further learned that capitalists of Melbourne and Sydney had recently obtained large blocks of land in the north, and were sending their flocks and herds into these new pastures. The climate was claimed

IN THE PASTURE LANDS.

to be delightful, and their informant quoted the words of a clergyman who averred that it was no exaggeration to say, generally speaking, that Western Australia possessed one of the most healthful climates in the world.

But in spite of its praises they had no wish to remain, and after strolling through the streets of Albany, looking from the heights in its rear upon the peaceful waters of King George Sound, and gazing upon the spot where, with much ceremony, ground had been recently broken for the railway to Beverley, they walked to the end of the long pier which juts into the harbor, and were soon once more on the deck of the steamer.

Just as the sun was dipping into the west the great vessel left her anchorage, passed through the channel at the side of rugged Breaksea, and then skirted the coast to the westward for several hours. In the morning Cape Leeuwin, the last headland of the island-continent, was dimly visible in the distance; before the sun marked the meridian the cape and all behind it had disappeared, and the great steamer, her only companions the sea-birds, ploughed the waters of the Indian Ocean, with her prow turned towards the shores of spicy-breezed Ceylon.

As Cape Leeuwin sank from sight beneath the waves our friends murmured a farewell to the land whose skies are stippled at night by the stars of the Southern Cross, and whose arid plains are cooled by breezes from antarctic seas. And their farewell was accompanied with the heartiest good wishes for the people whose enterprise and energy are so admirably exemplified in the populous and busy cities and the prosperous colonies which have been described in these pages by those veteran though still young travellers, Frank and Fred.

ROCKS AT THE CAPE.

THE BOY TRAVELLERS IN AUSTRALASIA.